NEWTON'S FIRE

Will Adams has tried his hand at a multitude of careers over the years. Most recently, he worked for a London-based firm of communications consultants before giving it up to pursue his life-long dream of writing fiction. His first novel, *The Alexander Cipher*, has been published in sixteen languages, and has been followed by three more books in the Daniel Knox series, *The Exodus Quest*, *The Lost Labyrinth* and *The Eden Legacy*. He writes full-time and lives in Suffolk.

D0049712

CALGARY PUBLIC LIBRARY

DEC   2013

Also by Will Adams

The Alexander Cipher
The Exodus Quest
The Lost Labyrinth
The Eden Legacy

WILL ADAMS

Newton's Fire

This novel is entirely a work of fiction.
The names, characters and incidents portrayed in it are
the work of the author's imagination. Any resemblance to
actual persons, living or dead, events or localities is
entirely coincidental.

Harper
An imprint of HarperCollins*Publishers*
77–85 Fulham Palace Road,
Hammersmith, London W6 8JB

www.harpercollins.co.uk

A Paperback Original 2012
1

Copyright © Will Adams 2012

Will Adams asserts the moral right to
be identified as the author of this work

A catalogue record for this book
is available from the British Library

ISBN: 978-000-742423-8

Set in Sabon LT Std by Palimpsest Book Production Limited,
Falkirk, Stirlingshire

Printed and bound in Great Britain by
Clays Ltd, St Ives plc

All rights reserved. No part of this publication may be
reproduced, stored in a retrieval system, or transmitted,
in any form or by any means, electronic, mechanical,
photocopying, recording or otherwise, without the prior
written permission of the publishers.

This book is sold subject to the condition that it shall not,
by way of trade or otherwise, be lent, re-sold, hired out or
otherwise circulated without the publisher's prior consent
in any form of binding or cover other than that in which it
is published and without a similar condition including this
condition being imposed on the subsequent purchaser.

MIX
Paper from
responsible sources
FSC C007454
www.fsc.org

FSC™ is a non-profit international organisation established to promote
the responsible management of the world's forests. Products carrying the
FSC label are independently certified to assure consumers that they come
from forests that are managed to meet the social, economic and ecological
needs of present and future generations, and other controlled sources.

Find out more about HarperCollins and the environment at
www.harpercollins.co.uk/green

To Jonathan and Sarah

PROLOGUE

St Martin's Street, London 1713

There was singing in the French Protestant Church as Erasmus and his companions turned into St Martin's Street, but it was evidently the last act of the service, for the doors opened as they trundled by, and the congregation began trickling out, singly, in pairs and in small family clusters, bracing themselves against the wintry night.

'You ain't trying to save our souls now, are you, Ras?' muttered Johann.

'Someone needs to,' he retorted.

'They will after tonight.'

Erasmus spat over the side of the cart, gave the horses a tickle with his whip, peering through the darkness for

1

the house. When he found it, he gave the reins a tug and they came to a halt.

The congregation had already largely dispersed, chased off by the cold drizzle. The church doors closed again, leaving the cobbled street empty, dark and silent, save for the creaking boards of their own cart and the muffled revelry of Leicester Fields. He passed the reins to Johann, climbed down. His left boot splashed in a puddle he hadn't seen, and the chill of it penetrated his sole almost at once, feeling peculiarly like fear. He scowled as he strode over to the front steps, both from irritation and the need to give himself resolve. Johann was right. For all the prestige and the fine title of the man who'd given them their orders, Erasmus didn't like this business one bit. Too many mysteries. Too much whispering in dark corners. But it wasn't for the likes of him to doubt knights of the realm; nor to turn down their guineas neither.

He knocked three times. Nothing happened. He banged twice more, cupped his hands around his mouth, gave a holler. Still nothing. He looked around at his companions, shrugged. Sir Christopher had been adamant there would be someone here. He called out again, and finally he heard something inside. Bolts were drawn; hinges creaked. The door opened to reveal a portly, elderly man of middle height with unkempt grey hair down to his shoulders. He was dressed in black and he was holding a five-branched candelabra, so that tiny sparks of light reflected from his dark eyes. 'Sir Christopher's men, I take it,' he said.

'He said you had something for us to collect.'

'Did he tell you what?'

Erasmus shook his head. 'No, sir. Only that it would need ten of us.'

'At least ten. If you're strong.'

'We're strong enough.'

The old man stared at him for several moments. It made Erasmus feel like a whipped child. Despite the chill of the night, a bead of sweat trickled from his nape down his back. 'Where's Sir Christopher now?' he asked.

'Waiting, sir. With his son.'

'Then how can I trust you're who you say you are? Did he give you a token to show me?'

'No, sir. Not a token. A word.'

'What word?'

Erasmus scratched his throat. There'd been a lot to remember this evening, and memory had never exactly been his greatest strength. 'The word was Polanus,' he said.

'Polanus?'

'Yes, sir. Polanus. Or Bolanus, maybe. Balanus.'

The old man gave the first hint of a smile; though no more than a hint. 'Close enough, I suppose.' He glanced across at the cart. 'Your men won't be much help over there, will they?'

Erasmus beckoned them over. 'Come on, lads. Work to do. Fees to earn.'

'Have them wipe their boots,' said the old man.

He led the way along a passage flanked by open doors, his candlelight offering brief glimpses of desks and tables strewn with papers, mirrors that stretched and shrank, dark oak-panelled walls with curtains red as slaughter-houses. Erasmus raised an eyebrow at Henry. For sure, they'd crack some jokes about this later, fortified by an ale or two; but right now he didn't feel much like laughing.

They passed out the back of the house. The old man unlocked and opened a cellar door, releasing a draught of foul-smelling air. He didn't even seem to notice, just went straight on down, taking the candlelight with him. They looked hesitantly at each other. It was absurd to be scared of an old man and his cellar; yet scared they were. Something here wasn't right. Something wasn't of this earth. The smell of it, sulphurous and evil, like a gateway to hell itself.

Erasmus shook his head at himself and his companions. He steeled himself and led the way. The cellar surprised him. From its stink, he'd expected something rotting and damp; but actually it proved clean and dry. The stench had to be coming from the jars, bottles and flasks that were crowded on the worktables and shelves, filled with colourful powders and liquids; or perhaps from the cold ashes of the great furnace against the far wall. But it was to the left-hand wall that the man went, to three oak chests lined up against it. He rested his hand on the largest, a little over five feet long, maybe three feet wide and high. It had four brass handles along either side for carrying, another pair at either end. But it had no obvious hinges, lock or lid, no way to open it.

'Is this it, then?' asked Erasmus. 'These three boxes?'

'These three boxes,' agreed the old man. He smiled at Erasmus's companions, hanging back at the foot of the steps. 'Come now, gentlemen,' he mocked. 'We're not scared of a few boxes, are we?'

Simeon came across, lifting his chin defiantly. 'Ten of us?' he asked. 'Just for these?'

'Try lifting it,' suggested the old man.

Simeon nodded. He was short of stature, but he had broad shoulders and monstrously powerful arms. He took hold of the brass handles and heaved it up, raising it barely an inch from the floor before dropping it again and rubbing his palms ruefully on his breeches. He turned to Erasmus. 'Hell's teeth,' he said. 'So that's what you did with your missus.'

Laughter settled their nerves. They clustered around the chest, took a handle each. When they were all braced, Erasmus gave the word and they lifted it up together, shuffled it over to the foot of the steps before setting it down again with a dull thump that sent shivers through the floor, shook dust from the walls. They stood there, massaging their backs and flexing their sore fingers, looking with dismay at the steep steps that faced them.

'In the name of Christ,' said David, staring balefully at the chest. 'What's in this thing?'

The old man smiled, as though he'd been hoping someone would ask. 'The end,' he said. 'Or the beginning of it, at least.'

They looked at each other with bewilderment, but it was Erasmus who voiced their shared thought. 'The end of what?' he asked.

The old man's smile broadened. 'Everything,' he said. 'The end of everything.'

ONE

I

A country house attic, Suffolk, England, Sunday June 5th
Luke Hayward was lifting a stack of documents from
the cardboard box when he glimpsed the sliver of sepia
paper about two thirds of the way down. It looked altogether more intriguing than anything he'd seen so far.
Stiffer and older and with a fractionally compressed edge,
as though it had been cut by a blunted guillotine. His
heartbeat accelerated slightly; but only slightly. Experience
had taught him not to get his hopes up at such faint
hints of promise.

He put the stack down on the dust sheet, lifted off
and set aside the top half, then a bit more, exposing
the front of a faded manila folder on which someone
had scrawled *S.I.N.* in smudged black ink. His heart

gave another kick, more pronounced this time, more warranted. His mouth was dry, he realized; he swallowed some saliva then paused to wipe his hands, deliberately taking his time. If disappointment awaited him, as surely it did, he could at least defer it a few more moments.

He crouched down, lifted up the front flap of the folder with his index finger, pulling the sheet with it a little way, too, as though glued to it by habit; but then he lifted the flap further and it released with a faint whisper and fell back and outwards; and Luke froze for a moment, staring down at it in disbelief.

Six months he'd been hunting. *Six months*. Yet not once in that time had he ever truly thought he was going to find anything. Not truly. Not in his heart. Not if he was honest with himself.

But he'd have recognized that handwriting anywhere.

He set the flap back down, rose to his full height, took a pair of white cotton archivist's gloves from his pocket and pulled them on over his fingers like a surgeon prepping for an operation. He smoothed the dust sheet out over the attic floorboards, brushed away some dust and grit of fallen plaster, then opened the folder all the way. There were four sheets of the paper, he could now see, not just one. He fanned them out a little. Each bore the tell-tale creases of once having been folded into quarters and slit along one edge to make a miniature notebook, much as he'd sometimes done himself as a child, playing at being a spy. Almost certainly alchemical papers, then, for it had been one of the great man's quirks to dedicate such notebooks to his alchemical studies. But the sheets had been unfolded many years ago, and the decades spent weighted down near the foot of this tall stack of papers had pressed them flat.

It was too gloomy here for Luke to read. He carefully picked up the top sheet, took it to the nearest window. The light was better here, but still not ideal, for the panes were small, dirty and obscured by fingers of ivy. Besides, the writing had blurred and faded a little over the centuries, perhaps from these less than ideal conditions, exposed to extremes of heat and cold and damp. Add to that the characteristic tightness and closeness of his handwriting, and the arcane subject matter of the text, and it took Luke a good two minutes just to make sense of the top three lines.

Saturn will put into your hand a deep glittering mineral wch in his mine is grown of first matter of all metals. If this mineral after its preparation wch he will show until thee is in a strong sublimation mixed, with three parts

The passage stopped abruptly mid-sentence. Beneath it, though upside down, thanks to Isaac Newton's quirk with the notebooks, was a citation from St. Didier's *Triomphe Hermetique*, one of the alchemical texts the great man had most admired. It had been published in 1689, if Luke's memory served, though Newton hadn't got hold of his own copy until 1690. Luke held the sheet up to the window again. When he squinted hard at the paper itself, he could just about make out a watermark: a horn at the top, the capitalized letters IR beneath it. He knew the paper well. Newton had bought a large stock of it in the mid 1680s; had used it, on and off, until around 1695. Put together with the Saint-Didier citation, it dated this paper to first half of the 1690s; most probably from autumn 1692 to late 1693, the most intense period of alchemical experimentation and study in Newton's life.

Luke's hand was trembling a little, he noticed. As an academic specialising in the Scientific Revolution, he'd seen thousands of pages of Newton's handwriting and annotations over the years; and many hundreds in the past year alone, when dismissal from the university had given him the time to begin the research for his long-planned biography. But none had affected him quite like this, for they'd all been in libraries and museums and private collections. They'd all been known about, studied, debated.

But this was new. This could be anything.

He turned the page over. Again the patchwork writing, passages in English, French and Latin. It had been Newton's practice, when studying any new field,

10

to read the acknowledged authorities in it, preferably in their original language, copying out any passages that particularly caught his eye. Luke recognized a citation from Philatheles and two lines from the Emerald Tablet, but otherwise the extracts were unfamiliar.

He returned the page to its folder, picked up the second sheet, hesitated. He'd promised Penelope Martyn he'd let her know at once should he find anything. He also needed to photograph these pages and email them to his client's lawyer. But he couldn't resist another quick look. This sheet too was filled with alchemical passages; but there was something else overleaf, something different: four words scrawled so fiercely near its foot that Newton had evidently damaged his quill while doing it, for the ink was thick and blotted.

Fatio O my Fatio

He set the page carefully down, conscious of a warmth in his throat and cheeks, flushing slightly with vicarious embarrassment, as though he'd walked in by accident on someone's private shame. And, just for a moment, he felt uncertain what to do.

No. That wasn't quite true. He knew *exactly* what he was going to do.

It was just that he felt wretched about doing it.

II

The Amalfi coast road, Italy

Vernon Croke could sense Irina struggling to maintain her silence as they wended the sharp, high hairpins just fast enough for their tyres to screech on the sun-baked roads, for she knew better than to question his tactics or to imply criticism, especially in front of other people, even if only his driver Manfredo. But they had to drop by the villa to pick up their things before heading on to Naples airport, and when they were safely inside he decided to let her off her leash.

'I didn't know you spoke German,' he said.

'I don't,' she said. 'Honestly, I don't. My grandmother lived in the Black Forest. I stayed with her sometimes. I'm sure I told you about her.'

Croke smiled reassuringly. 'So you got the gist, then?'

She nodded twice. 'I don't understand,' she said, with a curiously plaintive indignation. 'How could you do business with such a man?'

'You mean, how could *we* do business with him?' He went to the bar to fix them each a Bloody Mary. 'Very easily, my dear. He happens to be *exceedingly* rich.'

'And you're not?'

Croke shrugged. It was true that he *lived* rich, what with the villas and cars and the private jet; but those were the necessary trappings for his kind of business, and most were rented. But he couldn't say that without ruining the illusion; nor could he exactly hold Irina's reaction to their recent meeting against her, for fastidiousness was one of the qualities he liked her for. And their recent host had been one of the more repellent men Croke had ever met, bloated and pale, and glistening with expensive scents that couldn't quite disguise the noxious smells beneath, like so much bleach poured into a toilet. He'd kept glancing hungrily at Irina throughout their meeting, licking his lips as if she were the last pastry on the plate. And then, after uncapping his fountain pen and seemingly poised to sign the contract, he'd paused, looked up at Croke and had switched to German. 'Your assistant keeps *smirking* at me,' he'd said.

'I'm sure she doesn't.'

'She's been smirking at me this whole meeting.'

It had been the first time Croke had met his host, but he was familiar with the type. Deny the accusation, he'd protest about being called a liar, and then it would be a matter of face; and you never knew where you stood with such men on a matter of face. 'Irina is young and new,' he'd therefore replied, in his most emollient German. 'I'm sure she meant nothing by it. I'm sure she's extremely sorry for the offence she has given.'

'I don't like women who smirk.'

'What man does?'

'She needs taking in hand. That's what she needs.'

Croke had nodded. 'I'll see to it as soon as I get her home.'

'I'll see to it for you,' said the man. 'Consider it my gift. To celebrate our deal.'

Croke had glanced sideways. The faint sheen on Irina's forehead had been his first hint that she could speak German after all. He'd turned back to his host.

'Call me superstitious,' he'd said, 'but I never celebrate a deal before the ink's dry.'

'Call me superstitious,' his host had returned, 'but I never make a deal unless I have a bottle of champagne on ice.' And he'd looked around at his two bodyguards at that moment: nothing dramatic, just enough to put them on alert.

Irina had been with Croke since the debacle in Doha. She'd proved attentive, smart, discreet, loyal, quick to learn and fun to bed. Everything he could have asked. On the other hand, *his* safety was now at stake; not to mention a potentially lucrative relationship.

'Well?' his host had pressed, pen poised above the dotted line. 'Do we have a deal?'

Something unfamiliar had fluttered inside Croke's chest at that moment; and he'd realized, not without a certain perverse pleasure, that it was fear. It was an unexpected drawback of success, that it allowed you to cut risk out of your life. But risk was excitement; risk was *joy*. So he'd looked unflinchingly up into his host's gaze. 'Go fuck yourself,' he'd said.

A pinch of garlic salt in the Bloody Marys, a dash of Tabasco, ice cubes and a slice of lemon. He was a traditionalist when it came to drinks. He took the heavy crystal tumblers over to Irina, gave her hers. She took a large swallow. Her eyes gleamed and her jaw muscles tightened. 'You considered his offer,' she said bitterly. 'I saw you considering it.'

'I considered the *situation*,' he said mildly. 'It's not the same thing at all. Besides, if it makes you feel better, it wasn't about you.'

She snorted at that. 'It felt like it was about me.'

'I'm sure it did. But it wasn't. If it had really been about you, he'd never have signed the contract. We might not even have got out of there alive. It was about *me*. Specifically, he wanted to know if he could trust me, or whether I was the kind of man who could be bribed or bullied into giving up something I valued.'

'I thought you were going to say yes,' she said, the slight quaver in her voice betraying the way her world had trembled beneath her feet. 'I thought you were going to give me to that . . . that *monster*.'

'But that's the point,' said Croke. 'It wouldn't have been a gift. Not under coercion like that. It would have been *tribute*.'

She took another gulp, frowned and shook her head. 'I don't see—'

'Tribute is something demanded by the stronger party and paid by the weaker,' explained Croke. 'I don't pay tribute. I *never* pay tribute. It sends all the wrong signals. It lets people know you can be pushed around. Gifts, on the other hand, are what equals exchange freely and willingly. They're a valuable part of what I do; they're how I form bonds with other powerful people, how I build my influence. Here's a tip for you: in situations like this morning, where you find yourself at a temporary disadvantage, do whatever you can to achieve parity first, and *only then* show generosity. Otherwise it will be misinterpreted as weakness. Do you understand?'

She sat a little heavily down in one of the white leather armchairs. 'My head,' she murmured. 'I don't feel so good.'

'A reaction to the tension, I expect.'

'Yes.'

'Or perhaps to what I put in your Bloody Mary.'

She frowned a moment then looked in dismay down at her drink. But it was already too late. She tried to push herself up but collapsed back down again.

'You really should have let me know you spoke German,' he told her. 'I need to be able to trust the people around me.'

She tried to say something, maybe explain herself, but nothing came out. The tumbler slipped from her weakening grasp and shattered on the polished marble floor, tomato juice spreading like blood around the translucent shards. Her eyes glazed and her head lolled forward, a little pinkish drool leaking out onto her white blouse.

The door banged open, Manfredo and Vig sprinting in, handguns already drawn, alarmed by the tinkle of breaking glass. 'It's all right,' Croke assured them. He nodded at Irina, slumped unconscious in her armchair. He turned to Manfredo. 'Take her back to our friend from this morning, would you,' he said. 'Tell her she comes with my compliments, to celebrate our deal.'

Manfredo holstered his gun. 'Yes, sir. And afterwards?'

'Meet us at the airport. We wouldn't want to miss our slot.'

'No, sir. Anything else?'

Croke knocked back the dregs of his Bloody Mary, set his glass down on the counter. 'Yes,' he said. 'You'd better call Francesca in Geneva for me. We should probably let her know I'll be needing a new assistant.'

TWO

I

'You found them,' said Penelope Martyn in an awed murmur, when Luke tracked her to her kitchen. 'I don't believe it.'

Luke allowed himself a smile. 'I don't either,' he admitted.

'And? Are they . . . are they what you were hoping?'

He didn't quite know how to answer that. Her house was grand but badly rundown; and he'd got the distinct impression, when they'd chatted earlier, that a windfall would be more than welcome. 'They're alchemical papers,' he said carefully. 'Four sheets, written front and back. Citations from other authors, as far as I've been able to tell.'

'Oh.' She tried, unsuccessfully, to keep the shadow of disappointment from her expression. 'So not his original work then?'

'I'm afraid not.' He'd already explained to her the sliding scale of value for Newton's papers: the highly prized letters he'd written to both his famous and lesser-known friends; the coveted annotations for *Principia Mathematica* and *Opticks*; the significantly lesser interest in his theological and alchemical writings, especially those that didn't represent Newton's own thinking, but were merely his transcriptions of other authors. 'It could have been worse,' he said. 'They could have been his papers from the Royal Mint.'

'Newton was at the Royal Mint?'

'He joined just a year or two after he wrote these pages, as it happens. Ran the place for decades. Oversaw a complete recoinage of the realm.'

She shook her head. 'Why would a man like Newton take a job like that?'

Luke shrugged. It was a question that had vexed many academics over the years, and no one had really come up with a satisfactory explanation. 'The *Principia Mathematica* had made him a star,' he said. 'We think maybe he wanted to go to London to bask in all that glory. The Royal Mint was his ticket. And the money was pretty good too, especially after he was appointed Master.'

'Oh, well.' She touched the papers with her fingertip. 'Is there *anything* of interest in them?'

'I haven't been through them properly yet,' Luke told her. 'I wanted to show them to you at once. Besides . . .' He gestured at the cramped handwriting, the upside-down passages, the esoteric words, the passages in Latin and French, indicating how hard they were to read. 'But there is at least one thing.'

'Yes?'

He pointed out the four words to her. Then, unsure of her eyesight, he read them out aloud. 'It says "Fatio O my Fatio".'

'I don't understand.' She frowned. 'Who's Fatio? *What's* Fatio?'

'It's a who.' He stooped to unzip his laptop case, pulled out his digital camera. 'A he, to be precise. Nicolas Fatio de Duillier. A young Swiss mathematician who became a close friend of Newton's in the early 1690s. Perhaps even a *very* close friend.'

'*Very* close?' She tipped her head to one side. 'You're not implying . . .?'

Luke smiled. 'It's possible. Some people certainly think so.'

'Sir Isaac Newton? And some young Swiss man?'

'There's no evidence whatsoever that anything physical ever happened between them,' said Luke, setting the first page square on the tablecloth, the better to photograph it. 'Though they did spend a week together in London one time, when no one else even knew that Fatio was in the country.' He checked the image in his digital display, turned the page over to photograph its reverse. 'And Newton later implored him to live with him in Cambridge.'

'My word.' She let out a bark of a laugh. 'Maybe *that's* why Uncle Bernie wanted these papers.'

Luke set the second page in place. 'How do you mean?'

A little colour pinked her cheeks. 'They called them "confirmed bachelors" in my day,' she said, with just a hint of a smile, as though unaccustomed to revealing family skeletons, yet rather enjoying it. '"Not the marrying kind". I had no idea what that actually meant. I simply assumed Uncle Bernie hadn't yet met the right woman. I even hoped I'd be able to help find her for him myself. He was so *nice* to me. The only Martyn who *truly* welcomed me into the family. But then I called on him without warning one afternoon.' She gave another of her barking laughs and blushed even deeper. 'Well, I'm sure you can imagine.'

'Must have been a shock,' said Luke, photographing the third paper.

'For both of us,' she admitted. 'All three of us, I should say. We girls were so naïve back then. You wouldn't believe.'

He photographed the back of the last page, held up his camera. 'May I email these off? The sooner my client gets them, the sooner he'll make an offer. If he wants them, that is.'

'And I'm not obliged to accept, you said?'

'Of course not. All he asks is the opportunity to make the first bid.' His client's lawyer had been absurdly emphatic about that, repeating it at every opportunity. 'You'll be perfectly free to accept it, reject it or negotiate something better.' The house was too remote for his own WiFi service, but Penelope had assured him earlier that he'd be welcome to use the wired broadband she'd had put in to tempt her grandkids to come and visit. He plugged his laptop into her router, transferred the photographs, attached them to an email and sent them on their way. The high resolution files were big, however, and her connection was slow. 'This could take a while,' he said.

'We'll have a nice cup of tea,' said Penelope.

He toured the walls as her old kettle struggled to the boil, looking at family photographs. A surly lot, for the most part, with long noses and sour upper lips, posing grudgingly for the camera. But then he reached a picture of a young woman with short brown hair and an enchanting smile leaning against the driver door of an old grey-blue Rover.

'My great-niece Rachel,' Penelope said, appearing at

his side with a plate of shortbread biscuits. 'She's one of your lot.'

'My lot?'

'An academic. She's doing her doctorate at Caius College, Cambridge. She wants to be a lecturer like you.'

'Ah,' said Luke, a touch guiltily. He'd used old university letterheaded paper for his correspondence with Penelope; and somehow he'd neglected to let her know about their parting of the ways following his convictions for assault and offences against the Terrorism Act. 'What's her field?' he asked.

'The archaeology and history of the ancient Near East, I think. Something like that, anyway. Between you and me, I find it terribly hard to follow.'

'She looks nice.'

'As opposed to my own brood, you mean?'

'I didn't mean that at all,' protested Luke, a little too hotly. 'I just meant that she looks nice.' His laptop beeped, sparing his further blushes. He went to check it. The battery was running low. 'Mind if I recharge?' he asked.

'Be my guest.' She pointed him to a spare socket, cleared her throat, now suffering from awkwardness of her own. 'I hate to ask,' she said, 'but do you have any idea exactly *how* interested your client might be in these particular papers?'

Luke hesitated. He'd already given her a ballpark

estimate and was reluctant to do more. Go too low and she'd think he was trying to fleece her; go too high and he'd be setting her up for disappointment. He checked his screen to find that the photographs were on their way, gave her a blandly optimistic smile. 'I guess we'll find out soon enough,' he said.

II

Vernon Croke clenched a crystal tumbler of bourbon as he stared through the window of Naples' private jet terminal, watching airport security guards mill like ants around his plane.

It was like this everywhere.

The cabins of modern jet aircraft were pressurized as a matter of course. They flew so high that the thinness of the air would otherwise kill their passengers and crew. Their cargo holds, on the other hand, were often left unpressurized. In such aircraft the pressurized and unpressurized compartments had to be securely sealed off from each other lest some unfortunate accident provoke a catastrophic depressurisation.

There'd been times recently, however, when certain international agencies had found themselves frustrated by this. Times when they'd regretted the lack of an airlock system that would enable passage between the pressurized and unpressurized parts. Such a system could even allow an external hatch to be opened in mid-flight: to jettison potentially embarrassing evidence, say, or to parachute agents or supplies into hostile territory. Cargo planes were too slow, low and visible for such sensitive work, but no one looked twice at a private jet cruising at 25,000 feet. That was what the CIA had assured Croke, at least, when they'd offered him this plane ahead of a Department of Justice investigation into rendition flights. What with the generous discount, and its sophisticated comms systems, it had seemed too good an opportunity to refuse. But there were times he regretted his decision, for the plane's peculiarities of design invariably drew extra scrutiny wherever he went. 'How much longer?' he asked Vig.

'Five minutes, sir.'

'They said that ten minutes ago.'

The bodyguard shrugged. 'Another drink?'

Croke shook his head. 'I have calls to make,' he said. 'I can't make them here. Anyone could be listening.'

The door opened. An airport security guard beckoned. They were cleared. Croke strode briskly across the concourse. 'Are we secure?' he asked Craig Bray, his pilot, waiting at the head of the cockpit steps.

'Just done a full sweep,' Bray assured him. 'We're secure.'

The comms suite was towards the front. Croke had

turned it into his on-board office, from where he could manage his small empire in perfect confidence. He went there now, checked his messages. All were routine except for one from Max Walters, boss of his London office. He called him at once. 'What is it?' he asked.

'Just got an email from our Newton friend,' said Walters.

Croke sat up a little. 'Has he found something?'

'Four pages, sir. Up near Thetford in some old biddy's attic. I wouldn't have disturbed you, except that there's a list of twelve letters on the back of one of the pages, which is one of the things you told me to look out for, right?'

'Yes,' said Croke. 'Send them to me.'

'Already on their way, sir. I just wanted to alert you.'

'Good work.'

'Thanks. If you want the originals, I'm free this afternoon and I've still got that Riyadh cash. And I've put Kieran and Pete on notice.'

'Let me take a look,' said Croke. 'I'll call you back.' He downloaded and opened the email, found the twelve letters in four groups of three in a perplexing passage on the back of the third page. He brought up an online King James' Version, went straight to Exodus, scrolled down for the relevant passage and split the screen to check email against scripture. Then he sat back in his seat, his heart pumping.

A perfect match.

Over the past six months or so, his friends in Jerusalem and the southern United States had been increasingly in his ear, urging him to ramp up the hunt for these papers, claiming they needed them found by a very specific date. That date was the day after tomorrow, Tuesday 7 June.

Mostly, Croke was his father's son, feeling only mild disdain for religion and related superstitions. But there were other times, times like these, when his mother's blood would assert itself and he'd glimpse the vast hinterland of the unknown. He called Walters back. 'I want those papers,' he told him. 'I want them today. I don't care what they cost. Just get them for me.'

'What if she won't sell?'

'Find a way. That's what I pay you for, isn't it?'

'Yes, sir.'

'And I want all copies of these photographs destroyed. And this woman and your Newton expert are to keep their mouths shut. Understand?'

'Yes, sir. And when I get the originals, where do you want them sent?'

Croke hesitated. His father's seventy-fifth birthday wasn't until next weekend, and his flight-path back to the States would near enough take him over the UK. And what was the point of a private plane, after all, if not for moments like this? 'I'll try to do a fly-by,' he said. 'Are there any airports up that way?'

'Cambridge and Norwich for sure. There are bound to be others.'

'Fine. I'll let you know.' He ended the call then spent a few moments staring at Newton's cryptic message, trying to puzzle it out. But it was too obscure for him; he couldn't make head nor tail of it.

It was time to call in the expert.

It was time for Avram.

III

The Old City, Jerusalem
There was another aftershock that afternoon, half an hour or so after Avram Kohen returned from the hospital. It was mild, as tremors went; barely enough to rattle the crockery in his cupboards and set off an intruder alarm further down the street. Yet it sent a shiver through Avram all the same. What with the news he'd had earlier, it was as though the Lord Himself, praise His Name, had come into his home to tell him bluntly that there were to be no more deferments, no more excuses.

This was to happen *now*.

His heart swelled within his chest. His eyes began to water. And then, just like that, his phone began to ring.

'Shalom,' said Avram, picking up. He heard soft breathing and three distinct clicks before the caller disconnected. He put the receiver down, his heart racing, hands a little clammy. This was how he had to communicate these days, since learning that his security had been compromised. He went to his bedroom, rolled up the rug, levered up the terracotta tile to get at the steel safe beneath. He punched the password into the keypad, opened its door, took out the small laptop, the satellite modem and his security keys, and carried them all up the wooden ladder onto his flat roof.

The afternoon was cloudless and fiercely hot, exacerbating the stench seeping from all the sewers in the Old City that had been fractured by the earthquake, and hadn't yet been repaired. He sat with his back to the low perimeter wall as he aimed his modem north. From the corner of his eye he could see the Dome of the Rock, lording it over the Old City of Jerusalem like some conceited golden toad. But he didn't look away. He'd taken this house precisely because of this view, for he'd known it would act on him like a scourge.

Three thousand years before, King Solomon had built his temple upon that sacred mount. The Babylonians had torn it down some four hundred years later, but Cyrus had authorized its rebuilding and then Herod had renovated and expanded it. In 70 AD, the Romans had destroyed it again, punishment for the Jewish uprising. Then the Muslims had arrived. Aware that this was Judaism's holiest site, in 691 Abd al-Malik had built his wretched Dome upon it. And there it had remained ever since, a golden thorn in the heart of every Jew.

Many years before, Avram had dedicated his life to pulling that thorn free. Yet he'd gradually come to realize that bringing down the Dome wouldn't be enough. World opinion, after all, would be outraged; and Israel's craven leaders would doubtless succumb to pressure to rebuild it. And what sacrilege *that* would be! Not merely a Dome, but a Dome enabled by Jews. So he had come to the conclusion that it had to be brought down in such a way that only a Third Temple could be built in its place: in such a way that the Promised Land would be theirs forever.

The satellite modem finally acquired its signal. He typed in clearance codes from his security key to make the call. 'You've found the papers,' he stated when Croke picked up. 'Didn't I tell you that you would?'

'I've just emailed you photographs,' said Croke. 'Check the bottom of the sixth side and call me back.'

The file opened with teasing slowness on Avram's

screen, a courtesan at her veils. It was all he could do not to slap his machine. But finally the page appeared.

Received from E.A.
12 plain panels and blocks SW, 2 linen rolls
S T C, E S D, L A A, B O J
Papers J.D. J.T.
On completion, E.A. asks that ye whole be in
  SALOMANS HOUSE well concealed.

Something splashed against Avram's wrist. He looked up, half expecting clouds to have appeared, but the sky was of an almost impossible blue, so that he realized he was crying. He stood and paced around his roof, the tears now spilling freely down his wrinkled cheeks. He stopped, clenched a fist, shook it at the Temple Mount, at the insect workers striving so futilely to repair its earthquake cracks. Only now could he acknowledge, even to himself, how his faith had begun to falter this past year or so, despite his best efforts.

Never again, he vowed. *Never again.*

First things first. The message still needed interpreting. He was intimately familiar with Newton's studies of the Tanakh and the Kabbalah, with his writings on ancient kingdoms and the sacred cubit. But this lay outside that. He needed to talk to his nephew.

'Jakob,' he said, when the young man answered his phone. 'It's me. Uncle Avram.'

'Uncle? What is it?'

'You were right: the papers *do* exist. We've just found them.' He talked Jakob through what had happened, read out the cryptic message.

'"In Salomans House well concealed",' echoed Jakob, when he was done. 'Then that must be where we'll find it.'

'Yes. Of course. But where is Saloman's House?'

'It's here,' said Jakob. 'In London.'

'I don't understand.'

'It was Sir Francis Bacon. He wrote a book called *The New Atlantis*. Salomon's House appears in it: a kind of prototype research institute that was the direct inspiration for the Royal Society. And listen: *Newton became the Royal Society's president*. And one of his first big decisions was to move the Society out of Gresham College into two adjoining buildings in a place called Crane Court. He had them gutted and rebuilt to *his exact specifications*.'

'That's it, then,' said Avram, a little awed. 'We've got it.'

'It's not that simple,' cautioned Jakob. 'The Royal Society moved out of Crane Court back in 1780. And now no one knows which buildings they occupied there.'

'Someone must,' Avram protested.

'I give you my word, Uncle,' said Jakob. 'I tried to

find out myself two years ago. But its exact address isn't in any of the histories, there aren't any commemorative plaques outside and there's nothing online. Well, nothing definitive, at least. I spent *days* searching, I assure you.'

'What about old London directories and maps?'

'No use. Where they give an address at all, it's just the Royal Society, Crane Court, never a number. I even approached the Royal Society itself, asked to consult their old minute books and property deeds; but they'd shipped them all off to some storage facility in Wales to save money, only to lose them in the floods.'

'I don't believe this, Jakob. Someone must know.'

'I'm sorry, Uncle. They don't. And even if you could find the old address, which you can't, there's no guarantee it would help. Crane Court isn't what it used to be. They've demolished some buildings, knocked others together, turned some into offices and restaurants and apartment blocks. Even if we knew what numbers they had back then, the chances are high they'd have changed by now.'

'We'll find it,' insisted Avram. 'It's destined. And, when we do, you're going to have to escort it here personally. Are you ready? Do you have everything you need?'

'Yes, Uncle.'

'You'll have to arrange it with our friends. I'll be too busy myself.'

'As you wish, Uncle.'

'Shalom, Jakob. Till Jerusalem, then. It will be good to see you again.' He rang off, called Croke once more, told him what he'd learned.

Croke grunted in disappointment. 'That's too bad,' he said. 'But I can have my London people look into it next week, see if your nephew is right about—'

'*No*,' said Avram. 'This can't wait. Discovering these papers today, it's not a coincidence. It's a *sign*. The day after tomorrow is the seventh of June. That's the very day my people took Jerusalem back from the Muslims.' His mind flickered briefly to the moment nearly fifty years before when, as a young conscript, he'd stood outside the Golden Gate and stared in amazement up at the Temple Mount, waiting for the bulldozers that for some inexplicable reason had never come. 'The *49th* anniversary. The date foretold by the Prophet Daniel. The *exact* date.'

'I'm sorry. There's too much to arrange by Tuesday. You have to see that.'

'Not Tuesday. Monday.'

'But you just said—'

'The Jewish day begins and ends at dusk. We're going to need the cover of darkness for our assault. That therefore means tomorrow night. People will start rising for the first call to prayer around three a.m. our time, which is one a.m. London time. We have to have seized the Dome by then. And I'm not giving the order to attack unless I know it's already on its way. So you have a maximum of thirty hours to find it and get it in the air.'

'Thirty hours? It's not possible.'

'It *is* possible. It has to be.'

'I don't understand,' grumbled Croke. 'Why do you even have to seize the place at all? Why not just bring it down with those Predators I got you?'

Avram sighed. It was like talking to a boulder sometimes. 'You do know what this place is called?' he asked.

Croke sounded puzzled. 'You mean the Dome?'

'No. I mean the Dome *of the Rock*. The rock that we Jews know as the Foundation Stone. The same Foundation Stone from which Adam himself was made by the Lord, praise His Name. The same Foundation Stone on which Abraham offered his son Isaac in sacrifice. The same Foundation Stone on which, for hundreds of years, the Holy of Holies housed the Ark of the Covenant. The navel of the world, the place where heaven meets earth, the holiest site in all Creation. And you want me to *launch missiles at it*?'

'Ah,' said Croke.

'Yes,' said Avram. 'Ah.'

'So what did you need those Predators for?' asked Croke. 'Do you know how difficult they were to get hold of?'

'Turn on your television set tomorrow night. You'll see for yourself.'

'I don't know,' said Croke. 'I really don't think we've got enough time.'

'But we do,' insisted Avram. 'The Lord, praise His Name, makes hard demands of His servants; but He never asks the impossible. There has to be a way. Find it, my friend. Find it – and we'll both get what we want.'

THREE

I

Back upstairs in the attic, Luke worked his way methodically through the remainder of Bernard Martyn's belongings. He didn't expect to find anything more, and he didn't; but you had to make certain of such things. He finished the last box and was starting to replace things as he'd found them when he heard an engine outside, tyres crunching on gravel. Car doors opened and closed. Men bantered. He checked his watch. It was barely two hours since he'd sent off the photographs, so it seemed unlikely to have anything to do with him. He dragged a trunk across floorboards, scouring up dust that caught in his eyes and throat, making him blink and cough. An old cardboard box next, lifting it from beneath to make sure its bottom didn't—

'Doctor Hayward?' A woman calling up from below. 'Doctor Hayward?'

Luke put the box down. 'Penelope? Is that you?'

'Could you come down, please? There are some gentlemen . . .'

'On my way.' He wiped off his hands, wended between stacked tea chests, old furniture and other broken or discarded belongings. He reached the head of the steep attic staircase to find Penelope already near the top, gripping the handrail with both hands and climbing sideways, one step at a time.

'This is Steven,' she said, glancing back at the forty-something man with thinning fair hair in a slick pearl-grey suit right behind her. 'He's from your lawyers.'

Luke nodded to him. 'You got here quick.'

'You know clients,' shrugged Steven.

Footsteps below. A second man came into view. He was tall and dark with gold hoop earrings and a trimmed black beard. But the most startling thing about him was that he was carrying Luke's laptop in his left hand, tapping away on it with his right. 'Problem, boss,' he said, glancing up. 'Our friend here only went and sent those photos to someone else.'

Steven closed his eyes. He clenched both hands and took a deep breath, as though trying to control his rage. If so, he had limited success. He pushed past Penelope and marched to the top of the stairs, pressed

Luke back against the far wall. 'You did *what*?' he demanded.

Luke wanted to be indignant. These men were brazenly invading his privacy, after all. But he was simply too unnerved. 'I didn't do anything,' he said weakly.

'He logged out of his main account,' said Blackbeard, still down below. 'Then he logged back in to another account under a new name and emailed the photos to someone called Rachel Parkes.'

'Rachel Parkes?' demanded Steven. 'Who the fuck is she?'

'No one,' said Luke. 'I've never even heard of anyone called . . .' But then he remembered that photograph on the kitchen wall, the young woman with the enchanting smile, and he looked down at Penelope with dismay. She'd frozen on the second-top step, and was trying her best to shrink into invisibility, but her expression gave her away.

Steven saw it at once. 'You *hag*,' he yelled. 'You stupid fucking hag!' He went back to the top of the stairs and grabbed for her face. She cried out and leaned away from him. Her ankle turned on the step; she lost hold of the handrail and fell sideways. Luke pushed past Steven in an effort to save her, but her hand slipped through his and he had to watch in horror as she tumbled down the steps, pummelled by her own impetus. She hit the landing floor so hard that her neck audibly snapped, then she settled motionless on her back.

There was a moment of shocked stillness before Luke hurried down to kneel beside her. He felt for a pulse, for any sign of life. Nothing. Her eyes were already glazing. He felt sick, furious. He turned to Steven who was making his way calmly back down the steps. 'You killed her,' he said.

'She shouldn't have sent that fucking email, should she?' His callousness jolted Luke, reminded him how alone he was. That was when the third man arrived, and he really put the fear of god into Luke. It wasn't just his shaven head, or the shrunken white T-shirt that showed off his tattoos and body-builder's physique. It was the overt meanness of his face, the kind of man who met the world with cruelty and violence, because he liked it that way. Without a word, he went to stand beside Blackbeard, pointedly cutting Luke off from the main body of the house.

'I need to call an ambulance,' said Luke, his voice cracking just a little.

'I thought you said she was dead.'

'I'm not a doctor, am I?' He tried to push between Blackbeard and the bruiser, but they stood firm. 'This is ridiculous,' he said. 'Let me through.' But even he could hear his own fear.

'Boss?' asked Blackbeard.

Steven reached the foot of the steps. He didn't answer for another moment or so, thinking the situation through. But finally he came to his decision. 'Take him,' he said.

II

Naples Airport wasn't done with Vernon Croke quite yet. The control tower bumped him from his take-off slot to allow some Russian oligarch off first. He sat there seething. However much you earned, there was always someone left to kick sand in your face. It was how the game worked. And even trying to compete was dizzyingly expensive, especially when you found out how unforgiving a ratchet pride could be. Every car had to be faster than last year's; every boat fancier, every villa plusher. One step backwards and people would whisper that you were on the slide. Last year, as a consequence, Croke had spent three million dollars more than he'd taken in. *Three million dollars!* And this year was tracking even worse. He needed something good to happen, that was the blunt truth of it. He needed Jerusalem to come off. But there was no point undertaking so risky a venture unless he could guarantee a major payday. And that meant talking to Grant.

Croke had no way to contact Grant directly, for the man took his security far too seriously, but he sent word out into the ether, and it wasn't long before Grant called him. 'What do you want?' Grant asked.

'Our Jerusalem project,' said Croke. 'We've had movement.' He talked him through the day's developments, withholding Avram's absurd deadline and their ignorance of where in Crane Court to look until the end.

'Hell,' grunted Grant. 'You had me excited.'

'There's still one possibility,' said Croke. 'We search the whole block. Every building.'

'You're shitting me, right?' laughed Grant. 'How do you expect to pull that off?'

'By calling in a bomb threat,' said Croke. 'We'll have the whole place evacuated then send in people in to check it out. Which is why I needed to speak to you.'

'Forget it,' said Grant tersely. 'You know we can't have our fingerprints anywhere near this. That's why we hired you.'

'I don't need you for that. I'm going to go to our beloved Vice President.' With the president still in recovery from the recent attempt on his life, she was in charge of the administration, so it made sense to use her while they could.

'She'll do it for you, will she?'

'Not for me. For God.'

'Ah. Thaddeus.' Grant allowed himself a moment's thought. 'He'd have to talk directly to her, you realize?

Her team have gotten pretty good at running interference.'

'I thought they were all true believers too,' said Croke.

'They're DC insiders. They believe whatever will win them the next vote.' Grant paused then asked: 'So why the call? You don't need my approval for that.'

'There's no time for me to arrange covert delivery. Not by tomorrow night. So, if we find it, I'm going to have to take it in through the front door myself. And, to put it bluntly, I'm not doing that for free.'

'Fair enough,' agreed Grant. 'How much?'

'A hundred.'

Grant laughed loudly. 'A hundred? Are you crazy?'

'Let's not fuck with each other,' said Croke. 'I may not know your real name, or who you represent, but I'm not stupid either. We have to be talking the owners and CEOs of some *big* fucking corporations. Fortune 100 kind of big. The kind whose slush funds can buy small countries. That's what all this secrecy is about, because you can't risk word leaking about what America's business elite are up to.'

'Get to the point.'

'If this project succeeds, it'll be worth tens of billions in revenue to them. *Hundreds* of billions. You gave me five years to make it happen. Five years is an eternity for your modern CEO. I can deliver it on Tuesday. Doing so, however, will mean risking my reputation, my freedom and my life. And you expect me to do it for *free*?'

'There's a pretty big gap between free and a hundred million dollars.'

'A hundred's my price. Take it or leave it.'

'Then I'll leave it, thanks.'

'I'm impressed,' said Croke. 'I had you down as a spokesman, if I'm honest. Some kind of *lobbyist*. I didn't realize you had the authority to make trillion dollar calls without even asking.'

Grant sighed. 'Very well,' he said. 'I'll check. But don't expect an answer today, not on a Sunday. My friends are fierce about family time. Tell you what: why don't you set things rolling, and I'll call you back as soon as I get an answer.'

'Sure,' laughed Croke. 'And when will that be? On Wednesday, by any chance? Why hire me if you think I'm that stupid?'

Another sigh. 'Fine. Give me a few minutes. I'll see what I can do.'

III

Luke had no hope of fighting his way past Blackbeard and the bruiser. But Steven was another matter. He flung himself backwards, catching Steven by surprise, knocking him down. He scrambled over him, his feet on his chest and face as he sprinted up the steps.

Someone tap-tackled him. He went tumbling. He span as he fell, kicked out blindly, caught the bruiser in his throat, sent him crashing. He turned and scrambled up into the attic, zigzaging between broken furniture and dust-sheeted mounds that glowed like weary ghosts. He pulled over a stack behind him to hamper the pursuit and glassware and crockery shattered, littering the floor with shards. His jacket was hanging from a rusted nail, his mobile, wallet and keys in its pockets; but he didn't have time to stop for it. He ran down a short passage to a window that led out onto the roof. He tried to lift the sash but it was painted shut, so he smashed the glass out with his elbow and dived through its empty heart, twisting in the air to avoid the daggers of dirty glass on the sloped roof, hitting with his shoulder instead, tumbling down into the leaded valley between two gables. He thrust out his foot to stop his momentum and it went straight through an old red roof tile whose two halves snapped back together like a mantrap. The bruiser reached out the window for him but Luke pulled himself free, hobbled along the gable valley to the roof edge, took half a step back. The house looked incomparably higher from up here than from down below. And there was no easy way down. Its walls were thick with ivy, and there were iron drainpipes at either corner, but he didn't much fancy trusting his life to either of those.

He turned around. The bruiser had clambered out the window. Someone passed him a handgun from inside. No, not a handgun. A taser. Not that that was so much better. Luke scrambled up a gable, old tiles buckling and snapping beneath him, precipitating small terracotta avalanches. He crossed the ridge, descended into the neighbouring valley, then up another ridge. The far slope fell away to nothing. He'd reached the edge of the house. He had no option but to tightrope walk along the ridge towards the rear, arms out wide for balance. The old tiles were slick with moss; his left foot went from beneath him and he tumbled down the sloped roof. Desperately, he tried to stop himself but the camber was too steep. He fell over the edge, flinging out his hands to grab the ivy-tangled gutter. His momentum was too much for it. One end ripped free from its mountings, swinging him out and then back in a wild arc towards the house, so that he hit it like a wrecking ball, hard enough to make him lose his grip. He grabbed ivy as the gutter fell away behind him, shattering into shrapnel on the patio beneath.

Noises above. He looked up to see the bruiser peering cautiously over the edge. He wrested a roof tile free and hurled it down at Luke's face, but it veered at the last moment, bounced off his back before smashing on the flagstones. The bruiser stooped for another tile. Luke looked down. He was way too high to drop uninjured to the patio, but a few feet to his right the patio gave way to a grassy bank. He tried to edge along the wall to it, but clumps of ivy kept ripping away in his hands so that he had to scrabble desperately for grip with the sides of his shoes. Another tile smashed into the wall above his head, showering him with red dust and fragments. He kept edging sideways until finally he was above the bank. He kicked away from the wall, spinning in mid-air, bending his legs to brace himself as he hit the bank then tumbled down onto the lawn.

The impact punched all the air from his lungs, left him wheezing and dazed. He staggered to his feet, wobbled over to the sanctuary of the surrounding woods, sucking in air as he went, bewildered by how suddenly his world had been flipped on its head. The front door banged and footsteps raced across gravel. He could hear the bruiser yelling directions from the roof, like the helicopter pilot in a police chase. Luke fled deeper into the trees, hurdled a fallen timber. Earth clumped on his soles and he almost fell over a tripwire of ground ivy. Crows screeched from trees as he passed, giving his position away. The woods thinned. He burst out into open wasteland, knee deep with ferns, nettles and reedy grass, flecked with bluebells, dandelions and thistles. An abandoned compound of some kind lay ahead. Military, to judge from the rusting MOD 'Keep Out' signs, the fence topped with triple strands of barbed wire. Rabbits had burrowed fat holes beneath it, like intrepid POWs, but none were big enough for him.

There were vast fields of root crops to his left, far too exposed for him to risk crossing, so he turned right instead, ran alongside the fence. Someone had thrown a tattered green tarpaulin over the barbed wire – kids wanting to play inside the compound, no doubt. He tried to haul himself up and over, but the mesh was too old and too loose, so that it bellied out towards him and bit into his fingers. Then he heard voices shockingly close behind and he glimpsed colour and movement in the trees. No time to climb. No time to flee. As his two pursuers burst out into the clearing behind him, Luke threw himself down amid the ferns and nettles, and prayed that he hadn't been seen.

FOUR

I

Rachel Parkes rested the tea tray on an upraised knee as she turned the doorknob of Professor Armstrong's office, pushed it open and then hurried through, setting the tray down gratefully on the edge of his oak desk so that she could finally scratch the tip of her nose, which had been itching dreadfully all the way up the stairs.

'Not *there*,' sighed the professor, taking off his reading glasses as he looked up from his paperwork. 'The coffee table.'

'Sorry.'

'I mean, you do realize why they call it a coffee table? It's not just a *whim*, you know.'

'I had an itch,' she told him. 'On my nose.'

'How fascinating,' he said. 'Do you have any other bodily sensations you wish to tell me about?'

'Not currently, Professor,' she said, transferring the tray as requested. 'But I can keep you informed.'

He shook his head at her as he came over to the table, poured himself a cup. 'You call this tea?' he asked.

'That's what it claimed on the box.'

'I'll be glad when Karen gets back.'

'Me, too.'

His eyes narrowed; his lips pinched tight. 'How's the budget report?' he asked. 'I trust you'll have it ready for me this evening, as you promised.'

'I never promised it this evening,' she said. 'I promised it first thing tomorrow.'

'What's the difference?'

'If there's no difference, you won't mind waiting.'

'I'd like to look it over at home tonight.'

She shook her head. 'I'm sorry. I can't. I have my appointment.'

'Your *appointment*? Today may be a Sunday, Miss Parkes, but it's still a workday.'

'You knew about this. I cleared it last week.'

'Remind me.'

Behind her back, Rachel clenched a fist. He knew exactly where she was going, and why. He just wanted to make her say it for some perverse reason of his own, perhaps so that he could deliver another lecture on the folly of Afghanistan, graveyard of empires. Damned if she'd let him use her brother that way. *Damned* if she would. 'It's private,' she said. 'And the budget report will be on your desk first thing tomorrow, as I promised.'

'I plan to be in very early.'

'It will be waiting for you.' She nodded a little too curtly, tried to soften it with an afterthought of a smile. But he wasn't even looking at her any more. He simply waved her away with a patronising little flick of his right hand, then stirred a pinch of sugar into his tea.

II

Max Walters – the man who'd called himself Steven – burst from the trees expecting to see Luke; but there was no sign of him, just an overgrown glade bordered by fields and a derelict MOD compound. He swore beneath his breath. The fierceness of the chase had kept him from thinking about the old woman, but now his mind went back to her. He felt no remorse. She'd brought her fate on herself by sending that email. However, he did regret the shit-storm it was likely to kick off.

He tried to game it out. Luke would call the police, that was for sure, and the police would visit the house to check his story out. The smashed window, the broken roof tiles and guttering would all corroborate his account.

And they hadn't thought to wear gloves, so they'd have left their fingerprints everywhere. His own were on the police database for various youthful follies, and both Kieran and Pete had records too. This was a total fucking disaster. Then he remembered that Luke had form of his own. It was one of the reasons he'd hired him in the first place, for just such an eventuality as this. He had no idea of Walters' real name, and his only point of contact with him was via an anonymous email address that would be easy enough to scrub. He began to glimpse a way out of this.

'Any sign?' he called out to Kieran, who was wading through the ferns and nettles, looking for Luke.

Kieran shook his head. 'He has to be in here somewhere. If he'd gone for the fields, we'd have spotted him for sure.'

'But what if he *has* got away? What if he's calling the police right now?'

'How? His mobile was in his jacket pocket back in the attic.'

'What if he meets someone? What if he finds a house or a payphone?'

Kieran nodded gloomily. 'We need to get out of here.'

They turned, began jogging their way back.

'The email the old bat sent,' asked Walters. 'Any way to tell if this Rachel Parkes woman has seen it yet?'

'Not unless she replies. She hadn't when I looked.'

'But she's likely to, right? An email like that, a sweet old biddy asking her for help.'

'I'd have thought so.'

'Then let's assume she hasn't got it yet. So if we can delete it somehow, she'll never even know it was sent, right?'

'Easier said than done. We can't do it remotely, not unless she's been *incredibly* sloppy with her passwords. 123456. RachelP. Shit like that. I can run through the most-likelies, but we'd have to get extremely lucky. And her service provider will lock us out if we get it wrong too often. Then she'll know for sure that something stinks.'

'So give me a better idea.'

'We send her another email from the old bat. Have her say that her account's been hacked and that her last email was a virus, please delete it without opening. Or we could even attach a Trojan to it ourselves.'

'And what happens if Parkes finds out that the old girl was already dead when that email was sent?'

'There's no way of doing this clean *and* fast,' said Kieran. 'This is lesser-of-evils' territory we're in.'

'*Fuck*!' Walters made to punch a tree, but that wouldn't help. 'What if she lives locally? What if we could get inside her house?'

'Then it would be a piece of piss,' nodded Kieran. 'Everyone keeps themselves permanently logged in these days. Nine times out of ten, you just turn on the first device you find and you're in. Even if not, I can easily hack in or rig something up. Something untraceable.'

'You've got your kit with you?'

'In the car. Never leave home without it.'

'Good,' said Walters. 'Then let's get busy. We've got work to do.'

FIVE

I

A wasp had taken an uncomfortable interest in Luke's hair, buzzing around his collar and ears. And something large and ticklish was making its way up inside his trouser leg. But he lay absolutely still until his heartbeat had moderated a little, until he'd heard nothing but birdsong for at least five minutes. He got carefully to his knees, peered through the grasses and the ferns. No sign of them. He rose to a stoop then ran away from the house, chased by little flurries of panic.

Now what?

He needed to call the police, of course, but how? His mobile was back in the attic and he couldn't see any houses, not so much as a farm building. These were the Fens, after all, about the least-densely populated part of England. He checked his pockets, found some pound coins and other loose change; hardly enough to fund a new life in South America, but better than nothing. He headed onwards, listening intently. Engines kept screeching in the far distance, motorcycles at full throttle. He'd seen signs earlier for some biker festival; presumably they were gathering for it. He reached a farm track, followed it between fields of rape and wild poppies. An automated irrigation system began to spray, painting rainbows in the sky. A farmhouse ahead, a sagging roof and lichen shadows on its cream walls. He rang its doorbell, banged and shouted. No one answered. He considered, briefly, smashing a window. But it was too late to help Penelope, and his record would make life tough enough with the police without adding a burglary charge, so he turned and hurried on.

A flight of fighter jets queued to land at a nearby air-force base, noses up like snotty guests. Mildenhall, most likely. There had to be houses that way. He reached more woods, ground crackling with dried branches and twigs, emerged onto a winding country lane. It looked faintly familiar. He'd got a little lost earlier, trying to find Penelope's house. If this was the road he thought it was, there should be a T-junction ahead, with a road that led down to a hamlet with a pub.

There was no traffic at all. All those people moaning

about overpopulation should move here. He'd been jogging five minutes before he heard a car coming up fast behind. He stepped off the lane to wave it down when, looking back through a hedgerow on a bend, he glimpsed its black bodywork and tinted windows. He threw himself down and the SUV sped on by. He tried to catch its licence plate, but it was going too fast. It slowed for the T-junction, indicated right, and vanished from sight.

There were sirens in the distance as he hurried down the hill. He ignored them. The hamlet's pub was old, low and thatched, with a beer garden to one side and a car park on the other. He caught sight of his reflection in the front windows and was shocked by what a mess he looked. He decided to go around back in hope of a rear door and a payphone.

A handwritten sign offered a warm welcome to anyone attending *BikerFest*. That invitation had been gladly accepted, if the fifteen or so motorcycles parked outside the low, modern extension were anything to go by. Luke slipped inside. It proved to be a games annexe, large and gloomy except for two spotlit pool tables and a dartboard, plus a bank of fruit machines and arcade games. Middle-aged bikers with grey-streaked hair, black leather jackets and spotted bandannas drank pints of soupy ale. The payphone was next to a large varnished pine table, where two bikers were keeping an eye on a great mound of wallets and keys. One of them grinned at him as he passed, daring him to try his luck. Luke turned his back on him to dial the emergency services. A bored-sounding woman answered. 'Name?'

'Hayward. Luke Hayward.'

'Address?' she asked.

'Martyn's Hall,' he said. 'Near Mildenhall.'

'Is this about the fire?'

'Fire?' he frowned. 'No. This is . . .' Then he remembered the sirens and stopped dead. Steven and his friends must have set fire to the house, destroying any and all evidence that they'd ever been there. And his own car was sitting outside the front door! *Shit!* If they been smart enough to disable it before they'd left, the police would inevitably conclude that he'd killed Penelope himself, then had set fire to her house intending to cover his tracks only to find himself trapped there by a car that wouldn't start. They'd run his licence, get his name, learn of his convictions for assault and making threats against the authorities. And what would his defence be? An absurd story about a mysterious Newton collector, an anonymous lawyer and a generic email address. They'd laugh themselves sick.

'Sir? Are you still there, sir?'

He muttered a curse, slammed down the phone. This was a nightmare. He needed to think. If the police got hold of him now, they wouldn't bother looking for other explanations, they'd arrest him and charge him and lock him away, giving those three men all the time in the world to cover their tracks. He was screwed. He was completely screwed.

It was only then that he remembered the email Penelope Martyn had sent her niece. Not much, but something; a piece of evidence that would corroborate his account. And it had freaked those men out, that was for sure. But maybe it had freaked them out badly enough to do something about it. Cambridge was just forty minutes drive away, after all.

The phone took cards, not coins. He had just enough change to buy one from a dispenser. He called Directory Enquiries, had them put him through to Caius College. 'Rachel Parkes, please,' he said.

'She's not here,' said a man. 'May I take a message?'

'I need to speak to her now. Do you have a mobile number for her?'

'I couldn't possibly give out that kind of information.'

'Then can you at least get a message to her?'

Hesitancy in his voice. Anxiety that this might actually be serious. 'I'm afraid Ms Parkes is out of Cambridge this afternoon, and she doesn't have a mobile. I could ask her to contact you if she calls in.'

Luke hesitated. He could hardly wait here all day on the off chance. 'I'll try again later,' he said. He put the phone down, stood there in thought. What he really needed was someone to look for Rachel on his behalf, someone who knew Cambridge and who trusted him enough to do it without asking awkward questions.

Pelham, then.

He called Directory Enquiries again, asked for his friend's home number. It just rang and rang. Probably out with one of his women, though maybe he'd be at his lab, even on a Sunday afternoon. For all his protestations, the man was a workaholic. And why not? His company paid him a fortune to do the kinds of R&D he'd gladly done for free at his old college. But, for the life of him, Luke couldn't remember what his company was called. They'd moved into purpose-built laboratories at a Cambridge science park a couple of years back. Luke had taken Maria to the opening. But what the hell were they—

The pub doors suddenly slammed open. He span around to see policemen flooding in from the main bar and the car park, truncheons in their hands.

'*Raid*!' yelled one of the bikers. 'It's the pigs!'

II

'Twenty million,' said Grant, when finally he rang back. 'That's the highest I can go.'

'One hundred,' replied Croke. 'That's the lowest I can go.'

'Seriously, my friend. You don't know the people I work with. They think you're trying to take advantage of them. They hate people taking advantage. There's no chance whatsoever that they'd go for forty, let alone a hundred.'

'That's a shame,' said Croke. He looked out his window at the French Riviera thirty thousand feet beneath, the distinctive shapes of its marinas, the white specks of the cocaine super-yachts. It wasn't just how much they cost in themselves; it was their berthing fees and running costs. It was the salaries for their crews.

'So we're agreed, then? Twenty million.'

'I'm not risking my life for twenty mill.'

A beat of silence. Two beats. 'Thirty, then. I can probably go as high as thirty.'

'Ninety,' said Croke. 'For what your friends will be getting, ninety's a steal.'

'You know nothing about my friends.'

'I know they'll be getting a steal at ninety.'

'Fine,' sighed Grant. 'Call it fifty. But success-only, understood? No crying about near misses.'

They settled on seventy. Less than Croke had hoped; more than he'd expected. Now for the next stage. He called Avram in Jerusalem. 'I need you to speak to Thaddeus for me,' he told him.

'Why me?'

'Because I don't speak his language.'

'You don't speak American?' asked Avram, puzzled.

'I don't speak *Bible*.'

Avram grunted. 'And what do you want me to say to him?'

'Everything you told me before. Why you're so confident about finding it. Why this is the time. Why it has to be tomorrow night. I need him to do something he won't want to do. I need him excited. I need him *rash*.'

'Leave it to me.'

'Good. And when he's ready, have him give me a call.'

III

The police raid was surely meant for Luke; but the bikers didn't realize that. And they evidently had something to hide. A moment of stillness, as though neither side could quite believe the presence of the other. Then a pool-cue blurred and a policeman's cheek burst red. War cries of pain, anger, fear and defiance. The two bikers near Luke stood up and sent their table toppling, pint glasses, wallets and keys crashing to the floor. A wash of foamy ale swept a keychain to Luke's feet. He crouched and picked it up without even thinking, walked briskly into the washroom. The sash window was half up and he rolled beneath it, out onto the gravelled car park. He clicked the remote on the key-fob. The lights of a black-and-chrome Harley flashed. He straddled it, kicked it off its stand and started it up. Two bikers had escaped from the washroom after him. They yelled and tried to grab him. He twisted the throttle and squirted between them.

A police car screeched across the car park exit. Luke slithered to a halt, pulled a sharp turn, roared up a grassy bank into the beer garden, weaving between tables as men grabbed their pints and women grabbed their kids. He tore through a tangle of white and red roses, bumped down a bank onto a lane, raced away up a hill. He hadn't ridden a bike in years, not since his student days, and that bike had been nothing like this beast. Yet the skills returned quickly. He leaned into corners, trusting the bike a little more with every moment. But the spike of adrenalin soon began to ebb, allowing dismay to take its place. He was a fugitive now. The police would take it for granted he'd fled because he'd killed Penelope. Even more than before, he'd become his own only hope of proving himself innocent.

He came up fast behind a green Volvo as it slowed

for a blind corner, overtook it in a blur. At a junction, he glimpsed motorcyclists approaching from his right. They accelerated when they saw him, fell in behind, caught up fast. Of all the days to nick a Harley, he'd chosen *BikerFest*! He took a corner too fast, began fishtailing wildly, fighting desperately to regain control. A roundabout ahead, a long line of traffic to his right, held back by an old artic labouring up the hill towards it. He muttered a prayer and gave it everything, flashing past the lorry's bumper with nothing to spare, earning himself an indignant 'parp'. He was going so fast that he was late on the brakes and couldn't help but ride up the far verge, his back tyre sliding around, the casing pressing hot against his leg.

The line of traffic had balked the bikers behind him, earning him maybe thirty seconds grace. He hurtled past fields of mustard and barley, took a slip road down onto dual carriageway and swung straight out into the overtaking lane. A glance around, no sign of pursuit. He breathed a little easier. Sheer speed made him feel almost euphoric, stirring his spirits like a battle-cry. Wind buffeted his body, forcing him to hunker down and squint. He lost track of time and distance, simply putting in the miles. He overtook an accidental convoy of lorries, belatedly saw a sign for a place called Cherry Hinton. Cherry Hinton was the name of Pelham's science park, he was sure of it. He braked and cut across traffic, missing the slip road itself but managing to bump across a narrow strip of grass onto it. Then it was up through the gears and away.

SIX

I

Rachel found Bren out in the garden, reading an old copy of *Jane's* in the shade of an oak. She could tell he was angry from the stiffness in his posture and because he didn't look up as she approached, not even when she stooped to kiss his forehead.

'You were supposed to be here half an hour ago,' he said, turning another page with his right hand, holding it down against the breeze with the stump of his left elbow.

'I'm sorry.' She showed him the fronts and backs of her hands as witnesses for the defence, though she'd cleaned the oil off as best she could. 'More trouble with the Murcielago.'

'I wish you wouldn't call it that,' said Bren. 'I wish

you wouldn't keep making jokes about of it. It's a heap of fucking junk. Why can't you buy something that works?'

There was a bench nearby. She pushed him over to it then sat beside him, covered his hand with hers. 'You know why I can't,' she said.

'Then why not just get rid of the damned thing? There's a perfectly good bus service.'

'No, there isn't.' The nearest stop was two miles away, as Bren well knew, and the new timetable meant that she'd either have ten minutes with him each visit, or over three hours, neither of which was ideal. Besides, a car – even one as unreliable as hers – meant they could drive to a nearby pub or take an impromptu picnic in the woods. But she said none of this, for he was only letting off steam. Instead she reached into her bag. 'I brought you something.'

He took it from her, pulled away the flimsy tissue paper. He enjoyed presents but he found unwrapping them hard. When he saw the jacket, he couldn't prevent his smile, which made her smile too. It was from a charity shop, sure, but it was a book he'd mentioned as an aside during her last visit, his way of asking without asking. His smile quickly vanished, though; he looked, suddenly, ashamed. His eyes began to water, causing her far more anguish than his reproaches ever could. He bowed his head and covered his face and then his shoulders began to hump. She put her arms around him, held his cheek against her chest until he'd gathered himself once more. Then she gave him a moment or two longer to wipe his eyes. 'I'll get a better car soon,' she promised. 'As soon as the royalties start coming in.'

That made him smile. 'What was it called again?'

'*Cynic Philosophy in Second Century Anatolia.*'

'That's the baby,' he said. 'Title like that, it'll be flying off the shelves. And don't forget the foreign language rights. That's where the real money is.'

'I don't want you getting too excited,' she said, 'but I had a call from L.A.'

'I'm not surprised. It's got Oscars written all over it. And it's not just the box-office, you know, it's the merchandising.'

'That's what they say.'

'We'll sell little Diogenes dolls. When you turn them upside down, they'll shake a fist and yell "Get off my lawn!" That was Diogenes, wasn't it?'

'Close enough.'

They looked fondly at each other. Bren took her hand with his good one, interlaced fingers with her, shook his head. 'I don't know why I do it,' he said. 'You come all the way out here for me, and I just make you feel bad.'

'Shh,' she said.

'You do so much for me, and all I ever do is make you feel bad.'

'You're my brother,' she said. 'All you ever do is make me feel good.' She felt in danger of welling up, so she consulted her watch to clear her head, brace herself for the ordeal ahead. This place was only partly paid for by the Ministry of Defence; what remained was far too much for Rachel's paltry income from the library and her occasional bartending. Their lives, therefore, depended upon the continuing goodwill of the care home's management team. If they hardened their hearts today, Rachel didn't know what they'd do. Bren would go crazy without his army friends, yet the publicly-funded homes within any kind of distance seemed almost designed to drive costly veterans like him to suicide.

'We should head in,' said Bren. 'No point being late.'

Rachel took a deep breath. 'No,' she agreed. No point indeed.

II

There was no sign of Pelham's Alfa in the largely deserted Cherry Hinton Science Park; but, now that Luke was here, he might as well ask. He left the Harley hidden behind a line of wheelie-bins, hurried up the front steps into reception. An elderly guard was behind the desk, doing a crossword puzzle while listening to local radio. The way he looked Luke up and down reminded him of what a mess he was. He did his best to appear confident all the same. 'Pelham Redfern, please,' he said.

'And you are?'

The radio pipped the hour; the news came on. He belatedly realized he couldn't give his real name, lest the police already had put out an alert. Yet it had to be a name Pelham would recognize; someone he'd want to see. 'Jay Cowan,' he said.

The guard nodded, made his call. It seemed Pelham was here after all. He gave him Jay's name, raised an eyebrow in surprise at the warmth of the response. 'Mr Redfern will be down in a minute,' he said.

Luke nodded at the washroom door. 'May I? Been a hell of a day.'

The guard smiled. 'I'd guessed that much for myself,' he said.

Even though he'd been expecting it, Luke was still startled by the figure that confronted him in the washroom mirror. His face was filthy, his hair spiked, his shirt spattered. There were no towels, only a blow-dry machine, so he tore off handfuls of toilet paper, squirted soap from a dispenser, and went to work. He was still at it when the door opened and Pelham walked in, wearing a faded Zanzibar T-shirt and blue jeans that slouched around his hips like a gunslinger's belt. He was as tall, broad and shaggily handsome as ever, yet much heavier in the gut too, like a retired second-row forward making up for the diet years. 'Luke, mate,' he frowned. 'They told me it was Jay.'

'Yes. Sorry about that. Listen: do I have any credit in the bank with you?'

'Of course you do,' said Pelham. 'You know that. Why? What's going on?'

'Can we get out of here? I'll tell you on the way.'

Pelham nodded. 'Give us a minute,' he said. 'There's some stuff I need to shut down. Then I'm all yours.'

III

They hit turbulence over the *massif central*. The jet shuddered and dropped sharply enough for Croke to slop a little of his bourbon. He muttered irritably as he wiped it away. Then his phone rang. Thaddeus. 'Is it true what Avram tells me?' he asked breathlessly. 'That you've found it?'

'No. But we *have* found the papers. And we're confident they tell us where it is.'

'That's wonderful news! Just wonderful.' But then his tone became more guarded. 'Avram said you needed to speak to me. What about?'

'I need to know if you're in or not.'

'Of course I'm in.' He sounded baffled. 'Why would you even ask?'

'Forgive me, Reverend,' said Croke. 'But my experience has been that, whenever there's been an urgent decision to make, you've notified your colleagues on your Third Temple Committee. You've solicited their opinions. You've preached long and no doubt worthy sermons at each other. You've checked your scriptures for relevant texts and you've prayed for guidance. And by the time you've all reached a conclusion, the opportunity is across the border and into another country.'

'I sit on a committee,' said Thaddeus. 'That's how committees work.'

'Today's Sunday,' said Croke. 'As Avram no doubt explained to you, this has to happen tomorrow night or not at all. Let me say that again: *tomorrow night or not at all.*'

'I know the schedule.'

'Add in the time difference and we now have less than thirty hours to find this thing and ship it to Israel. So there's no time to notify your colleagues. There's no time for sermons or for prayer. It's go for it or let it slide. Me, I'm in. I'm all in. I'm on my way to England now, because I'll be needed there, my plane and me. But I need to know that everyone else is all in too; because if anyone holds back, we all go down.'

'God created our universe six thousand years ago, Mr Croke,' said Thaddeus. 'It says so in the Bible. Four thousand years before Christ, two thousand years since.

Those six thousand years are the first six days of God's creation. And on the seventh day He rested. *On the seventh day.* The thousand year rule of Christ on earth is about to start, Mr Croke. The Rapture and the Last Judgement. That is a plain biblical fact. Look around you. The signs are *everywhere*. Wars, famines, pestilence, earthquakes, the demise of the whore of Rome. I've been preparing for this my whole life. So yes I'm all in, as you put it. I was *born* all in. What do you need?'

'I need you to call the White House for me.'

Thaddeus laughed. 'You can't be serious.'

'You just said you were all in.'

'You don't understand how these things work,' said Thaddeus. 'There are rules. There are protocols. The biggest of which is that I *never* contact her. She contacts me.'

'You said last year that she knew about all this. You told me she was excited and had asked to be kept informed.'

'She was and she did.'

'Well, then. Inform her. Let her know that we've found the papers, that they're pointing us to some buildings in Central London. Tell her that you believe absolutely that we'll find it there, because this is God's plan and His seventh day is about to dawn, and He wouldn't have sent us all these signs unless He meant for us to succeed. Convince her that this is the mission God has appointed for her, that this is her time, that she is the one.'

'This *is* the time,' said Thaddeus. 'She *is* the one. She's the Esther for our age.'

'It's not me you need to convince, Reverend. It's *her*. And when you've convinced her, you're going to need to fly up to Washington to be with her and keep her strong, or her advisors will talk her out of it again.'

'I can't. I have duties here. My congregation.'

Same as it ever was, sighed Croke. *All in until he actually had to do something*. 'I remember the Book of Esther,' he said. 'My mother used to read it to me at bedtime. There was a Thaddeus in it, wasn't there? That old Jew who refused to bow to the prince, the one who sparked all the trouble.'

'His name was Mordecai.'

'Mordecai, Thaddeus. I knew it was something like that.' He shifted his phone to his other ear. 'And don't I recall that this Mordecai-Thaddeus guy had another important role in the story? Wasn't he was the one who, when Esther got scared, convinced her that God had made her queen precisely for that moment, that she needed to do His will *whatever the consequences*?'

Silence as Thaddeus digested this. 'You don't know her very well, do you,' he said. 'She isn't the kind of person you can give orders to.'

'I'm not suggesting you give her orders. I'm suggesting that you tell her what we're on the brink of, then see how she responds.'

'How do you expect her to respond?'

'I think she'll ask what she can do to help,' said Croke. 'And when she does, this is what you're going to tell her.'

SEVEN

I

The earthquake had torn fissures in many of Jerusalem's streets, yet the resultant congestion wasn't as bad as it might have been, for tourists had cancelled their bookings by the planeload, spooked by the threat of aftershocks, food shortages and riots, by reports of sewage on the streets and the first whispers of contagious diseases.

A bus took Avram from Jaffa Gate to King George. From there he had to walk. He hurried up Strauss into the ultra-Orthodox quarter of Mea Shearim. The streets here were strewn with torn fly-posters and other litter, and there was graffiti everywhere. The squalor dismayed him, as it always did, for it reflected so poorly on the devout, and gave unnecessary fuel to those who mocked the Haredim as all prayer and no fasting.

He paused outside a grocer's, picked up a lemon, glanced back. Only men in view, all of them dressed in the distinctive black frock coats and broad-brimmed hats of the ultra-Orthodox. This wasn't his favourite quarter of Jerusalem, sure, but it made it child's play to check for a tail.

He turned right at Yeshèskel. The earthquake had sheared the front off an apartment building, leaving the street narrowed by skips and scaffolding. He entered the religious bookshop to find Shlomo himself behind the counter. He looked startled to see Avram, but he covered it quickly. 'Yes?' Shlomo asked. 'May I help.'

'My great-nephew's bar mitzvah is next week,' said Avram. 'I'm looking for something special.'

'We keep our special stock in the back.' The bookseller handed over to an assistant, a plump and soft young man, beard wispy as undergrowth after a drought. Then he led Avram back to his office, where they greeted each other more warmly. 'This must be important,' said Shlomo pointedly. 'You wouldn't have come here otherwise.'

'It's time,' said Avram.

Shlomo nodded. 'And you decided this yourself, did you? Without consulting me or my men?'

'The Lord decided, praise His Name,' said Avram. 'It's tomorrow night. We need to start preparing now.'

'Tomorrow night? Are you crazy? Haven't you seen the extra soldiers they've brought in?'

'They're guarding the perimeter,' said Avram. 'We'll be attacking from inside the perimeter.'

'And the *Waqf*? They've doubled their numbers too.'

'The *Waqf*!' mocked Avram. 'Old men with sticks.'

'And the heifer?' asked Shlomo.

The question blindsided Avram. With everything else going on, he'd forgotten about the heifer. But he didn't let it show. 'What about her?'

'You have her?'

'Of course,' he said. 'How could we do this otherwise?'

Shlomo looked stunned. 'You never said.'

'No. Because last time we got anywhere close, we found her one morning with her throat slit. So this time I kept my mouth shut. Can you blame me?'

'How old?'

'Her third birthday was three weeks ago,' he said. 'The day of the earthquake. The *hour* of the earthquake.'

'Then it *is* true,' said Shlomo, awed. 'It *is* time.'

'What have I been telling you?'

'And the sacrifice? When do we do it?'

'Tonight.'

'No,' said Shlomo. 'I can't get my men together that soon.'

'Your men?'

'Of course. A perfect red heifer. The first for two thousand years. And you expect us not to be there?'

'I'm afraid there isn't time for—'

'Then we make time. For this, we make time. First thing tomorrow morning. I can have them ready by then. Where is she?'

'Near Megiddo,' said Avram. 'But I—'

'There's a car park by the archaeological site. We'll meet you there. Seven o'clock tomorrow morning.'

'Yes, but—'

'Seven o'clock.' He got to his feet, the meeting over. 'And then tomorrow night we'll do this thing, just as we've planned. Tomorrow night, we take the Mount back for Israel and the Lord.'

II

'What happened to the Alfa?' asked Luke, climbing in passenger side of a red BMW convertible. 'I thought you'd never sell that beast.'

'And I never will,' said Pelham, belting himself in. 'She's in the shop. Some bastard telephone pole leapt out in front of us, fucked her bonnet right up.'

'There ought to be a law.'

'There is, apparently. But I'm the one it holds liable, would you believe? One rule for us, another for telephone poles.' He turned on the ignition, made to lower the roof.

'You couldn't leave that up for the moment, could you?' asked Luke.

'Sure,' said Pelham. He glanced quizzically at him. 'Why?'

'There are some bikers out looking for me. And the police.'

'The police?'

'It's nothing to make you ashamed of me. I swear it isn't.'

'Of course not, mate. I know you better than that.'

Luke nodded. After the day he'd had, such a simple vote of confidence moved him more than he could say. 'If the police do stop us, just tell them I turned up out of the blue. You know nothing about anything. I'll back you up, I promise.'

'You quiet ones, eh,' grinned Pelham, pulling away. 'What was it? A bank?'

'That's where the money is,' agreed Luke.

They reached the junction with the main road. 'Where are we going?' asked Pelham.

'I need to find a woman.'

'What have I been telling you?'

'Her name's Rachel Parkes,' said Luke. 'She works at Caius College. But she's not there this afternoon. I already checked.'

Pelham slid him a glance. 'You haven't turned into some weird stalker-man, have you?'

'Look who's talking.'

'Fair enough.' Pelham pulled out his phone. 'Caius, right?'

'Yes. Why? Do you know someone there?'

Pelham grinned as he scrolled through his address book. 'Mate, I know someone everywhere.'

III

The man had a Midwest accent, and he sounded to be in his fifties or even his sixties, though Croke had been wrong in such assessments before. 'You don't need to know my name,' he said. 'But my boss was just called by a friend of yours. A *reverend* friend.'

'Ah,' said Croke. So this was the Office of the Vice President calling. Instinctively he set down his glass and sat up a little straighter, only to smile when he caught himself at it.

'We'll speak only this once,' said the man. 'If you ever breathe a word about it, you'll regret it.'

'I'll bet it turns your wife on when you talk like that,' said Croke.

'Don't get smart with me. You've already made a bad impression coming in through the back door like this.'

'Would I have got in through the front?'

'That's not the point.'

81

'Maybe not to you.'

'If we're going to work together—'

'We're going to work together just fine. You know why? Because your boss just ordered you to help us, or we wouldn't be talking. So stop wasting my time and get on with it.'

A rustling of paper. 'I'm reading your CIA file,' said the man. 'Fascinating stuff.'

Croke took a sip of bourbon. 'I do my best.'

'Front companies in D.C., London and Hong Kong. I'll bet they could do with an audit.'

'They're not front companies. They provide high-level business intelligence and security consultancy services.'

'That's not what it says here. It says here they're cover for your arms deals.'

'Is this really what you want to talk about?'

A page was turned. 'Your father is Dr Arthur Croke, I believe. The guy who used to run our USAF lab up in Rome.'

'He still runs it.'

'Really?' He sounded genuinely surprised. 'I thought he'd had to have retired by now. I mean, god, he was getting on when *I* met him. And that has to be twenty years ago, at least.'

'He's been running it thirty-three years,' said Croke, with genuine pride.

'A fine man. A real American patriot. His whole life dedicated to his country.'

'Yes.'

'So despite some of these . . . *startling* things I'm reading in your file, we'd have no reason to doubt that you're a patriot too; no reason to fear you'd ever do anything to harm our nation or bring shame upon your father.'

'Quite right.'

'Good. So the story's going to run like this: in your work as an arms dealer – forgive me, *as a security consultant* – you sometimes bump up against people of dubious character. It so happens that two of those people have recently and separately warned you of an attack being planned on our great ally Britain. As a loyal American citizen, you naturally passed this intelligence on to us. It happens to tally with some chatter we've been picking up ourselves. We're therefore about to warn the Brits that we fear some bad guys are planning an atrocity in and around Crane Court. The good news is that your sources are prepared to pass along new info as they get it. The bad news is that they'll only speak to you. But you've agreed to be our middleman, passing that information on in real time.'

Croke snorted. 'So if this turns to shit, you can put all the blame on me.'

'Of course. What did you expect? Now, you're already on your way to England, right? Which airport?'

'Cambridge.'

'We're shifting you to City of London. One of our people will meet you there. His name's Richard Morgenstern.' He gave Croke his cell and other contact details. 'He's seconded to a new counterterrorism group the Brits have just set up; but he's loyal to us. To us *personally*, I mean. To my boss.'

'Does he know what we're looking for?'

'He knows *what*. We had to tell him that much. But he doesn't know *why*. My boss just told him that finding it was her number one priority right now. That's all he needed to know. He's a true patriot.'

'Another one. Excellent. We can sing anthems together.'

'We're not going to talk again, you and me. Everything is to go through Morgenstern. And if you ever breathe one word about our involvement in all this, you're a dead man. Am I clear?'

Croke smiled. 'As crystal,' he said.

EIGHT

I

Before setting fire to Penelope Martyn's house, Max Walters had flipped through her address book to find out where Rachel Parkes lived. Now he pulled up opposite her front door. There was no sign of life inside, and when he tried her telephone he was switched over to voice mail. He glanced around at Kieran, who was monitoring the old bat's email account on his laptop. 'Any reply yet?'

'Nothing.'

'Okay,' Walters said. 'Let's do it.'

They waited for a cyclist to pass, crossed the road. The afternoon had grown sticky, hinting at storms. A communal front path led to a shared front door with buzzers for the top and bottom floor flats. He rang the ground-floor bell. No reply. An elderly couple walking slowly by along the pavement darted suspicious looks at them. Walters smiled cordially and wished them a good afternoon, but it did no good. They kept glancing around as they crossed the road and went inside a house opposite. Then their net curtains began to twitch. 'Shit,' muttered Walters.

'Maybe there's a back way in,' suggested Kieran.

They walked to the end of the street, turned left. 'What about those locks?' asked Walters. 'Any problem?'

'The Yale's a piece of piss,' Pete assured him. 'The Chubb'll be a bit harder. Say a minute for the pair. Plenty of time for those old farts to see us and call the cops.'

They turned up the next street. An unbroken terrace blocked any hope of breaking into Parkes' flat through a rear window. 'Maybe we'd better wait until dark,' said Kieran.

Walters snorted. 'Today's about the longest bloody day of the year. And what if she opens her email while we're waiting?' He took a deep breath. He hadn't yet reported this mess to Croke, hoping to sort it all out first. But he couldn't put it off any longer. He didn't want Pete and Kieran listening in, however, so he walked off a little way before calling Croke's number.

'Have you got my papers?' asked Croke.

'Yes,' said Walters. 'But there's been a hitch.'

'A *hitch*?' asked Croke.

Walters had meant to play it cool, but somehow the story came blurting out. Croke had that effect on him. 'We're outside the girl's place now,' he finished. 'But there are curtains twitching everywhere.'

'I don't believe this,' said Croke acidly. 'I ask you to buy me some papers, and instead I get arson and a dead woman. And now you're worried about *curtains*?'

'We work for one of your companies, sir. If we're arrested, it'll lead the police straight back to you. I wanted to make absolutely sure you think it's worth the risk.'

Silence. 'Okay,' said Croke finally. 'Stay where you are. I'll see what I can arrange.'

II

Pelham scrolled for a number then jammed his phone between shoulder and ear. 'Hey, gorgeous,' he said. 'It's me. Yeah. Listen, that friend of yours at Caius. Sonia, isn't it? You couldn't give her a call for me, could you? Brilliant. I need to get hold of a girl there. Rachel something . . .' He glanced across at Luke for a prompt.

'Rachel Parkes,' said Luke.

'Rachel Parkes,' relayed Pelham. He listened a moment, laughed loudly. 'No. Nothing like that, I promise. A favour for a mate.' He laughed again. 'What do you mean? I've got plenty of mates. I just won't introduce you or you'll run off with one of them.' He nodded vigorously. 'Yeah, anything you can get. Mobile, home phone, address, whatever. Thanks, sweetheart. Love you.' He killed the call, turned to Luke. 'Miriam,' he said. 'I think she might be the one.'

'You always think they might be the one.'

'Keeps the heart young, falling in love. Try it yourself sometime.'

'Maybe next week. This week I'm focusing on staying alive.'

'You'll need something to write on when she calls back.' He gestured at his glove compartment. 'Have a rootle around in there.'

'Jesus, mate,' said Luke, as he precipitated a small avalanche of candy bars and boiled sweets.

'Better give me one of those,' said Pelham. 'Wouldn't want to faint from sugar deficiency; not with all these telephone poles around.'

'Was that when the last one attacked?' asked Luke, finding himself a stubby pencil and a notepad. 'While you were feeding?'

'What are you? A claims adjuster?' He tore the wrapper off one with his teeth, stuffed the molten mess inside into his mouth. He was still chewing when his phone rang, had to give himself a couple of moments to swallow it away. 'Hey, sweetheart,' he said. 'Any joy?' He listened a moment, grinned. 'You're a star.' He called out phone numbers and an address for Luke to jot down. 'Thanks, gorgeous,' he said. 'And we're still on for tomorrow, yeah? Great. Then take care, now.' He ended the call and handed Luke his phone so that he could try the various numbers. Without success. 'Do you want to go sit outside her place?' asked Pelham. 'You can't consider yourself a proper stalker until you've done that.'

'How far is it?'

Pelham turned on his GPS, typed in her address. 'Other side of town,' he said. 'Twenty minutes or so.' He gave Luke a pointed look. 'Just about long enough for you to tell me what the fuck's going on.'

'Fair enough,' said Luke. He took a moment to order his thoughts. 'Remember that business with the Uni?'

Pelham nodded soberly. 'Of course.'

'I tried to get myself another job, but I was way too toxic. It was clearly going to be a year or two before the whole thing died down, so I decided to make a virtue of necessity, write my book. I'd been talking about it long enough.'

'Telling me.'

'I had some savings, but it was still going to be pretty

tight, you know; so I put the word out that if there was any work—'

'I asked around,' said Pelham. 'I swear I did. But you know how things are.'

'I wasn't having a go. I'm just explaining the background. Because around last Christmas this guy rings out of the blue. He tells me his name is Steven, though I doubt now that it really was. He says that he's a lawyer and that he's got a possible job for me. One of his clients is apparently a Newton obsessive.'

'You should get on famously, then.'

'This client had commissioned him to track down all of Newton's papers still missing from the Sotheby's auction. You know about that, right?'

'Do I?' asked Pelham. He pulled up at a set of lights, indicated to turn left. 'Tell you what: why don't you give me the refresher?'

III

Richard Morgenstern sounded young, enthusiastic, and distinctly Texan. 'Great to hear from you, sir,' he boomed, when Croke called him. ' I'm on my way to City Airport now. You're not there already, are you?'

'No. But I need something done and I hoped you'd be able to help.'

'If I can, I will. Anything for a man like you.'

'A man like me?'

'A friend of *hers*. She called me herself, you know? I mean, hell, I saw her a few times during the campaign, and once at the Academy. But I never *spoke* to her before. And she wasn't my Commander-in-Chief then. It's not the same, is it?'

'No. I guess not.'

'You know what she told me? She told me this is her number one priority right now. She said this trumps *everything*.' He laughed a little giddily, as though he still couldn't quite believe it. 'So tell me what you need. If it's in my power—'

'There's an email that could be problematic,' said Croke. 'I need it deleted.'

'Civilian or government.'

'Civilian.'

'Hell,' said Morgenstern. 'It would be. *Reading* an email's easy. We get copies of everything sent anywhere. But *deleting* one is hard. The service providers can be real assholes. They like evidence of threat or wrongdoing. They like *warrants*. Can we take this to the courts?'

'No,' said Croke.

'Then I don't know what to suggest.'

'How about the police?' asked Croke. 'Will they do what you ask without going to a judge?' He outlined his idea.

Morgenstern laughed. 'That shouldn't be a problem,' he said. 'I'll get on to it now. I'll call back if I have any trouble; otherwise you can assume it's taken care of, and I'll see you on the ground in thirty.'

'Thanks,' said Croke. 'I'll let my people know to expect company.'

NINE

I

It wasn't easy, giving an abbreviated history of the Newton papers. Luke had to start way back. 'Okay,' he told Pelham. 'Newton never married or had children, so he left all his papers to his niece Catherine. Her daughter married into the Portsmouth family, who offered them to Cambridge University back in the 1870s. Cambridge only wanted the scientific ones, so the rest were eventually auctioned off by Sotheby's in 1936. Sotheby's kept a record of who bought every lot. Most of the buyers were well-known dealers, but there were some private collectors too. The economist John Maynard Keynes bought a huge number of the alchemical lots; and a Sephardic Jew called Yahuda bought a bunch of theological papers that were later used to support the case for a Jewish homeland.'

'You what?' asked Pelham.

'I know it sounds strange, but the British were occupying Palestine at the time. Newton was the great man of British science, so his belief in the restoration of a Jewish state really meant something.'

'And Newton wanted a Jewish state, did he?'

Luke nodded. 'A lot of them did back then,' he said. 'They believed it was a necessary precondition of the Second Coming. But the point is that we know where the great majority of lots ended up. Keynes left all his to King's College Cambridge, for example. Yahuda's eventually went to the National Library of Israel.' He glanced at Pelham. 'Remember when Jay went to Jerusalem that time? That was to see the Yahuda archive.'

'But some of the Sotheby's lots have gone missing,' suggested Pelham. 'And this lawyer hired you to find them.'

'More or less. It was good money, it meshed perfectly with my research and it wasn't particularly demanding. I mean it's not exactly Sherlock Holmes. Mostly it's afternoons in reference libraries and public records offices, or writing letters and waiting for replies. The lawyer kept pushing me, but honestly there was only so much I could do. People have been hunting for the damned things for years, after all. It wasn't as if I was likely to do any better.'

'But you did?'

'There were these buyers we call the three Ms,' said Luke. 'They have no connection with each other, except that they each bought one of the missing lots, and their surnames all begin with the letter M. May, Manning and Martin. Not much to go on, but I figured I could narrow it down. For example, they most likely lived in or around London. Any further away, they'd likely have bid through a dealer. And if they'd made a special trip for the auction, then surely they'd have bought more than one lot.'

Pelham nodded. 'Makes sense.'

'So I went through various 1936 London and Home Counties directories for plausible candidates, then tracked descendants through obits and wills and the like.'

'Sounds a hoot.'

'It was, curiously. Or a distraction, at least. Anyway, I got no joy from that, so I tried alternate spellings instead. Mays, for example. Munnings. Martyn with a "y" rather than an "i".'

'Ah,' said Pelham. 'I sense we're getting somewhere.'

'A Bernard Martyn lived in an apartment in Bruton Place in 1936, just a short stroll from Sotheby's. I checked into him: a particle physicist with a special interest in light.'

'So bound to be interested in Newton?'

'You'd think so, wouldn't you? And likely to be pretty well off, too, with an address like that. Not that these lots were expensive; not for what they were. Ten to fifteen guineas, that kind of thing. About £500 in modern money. The entire collection only raised nine grand.'

'What would they be worth now?'

'God knows. They don't often come up for sale. And it depends massively on how interesting it is. Twenty or thirty grand for anything half decent. And if it's unusual, if it hints at original thinking . . .' He shook his head. 'A hundred grand easily. Quite possibly two or even three.'

'No wonder your client wanted them.'

'Anyway, Bernard Martyn died back in 1969. He was childless, so his estate passed to his nephew George. George died too, a few years back, leaving the residue to his widow Penelope. I tracked her down to the family pile in the Fens, so I wrote to ask her if, by any chance, she knew where Bernard Martyn's belongings were. They're up in my attic, she replied, covered by dust sheets. No one's looked at them in decades.'

'So you got in your car and drove on down?'

'And what should I find in one of the boxes,' agreed Luke, 'but four pages of Isaac Newton's alchemical notes?' He told Pelham everything that had happened since, finishing with his arrival at Cherry Hinton Science Park.

'Bugger me,' said Pelham. 'You *have* had a day.'

'So you see why I need Rachel Parkes. Her aunt's email and those photos are all I've got. If those bastards delete them, I'm toast.'

II

The policeman was uncommonly tall and thin, so that he looked disconcertingly like a marionette as he climbed out of his patrol car. And he kept dabbing at his septum with his index finger, as if tickled by allergies.

'Thanks for getting here so quickly,' said Walters, shaking him by his hand.

'Sod all else going on,' said the policeman. 'Never is, round here.' He folded his arms and leaned back against his car. 'So you're counterterrorism, right?'

'We can't discuss that, I'm afraid.'

'I've been thinking of getting a transfer myself, see if I can't get some proper action. What's it like with your mob?'

'I'm sorry. We really can't discuss it.'

He grunted and reached back inside his car for his cap. 'So what do you need me for?' he asked. 'The governor only told me where to come.'

'There's a house we want to look inside. But we can't have the locals complaining, so we need to show them we're on the side of the angels.'

'Mannequin duty, huh. Ah, well.' He gave the house a gloomy look. 'So this is part of the great terrorist nexus, eh? Should me and the boys be keeping an eye on it?'

Walters shook his head. 'It's information we're after, not bad guys.'

'If you say so.'

'And not a word about this, right? Not to anyone. We're talking national security here.'

'So I was told.'

'Good.'

Walters joined Kieran and Pete by Parkes' front door. The locks put up little fight. They spread out inside, taking different rooms. The kitchen was clean but cramped, with shabby units and a noisy fridge. Walters peeled himself a satsuma as he flipped through a stack of bills.

'Two bedrooms,' said Kieran, appearing at the door. 'One's an old biddy's; the landlady, I assume. The other is Parkes'. Her desk's set up for a laptop, but there's no laptop. She must have it with her.'

'Any other devices?'

'None that I can find.'

'Shit. Then what do we do?'

'They have broadband. I can put an intercept on the router. When she logs on, we'll piggyback in with her, then hijack her ID and disrupt her connection. She'll assume it's a glitch with her router or her machine. By the time she's turned everything off and on again, the email will be history. She'll never even know it was there.'

'How long to set up?'

'Five minutes. Maybe ten.'

Walters nodded. 'Then get to it,' he said.

III

Noxious smells and unnerving clanking noises were coming from beneath the bonnet of Rachel's Rover as she bunny-hopped along her street. She clutched the steering wheel tight and let out a heartfelt curse. Everything seemed to be going wrong today. The meeting at her brother's care home had been a near disaster. When you had nothing with which to bargain, you made rash promises instead. Ten grand by the end of the month. How on earth was she to find that? She was already pushing her luck at both her jobs. Her room was as cheap as Cambridge could offer, she'd pared every surplus expense from her life, had nothing left to sell. She could ask Aunt Penelope for help, but her pride revolted at the thought. If Penny's odious sons found out she'd given Bren any more money, they'd cut her off from her grandkids out of sheer spite. Rachel would never forgive herself if—

A police car was parked outside her house, a gangling officer leaning against it. And she could have sworn she saw movement in the front room, even though Betty was in Ireland for a fortnight. Her heart sank. They couldn't have been burgled, could they? Not on top of everything else. She parked and hurried across. 'What is it?' she asked the policeman. 'What's happened?'

'Do you live here, ma'am?' he asked.

'Yes. Why?'

The front door opened and three men came out; plain-clothes officers, presumably. They looked big and purposeful and more than a little mean.

'This young lady lives here,' the policeman told them.

The eldest of the three was blond-headed, about forty, wearing an expensive pale-grey suit. When he looked at her, he gave a little double blink that she found strangely unnerving. 'Rachel Parkes?' he asked, coming towards her.

'That's right. Why? Who are you? What's going on? Has there been a break-in?'

'No. Nothing like that.' He nodded at her front door. 'Perhaps we could talk inside.'

Something about him and his companions gave her the creeps. The last thing she wanted was to be alone with them. 'What's wrong with out here?' she asked.

'Very well.' He touched her shoulder to turn her away from the policeman, then adopted the falsely sombre expression of one about to deliver tragic news.

Her heart plunged. Bren had done it, the thing she'd feared he'd do, too proud to be a burden. 'My brother,' she said.

The man shook his head. 'Your aunt. Penelope Martyn.'

The relief was dizzying; she had to put a hand on the railing to steady herself. Then came a strange mix of grief and guilt and puzzlement. 'That's terrible,' she said. 'But why tell me? I'm not her next of kin.'

'There was a fire,' he said. 'We have reason to believe it was set deliberately. Do you know a young man called Luke Hayward?'

'Luke Hayward?' She shook her head. 'No. Why? Was it him?'

'Let's just say his name rang some rather loud bells. Let's just say we're *very keen* to talk to him. Which is where you come in.'

'*Me?*'

'You'll appreciate I can't tell you too much. This is an active murder investigation. But have you checked your email recently?'

The question took her by surprise. 'No. Why?'

'Your aunt sent you a message just before she died. It may be nothing. It may be everything. If so . . .' He spread his hands to indicate how self-evidently valuable it could prove, then beckoned to one of his companions, a man with gold earrings, glossy black hair and a trimmed black beard. He stepped forwards and opened up a laptop for her, like a waiter with a humidor.

'You want me to check? Out here?'

'I did suggest we go inside.'

'Do you guys have ID?'

The man shook his head. 'We were off duty when the call came in. All hands to the pump.'

'Leave me your details. I'll forward you the email if I find it.'

'This is a murder enquiry,' he said. 'Your aunt's killer might be getting away *right now.*'

Rachel sighed and turned to the policeman. 'And you vouch for this, do you?'

He shifted uncomfortably from foot to foot. 'I don't know the specifics, ma'am,' he said. 'But these gentlemen are with the security services, yes; and my orders certainly came down from on high.'

It wasn't the most fortunate choice of words. Rachel's brother had been sentenced to life in a wheelchair because of orders handed down from on high. Anger cleared her mind and gave her courage. She turned back to blond-hair. 'What were you doing inside my house?' she asked.

That double blink again. It gave him away. 'I beg your pardon.'

'You heard me. Why were you inside my house if it's an email you're after? Were you going through my things?'

'This is a time-sensitive investigation,' he said. 'Your aunt's killer is on the loose. Are you *trying* to help him?'

'Of course not.'

'Then just log in, will you?'

'Like hell I will!'

She span on her heel, squeezed between two parked cars, hurried back across the road, fishing out her car keys as she went. The man called out for her to stop but she ignored him. Something thumped into the small of her back and her whole body jolted. She fell into the road, her limbs twitching, her muscles drained and feeble, saliva leaking from her mouth to form a small pool on the sunlit black tarmac. Polished shoes arrived beside her face. The man crouched to grab her collar. He hauled her to her feet then pressed the nodes of his taser against her throat. Though still dazed, it occurred to Rachel how *bizarre* this all was, being assaulted so brazenly while a policeman just stood there and let them.

The waiter held out his humidor once more. She didn't want to submit, but she was scared and alone and she found herself complying. Her hands kept breaking into spasms so that she had to type with a single finger. She entered her username, was almost through her password when an engine roared in the street behind and a horn tooted loudly and she turned in bewilderment to see a red BMW hurtling with lethal speed towards their little group.

TEN

I

Avram crossed the Jaffa Road and was instantly in a different world, the ultra-Orthodox black uniforms of Mea Shearim replaced by the garish shorts and T-shirts of Ben Yahuda. He bought a card at a kiosk, found a payphone, dialled one of the several numbers he'd taken the trouble to memorize. 'It's me,' he said, when Danel picked up.

'It's happening, then,' said Danel. Half statement, half question.

'Bring everyone you can trust,' Avram told him. 'Netanya, tomorrow afternoon. Same place, same time.'

'It is,' said Danel. 'It's really happening.'

'Tomorrow afternoon.' He finished the call, walked briskly to another bank of phones. 'I need the truck,' he said, when Ephraim answered.

'When?'

'This afternoon. Tonight.'

'I sold the last one,' said Ephraim. 'I've got a new one. It's dark blue and a little bigger. But shabby. I was going to repaint it this week.'

'Shabby is fine. As long as it runs.'

'It runs beautifully. I'll leave it for you now.'

Avram moved on again for his third call. An abrasively cheerful young American woman answered. When he asked for Francis, she told him to hold, then went away singing a spiritual. Her voice faded and the minutes passed, so that Avram began to fear he'd been cut off. But then suddenly a man came on. 'This is Francis. Who are you?'

'You know who.'

'Oh.' Silence stretched out. 'What do you want?'

Avram lowered his voice, less from the fear of being overheard than from shame. 'I need a cow,' he said.

'That's why we're here,' said Francis.

'I need her by seven o'clock tomorrow morning.'

Francis laughed. 'That's not possible. You know it isn't. Not perfect. Not three years old.'

'You told me once that you didn't believe the nine previous heifers could all have been perfect reds. You told me once that if we couldn't breed even one, despite our huge herds, our varieties of cattle and our modern genetic techniques, then it defied credibility that the ancients had found even one truly perfect one, let alone *nine*. You did tell me that, didn't you?'

'And I believe it.'

'I believe it too.' He took a deep breath before diving headlong into the heresy. 'I think that many things claimed as absolute in the Tanakh were in fact not absolute. I think too many of my brethren use literalism to show off how devout they are. That is not how one honours the Lord, praise His Name. That is the way one defies Him.'

A beat of silence, then: 'Tomorrow morning?'

'Seven o'clock. As good as you've got. And at least three years old. We can honour that much. And her documentation will have to be convincing. My companions will want to check. Oh, and make it seem like she turned three at the precise hour of the earthquake.'

'You're asking too much. There isn't time.'

'And we'll need the whole place to ourselves. You should be there, to answer questions. But not your volunteers. They'll only say something stupid.'

'You're not *listening*. There isn't time.'

'No,' said Avram. '*You're* the one not listening. Call America if you need authority. Thaddeus will explain. But this *has* to happen. This is *going* to happen. Seven o'clock tomorrow morning. Be ready.' And he put the phone down before Francis could argue further.

II

Rachel was too groggy to do anything but stand there dumbly as the BMW rushed towards her. But the men were quicker, leaping out of its way. It swerved at the last moment, pulled up with a screech beside her. The passenger door flew open and an athletic-looking, dark-headed young man grabbed her wrist, pulled her sideways onto his lap, her legs still dangling out. Blond-hair lunged for her, but the driver stamped on the accelerator and the BMW surged away, acceleration banging the door against her shins. They reached the junction with the main road and passing traffic forced the driver to hit his brakes. The door flew open again, allowing her to bring her feet fully inside so that the passenger could close the door. She looked around. The three men were chasing hard, fury in their eyes. They were almost upon them when a barely-existent gap opened in the traffic and the driver squirted out into it, forcing oncoming cars to brake sharply, leaving them honking like indignant geese.

'Who the hell *are* you people?' asked Rachel, still in the passenger's lap. 'What's going on?'

'Those men back there,' said the passenger. 'Was that a policeman with them?'

'Yes.'

'Fuck!' he said.

The driver grimaced. 'You reckon they got my licence?'

'Don't know, mate,' said his passenger. 'Probably. Can they trace it?'

The driver shook his head. 'Won't be easy. The company rented it for me.'

'Hey!' Rachel had to shout for attention. 'Who *are* you people? What's going on?'

The passenger grimaced, uncertain how to answer. He offered her his hand to shake, which was somewhat awkward with her still in his lap. 'My name's Luke Hayward,' he said. 'I knew your—'

'Luke Hayward?' she said. She pushed away from him in horror, spilling over onto the back seats. 'You killed my aunt.'

'No,' he said, turning around to face her, holding his palms up to diminish any threat she might feel. 'That's not true. I swear it's not true. It was those men back there. That man with the fair hair.'

'They were police. You're saying the police killed Aunt Penny?'

'They weren't police,' he insisted. 'They were *with* a policeman. It's not the same thing.'

'He was on duty. He said his orders came down from on high.'

'They tasered you in the back,' said Luke. 'Are you really going to take the word of men who'd taser you in the back over the people who saved you from them?'

She sought for a good comeback, couldn't find one. 'What the *hell's* going on?' she asked weakly.

'I don't know,' said Luke. 'Not everything, anyway. But those men were at your aunt's house earlier. They found out that she'd sent you an email she wasn't supposed to send, and that fair-haired guy lost his rag. She was trying to get away from him when she fell down the attic stairs.'

'You were there? You saw it happen?'

'Yes.'

'Then why not report it?'

'I tried.'

He launched into an extraordinary story about rooftop escapes, a phone call from a local pub, swarms of police. She listened in mounting horror. Fifteen minutes ago, she wouldn't have believed a word of it. But now she did, she believed him completely. 'This email my aunt sent,' she said. 'That man was talking about it too. He wanted me to forward it to him.'

He shook his head. 'I doubt it. I'll bet he just wanted to delete it.'

'Why? What is it?'

'This is going to sound crazy,' he told her.

'Crazier than everything else?'

'Okay. It's photographs of some old papers that your aunt wanted valued.' He must have read bewilderment on her face, for he went on: 'They're valuable, don't get me wrong. They were written by Sir Isaac Newton. Your aunt's great-uncle bought them at Sotheby's back in the 1930s. His name was Bernard Martyn. He was a physicist who worked for—'

'Great-uncle Bernie,' nodded Rachel. 'Mum used to talk about him.'

'I'm a Newton scholar,' said Luke. 'Those guys hired me to find his missing papers. I tracked your great-uncle's lot to your aunt's attic. I took pictures and emailed them off because my client had first refusal. Your aunt was happy with that. But she didn't know what a good price would be.'

Rachel felt hollow. 'So she emailed the pictures to me?'

Luke nodded. 'I think she reckoned you could have them valued for her somehow. But then those guys showed up.'

'Who are they? Who's this client of yours?'

'I don't know.'

'But you were working for them.'

'They never told me their names. They never told me anything.'

'And you didn't think that *odd*?' said Rachel. 'You didn't think that *suspicious*?'

'These are the lost papers of Isaac bloody Newton we're talking about, not nuclear fucking secrets. I just assumed it was some cranky old collector. How could I know this would happen?'

'My Aunt Penny's dead,' said Rachel furiously. 'She's dead because you led those men to her.'

Luke blinked as though she'd slapped him. He was about to defend himself but then thought better of it. 'I'm sorry,' he said. 'I'm so sorry. If I'd had the first idea . . .'

The driver glanced around, spoke into the silence. 'Listen, love, I'm sorry too, and all that, but we weren't the ones who killed your aunt or zapped you with that taser. This email is the only evidence there is of what really happened this afternoon. If they can delete it somehow, they'll get away with this and maybe even put my mate here in the slammer for the rest of his life for something *they* did. Is that what you want?'

'Why should I trust you any more than them?'

He reached into his pocket, pulled out his mobile, tossed it to her. 'I got your address from a woman called Sonia, forget her surname, but she teaches law at Caius. She's mates with a friend of mine called Miriam. Call Sonia. She'll vouch for Miriam. Then call Miriam. She'll vouch for me.'

'And what's *your* name?'

'Redfern. Pelham Redfern.'

A bell tinkled faintly in Rachel's memory. 'I know that name,' she said. 'You're the bastard who went out with Vicky Andrews.'

'Ah,' said Pelham. He scratched his throat uncomfortably. 'Yes. Vicky. We did see each other for a—'

'You broke her heart.'

'Yes, well, sadly not every romance is destined to end in confetti and—'

'She found you in bed with her sister.'

'Oh, for god's sake, mate,' said Luke. 'You bedded her sister?'

'More accurate to say that she bedded me,' shrugged Pelham. 'Some serious sibling rivalry issues there, if you ask me, with muggins here caught in the middle. And somehow *I'm* the bad guy?'

Luke turned helplessly back to Rachel. 'Okay, fine,' he said. 'Maybe you *can't* trust us. Not like that. But we're not conmen or villains or anything like that, I swear we're not. We're people like you. Our friends are your friends.'

Rachel hesitated. She wanted to be angry with him, she wanted to be suspicious, but there was something about him that she instinctively trusted, and it would have been dishonest to deny it. 'Fine,' she said. 'Let's say I believe you. What now?'

ELEVEN

I

Walters had been so intent on catching the BMW that he'd neglected to memorize its licence number. 'The plates,' he said, whirling around on Pete and Kieran. 'Tell me you got their plates.'

'I did,' said Pete, jotting the number down before he could forget it.

'That was him in the passenger seat,' muttered Kieran. 'The one from the old bat's house.'

'I know.' Walters clenched a fist. He'd thought he'd been so smart setting that fire. He'd taken it for granted that the police would have nabbed Luke by now, would be scoffing at his story, preparing charges of manslaughter and arson. Instead, he now had the girl and the driver as witnesses for his defence; and even their tame policeman had become a liability, a thread that could be followed back through his boss, first to Croke and then to them. Walters looked at him. He was standing open-mouthed in the road, radio in hand, evidently wanting to call it in but not knowing what to say. Walters marched over to him, clapped him on his arm. 'Good work,' he said. 'If you still want to join us, I'll put in a word for you.'

'Yes,' said the policeman uncertainly. 'Thanks.'

'And keep all this to yourself, right? National security. Above even your boss's clearance. Can't say any more. Not until you join us.' He flashed him a smile, strode to the SUV. They all piled in and pulled away, leaving the policeman still standing there dumbly, doing his best mannequin yet.

'What now, boss?' asked Pete.

'We find that BMW and get rid of that fucking email.' He turned to Kieran. 'How much of her password did you get?'

'First six characters. Should be enough to break the rest.' He set a programme running, turned to Pete. 'Give us their licence number, then.' He tapped it in, ran a search. 'It's a rental,' he announced, thirty seconds later. 'Company called Jonson's Cars.'

'Where are they?' asked Walters.

'Head office is St Albans,' said Kieran, checking his screen. 'But they've got a dealership here in Cambridge.'

'Open Sundays?'

'For another hour.'

'Then give me their address. Let's pay them a visit.'

II

'What now?' asked Pelham rhetorically. 'What do you mean, what now? You check for your aunt's damned email.'

Rachel nodded. She logged in on his phone and there it was.

'My dearest Rachel,

The most extraordinary thing – some Isaac Newton papers have just been unearthed in my attic! It seems your Great-great uncle Bernard bought them at Sotheby's for next to nothing, and now they're worth a small fortune! And we always thought him the unworldly one! Anyway, I thought of you and your brother at once. Bernie doted on your mother, though she wasn't much more than a girl when he died. I'm sure he'd have wanted to help.

Now this is all supposed to be terribly hush-hush, but apparently some terrifically wealthy collector is about make me an offer. Naturally I haven't

*the first idea what the papers might be worth,
and the nice young man who found them will
only say they should fetch £20,000 or more. That
would be wonderful, of course, and I think I can
trust him, but he is here on behalf of this
collector, after all, and I'd never forgive myself if
I let myself be duped, not after that wretched
episode with the barn roof! Anyway, to cut a long
story short, I thought perhaps you or one of your
colleagues might have some idea, so I've attached
the photographs. Incidentally, not a word to
anyone, especially not my brood. They don't
know of this yet, so we'll be able to put the
proceeds towards your brother's care, and no one
will ever be the wiser. I'm sure that's what Bernie
would have wanted. How does that sound?*

   Your loving Aunt P

Tears threatened Rachel's eyes; she had to bite the
knuckle of her index finger to stop them. 'These papers,'
she asked. 'Where are they?'

'Those men have them.'

'Then why were they after me? If they've got the
originals, why would they want copies?'

'They don't. We think they just want to deprive access
to them to anyone else.'

'Because they back up your story about Aunt Penny?

Luke shook his head. 'There has to be more to it than that. They freaked out the moment they realized your aunt had sent you the email, which was before she even fell. So there has to be something in the papers themselves.'

Rachel held up the phone. 'No way can we read a manuscript on a screen this small.'

'We'll be at my place in a minute,' Pelham told her. 'Send it to print and it'll be waiting for us when we get there.'

'How? Do I need to download all these attachments?'

'No. I'm on my company's cloud network.'

'You're on what?'

'Give it here.' He took his phone back from her, worked it one-handed as he drove. 'All done,' he said, tossing the phone over his shoulder to her. 'And you might want to forward your aunt's email on to some friends. The more copies of it and of the Newton papers that are out there, the happier I'll feel.'

She nodded and set to work. The smart-phone was still busy with the printing, however, and was slow as treacle as she tried to type out a covering note. Then suddenly it froze altogether. The screen blinked black then began to reset. She tried at once to log back into her account but now it wouldn't recognize her. 'They've locked me out,' she said bleakly. 'Those bastards have locked me out.'

III

The lights were on in Benyamin's office. Avram was about to ring the buzzer when a young woman emerged, head in the air with laughter as she talked into her phone. He kept the door open with his foot, hurried up the steps. It was a while since he'd been here. The lobby had been painted cream and teal, the walls hung with works of characterless modern art. 'Who's there?' called out Benyamin, when he knocked.

'Me. Avram.'

Footsteps, brisk and purposeful. The office door swung open. 'What do you want?' scowled Benyamin, his voice low enough to suggest he had company.

'We need to talk.'

Benyamin nodded and beckoned him inside. A well-dressed Yemenite woman was studying architectural plans pinned to a slanted work table. 'Forgive me, Anna,' he said. 'We'll have to pick this up again tomorrow.'

'What if Zach calls?'

'Don't worry about Zach,' he assured her. 'I can handle Zach.' He escorted her out, locked the door behind her, led Avram over to a pair of tattered red armchairs slouching around a low glass table. 'Well?' he asked. 'What brings you here?'

'You know what brings me here.'

'It's on, then?'

'Tomorrow night.'

Benyamin nodded several times. 'I was beginning to think you'd never get around to it. I was beginning to think you were all talk, like the others.'

'We've been waiting for the right time.'

'And what makes this the right time? Have you had one of your signs?'

'We've had many signs.'

'I must have been looking the other way.'

'Even a sceptic like you must have felt the earthquake, Benyamin.'

'*That*?' snorted Benyamin. 'That was your sign?'

'It put fissures in the Dome of the Rock. What else would you call it?'

'I'd call it an earthquake,' said Benyamin. 'After all, if He is prepared to use earthquakes to get His way, why not bring the whole Dome down while He's at it? Or aren't His powers up to that?'

'He doesn't want to bring it down Himself. He wants *us* to do it. That's why we call it a sign.'

'Strange how your God uses earthquakes for signs only in earthquake zones,' he said. 'Why is that, do you think? Wouldn't it be more impressive if He made them happen in places without geological faults? And, while we're at it, why does He always bring down the cheapest housing, killing poor people by the tens of thousands, while leaving alone the houses and offices of rich people designed and built by structural engineers and architects like myself? Does He hate the poor that much, do you think?'

'I didn't come here to discuss theology, Benyamin,' said Avram. 'I know you don't believe. But I do, others do. Others who'll be moved to do the things we both want precisely *because* of their belief, *because* of these signs. And do you honestly care why they do those things, so long as they do them?'

Benyamin shrugged. 'You're right. I don't care. The earthquake was a sign. What do you need?'

Avram realized, a little too late, that he'd just set himself up for mockery. But there was nothing for it now. 'I want to be sure that our charges work,' he said. 'I want to make sure the Dome implodes completely.'

Benyamin shook his head. 'Implosion is a technical term,' he said. 'It happens when exterior pressure is greater than interior pressure. What you'll be doing is knocking out support pillars and letting gravity go to work.'

'But we'll bring it down, yes?'

'Oh, yes. You'll bring it down.' He frowned. 'Why would you even think otherwise? Has something changed since we last . . .' He realized the answer for himself, burst out laughing. 'It's the earthquake, isn't it? They've put up scaffolding and buttresses in case of another shock. And now you're worried that even if you take out the pillars, the Dome will stay up. That's it, isn't it?' He rocked delightedly back in his chair. 'Your sign!' he taunted. 'Your precious sign! What a perverse God He is, to make your task so difficult.'

'Please keep your voice down,' said Avram. 'Do you want people to hear?'

'Why? Won't your God protect us from eaves-droppers?'

'I'm getting tired of this,' said Avram. 'Will you help or not?'

'I don't see how I can. A situation like this, I'd need to get inside, examine the work up close. Not a chance in hell they'll let that happen. Not a chance in hell they'll let *any* kafir inside. Not with the repairs going on. It's your precious sign at work again, making life easy.'

Avram leaned forwards. 'Signs aren't meant to make things easy,' he said. 'They're meant to make them signifi-cant. They're meant to make our people receptive to His message, so that their hearts will flood with belief and they'll have the strength to do the hard things that will need doing. The things that need *steel*.' He forced a smile, let his anger subside, sat back in his chair. 'What if I could get you footage?'

Benyamin shrugged. 'It would be better than nothing. But not much. It's impossible to gauge structural strength accurately from video. You need to see the thing itself, the materials, the workmanship. My advice, just put charges on everything.'

'We don't have enough. Or the men to carry them.'

'Then you have a problem.'

Avram nodded. 'There is one solution I can think of.'

Benyamin gave Avram a sour look. 'One more than I can,' he said.

'Perhaps you're weakening,' suggested Avram. 'I could understand that. It's been three years now, hasn't it? Over three. Perhaps you don't feel so strongly any more.'

Colour flushed Benyamin's face. 'I feel strongly.'

'Then come with us tomorrow night. See the repairs for yourself. Examine the pillars and the scaffolding. Tell us where to place the charges. You can finally do something to avenge Elizabeth. It was Elizabeth, wasn't it?'

Benyamin's expression stiffened. 'You know it was.'

'And Judy and Rosanna?'

'I remember their names,' said Benyamin tightly. 'You think I could ever forget their names?'

Avram nodded. 'You don't have to decide now,' he said. 'All I ask is that you listen to my plan.'

'Go on, then.'

'Not now. Tomorrow night. I'll explain everything then, and I'll show you something that will make even *you* believe.'

'What?'

Avram got to his feet. 'Tomorrow night. Be ready when I call.'

'Very well,' said Benyamin. 'Tomorrow night.'

IV

'All done?' asked Walters, turning into the Jonson's Cars lot.

'All done,' nodded Kieran. 'I've changed the girl's login details, and I've deleted every mail and attachment in all her folders, including the one from her aunt, and those photos.'

'And she didn't forward them anywhere first?'

'She didn't forward it, no. But it's possible she downloaded or printed it.'

'Shit. Then we still need to find them.'

He parked by the rental office, went inside. A bored young woman with peroxide hair and vivid pink lipstick was slouching behind a cheap pine desk. 'Yes, sir?' she asked, sitting up a little straighter. 'Can I help you with something?'

'I'm after information,' said Walters.

'About our stock or about our prices?'

'About one of your cars. A red BMW soft top. I want to know who's driving it.'

She gave a gulping kind of laugh. 'Are you serious? I can't tell you that!'

Walters didn't have time for subtlety. He took out his wedge, counted off £500 in twenties, slapped them on her desk. 'Are you sure?' he asked.

She stared hungrily at the money. 'Do you have the

licence number?' she asked. He gave it to her. She tapped keys, checked her screen. 'It's a business rental,' she said. 'Goldwood Laboratories. They're over at Cherry Hinton Science Park. You know it?'

'I can find it.' He frowned at a thought. 'I don't suppose you put trackers in your SatNavs, do you?'

'I can't trace them for you, if that's what you're asking. Not from here. They handle all that out of Head Office.'

'Okay,' said Walters. 'Not to worry. And not a word, right?'

'Are you kidding?' she said, tucking her money away. 'They'd fire me in a heartbeat.'

TWELVE

I

Pelham lived in a converted malting house a short drive north of Cambridge. He parked in his designated slot by a grass bank and led them inside. Compared to the well-tended lawns and communal areas, his ground-floor apartment was a mess. He waved a hand in vague explanation or excuse for it as he led them into his shelf-lined study, crowded and dark with books and journals, many more stacked in precarious tall heaps on the floor, like a child's recreation of the Alps.

They went straight to the printer, fearful that the Newton papers wouldn't have made it; but they were there, waiting for them in the out-tray. The printer, however, had tried so hard to capture the lush sepia background of the originals that it had drenched the cheap printing paper in yellow and black ink, blurring Newton's handwriting badly, making it even harder to read and surely diminishing its value as evidence should they need to show it to a sceptic.

Pelham spread the pages on his desk, opened curtains to improve the light. 'What are we looking for?' asked Rachel.

'Anything that sticks out,' said Luke.

'That's helpful.'

Pelham tapped the bottom of the sixth page. 'How about this?' he asked.

Luke glanced over. Like the other pages, it was mostly alchemical citations. But Pelham was right: there was something very different in its bottom left quarter.

Received from E.A.
12 plain panels and blocks SW, 2 linen rolls
S T C, E S D, L A A, B O J
Papers J.D. J.T.
On completion, E.A. asks that ye whole be in
   <u>*SALOMANS HOUSE*</u> *well concealed.*

'E.A.?' asked Pelham. Who's E.A.?'

'No idea,' said Luke, squinting closer. 'You think it could be "F.A"? Newton was friends with a Francis Aston at Cambridge.'

'It's not an "F",' said Rachel. 'It's an "E".'

'Then I don't know,' said Luke. 'Newton's mother's maiden name was Ayscough, but I can't think of any Edwards or Elizabeths among his cousins.'

'Ebenezer?' suggested Pelham. 'Ezekiel?'

'Let's come back to it,' said Rachel. She pointed to the second line. '"*12 plain panels and blocks SW, 2 linen rolls.*" Any ideas?' Luke shook his head. Pelham too. 'Then what about these groups of letters?' she asked, pointing to the third line.

Luke pulled up a browser on Pelham's laptop. 'Read them out for me,' he said. He typed them in as she went, four clusters of three, then ran a search. But Google gave them nothing. 'What's the next line?' he asked.

'Papers J.D. and J.T.,' said Rachel.

'J.D. couldn't be my old mate Doctor Dee, could he?' asked Pelham. 'I mean he was a John, so to speak. And for sure it gives us an alchemical link.'

'He was dead eighty years by 1690.'

'*He* may have been. Not his papers. In fact . . .' He snapped his fingers. 'I think I know who E.A. is.'

'Who?' asked Rachel.

'A bunch of Dee's papers went missing after his death,' said Pelham. 'Notes on his conversations with Enochian angels mostly.'

'His *what*?' asked Rachel.

Pelham grinned. 'Dee was convinced he could use the

Book of Enoch to communicate with angels. He thought he could open the gates of heaven from the inside and so precipitate the Apocalypse and the Second Coming. But first he needed to find an honest medium.'

'Oh, was that all?'

'He tried a few. None worked. Then he hired the great Edward Kelley. A complete rogue and one of my major heroes. He wasn't satisfied with fleecing Dee rotten; he also convinced him that the angels had ordered them to swap wives for the night.' Pelham laughed loudly. 'Hats off, eh?'

'And Dee bought it?' asked Rachel, incredulously.

'Damn right,' said Pelham. 'You don't fuck with Enochian angels.'

Luke shook his head. 'What's this got to do with E.A.?'

'The Dee papers that went missing,' said Pelham. 'There was no sign of them for years. *Decades.* Then one day this old couple bought a wooden chest in an estate sale. It looked empty, but they kept hearing noises inside, so they jemmied off its bottom and found a secret compartment stuffed with strange bundles.'

'Dee's missing papers,' said Rachel.

'Give the girl a coconut,' said Pelham. 'Anyway, the husband dies and the widow remarries some new guy who knows a man who likes that kind of thing.'

'Who?'

Pelham tapped the initials. 'Elias Ashmole,' he said.

Rachel frowned. 'The founder of the Ashmolean Museum?'

'That's the one. And I'll tell you something else: Ashmole claimed some of the papers were burned by a maid.' He shook his head. 'Maids who value their jobs don't throw random sheaves onto the fire. So what if Ashmole kept certain papers back to send them on to Newton? What if he blamed the maid to explain the gaps in the record?'

'Were Ashmole and Newton friends?' asked Rachel.

Pelham nodded at Luke. 'He's the one writing the book.'

Luke shook his head. 'Not friends, no. But they *were* contemporaries, and they worked in the same fields; and for sure they knew of each other. They were both early members of the Royal Society, for one thing. And they were Britain's two leading alchemists. Ashmole published one of the great alchemical compendiums: the *Theatrum Chemicum Britannicum*.'

'And Newton would have known of it?'

'God, yes. His own copy is at the University of Pennsylvania. I saw it a couple of years ago when I was over there for a conference. Newton had dog-eared half the pages, and scrawled annotations over the rest, a certain sign that he thought extremely highly of it.'

'So Newton rated Ashmole,' said Rachel. 'Would it have been mutual?'

Luke laughed. 'Best I can tell, Newton wrote these pages sometime around 1693. That's four or five years after the *Principia Mathematica* came out, give or take. The *Principia* changed the world, particularly for the educated elite like Ashmole.' Hardly anyone alive had been able to follow Newton's mathematics, but anyone could grasp the basic point. The universe had been made mechanical. The heavens were suddenly predictable and therefore no longer to be feared as the message boards of capricious and wrathful gods. '"Nature and Nature's Laws lay hid in night,"' said Luke. '"God said Let Newton Be, and all was Light."'

Pelham squinted at him. 'Wasn't Pope paid to write that?' he asked.

'Doesn't mean it wasn't true,' said Luke. 'Trust me on this: if Ashmole had owned something extraordinary, something mathematical, particularly something *alchemical*, Newton would have been his man.'

Rachel had pulled up a biography of Ashmole on the laptop.

'Sorry to be the one to toss in the monkey wrench,' she said. 'But Ashmole was dead by '93. He died in May '92.'

'That still fits,' said Luke. 'It just makes whatever this was a bequest rather than a gift.'

'Something Ashmole couldn't bear to part from while he was alive,' suggested Rachel.

'Or something too explosive to share,' said Pelham.

Luke nodded. 'That would explain those guys from earlier.'

'But what the hell is it?' asked Rachel. Only silence followed her question, however. 'Maybe if we knew more about Ashmole,' she said. 'All it really says here is that he founded the Museum. What else did he do?'

'I know someone who could help,' said Pelham. 'Olivia something, forget her surname. Runs the Museum of the History of Science in Oxford. I put on an exhibition with her a few years back, about the transition from alchemy to chemistry.'

Luke shook her head. 'Why would she know about Ashmole?'

'Because her museum's in the original Ashmolean building,' said Pelham. 'And she's an historian of science. So she's bound to know something, right?'

'Or maybe there's an easier way,' said Rachel, pointing to the bottom line, reading it out aloud: '*On completion, E.A. asks that ye whole be in <u>SALOMANS HOUSE</u> well concealed.*' She looked up at them both with a mischievous grin. 'You don't suppose it could still be there, do you?'

II

A navy blue Range Rover was waiting for Croke on the tarmac of London's City Airport. A shaven-headed young man in pale slacks, a short-sleeved blue shirt and mirror sunglasses was leaning against it, hands casually in his pockets. Croke went over to him. 'Morgenstern, right?'

'That's me.'

'Thanks for arranging Cambridge.'

'No sweat.' Morgenstern was trying to play it extra cool, perhaps regretting his earlier gushing over the Vice President. He opened the Range Rover's rear door, invited Croke inside.

'What about my men?' asked Croke, as Manfredo struggled down the jet's steps with his suitcases.

'I was told to help you,' said Morgenstern. 'No one said anything about your crew.'

'Fair enough.' He went back to tell Manfredo to find rooms and wait for instructions, then joined Morgenstern in the Range Rover.

'Crane Court, yeah?' asked Morgenstern.

'Crane Court,' agreed Croke.

Morgenstern leaned forward to give their driver his orders then buzzed up the internal glass screen for privacy. 'We're evacuating it right now,' he said. 'Should be ready for searching by the time we get there.'

'How long will that be?'

He shrugged. 'We've had to close down Fleet Street. Traffic's going to get crazy. We'll use sirens where we can, but they're only so much help in a gridlock.'

'Give you time to explain how this works,' said Croke.

Morgenstern nodded. 'First thing you need to know is that counterterrorism in England used to be run by London's Metropolitan Police; but they kept screwing up, so it got split off into a new body.'

'The National Counterterrorism Taskforce?'

'That's the one. Second thing you need to know is that, around the same time as the NCT was being set up, the UK Supreme Court ordered the release of some highly-confidential documents that the CIA had shared with various agencies here. The intel itself was nothing, to be honest. Embarrassing rather than harmful.'

'But it was the principle,' suggested Croke.

'Exactly. It was the principle. The Brits had given us their word they'd keep this shit secret. Suddenly it's all over the front page. What are they going to release next? The name of one of our agents? The Internet companies and banks who share their customers' data with us? Footage of an enhanced interrogation?'

'Could be a problem.'

'Damned right. But what could we do? Britain's our ally, and we can't withhold intel just because their justices, in their supreme fucking wisdom, are complete pricks. Besides, the Brits have some top sources themselves. What if they cut us off in retaliation? In pissing matches, everyone gets their feet wet. So we put our heads together and designed a mutually acceptable solution into the new NCT. Still with me?'

'Yes.'

'It's British-run, of course; and all the full-time personnel are Brits. Mostly ex-policemen, from when it was part of Scotland Yard; though they're recruiting more and more from the SAS and MI5, places like that. Thing is, because of the Supreme Court decision, we can't risk giving them our best raw intelligence; so what we do instead is we second people like me from the State Department, the CIA, the NSA and Homeland Security. We all have high-level clearance and therefore unrestricted access to our best intelligence.'

'So if you learn anything of use to the NCT, you can let them know,' nodded Croke. 'And, because there's no physical documentation, the courts can't order it released.'

'Exactly,' said Morgenstern. 'Unfortunately, as it turns out, our intel is sometimes so ultra top secret that even that's too much of a risk. So what we do in those situations is we help our British colleagues plan their operations, then we tag along to make sure they have all the information they need in real time.'

Croke frowned. 'You're telling me that we get to plan and run NCT operations? And their guys just do the dirty work?'

'Essentially, yes.'

'And they go along with this?'

'Are you kidding? They're *grateful*. Amazing what fear will do. But this is pretty sensitive territory, as you can imagine, especially as there have been some malicious rumours recently, accusing us of using this arrangement to pursue our own agenda, go after low-level hackers, critics of our foreign policy, that kind of shit.'

Croke smiled. 'As if.'

'Exactly. As if.'

'So how will it work today?'

'Simple. We'll fix you up in an apartment in Crane Court, give you access to whatever you need. Me and my Brit counterpart will run the actual search. I'll come brief you every half hour. You tell me what you need done next, I'll make sure it happens.'

'And your counterpart won't object?'

'We have *extremely* good relationships with these guys,' said Morgenstern. 'Our arrangement stipulates that we only have to share our intel with people we've vetted thoroughly and feel comfortable with. Naturally, we only feel comfortable with those who share our broad outlook of the world; and then only after we've had them over in the States for six months' evaluation and training. Trust me. By the time they get back here, they might as well be ours, born and bred.'

Croke nodded. 'Are there many of you?'

'You mean Americans? Just twenty. But that's plenty, believe me. Think of us as project managers rather than operational staff. We get to draft in whomever we like: civilian contractors, the army, regional police forces. And they don't get to ask why or say no. The moment we cite national security, they have to give us whatever we want.'

Croke laughed. 'Now *that's* a Special Relationship,' he said.

THIRTEEN

I

Walters could sense Kieran growing uneasy in the back as they sped towards Cherry Hinton Science Park. He met his eyes in the rear-view mirror. 'What is it?' he asked.

Kieran scratched his beard. 'It's just, what are we going to do with them once we've found them?'

'We're going to make sure they can't blab, of course,' said Walters.

'Yes. But what does that mean exactly?'

'What do you think it means?'

'Fuck,' said Kieran, looking a little sick. 'Is that really necessary?'

Walters glared at him. 'You'd rather they put you inside for the rest of your life?'

'But they can't,' said Kieran. 'They can maybe do us for arson. That's about it.'

'What about the old bat?'

'That was an accident. She fell.'

'Sure. And you think that's what Luke what's-his-name will tell the filth, do you? Bollocks. He'll say we pushed her.'

'He'll say *you* pushed her,' muttered Pete.

'You think that will save you?' scoffed Walters. 'They'll charge us with being there in commission of a crime, meaning we'll all be equally liable for her death. And who was it that actually set the fire?'

'Only because you told us to!' Kieran protested.

'Yeah. And that worked wonders at Nuremberg.'

'Shit,' muttered Pete. He looked almost as unhappy as Kieran.

'Don't sweat it,' said Walters, turning into the science park. 'It's going to be fine, trust me. I've done this sort of shit before. I know what I'm doing. We just need to find them, that's all.'

He pulled up in front of Goldstone Laboratories, got out before they could argue, jogged up the front steps and through the sliding glass doors into reception, where an old granddad with watery eyes was sitting behind the desk. 'Listen, mate,' he said, striding up to him. 'Wonder if you can help me. You're not going to believe this, but my wife lent her Renault to my arse of a son last Friday.

Little bastard only comes home with a dent in the front bumper. Thought we wouldn't notice. Bloody eighteen year olds, eh?'

Granddad grunted. 'Tell me about it.'

'Anyway, I ask him where he did it, he spins me this load of old cobblers like you wouldn't believe. So I ground him, tell him he's not leaving his room until he comes clean. Takes him until this afternoon to talk. Got to give him credit for that, I suppose. He came here sometime last week, apparently, to pick up some new bird of his. But he managed to ding the back of this red Beemer soft-top in your car park while he was at it. Swears blind he didn't do it any damage, and also that he left a note. My arse. Why leave a note if you didn't do any damage, I ask. Didn't have an answer to that, did he? Anyway, I just wanted to check. If this Beemer needs any repairs, I'll make sure the little runt pays for every penny. You know anyone who drives a car like that?'

'A red BMW convertible?' frowned granddad. 'Mr Redfern is driving one at the moment. But I haven't heard anything about any damage.'

'Mr Redfern. That wouldn't be old Ronnie Redfern, would it? Is he working here now?'

'No. Pelham. Pelham Redfern.'

'He's not here now, is he?'

'He left a couple of hours ago.'

'But he'll be in tomorrow, yeah?'

Granddad shrugged. 'I'd imagine,' he said.

'Great. I'll give him a bell in the morning, maybe drop by. Thanks for the help.' He went back out, climbed back in the SUV. 'Name's Pelham Redfern,' he said.

Kieran tapped keys on his laptop. 'Got him,' he said. 'Apartment Two, the Old Maltings, Horningsea. That's just a couple of miles north of here.'

'Good. Then let's go finish this.'

II

'Saloman's House?' frowned Pelham. 'Why does that sound familiar?'

'Sir Francis Bacon,' said Luke. 'He wrote a book called *The New Atlantis* that contained a kind of blueprint for academic research institutions. He called it Salomon's House. Named after Solomon, of course, but with the first O changed to an A. It was the inspiration for the Royal Society. That's why they call you guys fellows. Because that's what Bacon called your equivalents in *The New Atlantis*.'

'*You* guys?' asked Rachel, looking incredulously at Pelham. 'You're not seriously telling me *he's* a fellow of the Royal Society?'

Pelham laughed cheerfully. 'What's the world coming to, eh?'

'It's how we originally hooked up,' Luke told her. 'I helped write a documentary on Newton for the Beeb a little while back.'

'That was you? I saw that. It was terrific.'

'Thanks. Anyway, we wanted to replicate some of Newton's alchemical experiments, so I asked the Royal Society if they had anyone interested in that kind of thing who might be prepared to help.' He nodded at Pelham. 'Bastards gave me him.'

'Alchemy's a hobby of mine,' explained Pelham. 'It's how I first got interested in chemistry myself, so I figured it might do the trick for other kids. There's this show I've put together that I sometimes take around the local schools.'

'A show?' asked Rachel.

'Yeah. You know the kind of thing. Put on the Harry Potter costume, mix some chemicals together, make things fizz and smoke and bang.'

'Sounds fun.'

'It is,' he agreed. 'And damned rewarding too.'

'Working with kids?'

'Fuck, no. Turning base metals into gold. So much easier than actually having to work.'

'You've cracked it, then?' asked Rachel.

'Any day now. Just waiting for Neptune to align with Mars.'

'Come on, guys,' pleaded Luke. 'A bit of focus, please. What do you think this means?'

Pelham shrugged. 'I guess that Ashmole left these papers and this other stuff to Newton so that he could hide it somewhere in the Royal Society.'

'But why wouldn't Ashmole just have hidden it there himself?' asked Rachel. 'You did say he was a member, right?'

'The note says that it needed to be "completed" before it was hidden,' said Pelham. 'Maybe only Newton could do that.'

'Ashmole was a bit-part player at the Royal Society anyway,' added Luke. 'Newton was its star. In fact . . .' He trailed off, went over to Pelham's desk, ran a search on his laptop, brought up the Royal Society's home page.

'What are you looking for?' asked Rachel, watching over his shoulder.

'The Royal Society didn't have a permanent home for its first forty or fifty years. They just switched between rooms in Gresham College and Arundel House. But then they made Newton president, and about the first thing he did was set about buying them a place of their own.'

'Carlton House Terrace?' asked Pelham.

'No. This was way before you guys moved there. I don't remember the exact address, but it was just off Fleet Street.' He reached the Royal Society's *Our History* page, scanned the text. 'Crane Court,' he said. 'That's it.' He pulled up a new tab, ran a new search. The top five links were all to breaking news stories, thumbnails of police officers in yellow bibs. 'What the hell?' he muttered. He clicked the top link. A newsflash from the AP, Crane Court being evacuated because of a bomb scare. He looked around in shock at Pelham and Rachel.

Pelham shook his head. 'It's coincidence,' he said. 'It has to be.'

'Bollocks,' said Luke. 'They did exactly what we just did: they worked out that Newton had hidden this thing in Crane Court, so they invented a bomb scare and closed the whole place down so that they could search it.'

Rachel looked stunned. 'Who *are* these people?'

'They're way out of our league, that's for sure.'

Pelham nodded grimly. 'If you're right about this, and they did get my licence, they'll be here in no time. I vote we get out *now*.'

'And go where?'

'My sister's got a place in the Cotswolds. Keys under the dustbin, linen in the closet. We can stay there until we work out what's going on and devise some kind of plan.' He picked up his wallet, car keys and phone, stowed them in his pockets.

'Not your phone, mate,' said Luke. 'They'll trace us through it.' Pelham nodded bleakly, pulled it back out. Luke touched his arm. 'Listen: it's me they want, not you or Rachel. If you two keep your heads down for a day or so, I'm sure they'll—'

'Fuck that,' said Pelham. 'You're my friend. But you'll owe me big for this. So next time I need you vouching that I kipped the night at your place, no more of that ethics bullshit you gave me last time. Okay?'

'Fair enough.' He turned to Rachel. 'How about you?'

'Those bastards tasered me in the back,' she said. 'But I want you to promise me something. I want you *both* to promise.'

'What?'

A touch of shame pinked her cheeks as she gathered the printouts together. 'If we ever get the originals back, they're mine. Aunt Penny wanted me to have them, and I need them. My brother needs them.'

'What for?'

She shook her head. 'He just needs them, okay?'

A siren in the distance. They turned towards it, bracing themselves for disaster. But almost at once it began to fade. 'Fine,' said Pelham. 'The originals are yours. Now let's get the hell out of here.'

III

It was a dismal drive in from City Airport through East London, dual carriageways punched through shabby housing estates and brutalist tower blocks. But at least it was quick. Then, however, they entered some long tunnel and the traffic started to congeal. By the time they finally emerged, it was pretty much locked solid. Their driver put a siren on their roof, used it to bully his way through. They passed St Paul's Cathedral, reached the bottom of Ludgate Hill. The police had shut off Fleet Street with metal barriers, forcing traffic to turn right or left, but another squirt of siren saw them through.

They nudged through thin crowds of Sunday afternoon sightseers. Digital cameras and phones pressed against their windows; flashes popped. Croke fought the urge to shield his face; it was too late anyway, and would only draw attention. They passed through more barriers into a cordoned-off area, drove beneath a canvas awning that allowed them to exit the Range Rover without being photographed. They walked through a short, arched brick passageway and emerged into Crane Court itself, a flagstoned alley with old, low and wide redbrick buildings to their right, taller, modern ones to their left, the ugly backsides of offices and other businesses.

A senior policeman, to judge from his age and uniform, was in heated discussion with a youngish man in a dark suit. 'Wait here,' said Morgenstern. He went to join the conversation, came back after a minute, brow furrowed. 'Problem,' he said.

'What?'

'That prick in the uniform. He's media liaison. I've dealt with him before. All he cares about is how good he looks on the TV news.'

'So?'

'So he's due to give a briefing. Says he won't do it until he knows why we're searching *all* the buildings. He says if our information is any good, surely we know which one to search. And if our information isn't any good, why go in so fast? Why not hang back and watch?'

Croke nodded. It was a sensible question. 'What did you tell him?'

'That the threat may not be very specific, but it *is* imminent.'

'That didn't work?'

He shook his head. 'I know this guy. He's going to background brief that this is all kabuki, designed to make Londoners scared. And if people start asking those kind of questions . . .'

Croke nodded. 'Can we escalate?'

'How do you mean?'

'Have your search teams put on HazMat uniforms, wave some Geiger counters around.'

Morgenstern squinted at him like he was crazy. 'You want people thinking we've got a dirty bomb on our hands?'

'It would explain why we couldn't risk waiting, wouldn't it?'

Morgenstern laughed. 'I'm going to enjoy working with you,' he said.

FOURTEEN

I

Even as Walters turned into the Maltings, he spotted the red BMW parked up against a grassy bank at the foot of the main building. 'Got them!' he exulted. But the building's main doors opened at that moment, and Luke, Rachel and Pelham hurried out and made straight for their car.

Walters maintained a steady pace, not wanting to attract attention. But Luke spotted him anyway. He yelled to the others and they sprinted for the BMW, climbed inside. Walters spurted the SUV forwards then braked sharply so that his front bumper was flush against their rear, blocking their escape. He jumped out, tried the BMW's back door. Too late. Already locked. He glared in through the back window. The girl, Rachel, was holding a sheaf of sepia-and-black pages, printouts of the Newton papers. Rage coursed through him. He punched the glass, but only hurt his hand.

Kieran tried the doors on the other side, but they were locked too. It was Pete who found the more practical approach. He clambered on to the soft top and tried to tear the fabric free from its moorings. But Redfern started up the BMW and shot it forwards up the grass bank until his bumper hit the Maltings' front wall. Then he swung the wheel hard around and reversed back down, clipping the SUV before racing away. He turned sharply, accelerating across the car park with Pete still on his roof before screeching to an abrupt halt and sending him tumbling down the BMW's bonnet and across the tarmac. Then they were off and away.

Walters climbed back into the SUV to give chase, but by the time he'd picked up Kieran and Pete, the BMW was nowhere in sight. They drove around for a little while in hopes of seeing it, but without reward. 'Now what?' asked Pete.

'We need to find them,' said Walters.

'How?'

'Maybe they left something back at Redfern's place.'

'What if one of his neighbours has called in the filth?'

'Have you got a better idea?'

They went back, watched the entrance for fifteen minutes. No sign of the police. No sign of anyone. They parked in a guest slot and Pete soon had them inside. Redfern's apartment was a mess, and they found little of any use. The smartphone on the desk made Walters curse, for they'd evidently got serious about covering their tracks. He pocketed it anyway; it would make it easy to identify Redfern's contacts. He checked the drawers next, found paperwork for the rented BMW. It gave him an idea, though making it happen was way above his own pay grade. He took a deep breath then called his boss.

'I don't believe this,' snapped Croke, when Walters had brought him up to speed. 'I thought you were supposed to be good at this kind of thing.'

'With respect, sir, we've been unlucky.'

'Unlucky!' scoffed Croke. 'These people can do me *damage*. I want them found before that happens. I want them silenced and I want their copy of the papers destroyed. Am I clear?'

'That's why I called, sir. The thing is, Redfern's BMW has SatNav. We should be able to track them through it.'

'SatNavs are receive only,' said Croke.

'Most are, yes,' persevered Walters. 'But this is a rental. Rental companies often fit receive *and* transmit systems to monitor their fleet, recover stolen cars. The girl in the office here as good as told me they use a system like that, only they run it out of St Albans. They'd never give that kind of info to a nobody like me. But you seem to have some pretty influential friends.'

A beat or two of silence. 'Okay,' said Croke, grudgingly. 'Give me Redfern's licence number. I'll see what I can do.'

II

In the back of the BMW, Rachel watched anxiously for pursuit. She couldn't see anything, yet her heart kept pounding all the same. That man on the roof; the noise of him trying to tear his way through the fabric. And the look on his blond companion's face when he'd seen the papers in her hand; she'd never before seen murder so plainly written on a human face.

She turned to face front, assuming that Luke and Pelham would be equally shaken. To her surprise, however, they both appeared almost calm. In the passenger seat, Luke was flicking between radio channels in search of bulletins from Crane Court, while Pelham was driving in characteristically negligent fashion, slouched in his seat with his legs splayed wide and his wrist on the wheel. Something in their manner proved contagious, and her own nerves began to settle.

They reached dual carriageway, headed west. The road's surface had recently been re-laid, and it was so tacky from the sun that it sounded almost like driving through shallow water. Luke finally gave up his hunt for news and turned the radio down low. Relative silence gave Rachel the opportunity to brood and reminded her of how little she knew about these two. If they were to be fugitives together, she needed to learn more. On the other hand, she didn't want to antagonise them with crude questions, so she leaned forwards between the front seats and turned to Pelham. 'I bet you get asked this all the time,' she said. 'But where did you get your first name?'

'The folks were Wodehouse fans,' he told her. 'How sick is that?'

'He was a wonderful writer.'

'So was Dickens. So was Tolstoy. No shortage of wonderful writers with cracking first names. I'd have made a great Leo, if you ask me. Big, king-like and extremely dangerous. But no, I get fucking Pelham.'

'It could have been worse,' she pointed out. 'They could have been Brontë fans.'

He laughed and threw her an admiring glance. 'So do you have a bloke, then, Rachel?'

Luke put his head in his hands. 'Jesus, mate,' he sighed.

'A bloke?' asked Rachel.

'A man. A boyfriend. You must have come across the

concept. Someone to rush home from work for, so you can do his ironing.'

'Ah. A *bloke*. Then no. Not just at the moment.'

'Outstanding,' grinned Pelham. 'Tell you what. When this business is all over and done with, how about you, me, Mozart and some moonlight? The chance of a lifetime, though I say so myself. I mean, how many Nobel laureates have you ever been out with?'

She looked at him in disbelief. 'You've won the Nobel Prize?' she asked.

'Of course he bloody hasn't,' said Luke.

'Maybe not technically,' admitted Pelham, 'but I assure you it's just a matter of time. And this way you get to say you knew me when.' He turned to face her again, letting the BMW drift alarmingly from their lane, so that Luke had to grab the wheel and course-correct them. 'Come on. How about it?'

'I'm really flattered,' said Rachel. 'But, honestly, I don't think I could go out with a man called Pelham.'

'Fucking parents,' scowled Pelham. 'I tell you something: that man Larkin knew what he was about.'

'Hey!' said Luke, holding up a hand for silence while turning the radio back up loud to catch a chaotic Crane Court press conference in progress, a crowd of reporters shouting out questions.

'What's in there?' yelled one of them. 'What are you looking for?'

'We don't know.'

'Then what's with the HazMat suits?'

'Purely precautionary, I assure you.'

'Precautionary for what? Anthrax? A dirty bomb?'

'Is this to do with the memorial service?' yelled a woman.

'The what?'

'The Royal Family are going to parade past here on their way to the memorial service at St Paul's on Tuesday night. Has this investigation got anything to do with that?'

'No comment. Now if you'll excuse me.'

The press conference ended in a bedlam of unanswered questions. A reporter summed up and handed back to the studio. Luke turned the volume back down. 'A dirty bomb. Jesus. They're not holding back, are they?'

'You reckon they've found it?' asked Rachel.

'I reckon we won't hear a peep if they have.'

'No.' She sat back and spread the Newton papers out on the rear seat beside her, read again the enigmatic note on the sixth page. 'And you guys can't think what it was that Ashmole might have left Newton?' she asked.

'I don't know a thing about Ashmole, apart from that Dee connection,' said Pelham. 'At least, there is *one* thing – but you'll think me terribly immature.'

'More than for owning a Harry Potter costume?' asked Rachel.

'Ouch,' laughed Pelham. 'Okay. Ashmole sometimes published under a pseudonym.'

'What's so immature about that?'

'I only remember because of the name he chose: James Asshole.'

Rachel couldn't help but laugh. 'You're not serious?'

'Sadly, no. It was actually James Hasolle. But close enough, you know. Hey, I was an undergraduate. And, to be fair, it is an anagram of his name.'

'They loved their anagrammatic pseudonyms back then,' said Luke. 'Newton called himself *Jeova Sanctus Unus*: One holy god.'

'No way is that an anagram of Isaac Newton,' protested Rachel.

'Of Isaacus Neuutonus, it is,' said Luke. 'If you allow a little latitude, at least: "i" for "j"; a "u" for a "v". That kind of thing.'

'One holy god,' smiled Rachel. 'Didn't think much of himself, did he?'

'He could be pretty conceited,' agreed Luke. 'He believed he was some kind of seventeenth-century counterpart of the prophets. An adept with special insight into the true nature of God and His universe. And not just *any* adept, but the greatest of the modern age, the successor of Moses, Elijah and Solomon, a man whose lifework was an important prelude to the Second Coming.'

'Honestly?'

'Scout's honour. He was convinced he had a destiny. Loners often do, of course; particularly the brilliant ones. And he was born on Christmas Day, which can't have helped. He kept it to himself, of course, along with his Antitrinitarianism and his other heresies, because you couldn't exactly go around talking about that kind of thing, not in polite company; but it's implicit in his private papers.'

Rachel was only half listening. Her mind had moved on. Or, more accurately, back.

'Anagrammatic pseudonyms,' she murmured. 'You don't have a pen, do you?'

'A pencil.' He rummaged through the glove compartment, handed it to her, along with a notepad. 'Why?' he asked. 'What is it?'

She shook her head. 'Probably nothing.'

'Come on. Share.'

'Okay. You said earlier that Bacon deliberately misspelled "Solomon" as "Salomon" by changing the first "o" to an "a". That's right, yes?'

'Yes. So?'

She tapped the page. 'That's not how Newton spells it here.' She held it up for him to see. 'He's changed the final "o" of Solomon to an "a" as well.'

'I wouldn't read too much into that,' said Pelham. 'Spelling was pretty arbitrary back then. An honourable tradition that I choose to follow myself.'

'Yes, but Salomon was *deliberately* misspelled. That's what Luke said. Newton would surely have known that. And he'd surely have known *how* Bacon had misspelled it too. Anyway, why put it all in capitals and then underline it if you don't want to draw attention to it? And isn't there something odd about the construction of that whole bottom line?'

'In what way?'

'I don't know. I mean, I know crosswords didn't exist back then, but doesn't it read almost like a cryptic clue? And when you were talking just now, I couldn't help notice that the letters in Ashmole are also in Saloman's House.'

Luke frowned and looked closer. 'You're right,' he said.

'I know I'm right,' she said. 'That's why I said it.'

'And if you take those letters out? What does that leave?'

Rachel jotted SALOMANS HOUSE down on the pad, struck out the letters A S H M O L and E. 'A, N, S, O, U and another S,' she said. They looked at it together, but nothing leapt out. 'Damn,' she said. 'I really thought I was onto something.'

'You are,' said Luke. He leaned over and took the pencil from her, his fingers just brushing her skin. 'But it's not Ashmole,' he said. 'It's Ashmolean.' He struck out the A and N, underlined the four remaining letters left sitting there already in the right order, just begging to be read out.

'Sous Ashmolean,' murmured Rachel, meeting his gaze with something akin to awe. 'Beneath the Ashmolean.'

III

Avram was in his bedroom when he heard his nephew Uri finally returning from work. He zipped up the second holdall then went down to greet him. 'Good day?' he asked.

Uri shrugged. 'Shimon wants to open in Haifa. We haven't even got Jerusalem running smoothly yet.'

'Shimon is an ambitious man,' said Avram. 'That's a commendable thing.' He beckoned him upstairs, put a finger to his lips, pointed to the bedside telephone and the ceiling light socket. He picked up a pad of plain paper and wrote on it: 'They may be listening. Take off your clothes.'

Uri frowned. He was about to say something but Avram shook his head and pointed again to the telephone and the light socket. Then he jabbed the tip of his pencil in emphasis against the words he'd already written.

Uri nodded and began to strip. When he was down to his underwear, Avram handed him a clean shirt, some workman's overalls and a new pair of sandals. He put them on. They picked up a holdall each and then Avram led him out the rear door onto the communal terrace. Whenever their neighbour Paul was away lecturing in America, as now, Avram kept an eye on his home. They went in through his kitchen, emerged from his front door out into the alley that ran parallel with their own.

'What's going on?' murmured Uri.

'Not yet,' said Avram, and led him through the familiar Old City maze.

The evening air was pungent with saffron, cinnamon and other spices as stallholders closed for the day, gloomy from lack of customers. A Hasid freewheeled with indecent glee down the narrow cobbled street, arms upraised to the Lord. They passed through Jaffa Gate. A helicopter rattled low overhead, as much to remind people of its presence as to do anything useful. They reached the car park. Avram didn't know precisely where Ephraim had left the truck, and there were several candidates, so he tried door handles until finally one opened. He felt beneath the driver's seat and found the keys.

'Whose is this?' asked Uri.

'A friend's.' Avram handed him the keys, gestured for him to take the wheel. 'He does removals. He lends me a van from time to time.'

'So what's going on?' asked Uri, climbing in. 'All that business with my clothes?'

'They can bug everything these days, so Shlomo says.

They can even trace clothes and shoes. Apparently, they have transmitters so small that they can sew them into your hem without you noticing; yet they can still track you wherever you go.'

'But why would they? Are we under suspicion?'

Avram nodded. 'Shlomo thinks one of his men may have been talking.'

Uri looked shocked. 'Does he know who?'

'No. Not for sure. But if anyone can find out, Shlomo can. And don't be too alarmed. He swears that none of his men know anything about me, let alone you. But it's only sensible to take extra precautions until we can be certain.' He smiled and patted the truck's dashboard. 'Especially when we have important business to attend to.'

'Yes,' said Uri. 'I was going to ask.'

'New supplies have just been delivered. Communications equipment.'

'You're showing me our supply route? I thought you didn't want anyone to know.'

'I'm getting too old for this,' said Avram. 'You're the only one I can trust completely.'

Uri nodded soberly. 'Thank you, Uncle. I won't let you down.' He belted himself in, turned on the ignition, began to pull out of his space, paused. 'Where to, then?' he asked.

'South,' Avram told him. 'We're going to the Negev.'

IV

Pelham pulled onto the hard shoulder of the dual carriageway, the better to look at the anagram for himself. 'Sous is French,' he said. 'Did Newton even speak French? I thought it was all English and Latin back then.'

Luke nodded. 'He taught himself so that he could read St. Didier in the original.' He turned to the first page to show them the citation from *Le Triomphe Hermetique*.

'This Museum of the History of Science woman of yours,' said Rachel. 'Olivia, wasn't it? Can we talk to her?'

'I don't know her number.'

'But she's in Oxford, yes?' said Luke. 'Why don't we go see her? It's pretty much on our way.'

'It's Sunday. Her museum will be shut by now.'

'Don't you know where she lives?'

Pelham shrugged. 'I know where she lived back then. Odd-something. It seemed so *apt* for her. Oddminster, maybe. Oddhampton.'

Luke typed the first three letters into the SatNav and let its predictive software go to work. 'Oddingley or Oddington,' he said.

'Oddington. That's it.' Pelham looked at them both. 'What do you reckon? Worth a visit?'

'Damned right,' said Luke. 'These people know who we are. The police and counterterrorism and god-knows who else are on their side. They'll be watching our friends and families, probably monitoring the Internet and the media too. They'll find us eventually. I say we fight back while we can. If we can find out what they're looking for, we can take the story public and maybe even be believed.'

Pelham nodded. 'Rachel?'

She nodded emphatically. 'The sooner we get started, the better. Oxford will be safe enough as long as they're still searching Crane Court.'

'Good,' said Pelham. 'We're unanimous.' He pulled a lever and the roof began to pack itself away in his boot, prompting Luke to give him a look. 'They're after a car with its roof up,' he said.

'Sure,' said Luke. 'This'll fool them.'

The papers began to rustle and flap on the back seat as they moved off. Rachel passed them to Luke to stow in the glove compartment. 'Sous Ashmolean,' she smiled. 'What on earth's down there? What was Newton working on when Ashmole died?'

'In May 1692?' replied Luke. 'Not much. He was still recuperating from the *Principia*.' It was understandable enough. Writing it had been arguably the greatest sustained intellectual effort in scientific history. And it had left him utterly exhausted. 'But he began working again towards the end of the year. On alchemy.'

'Triggered by whatever Ashmole left him,' suggested Pelham.

'The dates fit,' agreed Luke. 'And he worked himself sick over the next twelve months. And I do mean sick. He had a pretty severe mental breakdown, writing bizarre letters to Samuel Pepys and John Locke, accusing them of all kinds of fantastical stuff. Then he wrote them profuse apologies, blaming exhaustion and fumes from his experiments.'

'Two letters hardly constitutes a breakdown,' said Rachel.

'There were plenty of other indicators too,' said Luke. 'For one, it looks like that year broke him. He published some ground-breaking work afterwards, particularly *Opticks*, but his breakthrough thinking was largely done. And then he wrote this notorious paper called *Praxis* that . . .' He broke off, frowned.

'What?' asked Rachel.

'Nothing,' said Luke. 'Just coincidence. It has to be.'

'What has to be?'

'This paper he wrote. It's not dated, but we're pretty sure he wrote it in summer or autumn 1693, because it doesn't make sense unless he was going through some kind of crisis at the time.'

'Why not?'

'That's the thing. He claimed in it that he'd achieved multiplication.'

Rachel shook her head. 'Multiplication?'

'It's the ultimate goal of the alchemist,' said Pelham, answering for Luke. 'Newton was effectively claiming that he'd discovered the philosopher's stone itself.'

FIFTEEN

I

Office of the Chief of the General Staff, The Knesset, Jerusalem

It was the kind of briefing that the Chief of the General Staff Ysrael Levin had hoped he'd never have to be given, yet there was some little part of him that was perversely gratified despite that. People didn't make careers in the Israeli Defence Forces unless they enjoyed a good crisis. 'And you're quite sure about this?' he asked Judit Hafitz, his head of nuclear programmes.

'We're quite sure that we've found bits of code that shouldn't be there,' she told him. 'What we don't know yet is how they got there, or what they do. What we don't know yet is whether they're malicious or effectively benign. What we don't know yet is what they mean for our warheads and delivery systems.'

'How can you not know things like that?'

'Because it's the nature of such worms to separate into a million little pieces, each bit of which then embeds itself out of sight. If this truly is a worm, then it's brilliantly designed, better than anything we've got. It doesn't respond to simulations. We think it's been designed to lie dormant until launch commands are given for real. Only then will we be able to see exactly how extensive the infection is, what its effects will be. If we're lucky, it will be like the millennium bug: all anxiety and then nothing.'

'And if we're not lucky?'

'Then it could be . . .' She closed her eyes for a moment, as though trying to think of the right words: '. . . *truly significant.*'

'And what does truly significant mean? You can't seriously be suggesting that this . . . this *worm* could deprive us of our missile defence?'

'General, I'm saying that, for all we know, we could launch a strike at Tehran, only to hit Tel Aviv instead.'

Ysrael Levin could feel the blood draining from his face. No more did he feel that small thrill of gratification. All he felt in the pit of his stomach was an extraordinary dismay. 'When will you know for sure? When will you have it fixed?'

'With respect, General, I only just learned of this myself. I assumed you'd want to know at once. I'm here to advise you that we have a problem, not yet to tell you the solution.'

'How widespread is it? Will it affect our submarines?'

'We don't know.'

'You don't know?'

'The only way to tell quickly is by running diagnostic programmes. But we fear they may be one source of infection. If we run them, therefore . . .'

'You'll only spread the infection further.'

'Yes, General. My advice is that we close down everything while we study the code itself to learn precisely what we're dealing with. It's not as if we'll be completely without nuclear defences. We still have our artillery and our planes.'

The Chief of the General Staff didn't bother to say what they both well knew. Their guns only reached sixty kilometres and their few aircraft capable of delivering nuclear payloads were a generation out of date. 'How long before you fix this?' he asked.

'I can't say. Maybe days. More likely weeks or months. Possibly years.'

'*Years?*'

'General, it's possible that we'll *never* be able to fix it, not to the level of confidence we need for nuclear warheads. It's possible we'll have to strip out our systems and start again.'

The Chief of the General Staff shook his head. 'I don't understand. I thought we designed our systems in silos precisely to make sure this kind of thing couldn't happen.'

'We do.'

'Then . . .?'

'Someone got lucky,' said Judit. 'At least, we think that's what must have happened. The earthquake damaged several of our locations, and took out our firewalls, exposing our systems to infiltration. We think they must have had the worm ready, then took advantage. And then of course we ran our full suite of diagnostics to see if we'd suffered any damage.'

'Spreading this worm throughout our network?'

'That's what we suspect. But, as I say, we don't know anything yet. Not for sure.' She shook her head ruefully. 'If one of our technicians hadn't been on the ball . . .'

A moment of stillness, rage building inside. 'Who did this? Was it the Iranians? Is this payback for Stuxnet?'

'It's possible. The technology is light years beyond anything we thought Tehran had, but they've been building up their capability fast. My money would be on the Chinese, though, or possibly the Russians. You'd know better than I who'd benefit most from something like this.'

The Chief of the General Staff put a hand to his head. 'Will they know how much harm they've done?'

'They'll likely know that they've successfully infiltrated

their worm into our systems. They probably won't know how far it's spread, whether we've spotted it, what our countermeasures are like or how long it will take us to sort it out. Not unless there's some other vulnerability in our system we haven't yet identified.'

'And what's the likelihood of that?'

'At this time yesterday I'd have told you that there was no possibility whatsoever of there being a worm like this in our system.'

The Chief of the General Staff sat back in his chair. This would have been disastrous news at the best of times; and this was far from that. Three weeks ago, on May 15th, Arabs here and across the broader region had started making trouble, rioting and throwing stones in protest at the anniversary of Israel's independence. Usually, these *Nakba* protests lasted a day or two before fizzling out, but the earthquake that had wrecked their nuclear defences had also put fissures in the Dome of the Rock, sparking a massive increase in the scale, intensity and duration of unrest.

Marches in Damascus, Amman and Cairo and along their borders had turned into violent anti-Jewish riots – though quite how the Jews were to blame for the earthquake had never been made clear. Missiles had been lobbed into Jewish towns and villages from the Gaza strip and southern Lebanon. Israel's own forces had had no choice but to strike back. They'd bombed Hamas and

Hezbollah positions in Lebanon, Syria and Gaza, had sent in ground-troops to take prisoners. Alert levels had gone up on all sides, army groups had moved closer to their borders. Firebrand politicians and religious leaders had cursed each other from behind the safety of TV cameras. And everyone had been intensely aware that this was all prelude to the region's other great anti-Jewish anniversary: the week long festival of hate and rage that commemorated the Six Day War, which had kicked off earlier today.

Until now, however, this had all seemed to him part of the usual theatre: alarming, certainly, yet essentially manageable. But what if there was more to it this time? What if this were part of some larger plan?

He stared down at his desk. For some forty years, Israel's strategic defence had ultimately relied on nuclear deterrence. Their Arab neighbours, for all their bluster, had never truly contemplated Israel's destruction, lest Israel take the whole region down with her. Now, at a stroke, they'd effectively been reduced to conventional forces. And while Israel was a theoretical match for its neighbours' combined armies, hot wars chewed up armour and aircraft at a terrifying rate, depleting stocks of petrol and munitions rapidly. The Egyptians, Syrians, Lebanese and Jordanians could all expect swift if surreptitious resupply from Iran, China, Pakistan and Russia. Israel, by contrast, would be almost entirely dependent on the US. Yet tonight their Prime Minister was making a major foreign policy speech seeking stronger ties with the European Union at the expense of Washington, not least because they didn't want to be too reliant on a US administration led – since the botched assassination attempt – by a thin-skinned crazy woman who believed in the imminence of the Rapture.

He looked up at Judit. 'You're to work on nothing else,' he told her. 'You're to requisition any and all resources you need, but you'll find out the extent of this as soon as possible. And then you'll fix it. I'll want briefings twice a day until you do; and immediate updates if anything new emerges.'

'Yes, General,' she said. 'But, with respect, this happened under my command. This failure is my responsibility. I therefore wish to tender my—'

'Not yet,' cut in the Chief of the General Staff. 'Sort this mess out first, *then* make the offer. I might even accept.'

'Yes, General.'

'Good. Now get to work.' He watched her out the door, wondering who to take this to. By rights, he reported to the Defence Minister; but the Defence Minister was in South Africa this week, discussing nuclear security, of all things, and there was no time to waste. He picked up his phone, dialled an internal number. 'I need to see the Prime Minister,' he said.

'She's leaving for her speech in a minute,' said her assistant. 'I could fit you in afterwards or—'

'Her speech will have to wait,' said the Chief of the General Staff. 'I'm coming over now.'

II

There was something about having the roof down. Rachel's spirits lifted from the rush of open air and sunlight on her face, from the noise of the road and passing traffic. Her life had become drab with duty recently. That was the truth of it. To be whirled away from it, even under these extraordinary circumstances, felt bizarrely like release. And it was a pleasure, too, simply being with people that she liked. And she did like Luke and Pelham, she realized, rather to her surprise. She liked them a lot.

They passed Aylesbury, traded A roads for country lanes. Pelham slowed to a more leisurely pace, allowing her to admire the landscape, quaint villages separated by woods, pastures and fields of grain. It grew cooler. The late afternoon sun began a little alchemy of its own, turning a line of leaden clouds low on the horizon into streaks of glorious gold. Rachel leaned forwards between the front seats, as much for a windbreak as anything, and squinted against the windscreen's glare.

'Don't take this wrong, guys,' she said, 'but why on earth would a man like Newton fall for nonsense like the philosopher's stone? He didn't really believe transmutation was possible, did he?'

'Just because a theory turns out to be wrong, doesn't mean it was stupid,' said Luke. 'Alchemy was far more sophisticated than people think.'

'And it was immensely productive too,' added Pelham. 'The scientific method is hypothesis, experimentation, observation, inference, peer review, replication. All devised or developed by the alchemists.'

Rachel gave him a doubtful look. 'Yes, but turning lead into gold . . .'

'People didn't understand the nature of matter,' said Luke. 'They were brought up on earth, fire, air and water, with no real concept of atoms or molecules. The alchemists were doing their best to come up with a better model. And forget the get-rich schemes; those were for the charlatans. Gold wasn't even really seen as a precious metal by serious practitioners like Dee, Newton and Boyle. It was their symbol for light, for the sun, for the divine nature itself. Making it, for them, was like winning it for an Olympic athlete: not the accomplishment itself, merely proof of it.'

Rachel smiled at the analogy. 'So what were they after?'

'A unified theory of everything,' answered Luke. 'How the earth and heavens worked, the nature of substance, the secret of life itself.' He cocked an eyebrow at her. 'And don't make the mistake of thinking the philosopher's stone was some kind of magical gem. It was much more subtle than that. Alchemists also called it sacred fire or secret fire or even the animating spirit, all of which are far better ways of thinking about it. Newton originally thought it was magnetism or maybe even light. Ultimately he came to believe that it was electricity. And that isn't remotely stupid, if you think about it. Frankenstein's monster. The spark of life. Cardiac paddles.'

'But electricity had been around forever,' pointed out Rachel. 'Lightning was the weapon of the gods, remember? Not exactly *secret* fire.'

'Its *nature* was secret,' said Luke. 'No one understood it.'

'Yes, they did,' said Rachel, shifting in her seat to stop the wind whipping hair around her face. 'Not perfectly, I agree, but surely enough to demystify it. You get static everywhere, for one thing. And they knew it was connected with magnetism. The word electricity comes from the Greek for amber, electrum, because amber attracts or repels other objects when you rub it. And what about those Baghdad batteries?'

'What about those what?' frowned Luke.

'Baghdad batteries. You must have heard of them.'

He shook her head. 'What are they?'

'There was this excavation near Baghdad just before

the Second World War. They found these really weird earthenware jars with copper rods sticking up from their bottoms. Two thousand years old, give or take. Turns out they were most likely primitive electrical devices that used vinegar or some other acid to electroplate silver and other metals with gold.'

'Are you serious?' frowned Luke.

'Of course I'm serious. You think I'd make them up?'

But Pelham held up a hand for silence before Luke could answer. 'Oddington, guys,' he said, nodding at a sign. 'We're here.' He slowed almost to jogging pace as he searched memory and the twilit lanes for Olivia's house. 'There she is,' he said at last, swinging down a potholed track bordered by wild shrubberies before pulling up in front of a low thatched house of vivid pink that sagged perceptibly in its middle, so that the frame of the front door splayed out towards the foot, leaving gaps for the winter wind. They slammed their doors to give notice of their arrival, and Pelham rapped out Beethoven with the knocker.

'Who is it?' asked a woman warily. 'Who's there?'

'It's me,' boomed Pelham. 'Pelham Redfern the Third. Your friendly neighbourhood alchemist, remember? All lead turned into gold.'

Rustling inside, keys turning and bolts sliding and the door creaked open, revealing a tall, angular woman with silver hair swept back in a tight bun, reading glasses on a frayed grey string around her neck. 'Pelham,' she said, with the nervous warmth of a schoolmarm welcoming back some troublesome old boy. 'Whatever brings you here?'

'Hell of a story,' he said. 'I'm going to need a glass of your excellent whisky and water to help me tell it. But first let me introduce my two companions. This is Rachel Parkes of the great Caius College, Cambridge. And my old friend Luke Hayward, currently writing the definitive biography of Sir Isaac Newton.'

Olivia frowned. 'There was a flap in London last year about a Newton scholar called Luke Hayward.'

'Yes,' agreed Luke. 'There was.'

Olivia was silent a few moments, assimilating this information. 'I knew your Vice Chancellor at university,' she said finally. 'He was a prick then, too.' She stood aside to welcome them in, closed the door behind them, gestured them through. The passage was low with ancient beams, its walls crowded with portraits of the saints and religious curios. They reached a gloomy living room. She invited them to sit. 'Now, then,' she said, as they all settled into their various chairs. 'Which one of you three wants to tell me what this is all about?'

III

The Israeli Prime Minister took the news better than the Chief of the General Staff had dared hope. 'The Chinese, you say?' she asked.

'Most likely,' he told her. 'Maybe the Russians.'

'You don't think . . .' She hesitated, unsure whether to voice her thought.

'Yes, Prime Minister?'

'You don't think there's any chance the *Americans* might have been behind it?'

The General was surprised by the suggestion, but he took it seriously. Unlike many of his comrades, who mistook her dovishness for weakness, he respected his new Prime Minister. Her character, if not her policies. Nor did he romanticize Israel's relationship with the Americans, but saw it rather as the product of interests that were usually, but not invariably, aligned. 'Why would you suggest that?' he asked.

'They have the best engineers. They know our systems better than anyone, and therefore its weak points too. And I'm about to announce a more pro-European foreign policy. Could this be Washington's way of reminding us of just how badly we need them?'

'Worms like these take years to design,' he told her. 'And we think infiltration was only made possible by the earthquake. Your speech is a coincidence.'

'Good.' She looked relieved. 'But you're about to tell me to put it back in my bottom drawer, aren't you?'

'No, Prime Minister,' he said. 'I came here meaning to. But now I think that would be a mistake.'

'I thought you abhorred my new policy.'

'I do. But it's been too well trailed. Drop it now and you'll signal weakness. Whoever infiltrated the worm will know that we've found it, and that we're worried. The less information we give them, the better.'

The Prime Minister nodded. 'I'll take it down a notch.'

'Yes, Prime Minister.'

She sat back in her chair, stared up at the ornately plastered ceiling. 'What's your gut telling you?' she asked. 'About our neighbours, I mean. Is all their recent bluster and skirmishing just the usual nonsense. Or are they girding up for something?'

'I think it's the usual nonsense. A war would only work if they all came at us at the same time. They don't trust each other enough for that.'

'No.'

'Besides, their regimes are still too precarious. They need their people with them. And their people don't want new wars. They want jobs, food, the promise of things getting better.'

'Don't rely too heavily on that,' she said. 'They're frustrated and they're angry; and it doesn't take much to turn frustrated, angry people against a common enemy.

A stray missile on a wedding party. A firebomb in a mosque.'

'Some Third Temple fanatic taking down the Dome,' smiled the Chief of the General Staff.

She gave a little shudder, shook her head. 'Don't even joke about it,' she said.

'No, Prime Minister.'

IV

It was Luke who got the nod from Pelham. 'I found something earlier today,' he told Olivia. 'A folder of lost Newton papers.'

Her eyes glinted and she leaned forwards in her chair. 'One of the Sotheby's lots? How thrilling! But what do they have to do with me?'

He passed her the relevant page of the printout and directed her attention to Newton's cryptic message. Olivia put on her reading glasses, held it up to the light of an ebony lamp. 'Ah,' she said. 'Received from E.A. – and you're thinking Elias Ashmole?'

'Newton wrote this in 1692,' said Luke. 'At least, that's what the citations and watermark suggest. Ashmole died in May that year. So we think it was probably a bequest.'

Olivia shook her head. 'But why would Ashmole leave anything to Newton? They hardly knew each other.'

'We don't know that,' said Luke. 'Not for sure. They could easily have known each other well through the alchemists' network.'

'The alchemists' what?' asked Rachel.

'All the alchemists were in surreptitious contact with one another,' explained Olivia. 'They had to be, to trade their texts and furnaces, share their potions and theories. So we have overwhelming evidence for some kind of network, but sadly we know next to nothing about how it worked.'

Luke got to his feet and went across to Olivia to point out the bottom line. 'This is really why we're here,' he said. 'This bit about "in Salomans House well concealed".'

Olivia nodded. 'And you think that's the Ashmolean he's referring to?'

'Actually, we rather assumed it was the Royal Society? Why? Was the Ashmolean known as Saloman's House too?'

'Oh yes. Everything was back then. It was a real bandwagon for a while. We brought out a history a few years back: *Solomon's House in Oxford.*' She pushed herself to her feet to go fetch it when she paused, squinted at him. 'But why are you here if you didn't know that?'

'There's an anagram,' Luke told her. 'Rachel spotted it. Saloman's House comes out as Sous Ashmolean.'

'Sous Ashmolean?' Olivia looked at him with amused

consternation. 'You're not suggesting there's something beneath my museum floor?'

'We're suggesting that Newton's note implies it,' said Pelham, with uncharacteristic moderation. 'Why? Don't you think it's even possible?'

'No. I don't think it's even possible. The Ashmolean opened in 1683. It had been up and running for *nine years* by 1692. And the basement wasn't some abandoned storage area. It was one of the world's pioneering scientific laboratories. Then it became England's leading anatomy lecture hall. Don't you think someone might have noticed Sir Isaac Newton turning up one afternoon with a pickaxe over his shoulder? And don't you think that, during one or other of our various refurbishments, someone would have spotted some trace of this mysterious—' She broke off, put a hand to her chest, her breath suddenly coming a little faster. 'Oh my lord,' she murmured. 'Oh my good lord.'

'What?' asked Luke. 'What is it?'

'No. No. It's nothing. I'm sure it's nothing.'

'Then you won't mind telling us.'

She shook her head reluctantly. 'Very well,' she said. 'It's just that one of my predecessors as curator used to tell a story. But no one ever took it seriously. He was always telling stories.'

'And what was *this* story?'

She let out a long sigh. 'His name was Conrad Josten.

I knew him a little when I was an undergraduate. He was fascinated by Ashmole. He wrote his biography. Anyway, he oversaw a major refurbishment back in the 1960s. After the workmen had broken up and removed the old basement floor, but before they laid the new one, he ran a metal detector over it.'

'He found something?'

'So he claimed. Something *big*. Something *iron*.'

'And he didn't investigate further?'

She shook her head. 'You've no idea what it's like to run a museum, have you? Deadlines to meet, exhibitions to put on, absurdly tight budgets. Dig up a floor on a whim like that and you'd better find Sutton Hoo or start looking for a new job.'

'So whatever it was is still down there?'

'If there ever *was* anything there, which I doubt. Conrad was quite capable of spinning the slightest anomaly into some great mystery. And metal detectors were dreadfully crude beasts back then, minesweepers really, nothing like as sensitive as the ones we have today.'

'But that's a brilliant idea!' enthused Pelham. 'You're exactly right!'

Olivia looked startled. 'I beg your pardon?'

'We need to run a modern metal detector across your basement floor. Something state-of-the-art. Something infinitely more sensitive than what Josten had. What an inspired thought.'

'That's not what I meant at all!'

'Of course it was,' Pelham assured her. 'Maybe not consciously, but I'll bet it's what your id was thinking.' He grinned wickedly at her. 'Come on, Olivia. You know you want to.'

'I can't. I really can't. What if we found something?'

'What kind of attitude is that?' protested Pelham. 'Don't I remember you giving a talk about the virtue of relentless curiosity? That *was* you, wasn't it? My memory's not playing tricks?'

She gave him a look that could have burned toast. 'It would never work,' she said. 'We've laid far too much concrete over the years.'

'The latest remote sensing devices are extraordinary,' said Rachel. 'I spent two seasons mapping a site near Antioch with them. You wouldn't believe how much we found, and how deep. Ten or even fifteen metres, some of it. And we could still make out what metals the artefacts were made from and how big they were.'

'You've used them before, then?' asked Luke. 'You could do it at the museum?'

'Sure. If it's a model I know.'

Olivia shook her head. 'We've got a history of time running in our basement. I'm not moving all our exhibits and cabinets for this. I'm simply not. It's too absurd.'

'What kind of cabinets?' asked Rachel. 'Are they solid or on legs?'

Olivia pulled a face, unwilling to cede ground. But she was too honest to lie. 'On legs,' she admitted.

'Then they won't be a problem,' Rachel assured her. 'We can sweep beneath them, like vacuuming under the bed.'

Olivia gave a little wail. 'Where would we even get a metal detector at this time of night?'

'Come on, Olivia,' said Pelham. 'This is Oxford. You can barely walk down the street for archaeologists lugging around remote sensing devices. You must know someone.'

'Oh, Lord,' she said. 'We could try Albie, I suppose.'

'Perfect!' said Pelham. 'Albie's exactly the man.'

'You know him?'

'Not yet. And I never will, not unless you make the call.'

'I knew I was going to regret this,' said Olivia, 'the moment I heard your voice.' But her cheeks were flushed and there was a sparkle in her eyes as she went to her phone and flipped through her address book for Albie's number.

SIXTEEN

I

Parking anywhere near the centre of Oxford was always a challenge, but Pelham finally found a space in a residential street where he barely had to nudge the cars either side. They walked briskly and found Albie waiting by a side door of his college, pacing back and forth, checking his watch. 'This better be important, Olivia,' he said, kissing her briskly on the cheek. 'I'm supposed to be giving some wretched talk.'

'It *is* important,' said Olivia. 'And we're terribly grateful.'

He waved them inside, then led them with the cautious stoop of a tall man in an old building. They reached a stock room. He gave a courtier's wave at the array of remote-sensing devices on the shelves and slouched like problem youths against the facing wall.

'You've got a Mala!' said Rachel, going straight to it. 'Fantastic.'

Albie winced. 'Our moon-buggy is a fine machine too,' he said, steering her towards its neighbour. 'A real workhorse.'

'We'll look after it, I swear,' promised Olivia. 'We'll bring it straight back.'

Albie sighed. 'Tomorrow will be fine,' he said, as Luke and Pelham gathered up the Mala and its peripherals. 'So what are you looking for?'

'I can't say,' Olivia told him. 'Really, I can't. But if we find anything, you'll be the first to know.'

'I should damned well hope so.'

The old Ashmolean was closer than the car, so they headed straight there. Their route took them past the Sheldonian. 'Maybe it wasn't the alchemists' network,' mused Olivia, frowning at it. 'Maybe it was this guy.'

'You mean Wren?' asked Rachel.

Olivia nodded. 'One of Newton's closest friends. One of Ashmole's, too.' Her museum was bang next door. 'There's even a suggestion he may have helped design this place,' she said, leading them up its front steps. 'At least, that's what we tell people.'

Rachel smiled. 'Must add a bit of cachet.'

'And makes it harder for the council to tear us down.' She unlocked and opened the door, turned off the alarm, switched on lights. They found themselves in a display gallery that also served as reception and gift shop. An internal staircase led both up and down. They went down, passed through more doors into a large display room crowded with neat ranks of glass-topped display cabinets, and with sundials, grandfather clocks and other large chronometers against its walls. 'Conrad said it was in here,' she said. 'I don't know exactly where.'

'Great,' said Rachel. 'Then let's start looking.'

II

Walters had stopped off for a burger with Pete and Kieran. The mood was gloomy; the trail was cold. They were beginning to talk of giving up for the night and starting fresh in the morning when his mobile finally rang. He swallowed away a mouthful of dry bread and meat. 'Yes?' he asked.

'I don't know who the hell you think you are,' said a man.

'Makes two of us, mate,' Walters told him. 'You sure you got the right number?'

'This is the number I was given. I was told

you wanted information about one of our SatNav systems.'

'Ah,' said Walters. He beckoned to Kieran for a napkin and something to write with. 'Go on, then.'

'I don't know who the hell you think you—'

'Yes. I got that bollocks the first time. Where are they?'

'Oxford city centre.' He read out the GPS coordinates, gave the name of a road. Walters read it back to make sure he had it right. 'And they went straight there from Cambridge?'

'They stopped for a while at a place called Oddington.' He read out coordinates for that too.

'Thanks,' said Walters.

'This kind of thing shouldn't be allowed,' said the man, determined to get it off his chest. 'Honestly, I don't know who you people think you are.'

'We're the people you just shopped one of your customers to,' Walters told him, with a certain satisfaction. 'So I wouldn't go moaning about it if I were you.' He ended the call, picked up the remains of his burger and fries, examined them dispiritedly for a moment, tossed them back down. Then he nodded to Kieran and Pete. 'Come on, fellas,' he said. 'We're in business.'

III

Luke leaned against the wall and watched admiringly as Rachel assembled the Mala then set to work. No hesitation, no fumbling. It was always a pleasure to watch someone who knew exactly what they were doing. But then he sensed Pelham looking wryly at him. 'What?' he asked.

'Nothing,' smiled Pelham.

Olivia, meanwhile, had spread the Newton papers out on a glass-topped cabinet. 'The papers of J.D. and J.T.' she said, tapping the fourth line of Newton's enigmatic message.

'We think J.D. is John Dee,' said Luke, going to join her. 'We don't know who J.T. is.'

'I do,' said Olivia. 'And it's not a "he" so much as a "they". The John Tradescants, father and son.'

Pelham shook his head. 'Never heard of them.'

'Most people haven't,' said Olivia. 'Though they should have done. By rights, this place should have been named after them, not Ashmole. It was *their* collection that he left to Oxford, not his own.'

'The Tradescantareum hardly trips off the tongue,' said Pelham.

'Who were they?' asked Rachel.

'The father was a gardener. His boss sent him to Holland to buy some seeds and he caught the collecting bug. This was around 1610, when the world was really opening up. The Americas, China, India, Africa. He travelled to all parts, gathering specimens and other curiosities to put on display in his Lambeth home. The Ark, he called it. Charged a shilling a time. There was a huge market for curiosity shops back then. The more sensational, the better.' She nodded towards the rear. 'We found a mermaid's hand out back when we put the extension in.'

'A mermaid's hand?' asked Luke.

'So the Tradescants claimed,' she smiled. 'Turned out to be the paw of a manatee. Still. A wonderful find.'

'And the son went into the business too?'

'Took it over when his father died. Unfortunately for him and his wife, that's when Ashmole showed up. A really nasty piece of work, I'm afraid. He set his heart on their collection. The poor Tradescants never realized. Ashmole was an aristocrat, you see, so they trusted him. Then he got John blind drunk one night and somehow tricked him into leaving him the entire collection. Tradescant sued to get it annulled, but he died before his case could be heard. And then the court sided with Ashmole over Tradescant's widow.'

'Maybe Ashmole was in the right, then,' said Luke.

'Sure. Because courts always put poor widows ahead of wealthy aristocrats. Besides, there's a curious story about Ashmole just after the Civil War. He fought with the Royalists, so was in the doghouse. Then in 1646 he was inducted into a Staffordshire society of Freemasons. It's one of the earlier mentions of Freemasonry in English history, seventy years before the first Grand Lodge was formed in London. And within another week, he was swaggering around London like he owned it.'

'By virtue of being a Freemason?'

'That's how it looks. And, afterwards, Ashmole was forever taking people to court. He used to gloat about never losing a case. But then he wouldn't, would he? Not if he knew which courts had Masonic judges.'

'Maybe *that* was his link with Newton,' frowned Luke. 'There have been rumours forever about him being a Mason. One of his disciples even became Grand Master of—'

The Mala began suddenly to screech. Rachel muted the volume, checked the display. 'Your man Josten was right,' she told Olivia. 'There *is* something down there. Big and iron, just like he said.' She swept the detector left and right. 'And some kind of cavity too.'

'How deep?'

'Ten feet. Twelve feet. Something like that.'

'Pipes?' suggested Luke.

'Maybe.' She swept the GPR back and forth, mapping its edge, a rough circle perhaps ten feet in diameter. She adjusted the Mala's controls, the better to investigate the interior of this circle, checking data as she went. 'I'm getting something else,' she said, as she reached the centre. 'Another metal.' She checked the readings, frowned, checked again. Then she looked up at them all with the strangest expression on her face.

'What is it?' asked Luke.

'Gold,' she said.

SEVENTEEN

I

There was silence in the basement gallery, save for the ticking of clocks around the walls. Olivia folded her arms emphatically as they turned to her. 'No,' she said.

'No, what?' asked Pelham. 'You don't even know what we're about to suggest.'

'Yes, I do. You're about to suggest I dig up my floor. And the answer is no. This is a museum, not an oil field.'

'We've got to,' said Pelham. 'Don't you realize what a find this is? There could be anything down there.'

'Exactly. Which is why we're not going to risk damaging it.'

'But we—'

'No. I'm sorry. That's the end of it.'

'Then what do we do?' asked Rachel. 'We can't pretend it's not there.'

'And we won't. I'll call Albie first thing in the morning. He can verify your readings, put together a plan. And when we next have an appropriate window, he can excavate with the kind of care something like this demands.'

Luke glanced at Pelham. Pelham nodded. 'I'm afraid there's something about this business we haven't told you yet,' he said to Olivia.

Olivia's eyes narrowed. 'Go on.'

'We're not the only ones looking for this,' said Luke. He told her about his day: his anonymous client, Rachel's aunt, Crane Court and their narrow escape from Pelham's apartment.

Olivia listened in stony silence. 'How could you keep this from me?' she demanded, when he was done. 'Don't you realize how much trouble you're in? How much trouble you've put me in?'

'None of us are exactly here by choice,' said Pelham.

'You should have told me.'

'Yes,' admitted Luke. 'You're absolutely right. I'm sorry. We all are. But we're riding a bolting horse here. It's all we can do to cling on.'

'It doesn't make any difference,' said Olivia. 'You still can't dig up my floor. I don't care who's after you.'

Luke crouched, placed his palm flat on the floor,

tantalized by the mysterious gold just a few feet beneath. Yet he knew in his heart that Olivia was right. Even if they could get down, this was too important a site to risk. He smiled wryly at Rachel. 'Your aunt asked me something earlier. She asked me why a man like Newton would take a job at the Royal Mint. I gave her the usual reasons: status, income, London. But the truth is that no one really knows. What if *this* is why? I mean, Newton drove himself crazy with alchemical experiments in 1693. What if that wasn't pure research? What if he'd simply needed a large quantity of gold to complete whatever Ashmole left him? He was an alchemist; of course he'd have tried alchemy first. But when that failed him, where would he have turned?'

'The Royal Mint,' murmured Olivia.

'The position of Warden had always been a sinecure,' said Luke. 'But not under Newton. He designed new coining presses, invented new alloys. He oversaw an entire recoinage of the realm. And he was the greatest mathematician in British history, so I'm guessing he could have run rings around the auditors. He could have taken however much gold he'd needed and no one would ever have known.'

Pelham grinned down at the floor. 'Sir Isaac's stolen bullion,' he said. 'How cool is that?'

'All the more reason to treat it with respect,' said Olivia.

Rachel had gone to consult the Newton paper. Now she frowned. 'I think maybe we're missing a trick,' she said, tapping the text. 'I mean we're all pretty much agreed on what this means, right? Ashmole left something to Newton on the understanding that he'd complete it, bring it here and hide it beneath the floor. But this was a working laboratory by then. The foremost laboratory in England. And then an anatomy room. That's right, yes?'

'Yes,' said Olivia. 'Why?'

'So you were absolutely correct earlier when you said that Ashmole couldn't possibly have expected Newton to come here with a pickaxe and dig up the floor. Which means there must have been some other way down. A way that both he and Newton knew about.'

'There isn't,' said Olivia. 'We've rebuilt this place god knows how many times. If there were any secret passages or the like, we'd have found them long ago, believe me. And even if one had somehow escaped our notice for over three hundred years, do you honestly expect us to find it in just one night?'

'You can't think of anything?' asked Luke. 'No anomalies at all?'

She shook her head. 'We found an old septic tank when we put in the extension out back. But that was only a few feet deep, and we've concreted it up, anyway. And then there was the old well, of course. But that's it.'

'The old well?' asked Rachel dryly. 'You don't mean as in "Salomans House *well* concealed"?'

'Oh my good lord,' murmured Olivia, clasping her hands by her mouth. 'Yes, I rather suppose I do.'

II

There was little Croke could do to help search Crane Court, so he settled himself into a penthouse apartment and watched it live on a vast plasma TV. Speculative reports were interspersed with loops of footage, one of which even included a brief clip of himself and Morgenstern arriving earlier. But every so often they'd cut to aerial shots, and there was something perversely satisfying about being able to hear those selfsame helicopters clattering above his head.

His mobile rang. He checked the number. Walters. 'Are you in Oxford yet?' Croke asked him.

'On our way,' said Walters. 'But we may have found something. Thought you'd want to know at once.'

'Go on.'

'Redfern and the others stopped off in a place called Oddington. Kieran's been checking it out and the house nearest where they parked belongs to a woman called Olivia Campbell. An Olivia Campbell runs something called the Museum of the History of Science in Oxford, about fifteen minutes walk from where they parked. Thing is, they put on a History of Chemistry exhibition there a few years back. The programme's on their website. And guess who helped organize it? Only our friend Pelham Redfern.'

'Then that's where they've gone,' said Croke.

'So it would seem. We'll find out soon enough.'

'And you three can take care of them yourselves, right? Only I want to keep this to ourselves if we can.'

'Let us check it out. I'll call you back if we need help.'

'Good.' Croke finished the call, stood there frowning. A museum in the heart of Oxford. What an odd place to go to ground. He was still brooding on this when Morgenstern came in.

'Just completed the second scan,' he told Croke. 'Nothing. And we double-checked those anomalies against the plans, like you suggested. But they're all water or sewage or other utilities.'

'You're saying it's not here?'

Morgenstern gave a shrug. 'Police scanners are designed to find recent disturbances, organic remains, explosives, that kind of shit. For something like this, we should maybe get in some geological or even archaeological equipment.'

It was the word 'archaeological' that did it, for some reason. Croke held up a hand for quiet, to buy himself time to think. The Museum of the History of Science. What if Luke and the others *hadn't* gone to ground? What if they knew something he didn't? 'Bear with me a moment,' he said. 'I want to make a call.'

He tried Jerusalem first, but Avram wasn't answering, so he rang his nephew in London instead.

'Yes?' asked Kohen.

'The Museum of the History of Science in Oxford,' said Croke.

A moment's silence. 'Ah,' said Kohen. 'Yes.'

Anger descended upon Croke like the holy spirit. 'Tell me.'

'The Museum of the History of Science used to be the Ashmolean. The Ashmolean was also once thought of as Salomon's House. In fact, if the E.A. in Newton's message refers to Elias Ashmole, as seems plausible under this hypothesis, then it's probably more likely to be the . . .'

Croke held his cellphone down by his side to prevent himself from yelling. When he'd calmed a little, he raised it again. 'Are you telling me we closed down half London to search in the *wrong fucking place*?' he asked. He gave Kohen the chance to reply, but all he got was silence, so he ended the call before he said anything unforgivable.

'We're searching in the wrong place?' asked Morgenstern.

'So it would seem.'

'And this Oxford Museum of yours? That's the right place?'

'That's how it looks.'

Morgenstern nodded as he digested this. His lips tightened and a little colour rose in his throat. He could use this as an opportunity to distance himself from this fiasco, Croke knew, or he could remind himself that this was his Commander in Chief's top priority. Thankfully, he chose the latter option. 'Okay,' he said, 'then we'd better get down there, hadn't we?'

III

The well had originally been just behind the Ashmolean's rear wall, but the recent extension had brought it inside. Olivia led them to it. Its head was knee high and perhaps three feet across, and it had been fitted with a black-painted winch and handle to make it into a feature, even though its mouth was covered by a sheet of safety glass bolted to the brickwork.

'Back in a mo,' said Olivia. She vanished upstairs and returned heaving a battered blue toolbox. Luke found himself an adjustable wrench and went to work. The bolts didn't come easily, not even after oiling. But finally he had them. They lifted off the safety glass, rested it against the wall. A noxious smell oozed up from the darkness. Luke took a torch from the toolbox, aimed it down. Water glittered blackly from the foot, minutely disturbed by fragments of brickwork they'd dislodged while removing the glass. He pointed the torch at each section of shaft wall in turn, but it all looked perfectly normal.

'What now?' asked Rachel.

'One of us goes down, of course,' said Pelham. He gave Luke a pointed look. 'I can't think who.'

'Hey,' grinned Luke. 'I'd pay for the privilege.' A brass reflecting telescope was on display at the foot of the main staircase, roped off to discourage children from using it as a fairground ride. The rope was a ceremonial crimson, but it looked strong enough. Luke untied it and carried it to the well. He knotted one end around the winch, tugged it to make sure it would hold.

Rachel winced as she watched. 'Are you sure about this?'

'It'll be fine,' he said, tossing the rest of the rope down into the shaft. It uncoiled as it went, its end splashing into the dark water. The torch had a wrist strap, but he needed his hands uncluttered. There was a ball of string in the toolbox, so he cut off a length, fed it through the strap, and knotted it around his neck like an outsized medallion. He sat on the rim with his legs over the edge, grabbed the rope with both hands, gave it another tug. The winch's moorings creaked a little, as if to remind him they were mainly decorative. He looked down into the shaft, black and forbidding, turned to Pelham. 'If this thing starts to give, you'll grab the rope, right?'

'I'll certainly give it my fullest consideration,' said Pelham.

'That's all I ask, mate.'

Luke tightened his grip then committed himself, swinging across the shaft like the clapper of a bell, hitting the far wall harder than he'd expected, the cold rough brickwork scraping his shoulder and his side. The rope creaked and yawed, but it and the winch both held. He made circles with his right leg, twirling the rope around it before clamping it between his feet, allowing him to take weight off his hands. He began to lower himself. The torch banged off his chest and elbows, casting uneven light on the walls. The stone-work at the top had recently been cleaned and repointed; but soon it became blackened with decades or maybe even centuries of neglect. He glanced upwards and was taken aback by how far he'd already come, the mouth closing above him like the gullet of some prehistoric beast.

'Are you okay?' asked Rachel, her voice strangely thickened and deepened by echoes.

'Can you see anything?' asked Pelham.

'Not yet.' The rope was swinging more gently now, only occasionally nudging him against the sides, dislodging occasional pieces of grit that fell in soft whispers to the water beneath. He took his full weight on his feet again, the better to inspect the walls. Behind the moss and damp, the stones were granite grey, large as farmhouse loaves, shaped to fit into a ring. But he reached water without discovering a hint of falseness or abnormality.

'Come back up,' called Rachel. 'We need to rethink.'

'On my way.' He began to haul himself upwards. Foolish to rush. The rope creaked and twisted; his torch bumped against his chest, casting eerie shadows, painting faces in the moss and lichen. And was his mind playing tricks, or did the wall here bulge very slightly? If so, it was subtle enough that he'd missed it on his descent. He placed his palm on it. The stone was clammy, cold and unwelcoming. But there was no question: it bulged. There should be earth and hardcore on the other side, packing these stones tight together. For it to bulge like this, there surely had to be some kind of flaw or cavity behind.

'What is it?' called down Olivia.

'I don't know,' said Luke. 'Probably nothing.' He set his back against the opposing wall, placed his soles on the bulge, tried to push. Nothing. He tried until his calves and thighs ached. Still nothing. His hands were tired. He shouldn't waste energy like this, not with the ascent still to complete. But then he remembered the shriek of the metal detector, the stunned look on Rachel's face. This wasn't some crazy figment. There really was something down here.

He set his feet against the bulge for a third time and gave it everything he'd got. And was rewarded by the tiniest scrape of noise as the stone gave just a fraction. He allowed himself a few moments rest before he heaved again. It ceded even more this time, perhaps a full inch. Another effort and it gave up the struggle altogether, tumbled backwards. Both his feet vanished into the created space so that he swung wildly across the shaft, fighting to hold on to the rope. He recovered himself, pulled out his feet, reached his torch inside, illuminating an open space hacked out of bedrock, like some smuggler's burrow.

'Well?' asked Rachel. 'What is it?'

'Hard to tell,' said Luke. 'Maybe a passage.' The opening was too small for him, but he'd already loosened the neighbouring stones and he soon had them out. No question now. A passage of some kind. He set the torch on the floor and wriggled in after it, buffering his fall with his elbows and knees. He stood, looked around, anchored himself inside, leaned back out. 'It's a passage,' he called up. 'I'll check it out and come straight back.'

'Be careful,' said Rachel.

Luke laughed softly as he looked into the ancient darkness. 'Count on it,' he said.

EIGHTEEN

I

Rachel heard scraping and scuffing for a few moments after Luke vanished into the passage, but after that there was nothing, not so much as a glimmer of light. Staring down, she was taken aback by how anxious she felt on his behalf. She tried to tell herself that this was normal fellow feeling, but she knew in her heart it was more than that.

At one time, Rachel had enjoyed a string of boyfriends. But then Bren had returned broken from Afghanistan, and she'd put men to one side. Romance had struck her as selfish and frivolous, somehow, even disloyal. Having fun while her brother suffered. And her life these days was scarcely set up for it. She worked all the hours god gave, saved what money she could. But suddenly she realized how much she missed that kind of friendship.

'What's the deal with Luke?' she asked Pelham, keeping her voice low lest the acoustics of the well somehow carry it to him.

'The deal?' asked Pelham.

'Something bad happened at his university. You both know about it. What was it?'

'If Luke wants to tell you, he'll tell you.'

'But he doesn't want to, does he? And if he's got skeletons in his closet, they could have ramifications for us. I have a right to know.'

Pelham glanced at Olivia. Olivia nodded. 'You won't tell him I told you?' Pelham asked.

'On my word,' said Rachel.

'Okay,' said Pelham. 'But please bear in mind that I don't know the full story myself. He hates to talk about it.'

'I understand.'

'Right, then. There was this woman on the cleaning staff of his university. Gloria, I think. Congolese and lovely.'

'Ah,' said Rachel.

'No,' said Pelham. 'Luke was with one of his fellow lecturers at the time. Maria. They were thinking of getting hitched. It was his Vice Chancellor who couldn't keep his hands off Gloria.'

'My old friend Charlie,' said Olivia. 'The oiliest, nastiest man you could imagine. Born to privilege, never for one moment doubting that it was deserved.'

'I know the type,' said Rachel.

'Gloria's usually nothing but sunshine,' continued Pelham. 'Suddenly she turns overcast. Luke says something to cheer her up. She bursts into tears. He asks her what's going on. She won't say. He insists. She breaks down, spills everything. She's not illegal, exactly. She's one of the forgotten, lost between asylum and immigration. Charlie had found this out somehow and had bullied her into his bed.'

'His brother's a high-up at the Home Office,' said Olivia. 'He really could have had her deported.'

'Anyway, she fell pregnant,' said Pelham. 'She didn't have money for a kid, and abortion was against her faith. So she went to Charlie and he went crazy. He denied it all, threatened her with the first plane to Kinshasa if she ever breathed a word. All this now comes pouring out. Luke loses his rag. He charges off to confront Charlie, shocks him into a confession and a promise to support Gloria and her kid. Gloria's over the moon. Luke thinks it's job done. But then he doesn't see her any more. He asks about her; her colleagues won't meet his eye. And now Charlie denies the whole thing, threatens to have him fired.'

'I don't believe this,' said Rachel. 'What did Luke do?'

'He keeps looking. He hears word she's been taken to

a camp for expedited deportation. He drives straight over, demands to see her. They deny she's there. He sees her at a window. They still deny it. That's when he loses his head, tries to force his way inside. They hold him back. He makes threats; he pushes a guard. All of it caught on CCTV. So they charge him with assault and some absurd offence under the new Terrorism Act. First offence, good character, he gets a suspended sentence. But that's still enough for Charlie to have him fired and made unemployable. And then he forced Luke's girlfriend to choose. She chose her career.'

'And Gloria?'

Pelham shrugged. 'We tried private detectives. But there was no record of her leaving the UK or arriving in the DRC. No official evidence she ever even existed. Unless you believe Luke, that is.'

Rachel nodded. She looked down. It was a while since she'd climbed a rope, but it felt like one of those skills that stayed with you. She rummaged through the toolbox, found an old battery lamp, strapped it around her wrist. Then she sat on the edge of the well and gripped the rope tight.

'What the hell are you doing?' asked Olivia.

'Luke's on his own down there,' said Rachel. 'I think he deserves some help.'

II

The desert night was fabulous with stars, now that they'd left Be'er Sheva behind. And the road was almost empty of traffic, nothing but sand and rock either side of them until the Red Sea.

Avram Kohen glanced at his nephew Uri, his brow slightly furrowed as he concentrated on driving, on not letting himself be lulled by the relentless uniformity of the landscape. There was something so childishly serious in his expression that it provoked an unexpected pang of fondness in Avram. He'd never been tempted by fatherhood, but he did enjoy being an uncle, taking promising young men into his Jerusalem home, helping them find their true selves. Mostly, like Uri, they had some measure of blood-kinship; but all that he really asked was that their hearts and minds were open to the Lord, praise His Name. It was one of the most rewarding parts of his life, but it could break your heart when it went wrong.

In the darkness, it was hard to see the turning. He kept checking the odometer to see the distance travelled. Any moment now. The road rose sharply, kinked right. He motioned for Uri to slow. 'There,' he said, pointing to a delta of tyre marks in the sand. They bumped and lurched along a desert track for fifteen minutes, Avram pointing out silvery acacias, gaunt rocks and other minor landmarks for Uri to remember. They pulled up by a pair of boulders at the foot of a small hill. 'From here we walk,' said Avram. They went around back, took a flashlight and a pack each. They crossed a rocky ridge and descended a steep escarpment into a sandy valley. Avram unzipped the packs and handed Uri a shovel. 'That's it,' he said, pointing to the spot. 'Dig.'

They took it in turns, working by starlight, now that their eyes had adjusted. The sand was soft and dry and kept trickling back into the growing pit. It was Uri who struck steel. His excitement was obvious as he cleared the trunk's lid then tried unsuccessfully to open it.

'It's padlocked,' said Avram, tossing him the keys.

Uri stood back to lift its lid. He shone down his torch then looked in puzzlement up at Avram. 'It's empty,' he said.

Avram took out his handgun and aimed it down at his nephew. 'Not for much longer,' he told him.

NINETEEN

I

The passage had proved broad but not quite tall enough for Luke. He'd had to crouch his way along it, holding his torch out ahead of him both for light and to break the cobweb veils before they caught in his face and hair. The floor was so thick with dust that his shoes left moonwalk prints in it. After fifteen paces or so, the passage kinked left and he found himself at the top of a flight of steps that led down into a square chamber with a vaulted roof. But there was no sign of any iron, let alone gold.

Both sides of the chamber were hewn from bedrock, but the facing wall was brick. The mortar had dried to a crumble over the centuries, making it strangely satisfying to pick away. He jiggled a brick like a milk tooth until it came free. He set it down and shone his torch into the space, only to find another wall directly behind it.

A noise behind him made him jump. He'd become so engrossed in his work that he'd forgotten about the others. 'Hey,' said Rachel, coming down into the chamber. 'What have you found?'

He stepped aside, the better to let her see for herself. 'There's another wall behind,' he said.

'A dead end?'

He shrugged. 'Why brick up a dead end?'

Rachel gestured at the passage. 'I promised I'd let them know you were okay. I'll be straight back.'

He returned his attention to the wall, soon had a second and then a third brick out. There was still no sign of Rachel. He was beginning to wonder what was keeping her when finally she reappeared carrying a pair of white plastic bags. She set them down on the floor, pulled out a digital camera from one, snapped off a shot of him by the wall. The flash in the small chamber made him blink. 'For posterity,' she said, as it began the mosquito whining of a recharge. 'Olivia insists we document everything.'

'Good thinking,' said Luke. He checked her bag for other goodies. A claw hammer and a chisel, some chocolate bars from the gift shop and two large bottles of water that made him realize how dry his mouth had become. He swilled and spat some out, then drank so thirstily that it splashed down his shirt. He grabbed the claw hammer and went back to work, quickly revealing some kind of recess behind.

Rachel held up her lamp and peered. 'Is that wood?' she asked.

'Looks like it,' said Luke.

'A door?'

'Let's find out.' He freed another brick, provoked a creaking, splintering sound. Rachel grabbed his arm and dragged him tumbling backwards as the whole wall collapsed in a noisy heap, throwing up clouds of choking dust. Luke got to his feet, coughing violently, his eyes raw and streaming. He grabbed one of the bottles of water and followed Rachel up the steps and along the passage to clearer air. He uncapped the water and gave it to Rachel, took it back after she was done, gratefully swilling out his mouth. His torch had broken in his fall, so Rachel held up hers. Dust had turned their hair and faces prematurely grey. 'The future, huh?' he smiled.

'Granny and granddad,' she agreed.

It was the most offhand of remarks, yet somehow it struck Luke with unexpected force, almost with the power of prophecy. For the blink of a moment, he pictured them together fifty years hence, fulfilled, happy, still in love. His disaster with Maria had numbed his appetite for romance ever since she'd made her choice, but suddenly he felt hungry again. Suddenly he felt ravenous. He looked hurriedly away before Rachel could read his face.

'Is something wrong?' she asked.

'No,' he said, clearing his throat for effect. 'Just all this damned dust.'

They gave it another minute before heading back. The air was still ticklish, but their curiosity wouldn't wait. There was indeed a door behind the false wall. A pair of them, in fact, with great brass rings for handles and rusted iron hinges that suggested they opened out towards them. Rachel snapped off photographs while Luke cleared space for the left-hand door. Its hinges had stretched over the centuries so that its bottom screeched across the stone, but he pulled it far enough open for Rachel to squeeze through, and for himself to follow. He had the lamp in his trailing hand so that they were both in darkness for a moment before he brought it inside. Then he held it up to reveal what they'd discovered.

'My God,' said Rachel. 'I don't believe it.'

II

'Uncle,' said Uri in bewilderment. 'What are you doing? What's going on?'

'I took you into my home,' said Avram. 'I gave you shelter. I treated you like my son. What was mine was yours for the asking. And this is how you repay me? By going to the police? By telling them about my plans?'

'No, Uncle. No. I'd never have—'

'Yes.'

'No! I swear.'

'Did you really think that you could trust them?' asked Avram. 'Well, now you know better. They've been boasting to the Americans about infiltrating our group. Boasting about having an informer inside the ringleader's house. Unfortunately for you, we have Americans on *our* side too. Unfortunately for you, we've known of your treachery for months.'

'No,' said Uri desperately. 'You've got it all wrong. You have to believe me.'

'We haven't got it wrong, Uri. They even had your name.'

'They're trying to drive us apart. That's all. It's lies, misinformation. You know the games they play.'

'It's not lies, Uri. We both know it's not lies. But you're still my sister's grandson. You're still my blood. Come clean, tell me who they are, what they know and how you communicate with them and I give you my word that I'll try to find a way to let you live.'

'This is crazy, Uncle. I haven't told anyone. I swear I haven't.' Uri began to weep. He got down onto his knees in the metal trunk and clasped his hands in prayer. 'I swear it to the Lord.'

'This is your last chance,' said Avram.

'Please, Uncle Avram. I beg you. Don't do it. I don't want to die.' He looked around, as if in hope of miracle, but there was no chance of that. 'They knew already,' he sobbed. 'I swear they did. I didn't go to them. They came to me. And they knew everything. I never told them anything they didn't already know.'

'Go on.'

'I made them promise they wouldn't do anything to you, no gaol or anything like that. I made them sign an agreement. I was only thinking of you.'

'Of me?'

'You want to serve God. I know you do. But this has nothing to do with serving God. It's not for people like you and me to—'

Avram was surprised to find himself pulling the trigger. He'd intended to squeeze Uri dry before he killed him. But his anger was too intense. The four shots tumbled Uri backwards, leaving him lying on his side, obscuring the entry and exit wounds. Avram stepped down into the trunk, pressed the silencer against his temple and fired once more. Then he climbed back out, wiped the gun clean of prints, tossed it inside, closed and locked the lid.

It looked like they'd be needing a new supply route . . .

The irreverence of the thought made him smile. He felt, indeed, something unsettlingly like euphoria. Until this very moment, he hadn't known for certain that he'd have the strength of character to see this mission through. Now he did. Yet euphoria was an inappropriate reaction to such a solemn act, so he stamped down hard on it, picked up the shovel and almost in penance began the heavy work of burying his nephew and his makeshift coffin beneath the sand.

TWENTY

I

The room was maybe twelve feet tall and eight-sided, its walls rich with sculptures that stretched and shrank as Luke turned the lamp this way and that, making them seem eerily alive. There was an altar of some kind in the centre, or maybe a plinth, for it looked roughly the shape and size to hold a small sarcophagus. There was no sarcophagus on it at that moment, however, nothing but dust.

He glanced at Rachel to share the moment with her. She was staring raptly upwards. He looked up too. A great hemispheric dome of blue-black loomed high above them, a wondrous night sky inset into it: a silver crescent moon, galaxies of tiny diamonds, constellations of emeralds, rubies and sapphires, and comets with outstretched tails of crushed crystal that pointed them towards the peak and centre, where a dazzling golden sun presided like God over creation.

'Have you ever seen anything like it?' murmured Rachel, holding her camera down low to capture as much of it as she could.

'Never.'

But he tore his eyes from it all the same, for there was too much else to look at, and time was precious. The wall to the right of the door had been sculpted into some kind of mystical tableau. Between a pair of flame-topped pillars, four gowned men studied and discussed some kind of scroll unfurled on a table. Hammers, trowels, squares and compasses and other such tools decorated the walls, while in the far background tiny figures laid out the perimeter of a new city upon a distant hill.

'It looks Masonic,' murmured Rachel, taking a photograph.

'It *is* Masonic,' he agreed. Several letters and numbers had been chiselled along the foot of the wall. He crouched, the better to read them. 'BE 22108 BF,' he said. 'Any ideas?'

'Some kind of signature?'

'With BE and BF being the initials of the sculptors? Could be. What about the numbers?'

'The date, maybe?' suggested Rachel. 'The twenty-second of January, 1708?'

'Or the twenty-second of October, 1698? Or even '88?'

'Maybe.'

They let it lie, went to the next wall. It was carved in relief, too, borders of cascading flowers framing a life-sized portrait of an elderly man in scholar's robes. There were two lines inscribed at the foot of this one. The uppermost was simply the man's name: Elias Ashmole. And directly beneath it: BE 10460 BF. Luke glanced back at the first panel. 'Same initials,' he said. 'Different number.'

They moved together to the third wall. Another portrait, but this time shockingly familiar. Everything was there, from the intellectual high brow to the casually open collar and the exuberant cascades of curled hair. A direct copy from a Kneller portrait the great man had commissioned himself in celebration of the *Principia*.

'Sir Isaac Newton,' murmured Rachel, reading the inscription.

Luke glanced down. Curiously, unlike on the first two walls, the inscription didn't look quite centred, but was offset a little to the left instead.

Rachel now read out its lower line. 'BH 01256.' She gave a sigh. 'So much for my initials and date theory.'

'Maybe it's a cipher of some kind.'

'Saying what?'

'I don't know. It's in cipher.'

She laughed and gave him a playful slap. 'I thought maybe you'd know the kind of ciphers these guys used.'

He shook his head. 'Olivia might. Or my mate Jay. Newtonian ciphers are right up his street.'

'And he's in Oxford, is he?'

'London.'

'That's helpful, then.'

They moved to the next wall. Another portrait. 'John Evelyn,' read out Rachel. 'The diarist, right?'

'Among other things,' said Luke. Like so many notables of his era, Evelyn had been a polymath: a pioneer in horticulture, medicine and city planning, and one of the driving forces behind the Royal Society. He had a line of cryptic characters beneath his name too. BC 10484. Luke crouched down and ran his finger over them, as though touch might reveal their secrets, like Braille. But all he got was dust. He stood again, looked around. Someone had gone to extraordinary lengths to build this place and make a gallery of its walls. Yet they'd also bricked it up and hidden it down a well shaft so that no one would ever know it was here. Why?

Rachel was already on the next wall. 'Sir Christopher Wren,' she said.

'Makes sense,' nodded Luke. 'He wasn't just mates with Newton and Ashmole, but with Evelyn, too.'

'So he links them all together.' She stooped to read out the cipher. 'KD 11201,' she said, glancing up in case inspiration had suddenly struck. He shook his head.

They went together to the last two walls, a double-width

223

panel showing a single scene: a great tower at the heart of a walled courtyard. 'What the hell?' asked Rachel.

'The Temple of Solomon,' said Luke. 'Taken from one of Newton's own drawings, I think.'

'Newton drew Solomon's Temple?' frowned Rachel.

'He was one of the world's great experts,' Luke told her. 'He wrote a famous treatise on it. At least, it was ostensibly about the Sacred Cubit of the Jews, but in truth it was about the Temple. It needed to be rebuilt for the Second Coming, you see, and as the Bible gave its measurements in cubits, you had to know how long a cubit was, or you'd build it wrong. And who better to get it right than Isaac Newton, old *Jeova Sanctus Unus* himself?'

'And these other guys? Wren and Evelyn and Ashmole? Were they Temple geeks too?'

'Wren was,' said Luke. 'A couple of days after his daughter died, he got blitzed with Robert Hooke and spent the whole night talking about the Temple. And Evelyn would have known it as well. The Temple had been designed by God, you see, so it was, by definition, perfect. Any city planner worth his salt had to be familiar with it.' He turned the lamp back on the first wall. 'And it ties into that, too. Solomon's Temple is the basis of Masonic lore.'

'Olivia said Ashmole was a Freemason,' said Rachel. 'And you said there were rumours about Newton. What about the others?'

'I don't know about Evelyn, but Wren for sure. Freemasonry came out of the construction industry, remember, and London was the construction capital of the world at the time, thanks to the Great Fire. And guess who was responsible for commissioning all the main work?'

'Don't tell me: Sir Christopher.'

'They say he was the number two Mason for a while,' said Luke. 'And the first Grand Lodge met bang next door to St Paul's Cathedral. There's even a plaque to it.'

Rachel sighed deeply. 'So what is this place? A monument to these men?'

'Not *to* them. *By* them.' He turned the lamp on the central plinth. 'Maybe in honour of whatever Ashmole left Newton to complete, which was meant to go on that.' He went across, wiped away dust, found nothing beneath.

'Here,' said Rachel. Some lines had been inscribed in a panel of green marble halfway along the plinth's side. He crouched beside her to read them.

And as he journeyed, he came near Damascus: and suddenly there shined round about him a light from heaven:

   And he fell to the earth, and heard a voice saying unto him, Saul, Saul, why persecutest thou me?

   And he said, Who art thou, Lord? And the Lord

said, I am Jesus whom thou persecutest: it is hard for
thee to kick against the pricks.

And he trembling and astonished said, Lord, what
wilt thou have me to do?

'St Paul on the road to Damascus,' said Rachel. 'I
wonder if there's another on the other side.'

They went around to check and were rewarded.

Below as above, above as below
As it once was, so it will be
Look to my father, the sun, my mother, the moon
In the belly of the wind was I carried
Nurtured in dry earth
Up from this world I rise
So sayeth I, Thrice Great Hermes

'The Emerald Tablet,' murmured Luke.

'What on earth's it doing here?'

He shrugged. The Hermetic texts had caused intense
excitement when they'd been discovered during the
Renaissance. People had believed them written in
deepest antiquity, perhaps even at the time of Moses
himself. Their prestige had faded, however, once they'd
been correctly dated to the early centuries AD. Yet
alchemists had continued to revere them, especially this
particular text. Newton had been so intrigued by it

226

that he'd even studied Arabic in order to make his own translation.

Rachel raised an eyebrow when Luke told her this. 'Is this his?' she asked.

'No. But I think it's based on his. Just a lot shorter.'

Rachel sighed and shook her head, then she stood and worked her spine. 'Pelham and Olivia will be having kittens,' she said.

'Yes,' agreed Luke. 'It's time we were getting back.'

II

Walters had just reached the outskirts of Oxford when Croke called to let him know they'd come up dry in Crane Court and were switching their search to the old Ashmolean instead. 'What do you want us to do?' he asked.

'Hold off,' Croke told him. 'We'll be coming down ourselves. We'll take care of everything.'

'Including Luke and the others?' asked Walters. 'Only they can cause us real grief, remember?'

'I'm well aware of that, thank you. And I said I'll take care of it. Anyway, it's too late for you lot to do anything. My friends already have the place surrounded.'

'Whatever you say.' Walters ended the call and drove up Broad Street all the same. Sure enough, there were dark figures in a pair of cars parked across the road from the museum, and strange shadows in nearby alleys.

'I don't like this,' muttered Kieran. 'Too much bloody law.'

'The boss knows what he's doing.'

'Yeah. Looking after his own interests, not ours.'

'Our interests *are* his interests. If we go down, he has to realize we can take him with us.'

'If you say so.'

'I do.' But he didn't feel as confident as he made it sound. He drove on, guided by his SatNav, until he found the red BMW with the black soft top parked exactly where it was meant to be. Dark and unoccupied. He drove on a little way, found an empty spot with a decent line of sight and reversed into it. Maybe Luke and the others were hiding out in the museum. Maybe they weren't. Either way, if they ever made it back to their car, Walters intended to make them regret it.

III

Luke held the rope for Rachel, then leaned out into the well shaft to help her should she need it. But she made it back up easily enough, was greeted at the top by helping hands. He waited until she was clear then followed. Olivia shook her head sorrowfully at the state of them both, as if they'd let themselves and her museum down. 'I've a change of clothes for you, my dear,' she told Rachel. 'If you don't mind looking a bit dowdy. But Luke is beyond my help.'

They repaired to her office, a cluttered small space with three desks, a sink and an area for making tea and coffee. Rachel went off with a change of clothes, but Luke had to make do with the sink, staining the water brown. Olivia loaded the photographs onto a museum laptop, then she and Pelham began hurrying through them, firing questions as they went. They reached the first shot of the inner chamber and Olivia drew in a sharp breath. 'Good lord!' she murmured. 'The Rosicrucians.'

'I thought the Rosicrucians were a myth,' said Rachel, arriving back in the room in her borrowed blouse and tweeds.

'Not a myth exactly,' said Olivia. 'A hoax, maybe. Though it's hard to be sure even of that.'

'How do you mean?'

Olivia nodded. 'This was 1610, 1615, something like that. Copies of a mysterious letter called the *Fama Fraternitatis* began appearing in European cities. A Rosicrucian manifesto advocating a new world order run by natural philosophers. One passage of the letter described a multi-sided chamber discovered behind a false wall. It was topped by a dome, lit by an inner sun, and filled with treasure from around the world. It had a plinth too, and on it lay the body of Christian Rosencreutz.'

Rachel frowned. 'Are you saying we've found his tomb?'

Olivia shook her head. 'No, no, no. That was in Europe somewhere, and many decades before this. My only point is that Ashmole, Newton, Evelyn and Wren would absolutely have known about it. So this chamber isn't a coincidence. It's a reference. An *homage*.' She tapped her keyboard, brought up a word file, paged down. 'This is a talk I gave on the elder Tradescant,' she told them. 'He started collecting his specimens and curiosities right around the time the *Fama Fraternitatis* was published. Look at this bit.'

'A man admitted into the mysteries of heaven and earth through divine revelations and unwearied toil. In his journey through Arabia and Africa he collected a treasure surpassing that of Kings and Emperors, but finding it not suitable for his times, he kept it guarded for posterity to uncover, and appointed loyal and faithful heirs. He constructed a microcosm corresponding to the macrocosm and drew up a compendium of things past, present and future.'

'That's about Tradescant?' asked Luke.

'No. Rosencreutz. It's from the manifesto. But that's exactly my point, because it could easily be about either

Tradescant or even Ashmole. It was certainly how Ashmole saw himself. He used to tell this story about his baptism, how his godfather had had some kind of epiphany at the font, and cried out that his name should be Elias after the prophet Elijah. They were all expecting a new Elijah at that time. He was prophesied to bring strange things to light and begin a golden age of grace; which was what the Ashmolean was explicitly designed for.'

'And so Ashmole built himself a vault in order to be buried here with all his treasures,' suggested Rachel.

Luke shook his head. 'That plinth wasn't big enough, not for a grown man.'

Pelham was still peering at Olivia's text. 'Such an ambiguous word, isn't it?' he said. 'Treasure, I mean. Listen to this: "During his journey through Arabia and Africa, he collected a *treasure* surpassing that of Kings and Emperors." You all seem to be assuming that it was some great hoard of different things. But why shouldn't it refer to a single treasure? The proverbial pearl worth all the tribe.'

'A treasure that surpassed that of Kings and Emperors,' murmured Rachel. 'What could it be?'

'John Tradescant the Elder went on a famous voyage to the Mediterranean,' murmured Olivia. 'When word got out he was paying good money for curiosities, traders flocked from all across North Africa and Arabia to flog him stuff. He ended up with so much that he and his son lost track of it all. That's how Ashmole got involved. He catalogued their collection.'

'What if he spotted something while he was at it?' murmured Luke. 'What if *that's* why he set his heart on the collection?'

Rachel shook her head. 'Why take all of it? Why not just that piece?'

'Greed,' said Luke. 'Or maybe he was scared of tipping the son off.'

Olivia nodded. 'Ashmole only got to inherit the collection after Tradescant the younger and his wife both died. John went first. Guess what Ashmole did? He bought the house next door to the widow, then watched to make sure she didn't sell anything on the sly. He made her life hell, by all accounts, and then one day she was found drowned in her garden pond.'

Rachel looked shocked. 'He murdered her?'

'More likely hounded her to suicide. But the outcome was the same. And when he went to take possession of the collection, he flew into a rage and cursed her for hiding pieces from him. Then he took a lease on her house and searched it from top to bottom.'

'Looking for the treasure?'

'Makes sense, doesn't it? But he lost interest after a month or so, and sublet the house to someone else.'

'Implying that he'd found it,' said Luke. 'But he lacked

the skill to complete it, so he turned to his friend Wren who brought in Evelyn and Newton to complete their little cabal.'

'Good lord,' said Olivia. 'Yes. Of course. Their cabal!'

'I'm sorry?' said Luke.

'The word comes from Kabbalah, but it was made famous in England because of five Ministers of Charles II. Clifford, Arlington, Buckingham, Ashley and Lauderdale. Put their initials together and you've got yourself a cabal. Now look at our four lovelies: Ashmole, Newton, Evelyn and Wren.'

'Anew?' said Pelham. 'Not much of a message, is it?'

'You have to read the whole room,' said Olivia. She bought up the photo of the four Masons studying their plan while workmen laid stones on the hill behind. 'What's going on here?' she asked rhetorically. 'They're *building*.' Now she scrolled forwards to the final double panel. 'And here's the Temple of Solomon, eternal symbol of the holy city. Put our cabal in the middle and what have you got?'

'Christ,' muttered Luke. 'They were building a new Jerusalem.'

TWENTY-ONE

I

'A new Jerusalem?' said Rachel. 'Here in Oxford?'

'Or maybe not here,' said Olivia. 'Maybe that's why the vault's empty. I mean, don't get me wrong, *of course* Ashmole would have wanted it here. He was a vain man and this was his building. But he died long before Evelyn, and decades before Newton or Wren; and none of those three had any personal stake in this place. And, for people like that, Oxford was never the new Jerusalem.'

'Where, then?'

'London, of course,' she said. 'Capital city of the Church of England. And finding a suitable spot would hardly have been a challenge. Wren was rebuilding the whole damned place.' She shook her head in disbelief at the magnitude of it all. 'I need to call Albie,' she said. 'He has to see this.'

'No, Olivia,' said Pelham.

'Yes. Can't you see how *important* this is? There are implications. *Huge* implications.' She opened her address book, picked up the handset, began to dial. But then she stopped abruptly and dropped the handset like it had scalded her. 'It echoed,' she said. 'Isn't that what happens when people are listening?'

'Stay here,' said Luke. He hurried through the darkened lobby to the shuttered front windows, slid a shutter latch, opened it just enough to see shadows in the two cars parked across the street. He latched the shutter again, checked that the windows and front door were securely bolted, returned to Olivia's office. 'They're there,' he said.

'Our friends from earlier?' asked Pelham.

Luke shook his head. 'Different cars. And if they're tapping our phones, I'd say police.'

'How did they find us?' asked Rachel.

'Maybe they worked out Sous Ashmolean for themselves,' said Pelham.

'Then what are they waiting for?'

'Reinforcements?' suggested Luke. 'A warrant?' He turned to Olivia. 'Is there a back way out?'

Olivia nodded. 'There's a fire escape upstairs. It leads onto the alley.'

'Is it alarmed?'

'I turned it off when we came in.'

'I'll go check,' said Pelham. 'You guys get everything together.'

Luke zipped Olivia's laptop away in its case, pocketed the digital camera, went with Rachel to the door.

'Come on,' he said to Olivia.

'No,' said Olivia. 'I'm staying.'

'You have to come,' begged Rachel. 'These people are bastards.'

'I don't care,' she said fiercely. 'This is *my* museum. Damned if I'm going to let them run loose in here without being around to watch.'

Pelham came back in. 'They're out back too,' he grimaced.

'How many?' asked Olivia.

'I saw three. There could be more.'

'Oh, hell,' said Rachel. 'We're trapped.'

II

Croke sat in the back of the Range Rover as the NCT convoy sped west along the M4, passing other traffic in a blur. 'The police won't try to stop us, right?' he asked Morgenstern.

'We know what we're doing.'

Croke nodded. Morgenstern had impressed him not just with his swift switch of focus to Oxford, but also with his willingness to carry on searching Crane Court merely to keep the media distracted. They reached their exit. Roads narrowed, traffic thickened.

A call came in on Morgenstern's cell. He frowned as he listened, turned to Croke. 'Someone inside the museum started to make a call, then hung up,' he said. 'And they just checked out the fire escape.'

'They're on to us.'

Morgenstern nodded. 'Shall I send the police in?'

'How long till we get there?'

'Another four minutes. Maybe five.'

'If anyone comes out, have them grab them. Otherwise they're to hold off.'

He watched out the window as Morgenstern relayed the order. Sunday night in Oxford, everything closed, quiet, dead, the few pedestrians startled by the sudden rampage of their convoy, faces bleached by their headlights. They slowed before turning into Broad Street, not wanting to attract unnecessary attention, pulled up outside the museum. Croke got out along with everyone else. Morgenstern had hand-picked this team himself; with all the media still in London, there was no great need for him to stay covert. A few NCT men hurried around the museum's sides, while others went down to the basement door. But Morgenstern and Croke and the remainder marched straight up the front steps. 'What now?' asked Morgenstern.

Croke shrugged. 'We knock,' he said.

III

The double rap on the front door sent a shudder through Luke and the others. 'We know you're in there,' shouted a man. He sounded American. 'Open up or we'll come in anyway.'

They looked helplessly at each other. Only Olivia had anything to suggest. 'The well,' she said. 'You'll have hide back in the vault.'

'They know we're in here,' said Luke. 'They'll find us.'

'They know *someone's* in here,' countered Olivia. 'They don't know who or how many. If you three hide—'

'You two,' said Pelham to Luke and Rachel. 'They saw me on the fire escape. Besides, even if I made it down the well, I'd never make it back up.' He patted his gut regretfully. 'Wages of sin, and all that.'

'We're not leaving you,' said Rachel.

'Yes, you are,' said Pelham. 'Olivia and I can credibly claim to be working on a new exhibition. That won't wash if you're found here too. And if they think you're on the loose, they'll treat us better from fear of you raising the alarm. Speaking of which . . .' He scrawled a phone-number on a scrap of paper. 'My sister,' he told Luke. 'She's a lawyer and she's fierce. Call her if you possibly can.'

'Will do.'

Another knock on the front door, louder and more

insistent. They hurried to the well. 'How will we get back out?' asked Rachel, staring down.

'The rope, of course,' said Pelham.

'But we can't leave it dangling there or they'll be bound to see it. It'll lead them straight to us.'

'I'll take care of that,' said Olivia. 'Just get down there.' She turned and vanished back up the steps.

'You won't get anywhere looking like that,' said Pelham, nodding at Luke's filthy shirt. He stripped off his jacket and gave it to him.

'Thanks, mate,' said Luke. He felt Pelham's wallet and car keys in the pockets, offered them back.

'You'll need them more than me,' said Pelham. 'Just call my sister.'

Something crashed against the front door. They were breaking their way in.

'Quickly,' said Pelham.

Luke zipped Pelham's jacket inside Olivia's laptop case to keep it clean, slung the strap over his shoulder, grabbed the rope and slid down fireman style, the rope rubbing hot against his palms. He swung inside the passage and helped Rachel in after him, then began hurriedly to rebuild the wall. Footsteps above. Olivia. The rope slithered upwards. A few moments later it tumbled down again, a plastic bucket knotted to its end so that it danced like a hanged man a foot or so above the water, clattering the walls. Despite everything, Luke couldn't help but smile. Anyone looking down now would assume it was part of the feature.

The basement lights went out, leaving it pitch black. Rachel switched on the lamp but turned it away from the shaft so that it wouldn't give them away. A minute passed. He heard footsteps running above, men yelling. The lights flickered back on. He had only one brick left to complete the wall, but each time he tried to fit it in, it pushed its neighbours out into the well. He muttered a soft curse and gave up.

Through the small remaining gap he could see the rope swinging in slow ellipses, like the weight of a pendulum. Anyone who looked down would be bound to notice. He reached out through the small gap, let the rope nudge his fingers, moderating its motion a little. It swung away again, then back, allowing him to slow it a fraction more. But then he heard footsteps above and men talking and he had no choice but to withdraw his hand and watch as the rope continued its gentle oscillation, hoping against hope that it wouldn't be seen.

TWENTY-TWO

I

Croke was first through the splintered museum door, but the NCT search and secure team quickly left him behind. Four of them went upstairs; the remainder ran down, checking doors as they went, shouting instruction at each other, turning on lights. A yell from the staircase. Croke and Morgenstern hurried to check it out. A massively built thirty-something man and a grey-haired woman were sitting side by side at a desk in a cramped office: Pelham Redfern and Olivia Campbell, to judge from the descriptions he'd been given. They were both wearing headphones attached to a single small handset, and both were doing their very best to look shocked.

'What is this?' protested the woman, taking off her

headphones, getting to her feet. 'What's going on? Who are you people?'

'Skip the bullshit,' said Morgenstern. 'We're not in the mood.'

'What are you doing here? How did you get in? You haven't damaged my door, have you?'

'You should have answered when we knocked.'

'We didn't hear you.' She held up her headphones. 'How were we supposed to hear you?'

Croke walked over to the desk, put an earphone to his ear. Nothing. He gave her a wry look. She clicked the play button and a woman began explaining how to produce oxygen by chemical reaction. 'Our new audio-guide,' she said. 'I was showing it to Mr Redfern. We're planning a new exhibition and we'll need to do one of these for it.'

'Why bother with headphones?' scoffed Morgenstern. 'Who were you going to disturb?'

She picked up the handset. 'These things only work with headphones. We can't have people playing them out loud in the museum, or it would ruin everyone else's experience, wouldn't it?'

For the blink of a moment, Croke almost bought it. But then he remembered the aborted phone call, the figure scoping out the rear alley. 'Sure,' he mocked. He turned to Redfern. 'You were in Cambridge earlier today.'

'Is that against the law?'

'You picked up two people there. A man and a woman.'

'Your accent?' frowned Redfern. 'It's American, isn't it? I trust you won't mind my asking what authority you have to question me?'

Croke glanced at Morgenstern. Morgenstern nodded at the door. They went outside for a murmured conference. 'They're lying,' said Croke. 'The others were here.'

'Maybe,' said Morgenstern, nodding at his squad leader, who was indicating to them that the museum was clear. 'But they're not here now.'

'These two know where they've gone. We need to make them tell us.'

Morgenstern shook his head. 'If you mean what I think you mean, forget about it. The Brits are too squeamish. Especially as the woman really is curator of this place, and she's claiming Redfern as her guest.'

'Then what do we do?'

'We can put pressure on them. Charge them with obstructing justice, abetting a murderer. They're soft. They'll break soon enough.'

Croke shook his head. 'I don't want them entering the system. I can't risk them talking to lawyers.'

Morgenstern nodded. 'I can have them driven up to Birmingham for interrogation. Then have them transferred to London instead. We can bounce them around for at least twenty-four hours.'

'Good. Do it.'

An NCT officer approached, holding up some dust-covered women's clothes. 'Found these in the washroom, sir,' he said.

Morgenstern and Croke shared a glance. They matched what Rachel Parkes had been wearing. And some splashes of water on the blouse indicated she'd been there recently.

'How the hell did they get out?' scowled Croke.

'I don't know.'

'They can't have got far. I want everyone you can spare out hunting. Have them watch the train and bus stations. Taxi companies. And have them look for couples.'

Morgenstern passed on the orders, then they headed downstairs together into the basement where two NCT operatives were scanning the floor with ground penetrating radar. 'There's something down there,' said one. 'A chamber of some kind. And metal. Iron for sure. And I know this will sound crazy, but maybe gold too.'

'It's not crazy. How can we get down there?'

The man grimaced. 'It won't be easy. It's at least ten feet deep. We'll need specialist cutting and lifting equipment. If I put the order in now, we should be able to get it here by morning. All goes well, we can pop the floor early tomorrow afternoon.'

Morgenstern glanced at Croke. 'Will that work for you?'

Croke pulled a face. To meet Avram's deadline, he'd need to depart City Airport no later than midnight tomorrow. Allowing a few hours for transporting it there, and for the inevitable fuck-ups along the way, and they were pushing it tight. 'It'll work if it's down there,' he said. 'But what if it's not?'

'We could take a look first, if you'd like,' said the man.

'How?'

He put his hand on one of the display cabinets. 'First we move this thing,' he said. He crouched down and touched where one of its feet was bolted to the floor. 'Then we drill directly beneath here. A small-diameter hole all the way down to the chamber.' He made a circle with his finger and thumb. 'It'll have be about yea wide because of the width-depth ratios. Once we're through, we can feed down an endoscope. You know endoscopes, right? Miniature cameras with integrated lighting and a fish-eye lens on the end of a long fibre-optic cable, like the ones they stick up your arse when they're—'

'I know endoscopes,' Croke assured him.

'We use them a lot for surveillance,' said the man. 'They'll show us everything down there. If you still want to, we'll have time to take up the floor. If not, we just pull the endoscope back out, plug the hole with filler and bolt the cabinet back in place. No one will ever be the wiser.'

'Have you got everything you need?' asked Morgenstern.

The man shrugged. 'We've got a drill in the van, but isn't long enough. And we don't have enough cable for our endoscope. This is a *very* unusual job. But we can get started now and have the necessary extensions here in a couple of hours. That should give us a first look around sunrise, which is about the earliest we could hope to get the heavy cutting and lifting equipment here anyway.'

Croke glanced at Morgenstern. 'When does this place open tomorrow?'

'It doesn't. Not on a Monday. It's ours all day.'

'Okay,' said Croke. 'Let's do it.'

II

Luke and Rachel made their way back to the vault, on the basis that they were far more likely to be overheard if they stayed near the well shaft. They turned off the lamp to save its batteries, then sat in the darkness with their backs to the Emerald Tablet.

'So how come Newton?' asked Rachel.

Luke shrugged. 'He caught my imagination, I suppose.'

'You're writing a biography of the man,' she teased. 'You'll need to have something better than that on the blurb.'

Luke laughed. 'Okay. There's this story about him I first heard when I was a kid. It's kind of a nerd's fantasy. You'll find this hard to believe, I suspect, but I was a bit of a nerd myself back then.'

Rachel feigned shock. 'No. Get away with you.'

'This was 1697 or thereabouts. Newton was in a really bitter dispute with Leibniz over who invented the calculus. They both did, as it happens, but each was convinced the other had stolen the idea from them. The Brits supported Newton. The Europeans backed Leibniz. One of Leibniz's mates, an Italian called Johann Bernoulli, devised a pair of mathematical puzzles that proved too fiendish for Europe's top minds to crack, so he came up with a cunning plan. He sent them to Newton, hoping he'd fail too, thus wrecking his reputation for genius. Newton received them after a day at the Royal Mint. The following morning he sent off the answers to the Royal Society. They published them anonymously, but everyone knew. Even Bernoulli. You know what he said? He said: "You can tell the lion by its claw." I just loved that. I used to daydream people saying it about me. Mind you, I was ten at the time.' He laughed and tipped his head to the side. 'Your turn,' he said. 'How come archaeology?'

Rachel sighed. 'I don't know. I guess it meant something at the time.' The question seemed to make her restless. She stood and turned on the lamp, took a circuit of the walls.

'Tweed suits you,' Luke told her, as she came back around. 'You'll make a fine professor.'

'It itches like you wouldn't believe,' she said. Her gaze

slid from him to the Emerald Tablet inscription behind him, and then she frowned. 'How about that?' she murmured, to herself as much as Luke. 'An acrostic.'

He turned to read the first letter of each line. 'Balinus?' he frowned.

She nodded. 'It's what the Harranians called Apollonius of Tyana.'

'If that was meant to make things clearer for me,' said Luke, 'you might want to give it another shot.'

'Apollonius was a Turkish holy man from the time of Jesus. We found a lot of his cult objects on my excavation in Antioch. And one of my colleagues from the dig is *the* authority on the guy.'

'What's his name doing here?'

'The Harranians lived in Southern Turkey, right in the path of the Muslim Conquest. But they were allowed to continue with their own religion, which seems to have been almost alchemical in its nature. Their sacred texts were the *Hermetica*, which is how they survived until the Renaissance, and why Newton had to translate them from Arabic rather than Egyptian, Greek or Latin. And here's the thing: they revered this Balinus or Apollonius guy for having saved the Emerald Tablet before them. He was one of their heroes.'

'So our cabal decided to honour him too,' said Luke. 'But why use an acrostic? Why not just write his name?'

'Because Apollonius was a *very* controversial figure,

particularly among Christians. A male child whose birth was announced by heavenly beings, who embraced poverty and celibacy, who went everywhere barefoot and who refused to eat meat. A great moral teacher who healed the sick, raised the dead, cast out demons and predicted the future. Sentenced to death by the Romans but ascended into heaven instead.'

'Apollonius?'

'Which made him rather problematic for Christians preaching about the unique glories of Jesus,' said Rachel. 'Though I'm surprised to find that Newton was a fan. I always understood he was a devout Christian.'

'He was,' Luke assured her. 'But a very idiosyncratic one. He believed in the *teachings* of Jesus, but he didn't think him God. That was his great heresy. He loathed the doctrine of the Trinity, and therefore the Catholic church for foisting it on the world.'

'What about these other guys?'

Luke shook his head. 'All pretty conventional, as far as I know. But you had to be back then. Antitrinitarianism was a serious crime. At the very best, it would be the death of your professional and social life. No Antitrinitarian would ever have got to rebuild St Paul's, for example.'

'St Paul,' muttered Rachel. 'Yes, of course.'

'Of course what?'

'Here.' She beckoned Luke around the other side of the plinth and crouched in front of the second inscription. 'Apollonius wasn't problematic for Christians just because of his similarities to Jesus. He was even closer to St Paul. The name Apollonius comes from Apollo, which is close enough to mistake for Paul. He was born in southern Turkey, about thirty miles north of Tarsus, where St Paul came from. And he studied in Tarsus himself throughout his teens. So essentially you have these two men with similar names, born at the same time and place, both growing up to become itinerant preachers famous for the letters on morals they wrote to the citizens of major Mediterranean cities. Both had encounters with wild animals in Ephesus. Both wrote about sacrifices and ritual. And both were Roman citizens who crossed emperors and were sentenced to death.'

'You're saying they were the same person?'

Rachel shrugged. 'Plenty of people have thought so over the centuries. Maybe these guys did too. What do you think? Could they have believed in St Paul as Balinus, the secret alchemist who saved the Emerald Tablet?'

'I can't speak for them all,' said Luke. 'But Newton, sure. He didn't think of the prophets as mystics inspired by divine revelation, like most people seem to. He thought of them as immensely intelligent and informed, masters not just of religion but also of mathematics, astronomy, alchemy and all the other disciplines of natural philosophy. So Moses, Enoch, Elijah, Hermes Trimegistus, Solomon and the rest were great alchemists *by definition*.

That was what Newton aspired to for himself, so it would have made perfect sense to him that St Paul was the same. Especially as he was already a considerable figure among the alchemists.'

'How so?'

'You've heard of the Jesus myth, right? The idea that Jesus never even existed.'

'What about it?'

'A lot of that stems from St Paul, because he famously didn't write much about Jesus the man, only about Christ the spiritual force. And he wrote something very peculiar in a letter to the Corinthians, about the followers of Moses drinking from the spiritual rock that followed them; and the rock was Christ. Some alchemists interpreted that to mean that Jesus somehow *was* the philosopher's stone. Some even believed that if they found the philosopher's stone they could precipitate the Second Coming.'

Rachel looked around at the faces on the walls. 'What the hell were these guys trying to do?'

A dull buzzing noise sounded before Luke could answer. Dust motes shaken from the walls and ceiling began swirling in the lamplight. He looked bleakly upwards. 'They're drilling,' he said. 'They're coming down through the floor.'

TWENTY-THREE

I

The drilling stopped for a minute or so, giving Luke and Rachel hope that they might have given it up. But then it returned even louder. The air grew thicker with dust, making them blink and cough. 'We have to get away,' said Luke.

'What if they hear us?'

'We can't stay here.'

They headed back along the passage to the well, dismantled the wall. They couldn't risk the bucket banging on the sides of the shaft, so Luke untied it from the rope, set it down behind him. It was dark above, the basement lights off. That was something. He climbed as quietly as he could, though the rope still creaked as it twisted. The drilling grew louder as he neared the top, giving him cover. He peered over the rim. No sign of anyone. He hauled himself out and beckoned to Rachel. She began to climb, slowly and steadily, swinging from wall to wall as—

A door opened abruptly. Luke barely had to time to warn Rachel and duck down behind the well. Footsteps hurried to and up the main staircase. Silence for a minute or so, then a toilet flushed and plumbing groaned. More footsteps on the stairs, then the gallery door opened and closed once more. All clear. He beckoned to Rachel, dangling patiently. She looked weary by the time she made it to the top. He helped her out, gave her a few moments rest. They took off their shoes and carried them to the stairs. The drilling paused for a few moments and they could hear talking. Then it started up again. They climbed the stairs. The whole museum was in darkness except for a few emergency lights. A man was looking out one of the ground-floor windows, his back to them. They continued up to the first floor. The fire escape door had a locking bar so that it could only be opened from inside. Luke pressed down on it, his heart in his mouth lest it trigger the alarm. It didn't. A car passed by. Broad Street looked empty in its headlights. Luke slipped out onto the fire escape, held the door for Rachel. The locking bar clicked behind them. No going back now.

The wrought-iron steps were as cold as fear on Luke's soles. They crept down to the bottom, pulled their shoes back on and walked briskly but openly, as though with nothing to hide. A left turn took them into relative darkness, then out onto a square. A police car ahead forced them to loop around so that it took them twenty-five minutes to reach Pelham's BMW. They watched it for a while, saw no sign of ambush. Yet Luke felt anxious all the same. 'Stay here,' he whispered to Rachel.

Using parked cars for cover, he made his way along the pavement. Still no sign of danger. Footsteps approached, grew close. A young man lost his footing on the kerb and stuttered into an impromptu dance, laughing drunkenly at himself. Luke waited until he was almost level with the BMW then pressed the remote lock on Pelham's key-fob. It beeped loudly and its corner lights flashed orange. Almost instantly, the doors of a dark SUV down the street flew open. Three men jumped out and ran towards the hapless drunk. Luke turned and crouched his way back to Rachel, but a cry went up before he reached her. They'd been spotted.

Rachel had a few yards' head start. She turned left into darkness and he caught up with her. They reached a cul-de-sac. Automated intruder lights switched on as they passed, giving them away. Now the men were maybe fifty yards behind and closing fast. Two houses in relative darkness were separated by a narrow passage. Luke grabbed Rachel's hand and pulled her down it. The alley was overgrown with nettles, creepers and ivy. Luke put an arm up to cover his face as he bulled his way along, then his foot went straight through the rusted iron of an old dustbin lid, making a noise like a firecracker. They emerged into a small back garden, climbed a fence into a neighbouring property, then another. It was dark as sin back here, but they could hear the chase getting closer and closer. Luke pulled Rachel to the ground beside him just as two grunting shadows vaulted over the fence behind, crossed the lawn and then vanished. They gave it a few more moments then went to the rear of the garden. A wooden gate opened out onto a dark footpath that led to a lamplit street. They ducked their heads as they hurried away, ears pricked, pulses pumping hard. But they reached the end of the street without alarm.

A signpost pointed towards the train station. Luke looked at Rachel; she nodded. But there seemed to be police cars everywhere, driving at a dawdle to scan for couples to stop and question. They kept to back streets and finally made it. The station was closed for the night, its main entrance shuttered.

'I'll check for the first train,' Luke whispered. He was almost across the road when a side door opened and a policeman came out, carrying two mugs, concentrating hard on not spilling them. He walked over to a silver SUV, climbed inside. Luke swore softly, turned and retreated. 'Let's try the coach station.'

Rachel shook her head. 'They'll be there too.'

'A minicab?'

'They'll have thought of that.' A touch of desperation in her voice.

'Then *what*?'

'Let's call Pelham's sister. At least that way we know we'll have someone fighting for us.'

Luke nodded. They couldn't risk the bank of phones by the station, but they found another one nearby. Luke still had some credit on his phonecard. He rang the number Pelham had given him. A woman answered, groggy with sleep. 'Who the hell is this?' she groaned. 'Don't you know what damned time it is? If you've woken the kids—'

'I'm really sorry. My name's Luke Hayward. I'm a friend of Pelham's.'

'He's not here,' she said, as though struggling to believe she'd been woken up for this. 'He doesn't even live here.'

'I'm not trying to find him,' Luke told her. 'I'm calling on his behalf. He's been arrested.'

'He's been *what*?' Suddenly sharpness in her voice. Alertness. As if she'd sat up in bed. 'Who are you? *Where* are you?'

'In Oxford,' said Luke. He began explaining what had happened but hadn't got very far when Rachel grabbed his arm, pointed to a police car had just turned into their street and was now accelerating towards them. He dropped the phone and ran. They fled down a footpath and sprinted through a park until they couldn't run any more, just stood there in the shadows of a copse, heaving for breath.

'They're monitoring the payphones,' wailed Rachel. 'They're monitoring the fucking payphones. Who *are* these people?'

She sounded close to the edge. He put his arms around her, gave her a hug. 'We don't know that they're monitoring the phones,' he told her. 'It might have been a coincidence. And, anyway, we're still free, and now we've got Pelham's sister on our side. And he wasn't kidding: she sounded fierce.'

Rachel nodded. 'What do we do? They're everywhere.'

'I took the coach from here once,' said Luke. 'We stopped at least three times on our way out of town to pick up more passengers. They can't watch everything, so maybe they won't be watching those other stops. Let's find one and check it out.'

'You remember where they were?' asked Rachel.

'Pretty much. And they have to be on the way to the motorway, right?'

'Okay,' said Rachel. 'Let's try it.'

II

Walters briefly joined the chase of Luke and the girl, but Kieran and Pete were quicker and fitter than he was, and someone needed to stay behind in case they looped around and came back for the BMW. He went over to it. Luke had unlocked it to lure them from their hiding places, but had he locked it again? He tried the driver door. It was open. He knelt on the driver's seat and had a rummage front and back, but found nothing of interest except for some chocolate bars in the glove compartment. He ate one while he popped the bonnet and disabled the starter motor. They wouldn't be going anywhere in it now.

He checked his mobile for a signal as he returned to the SUV. Maybe Kieran and Pete would bring Luke and the girl back here themselves. More likely they'd pin them down somewhere and call in, so that he could go and collect them without their being seen. The last thing they needed right now, was the police putting them together with Luke and Rachel, for that would make disappearing them far harder. And Walters needed them to disappear. He *liked* his life. He had money, women and respect. No way was he going to let those two screw it up for him.

He'd been waiting the best part of half an hour when Kieran and Pete finally appeared out of the darkness. They were alone. 'What the hell?' he said, getting out. 'Where are they?'

'They got away.'

'For fuck's sake!'

'They're better at this than they've any right to be,' said Kieran ruefully. 'That trick with unlocking the car . . .'

'And I'm supposed to tell Croke that, am I? That they're better at this than we are? Screw that.'

'Then what do we do?'

Walters climbed back inside the SUV. 'We keep this fiasco to ourselves,' he said. 'Then we find the bastards and finish this.'

III

Making their way across Oxford frayed the nerves of both Luke and Rachel. There were police cars everywhere, and even unmarked cars held menace, particularly the SUVs. The back streets were no soft option, either, because taking them made it so hard to keep their bearings. But finally they made it to a coach stop. They watched for a few minutes but could see no sign of it being monitored, so they went to check the timetable. The first coach of the day was leaving for London in half an hour. At last something seemed to be going their way.

The coach stop itself was too exposed for comfort, so they waited in an alley across the road. Rachel shivered. The night had grown cool, but Luke sensed there was more to it than that. He wanted to comfort her, but feared that a hug would be taken amiss, so he touched her arm instead. 'Are you okay?' he asked.

'I'm fine,' she assured him. 'It's just that I realized something. The police have been looking for couples, right?'

'Yes. Why?'

'So what if they've asked the coach drivers to report any couples they pick up?'

'We have to get out of here before it gets light,' said Luke. 'It's worth the risk.'

'I know. I'm just saying that maybe we should get on the coach separately, pretend we don't know each other.'

'Good thinking,' said Luke admiringly. 'In fact . . .' He took out Pelham's wallet and gave her half the cash inside. 'The coach stops several times on its way out of town. If I get on at the next stop, they'll never put us together.'

Rachel's face became anguished. 'What if you don't make it in time?'

'Then I'll catch the next one. It's only another hour.' He handed her Olivia's laptop, as carrying it himself would only slow him down. 'You'll wait for me at Victoria, right?'

'Of course,' she said. Their eyes met for the longest moment and she gave his hand a squeeze. 'But please don't miss it.'

'I won't,' he promised. He nodded and headed off,

jogging eastwards along the road, glancing back for police cars, making sure the coach wasn't early. With all the evasive manoeuvres he had to make, the coach just about beat him to the next stop, but he waved frantically and the driver took pity. He was panting hard as he climbed aboard and paid. He pocketed his ticket and his change, walked down the aisle. Rachel was sitting across from the emergency doors, staring out of the window, pretending not to know him, yet not quite able to hide her smile. He slipped into the seat behind her as the coach pulled away.

He looked around. The coach was less than a quarter full. An unshaven man was stretched out along the rear seat, snoring lightly. A harried-looking executive in a rumpled dark suit was tapping away at his laptop, perhaps preparing the report he should have written over the weekend. A pair of prim elderly women clutched handbags in their laps. Four teenagers in shiny leather jackets took turns at a bottle of red wine.

They left Oxford without alarm, reached the motorway. The interior lights dimmed. Passengers rested their heads against companions or the windows, tried to sleep. Rachel turned on Olivia's laptop and went through the photographs once more, twisting slightly in her seat so that Luke could see over her shoulder. No one was paying them any attention, so he went to sit beside her. She set the laptop between them. Their legs and arms weren't quite touching, yet he could feel the radiated warmth of her all the same. He glanced sideways and felt a sharp stab of affection for her, an urge to take her hand, put an arm around her, hold her tight. Chance had thrust them together; yet it felt astonishingly like fate.

She became aware of his attention. 'What?' she asked, glancing up.

'Nothing,' he said.

She gave him a wry smile. 'Nothing?'

He felt himself blushing like a teenager. He had to say something, if only as cover. The wall with the Newton sculpture was showing on the screen, and he remembered the slight anomaly he'd noticed earlier, so he touched the inscription with his fingertip. 'These two lines,' he said. 'Don't they look a bit wonky to you?'

'Wonky?'

'Offset, then. Closer to the left of the wall than the right.'

She peered intently at it, frowned. 'Huh,' she said. 'You're right. But what does it mean?'

'I don't know. I don't suppose it means anything. I just . . .' But then he realized and snapped his fingers. 'Sir Isaac Newton,' he said. '*Sir* Isaac.'

She shook her head. 'I don't follow.'

'Newton wasn't knighted until 1705.' He zoomed in on the inscription, put his finger over the "Sir". 'See. *Now* it's centred,' he said.

She shook her head in bafflement. 'Are you saying that the inscription originally read just "Isaac Newton", and that the "Sir" was added later?'

'Yes. I suspect so.'

A woman in front of them sighed and turned in her seat. 'Please,' she said. 'Some of us are trying to sleep.'

Rachel held up an apologetic hand, dropped her voice to a whisper. 'But why? Was Newton really that vain? To go back to the vault just to add a Sir to his name?'

Luke shook his head. 'You know what Dr Johnson said about the Giant's Causeway? "Worth seeing, yes, but not worth going to see". I'd guess Newton's knighthood was much the same: worth doing, yes, but not worth going to do.'

'So he had some other reason for going back?'

'It wouldn't have been Newton himself, I don't suppose. He was into his sixties by 1705, and his legs were beginning to go. And Evelyn and Wren would both have been into their *seventies*. But they all had fiercely devoted disciples. Let's say they each sent one.'

'And Newton's decided to give him his knighthood while he was at it,' nodded Rachel. 'But what would their real mission have been? Bricking up the doorway?'

'That wall would scarcely have stopped anyone who'd already found the passage,' said Luke. 'I reckon that was just a nod to the Rosicrucians.'

'Then what?'

'What do we know? We know they took a hammer and chisel with them, or they wouldn't have been able to knight Newton so neatly. And why bring a hammer and chisel unless you plan to inscribe something?'

'The cipher,' murmured Rachel.

'That'd be my guess,' said Luke. He tapped the screen. 'See how this one is centred directly beneath "Sir Isaac Newton"? That surely implies they'd already added the "Sir" by then. Besides, the vault *was* the spot. Why mark it with an X unless the X leads somewhere else?' He jotted down the various elements of the cipher on a scrap of paper, and they wrestled with it for a few minutes; but their minds were too tired to get anywhere.

'How about your London friend?' asked Rachel, fighting a yawn.

'Jay?' Luke nodded. 'This is right up his street. And he lives just across the river from the coach station.'

'Let's go and see him when we get there.'

'Are you sure? You don't have to, you know, Rachel. It could be dangerous for you. And I can do it myself.'

Rachel looked pained. 'Don't you want my help?'

'Of course I do. But not as badly as I want you safe. You can go pretty much anywhere from Victoria. Lie low until this blows over.'

'There's nowhere so low that they won't find me eventually,' she pointed out. 'Besides, we owe it to Pelham and Olivia to solve this thing as soon as we can and then get the truth out. And we've got a far better chance if we stick together. Agreed?'

He couldn't help but smile. 'Agreed.'

'Good. Now how about catching a little rest?'

'Go for it,' he said.

She zipped away the laptop, set it beneath her feet, closed her eyes. Her head began to loll. It tipped against his shoulder only for the jolt to wake her. She sat up straighter, apologised with a rueful smile. But the tiredness soon got to her again; her head began to tip once more. He leaned to his left to give her a softer landing. A strand of her hair fell ticklish across his cheek. He had to put a finger to his nose to stop himself from sneezing. Lack of legroom and the way he was leaning made his posture uncomfortable, but he couldn't move just yet without risking waking her. Her hair rose fractionally with each exhale, then fell back again. She found sleep. The weariness on her face seemed to fade with every moment. Her colour improved. Still asleep, she felt for and took his arm, and a kind of peace settled over her.

Extraordinary to think that less than twenty hours had passed since he'd seen her photograph on her great-aunt's kitchen wall. They'd been through so much together since that he felt as if he'd known her forever. It occurred to him, however, that though he'd seen her smile and laugh and joke and tease in that time, he hadn't yet seen her light up from within in quite the way she'd lit up in that photograph. There was always something reserved about her, something withheld, perhaps from grief or stress or duty or simple tiredness. Whatever the reason, he had a sudden craving to see her smile like that again. He had a sudden craving to see her smile like that *for him*. And the mere thought of it provoked a painful twist of emotion in his heart: of sadness that he should have caught her up in this wretched business, mixed with an immeasurable gladness that she was here.

TWENTY-FOUR

I

Megiddo, Israel

Avram Kohen had slept in the same bed for so many years that he panicked a little on waking to find himself lying on a thin blanket on an unfamiliar hard floor in complete darkness. But then memories came to his rescue: his nephew Uri pleading for his life; his night-time drive north here from the Negev.

The truck's suspension creaked as he sat up. He felt stiff and tired and cold and filthy. He opened the rear doors, looked out at the broken concrete of the vast car park, and the hill that overlooked it.

Megiddo. Armageddon itself.

There was a payphone by the bus stop out on the main road. 'Are you ready?' he asked, when Francis picked up.

'Another hour,' said Francis.

'We'll be with you in forty minutes.'

He felt better for the modest exercise and the morning air as he walked back to the truck. He was a little hungry too, but Shlomo and his friends were the kind to be punctual. Indeed, a battered navy blue people carrier lumbered up the track a few minutes later. The doors opened and Shlomo and ten others got out. They all wore the distinctive beards, hair, hats and other garb of ultra-Orthodox Judaism, yet somehow they were different from the usual run: thinner and tougher and altogether more dangerous. A legacy of their army service perhaps.

'Where are the others?' asked Shlomo.

'They'll join us later.'

Shlomo frowned. 'They didn't want to be here for this? For the tenth heifer?'

Avram had deferred this moment as long as possible, to prevent defections; but now the time had come. 'Their motivations aren't your motivations,' he said.

'They're not religious?' asked Shlomo.

'They're good Jews,' Avram assured him. 'What more do you need to know?'

'What kind of Jews?'

'Settlers, mostly. From Hebron.'

There was silence. Haredim didn't mix easily with outside groups, particular secular ones. 'You lied to us,' said Shlomo.

'Did I?'

'You know you did.'

'Look at us,' begged Avram. 'Twelve men in a car park. You think we're enough to seize and hold the Promised Land? You think that we can bring down the Dome and then build a new Temple all by ourselves?'

'With the Lord on our side, praise His Name, we can—'

'The Lord, praise His Name, has been on our side forever,' snapped Avram. 'And yet the Dome still stands. So maybe we've been doing it wrong. How about that for an idea?' He looked around at them but saw only hostility and resentment in their faces so that he knew he needed a different approach or he'd risk losing them. 'Listen to me,' he said. 'Please listen. These past twenty-four hours, I've been talking with sympathizers from across the world. I've told them of all the signs that the Lord has sent us in proof that this is our moment. The earthquake. The heifer. The forty-nine years of the prophet Daniel. The simple fact that tonight there will be no moon. But there's one more reason we can be certain this is the time. A reason I shared with none of them, because they aren't capable of understanding. But *you* will understand. Because tonight isn't just significant in their Western calendar. Tonight is significant in our own calendar too. Tonight is *Rosh Chodesh Sivan*.'

There were murmurs among Shlomo's men at this.

They saw instantly where he was going. But he kept talking all the same, taking advantage of the moment. 'The people of the Exodus were a diverse people,' he said. 'They came from different tribes and families, different traditions and beliefs. Then Moses led them out of Egypt and into Sinai, to the foot of its holy mount; and it was there that, for the first time, we came together as one people. It was there that we became Israel.'

Avram knew they'd be familiar with the passage, yet it demanded being read out aloud, so he strode back to his truck for his battered copy of the Torah, turning to the Book of Exodus as he returned to them, reciting the verses as he walked.

> '"*In the third month of the departure of Israel out of the land of Egypt, on this day, they came in to the wilderness of Sinai. For departing out of Raphidim, and coming to the desert of Sinai, they pitched their tents in the same place: and there Israel camped against the mountain.*"'

He closed the book, held it aloft like triumph. '"*And there Israel camped against the mountain.*" The only instance in the Torah, in the entire Tanakh – *the only instance* – where our people are described in the singular rather than the plural. You all know that. And you all know why, too. Because, on that one day, we all of us became Israel — *one* nation with *one* mind and *one* heart joined together in *one* covenant with the Lord, the covenant that we kept in the sacred Ark in the tabernacle and in the Holy of Holies in the Temple of Solomon on Mount Moriah. So what other day could we possibly choose for this great enterprise, but *Rosh Chodesh Sivan*? And yet you would have the Haredim do it alone? No. A thousand times no. This is the day when *all* Israel comes together in covenant with our Lord. And who are we to say that these Jews or those Jews aren't worthy to be there with us? Who are we to put our own preferences ahead of the Lord's? This way, we will be a mirror of our nation. This way, when our fellows wake up tomorrow in Tel Aviv and Haifa, in Europe and New York, whatever kind of Jew they may be, they'll see people just like themselves on their television sets, striking a blow for our nation against the Arabs and their allies. And *all* Israel will flock to our side with passion and joy and courage and numbers because of it; and *all* Israel will demand that the Temple of Solomon is built once more upon Moriah. All Israel united as one again on *Rosh Chodesh Sivan*.' He came to a finish, half expecting to be greeted with acclaim and cheers, but all he got was a few grudging nods.

'Very well,' said Shlomo, interpreting the mood of his small company. 'Just as long as there aren't any women.'

Avram didn't let his expression so much as flicker. 'Of course not,' he said.

II

Luke woke to the harsh shriek of the coach's reversing alarm to discover his head resting on Rachel's. He must have dozed off too. He sat up as gently as he could, partly to allow her a few more moments rest, but mostly because he didn't want her knowing he'd fallen asleep. He didn't quite know why it should matter to him that she should think of him as having stayed vigilant; but it did.

She opened her eyes a second or two later, rubbed them tiredly. 'Are we here?'

'Yes, Victoria,' he said.

She closed her eyes again, leaned against his shoulder, snuggled up for a few extra seconds. Then the doors opened and the lights came on and she shook herself awake. He grabbed the laptop from beneath the seat.

'What now?' she asked, as they climbed down onto the concourse. 'Taxi?'

'Let's save our cash. He's only just across the bridge.'

She nodded at some payphones. 'Shall we warn him we're on our way?'

'Let him sleep,' said Luke. 'I can't remember his number anyway.'

The new day hadn't yet dawned exactly, but the sky was growing light. They walked briskly to the Chelsea Bridge Road and the Thames ran fat and grey beneath them. An impressively dedicated rowing eight heaved and grunted out of view beneath the bridge. 'A word to the wise,' said Luke. 'Jay isn't always the easiest person in the world.'

'How do you mean?'

Luke hesitated. It felt disloyal discussing his friend behind his back. 'He has a mild to moderate case of Asperger's syndrome. It's a high-functioning autistic spectrum disorder, the one that can sometimes make people exceptional at music and maths and—'

'I know Asperger's.'

'Jay's brilliant at pattern recognition. That's what makes him so good at codes. But he also has difficulty in reading people. He doesn't empathize easily and he tends not to spot irony or jokes unless they're heavily signalled. He doesn't do small talk, so he can come across as quite curt, and when he gets onto a favourite topic, or gets overexcited, he can be hard to stop. Occasionally he'll say something hurtful by mistake. And if he ever realizes afterwards, he'll beat himself up for days about it. So he's had to deal with a lot of self-hatred over the years. You can still see the hatching on his arms from when he used to cut himself. And I'm pretty sure he tried suicide at least once.'

'Jesus.'

'Don't get alarmed. Asperger's gets better with age. He's grown much more confident since I first met him, on that documentary I did. But he still gets edgy around new people. Particularly women. Even more particularly young and beautiful women.'

'Sure,' laughed Rachel. 'Because I'm a knock-out in borrowed clothes after a night on the bus.' But she adopted a more serious look. 'Would it be better if I waited outside?'

'God, no. I need you in there. And it'll be fine, truly. I just want you aware, so that you won't overreact if he says or does something odd.'

'Okay,' she said. 'Consider me aware. But how did he cope with your documentary? It can't have been easy for him, having a TV crew around.'

'It wasn't like that. He just checked our scripts and helped track down some interesting alchemical experiments for Pelham. This was before the bulk of Newton's papers were digitized, so he was invaluable. He knows them backwards – he can recite vast sections of Newton's *Chronology of Ancient Kingdoms Amended*. But for god's sake don't mention that to him, or there's every chance he will.'

'Must be a riot at dinner parties.' Her jaw trembled as she fought a yawn. 'Why's he so interested in Newton?'

'I think he sees him as a role model. Because of the Asperger's.'

Rachel squinted at him. 'Newton had Asperger's?'

'We think maybe. Diagnosis is impossible after three hundred years, but he certainly showed some signs. He pretty much taught himself mathematics from first principles, for one thing. Then he took it far beyond anything anyone had ever done before. You don't do that without a seriously unusual mind.'

'So all great mathematicians have Asperger's by definition, do they?'

'Of course not. But Asperger's is a syndrome. You diagnose it by looking for certain attributes and behaviours. One of those can be an extraordinary facility with numbers. Newton had that. So that box gets a tick.'

'And what's the next box?'

'Asperger's sufferers often have extraordinary visualisation skills. Remember that movie *Rain Man*? How the character played by Dustin Hoffman told at a glance how many toothpicks or whatever got spilled on the floor? According to a Cambridge roommate, Newton could do something similar. He kept a thousand guineas worth of coins in a huge bowl by his window just to see if anyone was stealing from him.'

'Wow,' teased Rachel. 'So he could be a suspicious room-mate. Lock the bastard up.'

'Okay,' said Luke. 'Asperger's shows itself very early. Infants with it have difficulty bonding with their parents. Newton's father died before he was born and his mother remarried when he was three years old. But the thing is, even though her new husband had plenty of room in his home, she didn't take Isaac with her when she moved in.'

'Maybe her new man didn't like children.'

'Then why marry her?'

'Ever heard of love?'

Luke shook his head. 'They hadn't even met when he proposed. He'd just heard good reports.'

Rachel looked startled. 'You're kidding me.'

'They were both recently widowed,' said Luke. 'It made good sense. But it certainly wasn't a marriage of necessity. So why not take Isaac?'

'What did she do with him?'

'Left him with her parents. They had a lovely farmhouse in Woolsthorpe in Lincolnshire, home of the famous apple tree. But he didn't get on with them either. He had a very strained relationship with his grandmother – and his grandfather actually cut him out of his will. As for the servants and farmhands, they popped corks when he finally left home: *Fit for nothing but the 'Versity*, as one of them put it. He didn't have many childhood friends, partly because he picked a lot of quarrels and held a pretty good grudge. Same thing at Cambridge. Later on, one of his disciples decided to track down Newton's contemporaries there, ask them what the great man had been like as an undergraduate.

None of them could even remember having met him. It was only in his thirties that he started making any real friends; but then people typically learn to manage their Asperger's better as they get older, like Jay's doing. And Newton never became comfortable with intimacy. In fact, he probably died a virgin. Anyway, I'm not saying Newton had Asperger's; I'm just explaining why Jay looks up to him.'

They'd reached Jay's street. Luke pointed across the road to a front door painted racing green. 'That's him,' he said. 'Let's go wake the bugger up.'

III

Croke was catching a few minutes shut-eye in the museum office when Morgenstern knocked and came in. 'Are we through?' Croke asked him.

Morgenstern shook his head. 'Still another hour. But I just had a call about your two fugitives. Thought you'd want to know.'

Croke stood up. 'They've found them?'

'Not exactly.' He gave a little grimace. 'We had people watching the coach station. But apparently there are stops on the way out of town too.'

'For fuck's sake. Didn't they think of that?'

'There wasn't enough manpower to cover everything.

But they did ask the drivers to report any couples they picked up.'

'And?'

'The first driver out picked up a woman at one stop, a man at the next. He didn't make the connection. But apparently they left Victoria coach station together. And their descriptions match Luke and the girl.'

Croke touched a finger to his temple. He wanted to yell at someone, but he couldn't see how it would help. 'Where are they now?'

Morgenstern shrugged. 'They left on foot. They could have gone anywhere. We'll try to track them through our CCTV network, but that's a bitch, believe me. We're more likely to find them when they break cover again, which they're bound to do, sooner or later. We've put taps on their families and friends, and we're monitoring the major media groups in case they go that route. And we'll keep a close eye on Twitter and the Internet too.'

'Okay. Good. Let me know if they surface. Or when we get through to the chamber.'

'Will do.' He nodded and withdrew.

Croke rested his head back against the wall, closed his eyes. Morgenstern should be able to stop Luke and Rachel damaging this operation before he left for Israel. But they could certainly still cause future grief, particularly for Walters and his men. And if those three went down, they'd likely take him with them. At some stage, he'd have to make sure that couldn't happen. But for the moment they were still too useful.

He called Walters now, briefed him on the Victoria coach station sighting. 'The NCT are out looking for them,' he told him. 'But I'd much rather deal with them in-house if we can.'

'Too right,' agreed Walters. 'We're on our way.'

TWENTY-FIVE

I

After the big build-up from Luke, Rachel was a little disappointed by Jay Cowan. She'd expected him to stand out in some way, yet he could scarcely have been more ordinary: slight, neat and generally unobtrusive. He had an oblique way about him, too, never facing either of them directly, or looking them full in the eye. He also held himself unnaturally still, as if someone had once told him to stop fidgeting, and he'd taken the words too much to heart. And while his green shirt and black drainpipe trousers and brown brogues were each perfectly fine in themselves, they looked awful in combination. Not ordinary, then, so much as trying his very best to appear ordinary, and falling strangely short.

'Luke,' he said, opening his front door. 'What are you doing here?'

'We didn't wake you, did we?'

'I was working.'

'Working?' asked Rachel, giving him her warmest smile. 'At this time of day?'

He didn't look at her so much as over her left shoulder. 'Yes,' he said. He turned back to Luke. 'What are you doing here?' he asked again.

'We need help, mate.'

'With what?'

'Can we come in? If I don't get a coffee soon, I'm going to keel.'

Jay stood there a moment longer, then nodded and let them in. A short corridor led to a dingy stairwell with worn brown carpeting. They went up to the first floor. Boxes stacked against the wall were covered by a white sheet. 'What's all this?' asked Luke.

'A project.' He led them inside his flat and into a large, book-lined room that should have overlooked the street, except that the thick crimson curtains were drawn across the windows, leaving it lit by a table lamp and an array of six computer screens stacked in two rows of three, each of which showed a hand from a different online poker tournament.

'That's your work?' asked Rachel. 'Poker?'

'This is the best time,' he said. 'People who've been

playing all night are tired by now. They make more mistakes when they're tired.' He began cashing out of the games one by one, switching off the screens.

'And you can make a living from it?'

'You wouldn't believe how bad some of them are. They bet in situations where there's no possible benefit to betting. Then they do it again.'

'Maybe they're trying to prove themselves,' suggested Luke.

'Or maybe they just want to go to bed,' said Rachel.

Jay looked directly at her for the first time. 'Then why wouldn't they just go to bed?'

With the screens gone black, the room suddenly felt a little spooky. 'Yes,' said Rachel. 'Good point.'

'How about that coffee?' said Luke, setting down Olivia's laptop. 'We've had one hell of a night.'

'Of course,' he said. He led them through to an impeccably neat kitchen, turned on the kettle. 'What do you need my help with?'

Luke fished his cipher text from Pelham's pocket. It was badly smudged and crumpled, so Jay found him a fresh pad of paper on which to write it out clean. 'Rachel and I found this last night,' said Luke. 'We think it's a cipher, perhaps devised by Newton.'

'A Newton cipher?' Jay's eyes opened a little wider. 'Where did you find it?'

'I can't tell you, I'm afraid. I gave someone my word.'

'You want my help and you won't tell me?'

'I'm sorry, Jay. If I gave you my word on something, you wouldn't want me to break it, would you?'

Jay considered this for a moment, like a boy with a scraped knee wondering whether or not to start bawling. 'It won't help me solve the cipher.'

'You can do it anyway. I've been telling Rachel how brilliant you are.'

For a moment, Rachel feared the flattery was too blatant, but Jay only nodded, so she decided to back Luke up. 'It's quite true,' she said. 'He's been bragging shamelessly about you.'

Jay's throat reddened slightly and he squinted at the architrave above the kitchen door. 'I can't promise anything.'

'Of course not,' said Luke, pouring boiling water into three mugs. 'Just give it your best shot.'

He nodded and set the pad square in front of him on the countertop.

BE 22108 BF
BE 10460 BF
BH 01256
BC 10484
KD 11201

'Five rows of five numbers,' said Jay. He turned to Luke. 'You've already checked for a grid, I assume.'

'For a what?'

Jay sighed. 'There are twenty-six letters in the Latin alphabet. If you treat I and J or Y and Z as one letter, you can fit the entire alphabet into a five-by-five grid. Code-makers have been using that for centuries. It would have been old hat to someone like Newton.' He pointed to the top row of numbers: 2 2 1 0 8. 'If that's what this is, then these numbers might indicate how many times each letter is used in the cipher text. This first 2, for example, would imply that the letter A appears twice.' He wrote two capital As at the top of a fresh sheet of paper. 'This second 2 would indicate two Bs.'

'I'm with you,' said Rachel. 'One C. No Ds. Eight Es.'

'How do you know the grid reads left to right?' asked Luke, a little piqued. 'Maybe it goes from top to bottom.'

'E is *by far* the most common letter in the alphabet,' said Jay. 'Eight Es therefore makes sense. Under *your* system, we'd have just one E, but eight Us. Are you really arguing that eight Us are more likely than eight Es?'

'I guess not.'

'Plus *my* way also gives us six Os, which I'd say makes rather more sense than *your* six Ws. Maybe you'd disagree? Maybe you'd prefer your six Qs to my six Is. At least it would give you something to do with all those Us. ' He glanced at Rachel, almost with a smirk, as though showing off for her. 'And I get four Rs and eight Ss, not to mention three Ns and two As, Ms and Ts, all of which make sense. That's why, incidentally, I can be confident that this is a YZ cipher rather an IJ one. Any other questions, or may I get on with it?' He didn't bother waiting for Luke to answer, but instead wrote out all the letters in sequence:

A A B B C E E E E E E E
F H H H H I I I I I I
L M M N N N N N O O O O O O
P R R R R S S S S S S S T T T T
U V W W Y/Z

'What about the pairs of letters before and after the numbers?' asked Rachel. 'What are they for?'

'The numbers stood for letters,' said Jay. 'So perhaps the letters stand for numbers.'

'I'm sorry?'

'A equals one. B equals two. E equals five. Add all the letter pairs up and what do you get?'

Luke shook his head. 'What?'

'My god, Luke! How long have you had this? Sixty. Now count up the numbers.'

'Sixty?' hazarded Rachel.

'Exactly. Well done. Sixty. *Now* do you see?'

'No,' said Luke.

Jay took a fresh sheet of paper, set it next to the list of letters. He wrote two dashes on the left of the page, followed by a space and another five dashes, as in in a game of hangman. 'There's your first B and E,' he said. He wrote two dashes and then six more on the right-hand side of the page. 'And that's your first B and F.' He repeated it immediately beneath, then followed it with a third line of two dashes followed by eight, a fourth line of two and three dashes, with eleven and four dashes on the bottom line. 'Now all we have to do is fit these sixty letters onto these sixty blank spaces until we've got a phrase that makes sense. Which would be easier if I knew where'd you found this thing, or what its context was.' But he said this more to make the point than in reproach, for he was clearly enjoying the challenge now and didn't want it made easier.

'Maybe we should each have a go,' suggested Luke.

'Yes. Or maybe you could allow me some silence in which to work.'

'Fine,' said Luke. 'We'll leave you to it.'

II

The farm was a few kilometres north-west of Megiddo Junction, an old kibbutz that had died twelve years before from internal rifts and a lack of new blood. Thaddeus and his friends had bought it cheap, sold off the surplus arable land and then switched its remaining cattle facilities from dairy to beef. They'd refurbished the dormitories for their American volunteers and had added state-of-the-art farming facilities, including a laboratory for testing, treating and preserving semen samples. Then they'd set about breeding themselves a red heifer.

The yard was dark and deserted when Avram parked outside the main house. But a light came on inside even as Shlomo pulled up alongside him, and then Francis came out, dressed with unusual modesty in tattered farm-hand clothes, deliberately downplaying his status here. Avram nodded at him. He beckoned for them to follow him to a cavernous barn, pungent with animal smells. Huge strip lights flashed and shuddered like a silent storm before finally coming on. Certificates, photograph albums and other documentation for the heifer lay on a pair of worktables inside the door. Another pair of tables against the end wall were arrayed with bowls, knives, vestments and everything else they'd need for the sacrifice itself. Water splashed into a ritual bath opposite the door, while the wall behind it was covered intriguingly by a vast white sheet. And, to their left, a wooden altar had been built beneath an expanse of open roof.

Yet, for all these marvels, Shlomo and his men had eyes for just one thing.

And the Lord spoke to Moses and to Aaron, saying: This is the statute of the law which the Lord hath commanded: Speak unto the children of Israel, that they bring thee a red heifer, faultless, wherein there is no blemish, and upon which there never came yoke.

A red heifer, faultless, wherein there is no blemish. And there she was, caged in a steel pen in the corner of the barn, trembling a little, shying away from the sudden light and the crowd of staring men.

Purity was impossible in this world. Try as one might, one simply couldn't avoid death and dirt and disease. Yet no observant Jew had been allowed to enter the grounds of the Temple while tainted. And certainly none would ever even contemplate intruding impure upon the Holy of Holies. That would have been a terrible sacrilege. On the other hand, Jews had still needed to visit the Temple. Before each visit, therefore, they'd cleansed themselves with ritual bathing and the anointment of ashes from a perfect red heifer.

Nine times in history such a heifer had been identified, sacrificed and burned. But then the Romans had destroyed the Temple and there'd been no more ashes. With the exact location of the Holy of Holies lost to human knowledge, few observant Jews would now dare walk upon the Temple Mount, let alone enter the Dome of the Rock, lest by accident they trespass on that most sacred space. Only by anointing themselves with the ashes of a new red heifer, therefore, could Shlomo and his men so much as venture onto the Mount. Only with a new heifer could they and their brethren bring down the Dome and build the Third Temple.

They edged tentatively towards her, almost as frightened as she was. They clustered around the small pen, leaned over the steel bars, yet not getting too close, as though scared that something cataclysmic might happen. But then one of them touched her by accident and instantly the spell was broken. Their hands were all over her, and they were babbling and laughing as they sought in vain the one white hair that might disqualify her, the one whisker.

Avram glanced at Francis. He looked serenely confident. Whatever dyes, tweezers or other tricks he'd used, they'd surely fool a dozen city boys like this. Reassured, he went to join them and share their joy as the truth dawned exultantly on them.

The heifer was real. The moment was real.

The time of the Third Temple had come.

TWENTY-SIX

I

Rachel opened the curtains a little way to allow some morning in. A cyclist wobbled by outside, and a yawning man trudged gloomily towards the river. Everything seemed so normal. She nodded at Jay's phone. 'You think he'd mind if we called Pelham's sister? See how she's getting on, if she needs any help?'

Luke shook his head. 'I wouldn't put it past them to be monitoring her phone. If they are, they'll be able to trace incoming calls. They'll be here in no time.'

She closed her eyes a moment. 'I keep forgetting.'

Reproductions of portraits of famous people were hanging either side of the kitchen door. Rachel hadn't noticed them in the earlier gloom, but now one caught her eye – the Kneller portrait Luke had mentioned earlier as the model for the Newton sculpture. She pointed it out to him. He grinned and murmured: 'Jay would give his right arm to see what we've seen.'

Rachel nodded. Jay liked his scientists, that was for sure. And neatness, too. Each picture had its counterpart on the other side of the door: Einstein matched with Newton; Faraday with Curie; Linnaeus with Darwin; Edison with Tesla. She went to his bookshelves. They were arranged primarily by subject matter but then by size, with the largest to the left. Five whole shelves were devoted to writings by or about Newton. He also had extensive collections on alchemy, chemistry and other sciences. Luke smiled mischievously and pulled down a history of electricity, flipped to its index.

'What are you looking for?' she asked.

'These Babylonian batteries of yours. I think you made them up.' He showed the index to her. 'See. Nothing here.'

'That's because they're *Baghdad* batteries,' she said, pointing out the entry to him.

'Damn it,' he said. He turned to the page and began to read. Then a puzzled look furrowed his brow.

'What is it?' she asked.

He closed the book. 'These batteries. How would you describe what they did? At their simplest level, I mean.'

She shook her head. 'I'm not with you.'

'They used acid to turn base metals into gold, right? Doesn't that remind you of something?'

Now she saw it. 'Alchemy?' she frowned.

'Alchemy was essentially based on texts written in and around Alexandria during the early centuries AD,' said Luke. 'But that doesn't mean the idea originated there. Baghdad was one of Alexandria's major trading partners. Is it really so far-fetched to imagine merchants gossiping about these miraculous vessels they'd seen that used acid to turn other metals into gold? And is it such a great leap to believe that Alexandrians would have coveted this know-how and sought to replicate it for themselves?'

'They'd have done anything for it.'

'They'd have failed, of course. But the effort was the thing. The belief that it was possible, if you just got the mix of ingredients exactly right, or if you used a particular mineral as a catalyst, or maybe if you were pure enough of heart or you waited until Saturn was in conjunction with Venus. And so they wrote down their ideas and aspirations and experiments, and *that's* the stuff that your Harranian friends preserved as their sacred texts, and which eventually reached Europe.'

'Alchemy based upon a misunderstanding of primitive electroplating?' Rachel gave a joyful laugh. 'What a wonderful idea.'

'It would mean awarding Newton the coconut for his theory about electricity as the philosopher's stone. And if it was part of what he was working on during 1693, it could even explain his breakdown too. Hallucinations, confusion and long-term cognitive damage are *exactly* the symptoms you'd expect from exposing yourself to a series of electrical shocks.'

Rachel nodded. 'So he stopped his experiments and his hallucinations stopped too.'

'He stopped doing them himself, at least. As President of the Royal Society, he appointed his own Curator of Experiments and had him concentrate almost exclusively on electricity.'

'Looking for the philosopher's stone by proxy?'

'Isn't that what you'd have done? Hire some poor wannabe to take the shocks and the visions on your behalf?' He glanced at the door. 'Maybe we're getting carried away. Let's run it by Jay, see what he thinks.'

They went through to the kitchen. Jay was so absorbed in his decipherment that he didn't even notice them. He simply carried on scribbling on his pad, trying out words then crossing them out. He gave a cry of excitement as he tore off a sheet of paper and started afresh. Luke and Rachel watched as he wrote rapidly and confidently, then clenched a fist in triumph.

'Success?' asked Luke.

Jay whirled around. He shook his head and made to turn over the pad, but Luke put his hand on Jay's to stop him, allowing him and Rachel could see what he'd written.

As above   it shines
So below   it shines
Ye monument
Of Sir
Christopher Wren

II

Croke returned to the basement gallery in good time to witness the drill breaching the chamber beneath. It took another fifteen minutes, however, to remove the various bits and then feed down the endoscope.

Morgenstern came to stand beside him. 'I spoke to our friend in Washington earlier. Our Vice President wants to watch live when we find it. But if he wakes her and there's nothing there, he'll have my ass for breakfast. So the way I figure it, we take a quick peek ourselves. If it's there, we pull the endoscope back up, give her a call and pretend like we've just broken through. Otherwise, we let her sleep. Agreed?'

'Agreed.'

They clustered around a laptop to watch the feed as the camera burrowed its way down, its integrated lighting flaring in the narrow borehole. Suddenly it emerged into the chamber and went dim. The operator adjusted his controls and the screen brightened once again. A block of stone came into view below, ghostly figures on every side. Yet it was hard to see anything clearly, making it both miraculous and frustrating at the same time.

The endoscope snaked lower and lower. Then Croke saw something that made him freeze. 'The floor,' he said tightly. 'Zoom in on the floor.'

The operator nodded; the camera focused. They all leaned closer to the screen. Yes. It was as he'd thought. There *were* footprints in the dust. *Trainer* footprints. He closed his eyes in disbelief. So that's where Luke and the girl had been hiding. Even more frustratingly, they must have sneaked away while they'd been drilling, or the coach driver wouldn't have been able to pick them up and drive them to London.

He turned abruptly, strode out of the gallery to the well. He noted in stony silence the dangling rope and the black gash in the shaft wall two-thirds of the way down. Anger washed over him in a great wave, but he didn't have time to indulge it. Whatever secrets were down there, Luke and Rachel already knew them. And they had a five-hour head start too.

He had some serious catching up to do.

TWENTY-SEVEN

I

'The Monument of Sir Christopher Wren,' murmured Rachel. 'That's the London Monument, right? I mean, Wren did build it, yes?'

'Yes,' said Luke. 'Him and Hooke.'

'You don't look convinced.'

'Hooke and Newton loathed each other,' said Luke. 'I can't imagine them willingly collaborating on a project.'

'What else could it be?' asked Jay.

Luke nodded and went through to the front room, looked out the window; but of course there was no view of it from there, hidden by the houses opposite and all the other buildings put up in the three hundred and fifty years since the Great Fire. 'As above it shines, so below it shines,' he said. 'What do you think it means?'

'If you'd give me some more context,' said Jay, 'maybe I could tell you.'

Luke glanced at his laptop, wondering whether the time had come. Then he recalled the grief he'd brought down on Pelham. The last thing he wanted on his conscience was more collateral damage among his friends. 'We think Newton may have hidden something valuable,' he said. 'We think this may tell us where.'

'The Monument has a flaming golden urn on its top,' nodded Jay. 'To symbolize the Great Fire. That must be the "As above, it shines".'

'And the "as below"?'

'There's a vault,' said Jay. 'Wren built it to conduct astronomical experiments. Or so he claimed. But he never used it much. All the traffic threw off his instruments.'

'Then that must be it,' said Rachel. 'Is it still there?'

Jay nodded. 'I tried to visit it once. They wouldn't let me in. The only access is through a trapdoor in the floor at the foot of the main staircase, so they have to keep it closed during the day. But they said I'd be welcome to see it if I ever got there before they opened.'

'And when's that?' asked Rachel.

Jay brought up the Monument's home page on one of his screens. 'Eight thirty,' he said. 'You can make it if you leave right now. You can catch a train from Queenstown Road.'

'Aren't you coming?' asked Rachel.

He shook his head vigorously. 'I can't,' he said. 'Not during rush hour. Too many people.'

'We can take a taxi,' said Luke.

'We'll never get one here in time. They're always booked up at this time of day. The train's your only hope, believe me. And you have to leave right now. Come back afterwards. Tell me about it.'

Rachel nodded. 'We'll take pictures.'

'Good. Great.'

'What if we have any questions?' asked Luke. 'You know Wren and Hooke far better than I do.'

'Call me.' He wrote down his numbers, gave them to Luke.

Queenstown Station was a ten-minute walk. They made it in five. They bought tickets at a machine, joined the platform scrum. The first train was too full for any more passengers, but they squeezed onto the second. 'Can't say I blame Jay,' murmured Rachel, her face jammed against Luke's throat. They changed at Vauxhall, headed north three stops. A great wave of commuters washed them out the exit, and there it was, a great Doric column topped by a gilded urn glowing brilliantly in the morning sunlight. Its door was locked, however, and no one answered Luke's knock. Fifteen minutes till opening.

Rachel beckoned Luke over to see some Latin text inscribed in the stone. 'Look at the date,' she said. 'Sixteen sixty-six comes out as MDCLXVI in Latin. Each letter used exactly once.'

'That's one reason they called it the *annus mirabilis*,' nodded Luke. 'Though actually they were expecting an *annus horibilis*. Six six six was the number of the beast, so people were pretty certain it was going to be bad. Then there was a comet in late 1664, another in 1665.' In fact it had been the same one coming back from orbiting the sun, but hardly anyone had realized that. 'People were expecting all kinds of terrors. Then the plague arrived. And the Great Fire. You can see why they thought it ordained. But the year wasn't all bad. It was Newton's own *annus mirabilis* too. The year he supposedly saw the apple fall and so solved all the secrets of the universe.'

'Supposedly?' asked Rachel. 'Are you saying the apple never fell?'

'No, it probably did,' admitted Luke. 'Newton certainly told the story himself, though not till he was an old man. And for sure he exaggerated its significance. He wanted to make it seem he'd had his breakthroughs early, because of that priority dispute with Leibniz I—'

He broke off as a portly, balding man arrived outside the Monument's door, popping the last bite of a croissant into his mouth even as he fished keys from his pocket. They hurried to intercept him. He held a hand over his mouth to prevent a spray of crumbs. 'Ten minutes,' he said.

'Please,' said Rachel. 'We don't want to go up. At least we do, but we're mainly here to see your basement.'

'My basement?' he frowned. 'There's nothing there.'

'There is to us,' said Luke. 'We're science historians. Your vault is scientific history.'

'Go through the City Authority. They can arrange it for you.'

'We're only in London for the day,' said Luke. 'We go back home this afternoon.'

'Please,' said Rachel. 'Just a quick peek. We'll be gone before you know it.'

He sighed extravagantly, as if they didn't realize the trouble they were putting him to. 'Fine,' he said. 'But not a word to your friends, okay? Or they'll all be here wanting to see it.'

'Our secret,' said Rachel. 'We promise.'

II

Deception and subterfuge didn't come easily to Jay. Apart from anything else, he found it hard to read on people's faces whether they believed him or not. He'd therefore become anxious that Luke and Rachel had seen through his efforts to send them on a wild-goose chase and were planning to double back to see what he was up to, so he'd followed them at a cautious distance all the way to Queenstown Road Station. Even that hadn't made him feel entirely secure. He'd kept expecting them to reappear from the station, so he'd found it impossible to tear himself away. He'd chided himself for excessive caution, but such compulsions were part of his condition, and there was little he could do about it.

When he'd finally convinced himself it was safe, he hurried back to his flat and bolted himself in. He drew the thick curtains to encase himself in the comforting cocoon of their privacy. Then he unzipped the case Luke had brought and set the laptop inside on his desk.

This was why he'd hustled them off earlier. This was why he'd sent them to the Monument.

He opened it up, turned it on, checked for recently opened files. It took him to a folder of photographs and a word document. He copied them to his own machine then zipped the laptop away again as it had been before, so that Luke and Rachel wouldn't know. Then he went through the photographs. What he saw amazed and gratified, yet ultimately disappointed, him.

It wasn't there.

He went through the photographs again, allowing himself enough time with each to imprint them onto his mind and build up a composite image of the vault. Then he sat back and let his brain whirr and hum with ideas and combinations, with deductions and inferences. He pulled volumes down from his shelves. He browsed the internet. He bought, downloaded and consulted various journal articles and e-books. And finally a feeling settled on him, a feeling of such perfect clarity that it was a joy. He knew where it was. He knew *precisely* where it was. And this time there was no possibility of a mistake. He smiled with satisfaction as he reached for his phone.

Uncle Avram was certain to be pleased.

III

The trap door was locked in place by a pair of steel bolts. The custodian grimaced as he stooped to release them. Then he raised the trapdoor by its handle. A steep stone staircase spiralled down into a small circular room. Luke ducked his head to avoid the stone lintel as he descended; but it was instantly obvious that there was nothing there but dust and an air-conditioning unit.

'Told you,' said the man.

They inspected and photographed the place anyway, but that was that. They thanked him and retreated back upstairs, brushing grit and cobwebs from their hair. 'Are you open yet?' asked Rachel. 'For going up top, I mean.'

The man shot the bolts and checked his watch. 'It'll be a fiver each,' he said.

They set off upwards. Slit windows at regular intervals allowed Luke to gauge their progress, as did a glance over the handrail at the lengthening corkscrew beneath. The stairs narrowed to single file as they neared the top. The breeze outside was surprisingly strong. 'What are we looking for?' asked Rachel, tucking hair back behind her ear.

'Maybe we'll know when we see it.'

The Thames lay grey before them, twinkling with morning sunlight. The London Eye and other buildings of the South Bank offered hazy reflections of themselves on its rumpled surface, as did a warship moored near Tower Bridge. Rachel peered through the safety mesh down at Pudding Lane, seat of the Great Fire. 'Can you imagine how that poor baker must have felt?' she asked. 'To have burned down half of London.'

'If he really did,' said Luke.

'How do you mean?'

'No one at the time believed it was an accident. They blamed enemy action. They actually strung up some poor French halfwit for it. But the powers-that-were needed it to have been an accident. So they held an inquiry and *hey presto*, a negligent baker.'

Rachel frowned. 'Why did they need it to have been an accident?'

'A quirk of the law. Landowners had to rebuild any property destroyed in an act of war, but tenants were on the hook for accidents. Parliament was made up of land-owners. Guess which side they came down on?'

Rachel laughed. 'You're kidding me.'

'A little,' admitted Luke. 'There was a genuine concern that if landlords had to pay, London would never be rebuilt. Tenants had little choice: they needed somewhere to live. Besides, it probably was an accident. Fires were common enough: all those wooden houses, all that open flame. And this one would have burned itself out, just like the rest, except for a brutal wind that kept scattering embers and starting new blazes. No arsonist could have arranged that. And even then the mayor could have contained it by knocking down some houses as a fire-break; but he was too cheap. My only point is that everyone takes it as settled that it was an accident, but it's not. And if it really was arson, there have been some pretty interesting names in the frame, not least our friends Sir Christopher Wren and John Evelyn.'

'No way!'

'Wren was a highly ambitious architect,' said Luke. 'He wanted a cathedral of his own, because that was how you made your name at the time. He'd already been commissioned to repair St Paul's before the fire, because Cromwell had left it in such a terrible state. But the Dean didn't have enough money to demolish and rebuild, as Wren wanted, so he insisted he mend and make do instead. Then came the fire.'

'And Evelyn?'

'He *hated* London. A loathsome Golgotha, he called it. He wanted it rebuilt on the European model, with great piazzas, avenues and parks; with a decent sewage system and the banishment of noxious trades.'

'Disliking pollution isn't the same as arson, Luke.'

He grinned. 'Did you know that within days of the fire, both Evelyn and Wren had come up with plans for completely remodelling the city?'

Rachel shook her head. 'I'm still not buying.'

'Me neither,' smiled Luke. 'Not while we can blame the French.'

The northern skyline was crowded with the blockish monsters of the City. To the west, the morning sun put a halo around the dome of St Paul's, while early-bird tourists on the outside galleries struck sparks with their camera flashes. They found themselves staring raptly at it. 'Are you thinking what I'm thinking?' asked Luke.

'St Paul does seem to keep popping up,' agreed Rachel.

'Our cabal inscribed both sides of that plinth to him. Once for the Damascene conversion, the other to Balinus the secret alchemist. But why settle for a plinth in a secret vault in Oxford when you've got a building with his name on it at the very heart of your new Jerusalem?'

Rachel gave a soft laugh. 'Have you ever taken the tour?' she asked.

'Not since school. Why?'

'I went on it last year. A friend from Turkey was over and wanted to see the sights. Wren's son composed an epitaph to his father. It's on his tomb and also around the rim of a great brass ring in the floor directly beneath the dome. I can't remember the Latin, but I do remember how our guide translated it.'

'And?' asked Luke.

She smiled at him, her eyes shining. 'It says: "Reader, if you want to see his monument, look around".'

TWENTY-EIGHT

I

Luke called Jay from a payphone by the tube station. 'It's not the Monument,' he told him. 'It's St Paul's. Apparently there's an inscription to Wren: "Reader, if you want to see his monument, look around".'

'Oh,' said Jay. 'Yes.'

'We're off there now. Just didn't want you worrying. Later, okay?' He put down the phone and hurried with Rachel along Cannon Street, dodging the morning's laggards, surly with weekend hangovers and Monday blues. They passed the southern flank of St Paul's churchyard and strode up the front steps. A pair of French school-teachers were struggling to corral a large party of unruly pupils and Luke and Rachel picked up their pace without a word, not wanting to get caught behind them, only to

307

run into four police officers by the main doors, bulked up with body-armour, automatic weapons held aslant across their chests. Sudden memories of last night's chase and fears of an ambush hit them simultaneously; but they held their nerve and the police gave them barely a glance.

It took Luke's eyes a few moments to adjust to the interior gloom of the great cathedral, for the familiar contours to come into focus. The organist and choir burst into a few bars of glorious noise as they bought their tickets, rehearsing Handel for some upcoming service. Walking down the main aisle, their eyes were irresistibly drawn upwards to the majestic cupola with its richly painted biblical scenes, the statues of stern-faced prophets around its base and the dizzying golden gallery at its peak. The *size* of it. Photographs and memory couldn't hope to do it justice. And all held up by the sixteen evenly spaced pillars that created a kind of inner sanctum in which wooden chairs had been arranged in concentric circles around a vast marble mosaic in the floor, a star-burst of thirty-two points around a gleaming brass disc. And, around its rim, just as Rachel had said, a Latin phrase was inscribed.

Lector Si Monumentum Requiris Circumspice

They gazed down at it for a few moments, as if expecting enlightenment to descend upon them like the

Holy Spirit. It didn't. Rachel sighed. 'This is hopeless, isn't it?' she said. 'We haven't got a prayer.'

'If it were easy, someone would have found it already.'

'Maybe they have. Maybe they found it centuries ago.'

He shook his head. 'Those people last night didn't think so.'

'No.'

'So let's assume they know what they're about. Let's assume that further progress isn't impossible. Let's assume we're missing something.'

'Like what?'

He slid her a wry look. *If I knew that . . .* 'How about John Evelyn?' he said.

'What about him?' she asked.

'There were four of them on the vault's walls. We know Ashmole's role: he acquired papers and some other stuff from Dee and the Tradescants that he passed on to Newton. And he was also presumably responsible for organising the vault beneath the Ashmolean. We know Newton's role. Ashmole needed him to complete and then hide whatever it was. And we know Wren's role. Maybe he designed the Ashmolean vault. For sure he designed *this* place. And he linked the others together. But what about Evelyn? How did *he* earn his spot on the roster?'

'Maybe he was the brains of the outfit.'

'Sure,' said Luke. 'Because that was what a cabal with Newton and Wren was lacking: brainpower.'

Rachel laughed acknowledgement. 'Okay. Brains is the wrong word. Leadership. Vision. *Drive*. Whatever you want to call it. I mean, weren't his great loves city planning and horticulture?'

'So?'

'I don't know. Designing parks, planting acorns, campaigning against pollution. Maybe I'm romanticising him, but he sounds the kind of person to whom long-term outcomes mattered more than taking credit.'

'An *éminence grise*,' said Luke. 'I could buy that. But where does it get us?'

'You asked about his role,' said Rachel. 'That was my suggestion. I never promised it would get us anywhere.'

Luke looked upwards. Sunlight flooded through the plain glass windows that girdled the base of the dome. The organist struck up again, and then the choir, a growing swell of joyous sound; and he felt a mild, toe-tingling vertigo at the sheer scale and glory of this place, mixed with awe at the courage and skill of the masons and carpenters and painters who'd risked their lives on precarious wooden scaffolds, just a stumble away from certain death. The *weight* of that thing. It was unimaginable. And all resting on this ring of sixteen slender pillars. But then he frowned. The pillars weren't actually in a ring after all, but rather in eight pairs. An octagon holding up a dome; he shivered with the ghost of an idea. But then Rachel touched his forearm and it vanished.

'Let's go up,' she said.

'Up?'

She nodded down at the brass disc in the floor. '"As below, it shines".' Then she looked up at the dome. '"As above, it shines." They do call that thing the great lantern, don't they?'

'These places needed light,' said Luke. 'You couldn't just flip a switch.'

'I know,' she said. 'But even so. It's a *theme*, isn't it? Something to investigate.'

Luke hesitated. The longer they stayed here, he knew, the greater would be the risk that those men would pick up their trail again. Yet the urge to find the truth proved stronger than caution. 'Let's do it,' he said.

II

Jay Cowan kept trying his uncle's telephone numbers, but his uncle wasn't answering and he couldn't wait forever. He put the phone down once more and went to stand in the centre of his living room. He clasped his hands lightly behind his back and stared intently at the wall. Doing this sometimes helped him clear his mind of clutter when he had consequential decisions to make.

Jay knew he wasn't quite like other people. It had taken him many years to come to terms with this, but now he welcomed it. His uncle Avram had shown him that he was *special*. Being special meant carrying special burdens, but it also meant enjoying special gifts. Most of all, it meant he had a purpose; because why else would you make something special? His uncle had shown him what that purpose was too and he had embraced it with all his heart. Now it was up to him to make it happen – even if that meant allying himself with people he didn't much care for; people like Vernon Croke. Even, indeed, if it meant deceiving friends like Luke and the woman Rachel. For Jay had liked Rachel very much. She'd been kind and pretty, and she'd smiled warmly at him and she'd been inside his home. Not that many pretty women had ever smiled warmly at Jay, or had been inside his home.

Perhaps she would marry him one day. It was possible.

Jay had known full well that there was nothing in the vault of the London Monument. Contrary to what he'd told them, he'd actually visited the place twice. He'd sent them there, hoping to keep them out safely out of the way. Unfortunately, they'd made the correct deduction by themselves and would already be in St Paul's by now. Telling Croke what he'd deduced would inevitably put them in danger. Yet failing to tell him might damage his uncle's mission; a mission that Jay had committed himself to helping succeed.

It was what they called a quandary.

His eyes narrowed. His lips tightened. Life missions, if they were to mean anything, had to take precedence over friendships, even friendship with the woman one might eventually marry. And it wasn't as if he was without power in this business. He had the power to protect them. In fact, by protecting Rachel, he could prove his worth to her, making their eventual consummation all the more likely.

He walked back to his desk. He picked up his phone and made the call.

III

Curiosity and dignity had fought like rival angels over Croke when invited to climb down the rope to see first hand what lay in the underground chamber. Dignity had won.

He watched the feed on a laptop screen. The passage. The antechamber. The vault itself. No sign of it anywhere. He hadn't expected it, not after having seen the empty plinth. Yet it was another major setback. And time was running out fast.

His mobile rang. Avram Kohen's nephew Jakob. The one who'd sent them here. 'What do you want?' he asked him tightly.

'I know where it is,' said Jakob. 'I know *exactly* where it is.'

'That's what you said last time.'

'No. I only said it made sense. This time I'm sure.'

'Go on, then. Where?'

'I want your word on something first. Luke Hayward and Rachel Parkes are my friends. They're not to come any harm.'

Croke scowled. So that was where they'd gone from Victoria. To see Kohen. 'Fine,' he said. 'You have my word. They won't come to any harm at our hands. Now where is it?' He listened as Kohen talked. 'You're quite sure about this?' he asked, when he was done. 'You've already steered us wrong twice.'

'I'm sure,' said Kohen. And he launched into a confusing explanation of the vault beneath Croke's feet, of ciphers, of iron anchors and state funerals.

'Okay,' said Croke, cutting him off. 'We'll take a look. If we find it, you'll be coming with us, right?'

'Yes.'

'Your uncle said something about supplies. Anything you need will have to be at City Airport by mid-afternoon.' He gave him contact details for his pilot Craig Bray then ended the call and stood there thinking through next steps. He tried Walters first. 'I told you they'd break cover,' he told him when Walters answered.

'Where?'

'St Paul's Cathedral. But listen: I gave Kohen my word that they wouldn't come to any harm. Not at our hands.

314

And we need him on our side, for the moment at least. So if anything should happen to them, it can't look like it was us.'

'Got you, boss. Leave it to me.'

Croke went over to the well shaft, shouted down for Morgenstern. The NCT man clambered athletically back up top again. 'I just got a call,' Croke told him, leading him to a secluded corner. 'It seems it's in London after all.'

'For fuck's sake!' scowled Morgenstern. 'How many more dead ends are we going to hit?'

'This wasn't a dead end,' said Croke. 'They built this place to hold it; they simply found somewhere better. And now we know where that is.'

'Where?'

'St Paul's Cathedral.'

'No way. No. Fucking. Way. It's miles beyond my authority.'

'Your authority comes from your Commander in Chief,' said Croke. 'Are you planning to let her down?'

Morgenstern bit his teeth together, brought his anger back under control. 'It's not like that,' he said. 'I'd do it if I could. But I can't. I just can't. I don't have that kind of pull. Crane Court was different. I could do it on my own initiative, explain myself afterwards. But not St Paul's. We'd need explicit ministerial approval. And they'd want some kind of in-person briefing. With evidence too. Hard evidence. Not some mysterious phantom source.'

'My informant has just assured me that the terrorists from Crane Court have planted a dirty bomb in the crypt of St Paul's Cathedral. There's a national memorial service tomorrow night at which the Prime Minister, his cabinet and the whole royal family are going to be honoured guests. Are you honestly telling me you're prepared to let that service go ahead without first making absolutely sure it's safe?'

Morgenstern nodded, seeing how he might be able to make it work. 'An attack on the Royal Family,' he said. 'On the British government. On democracy itself. We couldn't possibly risk that.'

'No,' said Croke. 'We couldn't.'

TWENTY-NINE

I

It was quite a climb to the top of the dome, particularly with the Monument already in their legs. Luke and Rachel allowed themselves a minute's respite on the stone gallery, savouring the breeze as they looked out between fat stone balusters down over the river and south London.

A man bumped into Luke's back, not looking on where he was going, too intent on his companion, a charming redhead. 'Quite something, huh?' he commented to her. 'How often in life do you get to stand on a miracle?'

'A miracle?' asked the redhead.

'The Germans threw everything at this place. *Everything.* Didn't hit it once. If that's not a miracle, what is?'

Beside Luke, Rachel stiffened. He glanced curiously at her. Her eyes were tight and her lips were clamped

317

together. He raised an eyebrow. She shook her head, waited until the couple were gone. 'I'm sorry,' she said. 'But I *hate* that bullshit story. St Paul's was hit multiple times. It survived because of the wardens who risked their lives staying up here during the raids to put out fires before they could catch. And, anyway, who the hell wants to believe in a God who'd save his precious building from the bombs, while letting tens of thousands die?'

Luke nodded. He agreed with her viewpoint, yet it didn't explain her intensity of reaction. 'You never did tell me about your brother,' he said.

'No,' she agreed.

'What was it? A bomb?'

'Please.'

'Was it in London? Some terrorist attack?'

She shook her head. 'No.'

'The army, then?'

She gave a little grimace. 'Afghanistan.'

'And it's not getting better?'

'It's not going to get better. It's his life now. *Our* lives.'

'And that's why you need the Newton papers? To pay for his care?'

Her eyes began to water. She blinked furiously, wiped them with thumb and finger, as though ashamed of her weakness. 'They say he's fit enough to work. He's not fit enough to work. He's nothing like fit enough. He's lost his legs and his hand, and the blast fucked up his insides and his mind. He can't concentrate. His memory plays tricks on him. He gets frustrated. He gets angry.'

'Aren't there schemes?'

'There are a thousand schemes. There's just no money in them. The government keeps reneging. And now they're trying to buy us off with a lump sum. But it's not enough. It's not even *close* to being enough. Do you have any idea how much a lifetime of care costs?'

'No.'

She sighed, held up a hand in apology. 'They owe Bren better, that's all I'm saying. They owe everyone in his situation better. They took their legs and arms and guts and brains for their absurd fucking wars, but now that the bill's due they're not only refusing to pay, they're trying to hide their victims out of sight so they don't have to look at them and have their precious consciences troubled. Well, fuck them. Fuck the lot of them.'

'Are you suing?'

She gave a nod. 'They keep postponing our hearings. It's just a ploy, of course. They want us to run out of money so that we'll have to accept their offer. But Bren will be screwed if we accept. All his comrades will be screwed. So we need enough to see us through. But I can't seem to make it happen.' She shook her head helplessly. 'I already have nightmares about how much debt I'm in. No one will lend us any more, except at such ridiculous rates of interest that we might as well give up. So yes, I need those papers.'

He touched her arm to express both his sympathy and his willingness to help her once they were through this, but also to steer her towards the steps. They trudged up to the golden gallery. A woman guide was sitting on a fold-up wooden chair outside the door, welcoming new arrivals with a smile and an invitation to ask questions. They were amazingly high. The grey stone balustrade was crumbling a little and discoloured with small islands of damp. Luke turned his back to it, leaning against it as he looked upwards and inwards, in case the answer to their quest lay at its peak; but the camber of the dome concealed it from their view.

'Thank god for the balustrade,' murmured Rachel, as she leaned back beside him.

'Thank Wren, you mean,' smiled Luke.

'Actually,' murmured the guide. 'Wren *hated* it.'

'Really?'

She stood and came to join them, bashful of being overheard. 'He thought it broke the harmony of the whole machine. That was how he put it himself: the harmony of the whole machine. It always stuck in my mind, that phrase, for some reason. Like he saw this place as a fearfully clever contraption for bringing about the will of God.'

Luke touched the balustrade. 'He lost the argument, then.'

'Newton talked him round.'

'Newton?' frowned Rachel.

'It was after they'd put Wren out to grass,' she told them. 'Newton was his close friend, and he sat on the committee to complete the cathedral, so he became their go-between, explaining decisions like the balustrade to him, making sure there weren't any technical reasons not to do them.'

'This committee to complete,' said Luke. 'How would we find out more about it?'

'You'd have to speak to Clarence,' she told him. 'He's our head librarian.'

'And where would we find him?'

'I'd imagine the library might be a good place to start.' She must have realized how tart she sounded, for she blushed and put a hand to her mouth. 'Do forgive me,' she said. 'I don't know what it is. These things just pop out.'

'It's okay,' laughed Luke. 'How do we get there?'

'It's on the Triforium level. Back below the Whispering Gallery.'

'What do you think?' Luke asked Rachel.

'Let's give it a go,' she said.

II

And ye shall give the red heifer unto Eleazar the priest, and she shall be brought forth without the camp, and she shall be slain before his face. And Eleazar the priest shall take of her blood with his finger, and sprinkle of her blood toward the front of the tent of meeting seven times. And the heifer shall be burnt in his sight. Her skin, her flesh, her blood and her dung, shall be burnt.

Avram stripped naked to purify himself in the chamber of immersion then dried himself with towels of white linen from the table of vestments.

The Talmud says: *When they are clothed in priestly garments, they are priests; but when they are not clothed in priestly garments, they are not priests.*

The white garments first, the woven six-ply linen tunic and trousers. The belt next, then the turban.

When he'd first started on this quest many years before, Avram had hoped to bring about the new Temple within the confines of strict Judaic law. He and his fellows had therefore obsessed over what chemicals to use for bleaching the linen and the precise array of the twelve stones on the ephod. He'd become intoxicated with textual analysis, the sense that he was studying the mind of God.

One afternoon, at a friend's house, they'd all got into a furious debate about the person who'd carry out the actual sacrifice. The texts seemed clear enough: it had to be a male of the priestly line, a Kohen like Avram himself. He had to be past Bar Mitzvah age, and he could never have been in contact with death. That was to say, not once in his at least thirteen years could he have trodden on an ancient grave or been inside a building in which anyone had ever died. But the modern world made such conditions impossible. The solution, therefore, had been to raise such a child *outside* the modern world. The discussion that afternoon had been about how. How to identify which male infants should be taken at birth from their parents; how high off the ground they'd need to build the compound in which the child would be reared to maturity; how then to get him from his compound to the place of sacrifice without contamination. The discussion had become increasingly heated. Voices had been raised, insults hurled. Avram had stopped participating after a while, had instead watched with a growing sense of the absurdity of it all – these fantasies of raised compounds and babies snatched from mothers' breasts, and it had culminated in a moment of insight so blinding that it had been almost painful: these men were lapdogs yapping from behind a fence. Open the gate for them and they wouldn't know what to do.

He'd left without another word and he'd never been back.

The ephod next, then the breastplate. The turban and the crown. By rights they should be doing this on the Mount of Olives, looking down on Mount Moriah and the Temple itself. But the Temple wasn't yet there, and to look down on those Muslim obscenities was unthinkable. He went therefore to the wall covered by the great white sheet. He paused a moment, to add a little drama, then gave the rope a tug. The sheet flapped as it fell, revealing a plastered wall behind, painted into a dream landscape with bright acrylics: Mount Moriah cleansed of the Dome and the al-Aqsa mosque, the Third Temple standing gloriously in their place.

The cries from Shlomo and his men were cries of exaltation. And Avram raised his arms high and wide in triumph, for all the world Moses winning battles on the mountaintop.

THIRTY

I

The Triforium had only recently been opened to the public, and it showed in the washed stonework, the waxed display cases, the fresh white gloss of the window-frames. By contrast, the library itself was deliberately gloomy thanks to the tattered drapes that had been hung over the tall windows to protect the old books from direct sunlight.

The only person inside was a man in clerical garb with ruffled grey hair and a fluffy beard who was studying tiny holes in a leather binding through a magnifying glass. They went to stand across his worktable from him. He evidently hoped that they'd leave if he ignored them long enough, but they waited him out and finally he sighed and looked up. 'Yes?' he asked.

'What are those holes?' asked Luke, in an effort to break the ice.

'What do they look like?'

'They look like woodworm.'

'Well, then,' he said.

'In leather?'

'The leather's only a thin cover,' murmured Rachel. 'There are actually thin panels of wood beneath.'

The man smiled in surprise. 'Very good, my dear,' he said.

'Maple?' she asked.

'Oak.'

'How can you tell?' asked Luke.

The man nodded at Rachel, inviting her to answer. 'The grain imprints itself on the leather,' she said. 'Each wood has a different signature.'

'I never knew that.'

'Why would you?'

The man set down his magnifying glass, finally prepared to give them his attention. 'What may I do for you?'

'We're looking for a Clarence,' said Rachel. 'You wouldn't be a Clarence, by any chance?'

'Dear me, no,' he said. 'I'm not a Clarence. I'm a Trevor. A Clarence is in Finland, I'm afraid. Finland or Norway. One of those places. The eagle owls are about to fledge, I'm told. But maybe I can help.'

'We're trying to find out about Isaac Newton's involvement with the committee to complete St Paul's.'

'Oh, yes. That really is a matter for a Clarence, I'm afraid. Not at all the right area for a mere Trevor like myself.'

'When will he be back?'

'The week after next, I believe. Eagle owls are no respecters of schedules. They fledge whenever they damned well please. But you could always consult the records of the Wren Society if you're in a rush. They'll have what you need, I imagine.'

'You don't have a set here, by any chance?'

'We do, we do, we most certainly do; but I'm afraid to say we're not *that* kind of a library. Try the British Library or the Guildhall. *They'll* let just about anyone read their books.'

Luke thanked him and made to leave, glad to get away before impatience got the better of him. But Rachel wasn't quite done yet. She paused at the door, glanced back. 'I don't suppose you Trevors would know anything about a man called John Evelyn, would you?'

'A man called John Evelyn?' said Trevor. 'A *man* called *John Evelyn*!' He shook his head with great good humour, pushed himself to his feet, came round to join them. 'I once wrote an article for the *Church Times* on a man called John Evelyn. On his book comparing ancient and modern styles of architecture, to be precise. At least, not

Evelyn's book so much as his translation of the essays put together by de Chambray. But you get the idea. It caused a tremendous sensation.'

'Your article?' asked Rachel sweetly.

Trevor laughed affably, as though to acknowledge that he'd earned a little chaffing. 'No. Chambray's book, and Evelyn's translation of it. I couldn't even interest my own dear mother in my article.'

'So what was it about?' asked Luke. 'Evelyn's book, I mean?'

'He liked architecture to reflect the divine mind. That was why he was so bullish on Corinthian columns. Designed by God Himself for Solomon's Temple, you know.'

Luke shared a glance with Rachel. 'Is that right?' he asked.

'Oh, yes. And his plan for rebuilding London after the Great Fire was based on the Kabbalah. The original Kabbalah, I mean, not the ridiculous red-string bracelet travesty so favoured by Madonna and her ilk. Specifically, on the *Sephirot*, the Jewish Tree of Life. You've come across it, I imagine.'

'Not in connection with city planning.'

The Trevor looked around for something to write on, but there was nothing to hand, nothing that he dared use at least. 'It's essentially an arrangement of ten or eleven small circles along three parallel lines,' he said.

'Three circles along each of the outside lines, four or five along the central one. Now lay the whole thing on its side and join the circles together like in a map of the underground and that's pretty much Evelyn's plan for London. All the circles were existing landmarks, of course, with St Paul's in pride of place bang in the middle. We corresponded with the *Sephirah* for *Tipheret*, if I recall correctly, which represents the sun.'

Shrieks of laughter sounded in the corridor outside. Heels slapping on tiles, schoolchildren testing the bounds of discipline. They waited until they'd passed and silence was restored. 'So what happened?' asked Rachel. 'To Evelyn's design, I mean?'

'Nothing.'

'Nothing?'

'It was too ambitious ever to be workable, frankly. Landowners kicked up too much of a fuss. So they gave it up and settled for widening the streets a little instead, improving the building codes.'

'And that was the end of the Tree of Life?'

'Yes. Unless you listen to a particularly exasperating correspondent of mine who insists that Wren incorporated Evelyn's ideas into St Paul's.'

'Really? How?'

'Send him a letter and ask. He loves to receive a letter.'

Rachel touched his wrist. 'Can't you just give us a hint? Please.'

'I can't believe you'd have me make his case for him,' sighed Trevor. He looked around furtively, almost as though fearful of being seen. 'Very well, then,' he said. 'Come with me.'

II

And the priest shall take cedar-wood, and hyssop, and scarlet, and cast it into the midst of the burning of the heifer. Then the priest shall wash his clothes, and he shall bathe his flesh in water, and afterward he may come into the camp, and the priest shall be unclean until the even.

The altar was a latticework of unblemished planks of cedar and cypress three good strides long by two wide. It was sloped slightly inwards, like the bottom two courses of a pyramid, and it was high as Avram's hip.

Shlomo and his men bound the heifer with ropes of reed then heaved her over to this low wooden tower and half-placed, half-threw her on it. Avram climbed up too. It was trickier than he'd anticipated, weighted down as he was by heavy robes and with a full-grown cow struggling against her cords. His foot slipped and he banged his ankle hard, provoking such a fierce spike of pain that he had to pause and close his eyes until it passed.

He took the ceremonial knife from his belt, pinned the heifer's head with his left arm. He paused a moment for effect then cut her throat. Blood gushed. He cupped a hand beneath the stream, stood tall, and turned to face Shlomo, his men and the painting of the Temple Mount. He flicked his fingers seven times, the blood cooling and caking as he was at it. He wanted to wipe his hand on his robes, but he restrained himself. He climbed down, lit the wooden torch with a lighter, then held it to the kindling until it caught and began to blaze. He picked up the log of stripped cedar. 'This cedar?' he asked.

'Yes,' said Shlomo and the others.

'This cedar?'

'Yes.'

'*This* cedar?'

A shout now: 'Yes.'

He set it back down, picked up the hyssop. 'This hyssop?' he asked.

'Yes,' they said.

'This hyssop?'

'Yes.'

'*This* hyssop?'

'Yes.'

He picked up the bowl of crimson dye next, repeated the invocations. Then he wrapped the hyssop and the cedar in wool and threw it on the fire. It was already so hot that he had to step back and avert his face. Smoke gathered in a thick, black canopy underlit by orange flame, like hell seen from beneath. Yet in his mind Avram was watching something else: the Dome as it collapsed, the Temple Mount engulfed in purging fire. And all around him they began to chant and cry out with joy, as though the Messiah himself was come.

THIRTY-ONE

I

There was an organ gallery and walkway at the rear of the Triforium that enabled passage from one side of the cathedral to the other without first returning back downstairs. Nearly a hundred feet above the cathedral floor, it offered a magnificent view along the main aisle to the altar; which was no doubt why a TV gantry was being assembled as they crossed, and why two women were scrubbing the floor while another waxed the black-and-gold balcony rail.

'Our poor Dean has been having nightmares,' confided Trevor. 'He thinks the whole world will be watching tomorrow night, and snickering at our stonework.'

'It must be stressful,' said Rachel, 'putting on an event like this.'

They reached the far side. Architects' plans hung along the wall. Trevor led them to the fourth, a bird's eye view of the cathedral. 'See these,' he said, pointing out a number of circles. 'They're open areas designed to echo the main dome. Three on either flank with a spine of them running down the centre. There's your Tree of Life.'

'There are more than five circles on the centre line,' pointed out Luke.

'You asked me what my correspondent would say,' retorted Trevor. 'This is it. Like I said, his theory is bunk.'

'How would he explain the discrepancy?' asked Rachel.

Trevor sighed. 'Wren had less control over his plans than people imagine. The Dean and the King forced him into countless alterations. Everything changed but the dome itself. It features in all his designs.'

Rachel frowned. 'Wren did multiple designs of St Paul's? I didn't realize.'

'Oh, yes. What we're in today is actually his *fifth* design, depending on how you count them; and far from his favourite.' He led them across the corridor, unlocked a door, ushered them into a large room dominated by a vast model of a cathedral. 'This is the Warrant Design,' said Trevor. 'It cost Wren a small fortune to have it made. The Commission turned it down flat.'

'And this was Wren's favourite?'

'No. He preferred it to what we've got, but his favourite was more radical still. You know, of course, that churches and cathedrals are traditionally laid out like a Latin cross, to commemorate the crucifixion. Wren decided to base his design on the Greek Cross instead, effectively an octagon with every other side indented.' He led them to a yew-wood map case, pulled out the wide shallow drawers in turn, checking the labels on the acid-free folders inside until finally he drew one out. He set it on top, untied its red string bow.

'Are these Wren's originals?' asked Luke.

'Good heavens, no. You don't honestly imagine I'd trust *street people* near his originals, do you? But they are *early*. And they are *important*. So no touching.' He opened up the folder, pulled out a sheet, laid it on top. 'Here we go. An indented octagon, as I said.'

'I love it,' said Rachel.

'The King did too. But not the Dean. It wasn't enough for it to *look* good, you see. It had to work too. A church needs a focal point for services and sermons. The focal point of an octagon is its centre. But that means having your congregation seated all around you, leaving many unable to see properly, or even hear. You could, of course, put the altar against a wall, but that would rather negate the purpose of the design. And then there were the acoustics! My Lord! Don't get me started on the acoustics!'

Luke nodded. 'Strange that he should even have suggested it.'

'Yes. Well. Paris was the great centre of architectural fashion at the time. Wren had his head turned by the buzz there about a Bourbon chapel planned for St-Denis. *That* never got built either. Such designs work best on paper. And the technical challenges would have been enormous. To accommodate the same number of people, the dome would have needed to be even bigger that it is now. And it weighs nearly seventy thousand tons as it is. *Seventy thousand tons!* And even that almost proved too much.'

'How do you mean?'

'The piers and pillars started to crack and burst from the weight. They got so bad that Wren had to dig up the crypt floor and anchor them to each other with huge iron chains.'

'Wren dug up the crypt?' asked Luke, glancing at Rachel. 'When?'

'They began noticing the cracks in the 1690s, I believe. But Wren spent years in denial. He couldn't bear to acknowledge that he'd made a mistake. Besides, the obvious solution was these iron anchors I mentioned, yet Wren had mocked other architects for such tricks. Pride's a terrible thing, isn't it? But by around 1705, I think, it got so bad he had no choice. It's still a taboo subject among Wren fans. He or his disciples even spread rumours that he'd had the iron anchors cut through, just to prove that they weren't really necessary.'

'What bit of the crypt is beneath the dome?' asked Luke.

'Nelson's tomb,' said Trevor, returning the folder of plans to its place. 'They lowered his coffin through a hole in the main floor during the service. A fine looking thing, though frankly far too *black* for my taste. I know death isn't the cheeriest of events, but I'd still fancy something lighter myself. A good pine, if you'll forgive the pun. Though why should you?' he added gloomily. 'It's an *awful* pun.'

'I've made worse,' said Luke.

'Very kind of you to say so, but I'm not altogether sure that's possible.'

'Nelson didn't die for another hundred years after 1705,' pointed out Rachel. 'What was in the crypt until then?'

'Nothing much, as far as I know, other than Wren's own tomb. It only became *the* place to be buried after Nelson. Then everyone wanted in.'

'And Nelson's coffin?' asked Luke. 'Is it beneath or above the floor?'

'Above,' said Trevor. 'But why do you ask?'

'No reason,' said Luke.

II

Avram packed the jar of ashes safely into the passenger footwell of his truck then bade farewell to Shlomo and his men and drove southwest towards the coast. His back and ankle began to ache from the accumulated driving, yet it was lack of sleep, engine fumes and the heat of the day that really got to him. He kept having to pinch the skin on the back of his hand to keep himself awake.

He reached Netanya in good time, however. He stopped for something to eat then continued to the warehouse. He entered the passcode into the keypad and the steel shutter clanked slowly upwards. He parked inside, lowered the shutter again, and turned on the lights. The warehouse was packed with the detritus of a hundred house clearances: old washing machines and refrigerators, boxes of books, rolled up carpets, beds and sofas. The only items that looked out of place were three dust carts he'd had stolen several months before from the streets of Jerusalem.

He checked his watch: still half an hour until Danel arrived. Plenty of time to check in with Croke. He set up the satellite phone outside and hurried through the security protocols.

'Finally,' grunted Croke. 'I was beginning to think you'd bolted.'

'I've been busy.'

'We've all been busy.'

'You've found it, then?'

A grunt of laughter. 'How the hell are we supposed to find it when you and your idiot nephew keep sending us to the wrong damned places?' And he ran Avram through recent events, including the switch back to London.

'You'll find it,' said Avram, unperturbed. 'What's destined is destined.'

'Maybe. But we're cutting it fine. Incidentally, we'll be filming it live for our friends in the States. Will you want to watch too?'

'Of course,' said Avram. 'And my nephew is to be there as well.'

'I'll see what I can arrange.'

'No,' said Avram. 'He is to be there. And then he is to accompany it on every step of its journey.'

'Like I said, I'll see what—'

'You're not listening to me,' said Avram. 'I know what can be done with technology these days. I know about special effects and computer-generated imagery. I know about switches and decoys. So let me make it clear: this won't happen unless my nephew verifies it to my complete satisfaction then stays with it all the way. Do you understand?'

'Fine,' sighed Croke. 'I'll see to it.'

There was still no sign of Danel, so Avram now took care of another piece of business. He set up a new Hotmail account on his laptop and filled its contacts list with email addresses for as many journalists, media companies, embassies and pressure groups as he could find. Then he opened a new Word document and drafted his two sets of demands, searching the net for the names of suitable prisoners for the first, double-checking the registration number of Croke's jet for the second.

He was just about finished when Danel finally arrived at the wheel of a white minibus. Avram waved in welcome. They'd first met some four years ago while he'd been on a tour of the settlements, lecturing on the Third Temple. Danel had stood up during the Q&A and asked bluntly why so many Jews *talked* about bringing down the Dome, yet never *did* anything. A common enough question, but while everyone else had laughed, Danel himself had remained stonefaced. Avram had intercepted him at the door, had asked him whether *he* was prepared to do something about it. Not only he, it had turned out, but his fellow settler also, enraged by the recent demolition of their Havat Gilad homes.

They climbed down from the minibus, stretched and joked. Ten of them in all. In their T-shirts, shorts, trainers and sunglasses, they could scarcely have drawn a starker contrast with Shlomo and his Haredim. They even had two women with them. Yet, though young and seemingly casual, they were in truth tough, disciplined and incredibly angry.

Avram nodded greeting to them all. 'Let's get busy,' he said. 'We've got work to do.'

III

Police officers were decanting from three vans outside St Paul's as Walters and his men arrived. They gave no sense of imminent action, however, but were standing around chatting among themselves, awaiting orders.

'What now?' asked Kieran.

Walters shrugged. Snatching people was hard at the best of times. A double snatch in a tourist spot surrounded by police . . . Yet they had to shut Luke and Rachel up if they could. 'Let's find them first, eh?' he said, buying tickets and leading the way along the aisle.

'And then what?'

Walters nodded up at the whispering gallery that encircled the base of the dome a hundred feet or so above them. 'The boss and his mate are about to have this place cleared,' he said. 'They're going to give the police orders to secure the perimeter then stay outside until the NCT guys arrive. That means it'll soon be completely empty in here. Wouldn't it be a terrible shame if a couple of people panicked during the evacuation for some reason, and fell from way up there?'

'Fat chance we'll be lucky enough to find them up there,' said Kieran.

'Who said anything about luck?' asked Walters. 'Do this right and they'll go up there of their own accord. It's just a matter of finding them and showing ourselves to them in the right way. We can herd them like sheep wherever we want.'

Pete grinned. 'Then we just wait until the place is clear, and finish this.'

THIRTY-TWO

I

The floor of the crypt was crowded with memorial plaques for the great and the good, so that picking one's way between them seemed like a macabre game of hopscotch. That impression was heightened by the gloomy lighting, for though there were chandeliers and wall-lamps everywhere, they were all turned atmospherically low.

Luke and Rachel found Nelson's ebony coffin easily enough, high on a marble plinth between Wellington's tomb and the Churchill Gate. It wasn't the coffin that caught Luke's attention, however, but rather the layout of the place itself, a small dome supported by eight pairs of pillars, just like the main cupola on the floor above.

'So?' asked Rachel, when he pointed it out to her.

'The tomb of Christian Rosencreutz,' said Luke. 'The vault beneath the Ashmolean. The dome upstairs. The Greek Cross design. Now this. Everywhere we go, eight sides topped by a dome.'

She nodded. 'What does it mean?'

'I don't know. But it can't be coincidence, can it?'

The floor around the tomb was laid with geometric mosaics. He crouched by one depicting the mystery of the Trinity, and smiled to himself. Newton would have just loved that. 'So what are we thinking?' he asked, looking up at Rachel.

'You first.'

'Okay. How about this: Tradescant the Elder is on his travels when he acquires something extraordinary. Maybe he comes to believe he's been sold a fake, and is embarrassed by it; or maybe he thinks it's just too precious to declare. Whatever, he doesn't put it on display, doesn't even tell his son about it. But then Ashmole comes cataloguing and recognizes it for what it is. He sets his heart on it and tricks Tradescant the Younger and his wife out of it. Then he brings in the other members of the cabal. He can't bear to part with it until he dies, however, at which time he leaves it to Newton. But Newton, Wren and Evelyn want it in London rather than the Ashmolean. They want it here beneath the dome.'

'But they can't bring it here until Wren has built a vault for it,' said Rachel, picking up the thread. 'And that's not so easy, what with this place on a schedule and a budget. So he starts muttering about cracks in the piers, giving himself the perfect excuse to dig up the floor. But now he can't bear the thought of people mocking him for his mistake, so he spreads a rumour about cutting through the anchors before laying them. And he and the others also arrange for a cipher to be left in the Ashmolean vault, perhaps as a kind of apology to Ashmole for having reneged on their—'

Alarm bells began to sound at that moment, screeching like a natal ward. Everyone stopped what they were doing, but calmly, assuming it was a malfunction or a drill. But the noise went on and on, and the guides and wardens began hustling visitors towards the exits. Luke glanced at Rachel. 'It's those bastards again,' he muttered. 'I'll bet it is.'

Rachel grimaced. 'How did they find us?'

'Maybe they didn't. Maybe they just cracked the cipher themselves.'

'If they've found the cipher, they have to know we were in the vault before them. They're bound to be looking for us.' Even as she spoke, she recognized a man near the exit, scouring the crowds as they filed out. She grabbed Luke's wrist and pulled him behind a pillar. 'Our fair-haired friend,' she whispered.

'Hell,' said Luke.

'What do we do? They'll be watching all the exits.'

He nodded towards the Triforium steps. 'Let's try Trevor. Tell him everything, throw ourselves on his mercy.'

'You think he'll believe us?'

'Only one way to find out,' said Luke.

II

When Avram had first resolved to bring down the Dome, he'd taken it almost for granted that the hardest part would be the assault itself. But as he'd studied the various problems, he'd quickly changed his mind. The Temple Mount was surprisingly thinly protected: a hard shell of Israeli police checkpoints around a soft centre of *Waqf*, the Muslim religious trust's guards, armed only with batons and the like. No. The hardest parts were recruiting the right personnel, arranging the necessary supplies and then – most difficult of all – getting them all into position at the right time. For the Old City was the worst place in the world from which to launch an attack like this. Its compressed nature, heritage status and paranoid atmosphere made it almost impossible to stash munitions for any length of time. And the surrounding new city was little better, infested as it was with snoops and gossips, with police and soldiers.

Two of Danel's men heaved the last of the washing machines aside. 'Is this it?' asked Danel, kicking a roughened patch of re-laid concrete with his heel.

'That's it,' agreed Avram.

They attacked the concrete with hand drills, quickly breaking it up and clearing it away to reveal the hatchway of an old fuel sump. Three of Danel's men climbed down inside and passed up supplies that the others laid out on the warehouse floor: nine Predator short-range assault weapons fitted with anti-bunker payloads; body-armour, night-vision goggles, assault rifles and handguns; explosive charges and detonators; military clothing and boots; laptops and cameras; a roll of blue silk, two deflated neoprene mattresses and six canisters of industrial foam.

Avram plucked at Danel's sleeve while this was going on. 'I need a word,' he murmured.

'About what?'

'About Ana and Ruth. Our friends tonight won't have women.'

Danel scowled. Like many settlers, he despised the Haredim as parasites and cowards. Only by assuring him that Shlomo and his friends had been volunteers in the IDF's *Yeshivat Hesder* had Avram persuaded him to accept them as allies at all.

'Ana is the best I've got,' Danel protested. 'And Ruth is *hungry*. They murdered her man.'

'She'll still get to eat,' said Avram. 'But with the Predators instead.'

Danel nodded. It wasn't exactly a surprise, for they'd discussed and planned for the possibility. 'I'll let them know.'

'Thank you.'

They returned to the others. Avram checked the supplies against his list. No point taking more than they needed. They returned the surplus to the sump then packed everything but the missiles into a mix of tourist and army backpacks. The tourist backpacks went onto the minibus, so that a cursory inspection would find nothing more sinister than a group of kibbutzim on their way for a night or two in Jerusalem. He turned on the Predators, entered the GPS coordinates for their targets, then had them loaded, along with the three dust carts, onto the back of his own truck. They packed the army backpacks into the dust carts then laid the assault rifles, handguns and spare clips on top of them, before covering them up with sanitation workers' jackets, caps and bibs. It was a tight fit, but Avram had calculated well. They packed all this contraband as far inside the truck as it would go, then hid it behind a false wall of old white goods and second-hand furniture.

Avram checked his watch. By some miracle, they were half an hour ahead of schedule. Just as well, considering Jerusalem's traffic. 'We should leave,' he said.

Danel shook his head. 'Not yet. You still owe us something.'

'The rest of your money?' Avram pulled a face of distaste. 'I told you: *after* this is done.'

'I'm not talking about the money,' said Danel. 'I'm saying isn't it time you told us the fucking plan.'

III

Climbing the steps to the dome was like fighting a water-fall, hundreds of tourists pouring down on them, many a little bit panicky from the continued shrieking of the alarms. Luke forced a passage for himself and Rachel, ignoring the guides and wardens who kept trying to stop them, making theatre with his hands, pointing upwards and shouting that they were looking for a friend. They reached the Triforium door, slipped inside, and walked briskly along the deserted corridor to the library. But it was closed and locked and there was no sign of Trevor, no sign of anyone.

A door banged behind them. They turned to see the fair-headed man walking purposefully towards them along the corridor, shouting into his mobile to make himself audible over the still-clamouring fire alarm. Luke swore as he and Rachel hurried away. The door to the rear gallery was locked, so they went left instead and found themselves at the top of a spiral staircase with a dizzying view down to the ground below. They'd barely started down it when Blackbeard appeared at the foot and began climbing. Luke hesitated. He didn't much fancy taking on fair-hair, but he had far more chance against him than against Blackbeard.

'Back up?' asked Rachel.

'Back up,' he agreed.

There was a small fire extinguisher on the stairs. Luke grabbed it to use as a weapon. Fair-hair stopped when he saw them, even took a step backwards, doing wonders for Luke's confidence. But then he drew his taser and a moment later the bruiser appeared behind him at the far end of the corridor. They were cornered.

A large oak door had a vast No Entry sign on it. It looked as though it hadn't been used in decades. Rachel slid the bolts, lifted the latch and pulled it open. The reason for the No Entry sign immediately became apparent. There was an organ on the other side. She got down onto her hands and knees and crawled beneath the keyboard, Luke following immediately behind. He stood up on the far side and found himself on the balcony that girdled the inside of the cathedral like a belt. Far below, two guides were helping the last of the stragglers out the main doors. Luke shouted for help, but the alarms drowned out his voice. And then they were gone.

The balcony to their left was blocked by fat organ pipes, so they headed right instead. But then a door opened ahead of them, and the bruiser came out. They turned back. They couldn't escape back beneath the organ, for fair-hair was on guard with his taser. Luke looked over the railings. The balcony floor jutted out a couple of inches or so. Not much of a toehold. But by clinging to the rail, they could crab their way along it, bypassing the organ pipes to reach the rear gallery. And from there they could cross to the other side of the cathedral and make their escape. It meant braving an eighty-foot drop to the cathedral floor, however, and one false step would be the end of them.

Rachel shook her head. 'I can't,' she said.

'We have to,' he said. 'We're out of options.'

Her face was pale, but she nodded. He clambered over the rail first, then helped her. He let her go first so that she could set her own pace. The narrow stone ledge was hard on their toes as they sidled along. Organ pipes protruding over the balcony forced them to hunker down like backstroke swimmers before a race. The sharp edges of the wrought-iron stanchions were cruel on their fingers. Still crouched, they reached the junction with the rear gallery. Rachel slipped as she made the awkward turn, lost her footing. She clung to the stanchions and scrabbled stonework with the sides of her shoes. Luke anchored himself with one hand, grabbed her wrist with the other. He tried to lift her but he didn't have the right posture. She'd have to do it herself. She hooked one foot back up, then the other. But she slipped again and the jolt ripped her grip from the stanchions. She'd have plunged to her death had Luke not had her by her wrist, but her sudden weight forced him down onto one knee on the narrow ledge, so that now he was holding her swinging above the drop, screaming and screaming. He tried to lift her back up, but he couldn't, not with just one hand.

The strain on his fingers, arm and shoulder was extra-ordinary. His tendons stretched; his grip grew weaker. He grimaced and cried out with the unbearable knowledge that this was a battle he couldn't hope to win.

Throughout it all, he'd been vaguely aware of scrabbling noises at the rear gallery's locked door. He'd hoped the lock would buy them time to make good their escape, but now the hinges creaked and he looked up to see Blackbeard arrive on the other side of the balcony. All he had to do now was break Luke's tenuous hold on the stanchion to send both him and Rachel plummeting to their deaths.

That decision was evidently above his paygrade, however. For, even as Luke watched, he glanced across at the balcony behind him, for all the world like a gladiator looking up from the Coliseum floor for his emperor's thumb.

THIRTY-THREE

I

'You know the plan,' said Avram. 'We've been through the plan a dozen times.'

'We know the plan for getting in,' said Danel. 'We know the plan for placing the charges so that they bring down the Dome. What we don't yet know is the plan for getting away afterwards. It seems to us that if we're still inside when it comes down, we'll be crushed to death. It seems to us that if we're *not* inside, then we'll be outside being ripped limb from limb by ten thousand Arab scum. You may think us cowards, Avram, but neither of those options exactly appeal.'

'And neither will happen.'

'You've always said that you couldn't tell us until the day itself, because it would put too many other people in jeopardy if any of us were captured and interrogated. Fair enough. We accepted that. But today is the day itself and now we want to know.'

'It's still too early.' He held up his hands to quell their protests. 'You all knew there'd be risks. We're about to take one of the biggest right now: driving two vehicles filled with munitions and other supplies into the heart of Jerusalem, then hoisting them onto our backs and carrying them in plain sight into the Old City. Anything could go wrong. *Anything*. And if it does, the more of us who know the whole plan, the more dangerous it will be for our other partners.' He turned to Danel. 'You didn't believe that I'd get you your first tranche of money. I did. You didn't believe that I'd come through with the missiles, the explosives, the guns and all our other supplies. I did. Everything I've promised, I've delivered. So please trust me just a little longer. Wait until we're safely inside the Old City and—'

'Once we're inside the Old City it will be too late for us to back out.'

Their faces were implacable. Avram knew he had to give them something. 'Very well,' he sighed. 'What exactly do you want to know?'

'I just told you: we're going to be in a building that's set to blow, completely surrounded by the police and the army, with an Arab mob baying for our blood. You promised us a foolproof plan for getting away, free and clear. We want to know what it is.'

'Ah,' said Avram. He smiled around at them all. 'Then I'm afraid I may have misled you a little. We're *not* going to be getting away free and clear. We're going to be giving ourselves up.'

II

The woman at the minicab company had promised to have a driver at Jay's house within ten minutes. It had actually taken twenty-four minutes and thirty-seven seconds from the moment he'd put down the phone. Jay had therefore sat wordlessly in the back as they'd headed north, his arms folded, glaring daggers at the driver's nape. Roadworks around Elephant & Castle squeezed traffic into a single lane, bringing them to a virtual stand-still. And now, to cap it all, Blackfriars Bridge had frozen up altogether.

Anxiety was a mangle inside his chest. He didn't trust Croke, that was the truth of it. Which meant that Luke and Rachel weren't safe. He couldn't just sit passively in the back of the cab any longer. 'I'm walking,' he told the driver, handing him the exact sum on the meter, for he knew it was important not to give tips for shoddy service.

'Fuck you too, mate,' said the driver.

Jay half walked, half ran across the remainder of the bridge then up Ludgate Hill to St Paul's, the obvious cause of the gridlock. The police had surrounded it and an evacuation was in progress, hundreds of tourists milling around on the plaza while fire alarms shrilled away inside. He looked for but couldn't see either Luke or Rachel. Maybe they'd got away. Or maybe they were still in there. He nodded good morning to the police officers by the main entrance as he tried to walk between them. They laughed and told him to scram. He went around the corner. A teacher, in tears, was counting pupil heads. Apart from her, everyone seemed remarkably calm, almost jovial. But then he heard a cry by the Paternoster Square exit. A ring of spectators quickly formed around an elderly woman who'd collapsed on the flagstones. Police officers from the crypt café entrance came to help, leaving the door unguarded. Jay glanced around then ducked his head and slipped inside.

'Oi!' shouted one of the policemen. 'Come back!'

'I'll only be a moment,' Jay assured him. He hurried down the steps and through the café. He heard noise behind him and looked to see three policemen chasing hard. They looked so red-faced and mean that some primal instinct kicked in and Jay simply fled. He stumbled up some steps and spilled out onto the cathedral floor. He reached the aisle and ran along it towards the main doors.

He was halfway down when the alarm finally switched off. It had been ringing so loudly that Jay could hear it still in his ears. Then he realized it wasn't ringing. It was screaming. He looked up and saw Luke clinging to the balcony rail high above, fighting to hold on to Rachel as she dangled helplessly beneath him, while a black-bearded man on the gallery watched them as if it was entertainment.

Behind Jay, the policemen slowed too. Slowed and looked upwards. And still Rachel screamed out for help. And still it didn't come.

III

They said your life would flash before your eyes at the moment of maximum danger. But as Rachel looked up at Luke, straining with everything he had to hold on to her as she flailed above the cathedral floor, all she experienced was a terror so complete that it left no room for anything else. All she experienced was the certainty of her own imminent death and the knowledge that she was powerless to prevent it.

Then the alarm stopped and she heard shouting and she looked down to see Jay and the police arriving like a miracle on the cathedral floor beneath her; and their presence gave Blackbeard no choice but to reach down between the stanchions, take her free hand, and help Luke hoist her back up and over the balcony rail to safety.

She fell onto her knees on the cold stone, arms across her stomach, retching and retching as her gut tried to expel its surfeit of chemical fear; but nothing came out. Luke knelt beside her, hugged her tight against him. 'It'll be okay,' he kept saying. 'I promise.' But his words did little to reassure her. Her father, after all, had said something similar when he'd first broken the terrible news of his diagnosis, and *that* hadn't turned out okay. His slide had been astonishing in its speed and remorselessness. And then, in the weeks after his death, her mother had simply fallen apart from grief and loss and fear and guilt at having spent the family's small wealth on futile quack remedies. And so, two months to the day after her husband's funeral, she'd parked her battered old Renault by a level crossing, fortified herself with a bottle of gin, then had walked out onto the tracks. And, just seven months after that, Bren's body had been shredded by an IED.

Never show weakness; never show vulnerability. An irony of human nature, that the more you needed help the harder it was to ask for. In the wreckage of her family, Rachel had built a shell around herself in which she'd learned to rely on nobody but herself. But that shell had been shattered into a million tiny pieces as she'd hung there looking up at Luke, utterly dependent upon him, the strain of holding her written so clearly in his grimace and the blood rushing to his face and the tendons like

stretched steel in his shoulders and throat. And now all
the unexpressed grief and loneliness and despair of recent
years sobbed itself out onto his shirt, while he held her
tight and whispered words of comfort.

Blackbeard proved to be neither a sentimental nor
sympathetic man, however. He took her wrist and twisted
it fiercely enough to tear her away from Luke. 'This way,'
he said. He dragged her along the Triforium corridor
into the room with the model cathedral and handcuffed
her to a cast-iron radiator beneath a window. His
companions frogmarched Luke in a moment later, cuffed
him to the next radiator along. Their captors then went
out again and there was shouting, though too muffled
by doors and distance to make sense of.

She became, suddenly, exquisitely aware of Luke; of
being alone with him, of the weakness she'd just shown.
She glanced his way. He was looking at her with a pained
and empathetic expression on his face, as though worried
by the scars the experience was sure to leave. 'I thought
I was gone,' she said. 'If you hadn't held me . . .'

'Nothing to do with me,' he told her. 'Your watch strap
just caught on mine, that's all.'

Under the circumstances, Rachel's laughter wasn't far
short of a miracle. 'Thank you,' she said.

THIRTY-FOUR

I

Croke arrived at St Paul's to find it the heart of a perfect storm. Scores of police officers in fluorescent bibs were struggling to hold back a crowd of sightseers, thousands strong, while media helicopters swarmed above and windows and roofs sparkled with flash photography. Their driver bumped the Range Rover up onto the front plaza and parked beneath a police canopy. Walters was waiting inside the cathedral. 'Nice work,' said Croke acerbically.

'We were unlucky,' said Walters. 'If the little brat hadn't turned up trailing all those police . . .'

Morgenstern held up his hands to stop them. 'I can't hear this,' he said. 'I'll go check the crypt, see how the scanning's coming along.'

'I'll join you in a minute,' said Croke. He waited till he was gone, turned back to Walters. 'What's the damage?'

'Could have been worse,' said Walters, leading him up a spiral staircase. 'The police wanted to speak with Luke and Rachel, make sure they were okay. We told them that they were wanted in connection with a planned atrocity, which was why they'd been trying to escape; and that the NCT insisted on talking to them before anyone else. But holding them off was still touch and go until your mate got on the case. I don't know who he is, but Jesus he's got some pull. He yanked the police out of there like they were on a string.'

'Good.'

'Yes. But they saw us with them. If anything happens to them now . . .'

'Don't worry about it,' said Croke.

'We could go down for life,' said Walters. 'How are we supposed not to worry?'

'Did the police see our two friends up close? Close enough to identify?'

'No.'

'And neither of them have family to kick up a fuss should they disappear, right?'

'The girl's got a brother,' said Walters.

'I thought you told me he was in a wheelchair.'

'So?'

'So no one will listen to him, will they?'

Walters shrugged grudgingly. 'What about those two from the museum? Redfern and the curator? People will listen to them.'

'We're still holding them,' said Croke. 'Shunting them from jurisdiction to jurisdiction. Something tragic is about to happen to them, I can just sense it. Then we can take care of our two friends and leak it that they escaped. Dispose of them properly and everyone will take it for granted that they're simply on the run. You can arrange that, right?'

They reached the top of the stairs and crossed a gallery. Pete was standing guard outside a door that he opened at their approach. There was a vast model of a cathedral inside, and Luke and Rachel cuffed to neighbouring radiators. Kieran was keeping an eye on them, and Kohen was there too, his arms folded and his mouth a sulky bow. 'You promised they wouldn't come to any harm!' he protested, coming to the door.

'And they haven't,' said Croke.

'Only because I—'

'Shut it,' said Croke. 'This is man's work. If you're not up to it, perhaps we should let your uncle know.'

'I didn't say that. I just said—'

'Good. Then come with me. He wants you downstairs.'

'I'm not leaving them. I don't trust you. I don't trust *any* of you.'

'Suit yourself. But then you'll have to tell him it was your own choice, okay?' He waited for a grudging nod, turned to Kieran. 'You're the electronics' expert, right? I need some advice.' They left the room together. Croke briefed him as they made their way to the steps. 'The guys downstairs are going to be filming for the White House to watch live. They've agreed to share the feed with us, so that our friends in Israel can watch too. But they won't give us audio. The thing is, I *need* audio. I need their voices. Otherwise all I'll have is footage of a bunch of guys with flashlights.'

Kieran bit his lip. 'I could maybe hack their system if you got me time alone with it,' he said. '*Maybe*. But if I were them, I wouldn't let that happen, not for a millisecond. Not with the White House on the other end.'

'Then what do you suggest?'

'Easiest thing, I fix you up with a buttonhole camera and mike. Won't be as good as a primary feed, but it'll hear everything you hear.'

'Have you got the kit?'

'In the office. It's only a stone's throw.'

'Then go fetch it. And get passports for yourself and the others while you're at it. Preferably not in your real names. You've got spares, right?'

'Of course,' nodded Kieran. 'Where are we going?'

'Israel,' said Croke.

II

Cries of outrage filled the warehouse. 'Give ourselves up?' demanded Danel. 'Are you crazy? They'll send us to prison forever.'

'No,' said Avram. 'They won't.'

'Of course they will. They'll lock us up and throw away the keys. And we wouldn't even have brought down the Dome.'

Avram held up his hands against the protests. 'Please,' he said. 'Think about this for a moment. Think about it *strategically*. What are we hoping to achieve tonight? What would count as a success?'

'We bring down that damned Dome,' said Uri, to nods of approbation. 'And then we get away.'

Avram frowned. 'Why would that count as a success?'

'What are you talking about?' asked Danel.

'Let me tell you what will happen after we bring it down. There'll be global outrage. You must realize that. All Europe and Asia and the whole Muslim world will revel in their outrage. They'll convene emergency UN meetings and pass resolutions denouncing us. They'll summon ambassadors and review aid packages and cancel trade agreements. They'll put all kinds of pressure on our new Prime Minister, and they'll dangle a Nobel in front of her nose too. You all know how pathetic she is. She'll crumple like so much tinfoil, because crumpling is her nature. And so she'll promise to have our own people – *our own people* – help the Arab scum build a new Dome in exactly the same place as the old Dome.' He looked around at them, challenging them to say he was wrong. None of them did. 'Think about *that* for a moment,' he went on. 'Not just the Dome being rebuilt, but being rebuilt *with the help of Jews*; because the third most holy site in Islam should obviously have priority over the holiest site of Judaism. *That's* what's going to happen. You know in your hearts it is. The question is, is that what you want?'

'Of course not,' said Danel. 'But if that's what you think, why are you even doing this?'

'That's what I'm trying to tell you,' said Avram. 'Because our job tonight isn't to take down the Dome. It's *never* been that. Our job is to take the Dome down *in such a manner that the Third Temple gets built in its place.* It's to take it down *in such a manner that it will bring about a Jewish Greater Israel forever.*'

'That's out of our hands.'

'No, it's not,' insisted Avram. 'It's absolutely not. Let me paint you a picture. We're all inside the Dome. Our explosives are set and ready to go. Outside, the police, the army and the *Waqf* are holding back lest we trigger our charges and bring it down. Then we give them our list of demands.'

'Our demands?' frowned Danel. 'What demands?'

'Prisoner releases; though that doesn't really matter. All that matters is that they believe they can talk us out of it. They'll send in their best negotiators. We'll bargain. We'll weaken. Finally, reluctantly, we'll agree to surrender, though only to the Israeli army, and only if there are enough of them to protect us from the vengeance of the mob. Then, just as we're being driven away . . .' He mimicked with his hands the charges blowing, the Dome collapsing. 'Can't you see it? It will drive the Arabs *crazy*. They'll *hurl* themselves at the army in their lust to tear us limb from limb, as you put it. And the army *will have no choice* but to fight back in self-defence. And all of this will be being broadcast live to the world, remember. It will make the usual riots look like school parades. There'll be uprisings in Gaza and the West Bank. Our neighbour governments will be forced by their outraged publics to intervene, to throw their armies against us, and then we'll be at war, with a clear line drawn. And all the children of Israel will be on our side of that line *whether they want to be or not*. It will be Jew against Arab, Israel against the world. And we will win, because the Lord is on our side, praise His Name. And when we do win, there'll be no more Arab vermin here, no more concessions, no more talk of one state or two state solutions. There'll just be Israel, as was promised to us millennia ago. We'll build ourselves a Third Temple and we'll proudly proclaim our identity and our faith. And do you honestly fear for one moment that anyone will keep you in gaol while all of this is going on? The patriots who made possible a Greater Israel? The patriots who made possible the Third Temple. Gaol? They'll be naming streets after you. They'll be building statues. You'll be *heroes*.' He looked exultantly around at them, yet still saw doubt on their faces.

'You're asking us to trust our lives to crowd psychology?' asked Danel. 'What if the Arabs *don't* charge? What if our neighbours *don't* declare war?'

'They will,' insisted Avram.

'How can you be so sure?'

'Because there's something else,' he said. 'Something that's happening right now.'

'And what's that?'

Avram hesitated. Danel and his comrades were secular Zionists. They wanted a greater Israel as much as he did, but for political more than for religious reasons. Tell them what they were about to find in London, they'd laugh in his face and walk away. But *show* it to them . . . 'Not yet,' he said. 'It would put too many others at risk. But come to Jerusalem and you'll see it for yourselves, I swear you will. You'll see it long before we go in.'

Danel looked around to gauge the mood of his comrades, nodded grudgingly. 'Fine,' he said. 'But we see this thing of yours or it's off. Understood?'

Avram nodded. 'Understood,' he said.

III

Morgenstern came to greet Croke as he arrived down in the crypt. His face was flushed and it was immediately obvious they'd found something. 'Looks like your boy was right,' he exulted. 'Another cavity. Amazing these damned buildings stayed up, all these holes beneath them.' He pointed to a triangular mosaic midway between the tombs of Wellington and Nelson. 'It starts about six or seven feet down, best we can tell. Then there's a landing of some kind at the head of a ramp or flight of steps.' He gestured at the granite block holding up Nelson's black coffin. 'It leads beneath that thing.'

'Can you tell what's down there?'

'No. We'd have to shift the coffin and the plinth to sweep the floor; and then we'd be asking our scanners to work through sixteen feet of mortar and hardcore. No chance of getting anything reliable.'

'So what do we do? Another endoscope?'

Morgenstern shook his head. 'That won't help either, not if the good stuff's at the bottom of the ramp, as you'd expect. Besides, we don't have time to drill and then take up the floor. Not if you want this done by tonight.'

'And you're sure this is the only way down?' Croke asked drily. 'I mean there aren't any wells in the vicinity?'

'Do you see any?' asked Morgenstern. 'Seriously, we've

looked everywhere. There's nothing. It's pop the floor or forget about it.'

'Pop the floor?'

'We're going to need a shaft at least four feet square if we're to get it out, right? The quickest way is jackhammers, but what kind of idiot goes looking for a bomb with jackhammers? People are watching. The government is watching. There's a limit to how far I can push this. So we're going to have to cut and lift. My guys tell me that if we angle slightly in as we go down, we can cut ourselves a slab like a giant cork. That way, when we're finished, we can slather its sides with cement and slot it back in. Then we level it off and let the restorers go to work. Give it a week or two, it'll be good as new.'

Croke slid him a sceptical look. 'Sure. And no one will ever know we were even here.'

'Of course they'll know we were here; but they won't know *why*. And unless they're prepared to tear the floor up again to go look, they never will. They'll just have to accept whatever story we give them.'

Croke nodded. It was crude but it could work. 'How long will it take?'

'We can start the cutting now while we're arranging for a workshop crane. When it arrives, we'll pin bolts into the sides of our cork then lift it up and out, go down and take a look.' He gave Croke a meaningful look. 'If you still want to, that is.'

'You're saying it's my call?'

'No. Something this big, I'm going to need clearance from back home. But there's no point asking unless you're still up for it.'

Croke took a deep breath. Until now, he'd always had a way out: to throw up his hands and insist he'd simply been passing on bad intelligence in good faith. That defence ran out here. No one would accept bad intelligence as an excuse for digging up the crypt of St Paul's Cathedral. If they did this and found nothing, he'd be screwed. No money, no friends, no alibis. Everyone's scapegoat. Thinking about it rationally, it was madness to go on. His only sensible course was to cut his losses and get away.

But a strange thing happened as he stared down at the mosaic floor. He saw that it had an almost Masonic-looking device on it: a triangle within a pair of concentric circles within two squares. The words 'DEUS EST' were at the very heart of it, with 'PATER' 'FILIUS' and 'SPIRITUS' in the surrounding circle, one at each point of the triangle, and the words NON EST between them. God is the father. God is the son. God is the holy spirit. But the father is not the son, and the son is not the holy spirit. And he experienced a sudden and vivid memory of a childhood afternoon in his mother's lap, her arms around him and her intoxicating perfume as she explained to him the mysteries of the trinity with the help of an illustrated children's bible. He could almost hear the wonder in her voice. She'd always liked things that defied logic. For her, irrationality had merely added to their power.

The father is not the son, and the son is not the holy spirit.

He took a deep breath. He'd got in to this business for Grant's seventy million dollars, but that wasn't what he was thinking about right now. Right now, he was thinking about destiny. Right now, he was thinking about immortality. 'I want to see it,' he told Morgenstern. 'I think it's down there, and I want to see it.'

'Me too,' grinned Morgenstern. He held up his cellphone. 'But I'm going to need to clear it back home, like I said. So if you'll excuse me . . .'

Croke nodded. 'They'll try to fob you off with flunkies,' he said. 'Don't let them. Not for this. For this, you're going to need to speak to the lady herself.'

THIRTY-FIVE

I

It had been a shock for Luke to see Jay first talking with their captors, then intervening on his and Rachel's behalf. He'd tried to resist the implication that his old friend not only knew these people but was working with them, had been working with them from the start. But the inference became inescapable. He glanced at Rachel. Her eyes were closed and her head was bowed slightly forwards, as if in prayer. She'd recovered some of her colour since her ordeal on the balcony, but she still looked shattered. And he didn't feel so good himself, though he tried not to let it show. He wanted to give her confidence, make her think he had a plan. Yet his only plan involved using Jay somehow, and the thought of that sickened him, for Jay had sold them out.

The bruiser on sentry duty across the room,

playing games on a tablet. He grew bored, went to the door to talk to whoever was on guard outside. Luke glanced across at Jay and jerked his head in summons.

'What is it?' asked Jay, coming across.

'You know these people,' murmured Luke. 'How do you know these people?'

'My uncle,' said Jay, glancing at the door, clearly nervous of overstepping some obscure line. 'This is his project. That's how come I can protect you, because tonight won't happen without him.'

'Tonight?' asked Luke. 'What's tonight?'

Jay shook his head. 'I can't tell you that. But everything's going to be okay. Trust me.'

'Trust you?' scowled Luke. 'You've been working with them all along. You *gave* us to them.'

'I tried to keep you out of it,' said Jay. 'I swear I did. That's why I sent you to the Monument.'

'Oi!' said the bruiser. 'Shut it, you two.'

Luke ignored him. 'You got these people to hire me in the first place, didn't you? To find the Newton papers, I mean.'

Jay looked anguished. 'You said you needed work. I thought I'd be helping.'

'But why?' asked Luke. 'Why not do it yourself?'

'I hate that kind of thing,' said Jay. 'Dealing with strangers. I'm no good at it. And, anyway, I was too busy double-checking all Newton's other manuscripts.'

'Enough,' said the bruiser. He strode across and pressed the taser against Luke's throat. 'Or maybe you'd rather have a taste?'

'No,' said Luke. 'I'll be good.'

II

While Morgenstern called the White House, Croke attended to some business of his own. He set up office in an empty room then sent Avram an email detailing latest developments plus a link for the video-feed. After that, he checked to see if Grant had yet honoured his part of their deal.

He logged onto the website of Rutherford & Small's, a boutique British Virgin Islands bank. He entered the account number, password and security code. And there it was, enough to jolt his heart into a pleasurable canter.

$70,000,000.00

It wasn't his yet, however. Not by any means. He and Grant used a three-stage payment system for jobs like these. In this, the first stage, Grant would lodge the full sum in an existing, mission-specific account, allowing Croke to check that it was there. But all he could do for the moment was look. Later tonight, once Avram had launched his assault, Grant would send Croke new pass-words giving him veto power over all future transactions, effectively turning this into an escrow account. Only then would Croke deliver his cargo and so fulfil his side of the deal, at which point Grant would give up his residual control of the funds, and the money would be Croke's.

He logged out and returned to the crypt. A pair of diamond-tipped saws were screeching and sparking against the mosaics, throwing up small clouds of grit and dust. 'She said yes, then, I take it?' he asked Morgenstern, almost having to shout to make himself be heard.

'She said yes,' grinned Morgenstern, handing him a pair of safety goggles. 'I knew she would. It's her destiny.'

'If you say so.'

'I told her we'd be through by eight p.m. our time. She's cleared her schedule to watch it live. And she's promised to have a word with Downing Street, make sure they don't give us any grief.'

'Can she swing that?'

'So she says. Apparently we've got footage of the new PM.'

'Footage?' Croke squinted incredulously at him. 'You don't mean *girl* footage?'

'Even better. *Boy* footage.'

Croke laughed happily. 'Outstanding.'

'We're going to pull it off,' said Morgenstern. 'I can't believe it: we're really going to pull it off.'

'We're not home yet,' warned Croke. 'We don't even know it's down there.'

'It's down there,' said Morgenstern. 'I told you: this is destiny.'

'Maybe. But destiny won't get it to City Airport.'

The NCT man frowned. 'Why will that be a problem?'

'Are you kidding? The whole world's watching. Anything leaving here in a truck is going to take a trail of media like you wouldn't believe. And I don't just mean helicopters and cars and vans that maybe you can block off or pressure to look the other way. I mean every Londoner with a camera-phone and a Twitter account. If we're seen going to the airport, if we're seen boarding my plane, this is over. The PM may control British airspace, but it's not British airspace I'm worried about.'

'Then what do we do?' asked Morgenstern.

Croke nodded at Nelson's tomb. 'What would you do if there really was something down there? I mean, imagine that terrorists had used the sewers or the underground or whatever to mine their way beneath the crypt and plant some kind of dirty bomb.'

'Are you serious?'

'Humour me. You must have contingency plans. What would they call for?'

Morgenstern frowned. 'We'd evacuate the area, as we've already done. We'd bring in experts to assess and then disarm the device. We'd load any radioactive materials into a nuclear container, then take it to a suitable facility for analysis and disposal.'

'Civilian or military?'

'Depends. A warhead would have to be military. But dirty bombs are typically just TNT packed inside some spent fuel rods and other high-grade waste. Power stations deal with that kind of shit all the time.'

'Where's the nearest?'

'Sizewell, I think. On the Suffolk coast.'

Croke nodded. He'd visited Suffolk many years before, on one of his father's tours of the USAF bases there. 'And you'd give this container the full escort, right? Police cars and bike outriders, maybe a security truck or two. And you'd clear the roads so there was no danger of getting stuck in traffic?'

'What are you getting at?'

'When we came in from the airport yesterday, we passed through a long tunnel.'

'The Limehouse Link,' said Morgenstern.

'That's on the way to Suffolk, isn't it?'

'It could be. But why would that . . .' He laughed out loud when he saw the answer. 'Yeah, it could work. But what about when we get to Sizewell and they find nothing in the container?'

Croke shrugged. That wasn't his problem. 'Can't you find some old fuel rods to put in it?'

'Not a chance. Not at this notice.'

'Then why not take it to a USAF base instead? They're up that way, aren't they? And nuclear equipped?'

'Not any more. We shipped the warheads home.'

'But the bases still have handling capability, right? In case they ever wanted to bring them back?'

'So?'

'Imagine something were to happen on your way to Sizewell. Imagine getting a tip off that terrorists are planning to attack your convoy, say. So you make an executive decision to divert to the nearest USAF base instead, because the bomb will be safe there. Once you're inside, you're as good as on US soil. Home free.'

'The Brits will go ballistic,' said Morgenstern.

'Is that a problem?'

'Fuck no,' grinned Morgenstern. 'More like a bonus.'

III

Avram and Shlomo parked side by side in a new lot off Ma'aleh Shalom, south of the Old City. The most direct route in was through the Dung Gate, but they couldn't risk the extra security of the Western Wall Plaza, so they entered through Zion Gate instead. Avram led the way, not once looking back at Danel and his companions. Twice he saw squads of police ahead, but he knew these alleys so well that avoiding them was no problem.

The safe house was a one-bedroom basement apartment. He unlocked the door and left it ajar behind him. It was dark, stuffy and smelly inside. Apart from his own sporadic checks, no one had been in here for a year. But the place had everything he needed, including electricity, running water and a connection to a satellite dish. He hooked the laptop up to it now, while Danel and the others came in and bolted the door behind them, then he checked for messages from Croke. He had two, one with a link for video-feed, the other telling him to tune in at 8 p.m. London time.

'Show us, then,' said Danel. 'This thing of yours.'

'Not yet,' said Avram, showing him Croke's email. 'And we need to go through the plan again anyway.'

'We've already *been* through the plan.'

'Not with the others, we haven't.'

'Where are they?'

'I'll fetch them now. But Ana and Ruth can't be here when I come back. We'll meet them later by the truck.'

Danel scowled. 'Who do these people think they are?'

'I'm sorry,' said Avram. 'They can't be here.'

He patted himself down to make certain he wasn't carrying anything compromising and headed out for the Western Wall. The plaza was thronged when he arrived, buzzing with the euphoria of faith. Monday nights were usually desultory affairs, but the anniversary of the Six Day War had brought out the crowds. His heart swelled as he looked around: these people didn't know it, but their long exile from the Mount was almost over. An old acquaintance waved to him. He nodded back, but with a studiedly sombre expression to make it clear he wasn't free to talk.

Shlomo and his men were standing in a small knot by the foot of the steps. He didn't look at them, but walked slowly past them to make sure he was seen. Then he went to the wall itself.

He'd already composed his brief imprecation. Or, more accurately, Isaiah had composed it for him, and he'd merely copied it out.

And it shall come to pass in the last days that the Lord's house shall be established in the mountains, and shall be exalted above the hills.

He folded the paper into tight fractions of itself, fitted it into a crevice high in the wall. For the first time in his adult life he felt something like peace as he prayed here, that nagging internal voice finally stilled. The Lord, praise His Name, had granted him the gift of life. Now, at long last, he'd have his chance to show his gratitude.

THIRTY-SIX

I

The afternoon was brutal for Luke. The floor of their makeshift prison was cold and hard, the cuffs chafed his wrists raw, and every time either he or Rachel said anything to Jay or to each other, the bruiser would threaten them with his taser. And then there was the fear. It had been one thing coping with occasional spikes of it over the past day or so, but now it was a constant, crippling dread. And not just for himself. The thought that something terrible might happen to Rachel because of him was a special kind of torment.

Shadows on the facing wall marked the slow passage of time. Day ceded to evening. The room grew gloomy enough for the bruiser to turn on lights. Others came and went, murmuring by the door. They didn't realize that the room's acoustics made snatches of their discussions sufficiently audible for Luke to learn their names. The bruiser was Pete, Blackbeard was Kieran, and their fair-haired boss was Walters. The three of them seemed to work for the American called Croke, who now appeared at the door and beckoned to Jay. 'We're almost through,' he said. 'Time to come with me.'

'I'm not leaving my friends,' Jay told him.

'You have to. Your uncle insists.'

'I'm not leaving them.'

Croke sighed. 'Don't make me use force.'

'Force may get me downstairs,' Jay said prissily. 'It can't make me talk to my uncle.'

Croke nodded to Pete. Pete grabbed Jay by his wrist. Jay began to wail and shriek like a spoiled toddler. Pete shrugged and looked to Croke for permission to teach him manners. Croke shook his head. Rather to Luke's surprise, Jay did indeed have real leverage. That was a limited consolation, however, so long as he and Rachel were held up here, far from safety. He spoke without really thinking. 'Take us down with you,' he said. 'We won't cause any trouble. We give you our word.'

'Your word!' scoffed Croke.

'Yes,' said Luke. 'Our word.'

Croke walked over, crouched down in front of him. 'I want you to remember something,' he said. 'We're still holding your two friends from Oxford. Fuck with me and it won't just be your own neck you'll forfeit. Understand?'

'We understand,' said Rachel.

Croke stood up again, turned around to Walters. 'Can you handle them?'

'As long as they're all friendlies downstairs,' said Walters.

'They're all friendlies,' Croke assured him. 'But they might not exactly welcome spectators.' He bit his lower lip. 'Take them to the cathedral floor; only bring them down to the crypt once we've broken through. That way we'll present them with a *fait accompli.*'

'How will we know when you break through?' asked Walters.

Croke laughed. 'We're taking up half the floor. I imagine you'll hear us.'

Jay came across once he was gone. 'I told you they needed me,' he said.

'Your uncle, more like,' said Luke. 'Who the hell is he?'

'A great man, Luke. A *great* man.' He sounded exuberant now that the skirmish had been won. 'You'll like him. You'll both really like him. He's not a scientist or a historian, but he knows his Newton, honestly he does.'

'You never mentioned him before.'

'I didn't know him until recently. He's not really my

uncle. My third cousin twice removed. He just likes us to call him Uncle.'

'Us?'

Jay shook his head and turned more towards Rachel. 'You have to understand,' he said. 'Not every page that Newton ever wrote has been checked and translated and understood. Not *properly*. Not by a Newton expert. Not by someone who knows Greek, Latin, Hebrew and French as well as English. Not by someone familiar with his handwriting and abbreviations, who understands his natural philosophy, theology and alchemy. That's *my* project: to study everything he ever wrote. Every page, every sentence, every word.'

'Out of my way, kid,' said Walters. He uncuffed Luke and Rachel from the radiators, allowing them to stand, stretch, flex their fingers. 'No games,' he warned.

'No games,' agreed Luke.

Jay walked alongside them to the door, eager to finish telling them about his self-appointed mission. 'Every word that Newton ever wrote,' he said. 'Mostly, it's easy. The papers have all been photographed and put online. I never even have to leave my flat. But not everything's like that.' They reached the steps, began heading down. 'Not all the Yahuda Archive is available online, for example. That's why I had to go to Jerusalem, to see the rest for myself. I *hate* going to new places. But I have family there, so I got in touch with them. That's when

Uncle Avram offered me a room. He even arranged a special pass for me at the National Library of Israel. And that's where I found them, on the reverse of a pair of pages about the ancient cubit: faint traces of ancient texts and sketches that Newton had himself rubbed out, but not perfectly—'

'Shut it,' said Walters, as they neared the foot of the steps. 'I want silence.'

They emerged onto the empty cathedral floor a few moments later, went over to the crypt stairs. They could hear hammering and drilling below. It wasn't yet time. They milled around as they waited, looking at the altar, the pillars, upwards at the great cupola.

'So have you worked it out, then?' asked Jay.

'Worked what out?' asked Luke.

'What this is all about. What we're about to find.'

'No,' said Luke. 'What are we about to find?'

Jay gave a reproving cluck of the tongue. 'Come on, Luke. Haven't you even noticed the *geometry* of this place?'

'Eight sides topped by a Dome,' said Luke. 'What about it?

'Oh.' He looked downcast for a moment. But then he cheered up. 'But I bet you don't know where Wren got the idea from, do you?'

'You mean the tomb of Christian Rosencreutz?' said Luke.

'No!'

'That Bourbon chapel in Paris, then?'

'St-Denis?' exclaimed Jay excitedly. 'Of course not St-Denis. How can you be so obtuse? Don't you know what the English believed back then? They believed themselves descended from a lost tribe of Israel. It was almost an article of faith.'

'What are you talking about?' asked Rachel.

'A lost tribe of Israel,' said Jay. 'London was their new Jerusalem, and this spot right here its most sacred site. The high point of the city, the focus of their worship. Did you know that St Paul himself reputedly came here and preached at this very spot? *This very spot.*' The drilling and hammering grew so loud that Jay had almost to shout to make himself heard. 'And what, in Wren's day, did Jerusalem have on the Temple Mount, on its most sacred site?'

'The Dome of the Rock?' hazarded Rachel.

'Yes!' cried Jay. 'The Dome of the Rock! Now do you see?'

Luke went a little numb. 'An eight-sided building topped by a dome,' he murmured.

'An eight-sided building topped by a dome!' Fervour flushed Jay's face. 'Have you ever seen Perugino's painting of the Virgin? It shows the Temple of Solomon in the background, and it's *exactly* like the Dome, eight walls topped by a dome. And Raphael too. The same thing. Eight walls topped by a dome. And yet you

386

somehow think that Wren's design for this place was a *coincidence*? That it was just dumb luck that he settled on the *exact same formula*? No. A thousand times no. He designed it like this precisely because—'

A great cracking and splintering noise came suddenly from below, like hell splitting open. 'I guess that's our cue,' said Walters, herding them towards the steps. They went down together, turned left towards Nelson's tomb. Even as they arrived, a great slab of floor began to rise, hoisted by a yellow workshop crane, steel cables creaking and groaning with the strain, so that the people nearest took an instinctive half step back. But everything held and the slab of mortar and hardcore inched upwards, bumping and scraping the sides as it came, throwing off a cascade of ancient dust that spread in a thick, low mist and set off a round of throat-clearing coughs.

The slab lifted clear of the floor. It was massive, not just fat but tall, a good foot taller than Luke himself. The operator swung it sideways above a makeshift mattress of blankets and dust sheets laid as a buffer on the mosaic, bumped it down. Everyone edged to the brink of the great black pit in the floor and stared seven or eight feet down to a pair of rotted wooden beams laid parallel across the shaft, then another eight feet or so of open space to a dusty flagstone floor at the head of a flight of stone steps that led into the darkness below Nelson's tomb.

Jay turned to Luke again, his voice barely a whisper now. 'London was the new Jerusalem,' he said. 'And Wren wanted his cathedral to do the same job as the Temple of Solomon did in the old Jerusalem. The same job that the Dome has been doing ever since.'

It was hard for Luke to concentrate on what Jay was saying, so mesmerized was he by the pit, by all the torches being shone down into it. 'Protecting the rock?' he asked.

'No,' said Jay impatiently. 'Protecting the Holy of Holies. The place where it used to be, at least. The *exact* place.'

'But why?' asked Luke.

'Why do you think?' demanded Jay. 'My God! What was the Holy of Holies *for*? What was its *purpose*? What was it designed to *house*?'

Jay had Luke's full attention now. He turned and stared at his old friend in disbelief. 'You can't be serious,' he said.

Jay's eyes glittered triumphantly. 'Oh, but I am,' he said. 'And you're about to see it for yourselves.'

II

No one seemed to be in charge. Morgenstern had headphones and a throat mike on, the better to describe what he was seeing to the Vice President and answer her questions. Everyone else was staring raptly down, forgetting that they had work to do. Croke therefore stepped up to the plate. He turned to an NCT man. 'Get the ladder,' he said.

The man nodded and fetched it, lowered it into the hole, twisting it sideways to feed it between two beams before setting it on the floor. The chamber was deeper than they'd anticipated; only the top rung protruded above the mouth, making descent somewhat precarious. 'I'll go first,' said the NCT man. 'I can hold it from the bottom.'

'No,' said Croke. '*I'm* going first.' He sat on the floor, felt for a rung with his foot, turned around and steadied himself before he began his descent. It grew dark more quickly than he'd expected. At the foot, all he could see was a few marble steps leading down into the blackness, and pale walls that glowed like ghosts around him. He was about to call up for a flashlight when he saw Morgenstern already on his way down with two of them, though both were turned off at present, presumably so that the Vice President could share the moment of revelation with them. And now the cameraman joined them at the foot, taking pains not to film their faces.

Morgenstern passed Croke the spare flashlight. 'Ready?' he grinned.

'Ready,' agreed Croke.

They turned on and raised their flashlights together. Their beams pierced the darkness, their flare making

Croke blink. The marble steps fanned out as they led down to a large chamber directly beneath Nelson's tomb, perhaps eight paces square and twelve feet tall, its walls inlaid with mosaics of a garden paradise, sunlit orchards heavy with fruit, streams cascading into lily-pad lakes while gorgeous birds thronged the cloudless skies. But that wasn't what grabbed their attention. For there was a second, smaller chamber nested inside the larger. Its walls were of flawless white marble and it was fronted by a pair of tall ebony doors. Croke advanced, mesmerized, down the staircase towards it. He stepped up onto its dais, took hold of the twin golden handles, tried to pull the doors towards him. The hinges had stretched over the centuries, however, so that the doors dragged across the floor, screeching and scoring tiny marks in the marble. He took them one at a time instead, lifting the right-hand door then shuffling backwards before setting it down again. Christ, it was heavy. He still couldn't see inside, for a white linen curtain was draped across the mouth. Rather than drawing it back straight away, he opened the left-hand door instead. Now he glanced at Morgenstern. Morgenstern nodded. Croke took a deep breath and swept the curtain aside. 'My god,' he muttered, when he saw what was inside. And it sounded, even to his own ears, like a prayer.

The walls, floor and ceiling of the inner sanctum gleamed with gold, dazzling as dawn in the sudden torchlight. And on a low marble central plinth, there it stood, the Ark of the Covenant itself, a chest of wood and gold, smaller than Croke had anticipated, smaller than the legends that surrounded it, but beautiful nonetheless, and extraordinarily potent, with its carved panels and the pair of golden cherubs kneeling in adoration on its lid, facing each other with their wings outspread and almost touching.

Something touched Croke's heart then, a childlike awe he hadn't expected to feel again. A sense that there was so much more to the universe than he understood; more to destiny and the divine. And he found himself, to his own surprise, crying out to the Lord and falling to his knees before it; and then Morgenstern and the cameraman did likewise, and the others behind, all falling to their knees and crying out to the Lord.

III

The tension in the Jerusalem basement had grown like closeness before a storm. Avram had hoped that a shared sense of purpose would overcome the manifold differences between Shlomo's and Danel's parties, but he'd quickly been disappointed. It had taken all his energy and diplomatic skills to keep them together. And then his architect friend Benyamin had arrived. One look at all the squabbling and sniping and he'd spun on his heel and had almost left before Avram had been able to stop him.

But at last something was happening in London. The black screen came to life, showing a great slab of stone and mortar being winched from a mosaic floor. There was no sound, however, and impatient mutters told Avram that the show wasn't impressing its audience. The slab was set aside. The camera peered down into the gaping hole. A ladder was fed into the darkness. The feed jerked and jumped as the cameraman made his descent. The lighting became ever more darkly atmospheric. Blacks and greys erupted in flares of golden torchlight. The very roughness of the pictures somehow added to their authenticity and mystique, and the basement fell quieter and quieter.

The cameraman walked down a flight of stone steps. There were gasps as the inner sanctum of white marble and ebony doors came into focus. The doors parted reluctantly. A curtain was swept aside. For the longest moment, total silence fell in the basement, astonishment and awe. But it didn't last. The place erupted with cries of joy, jubilation, even ecstasy. Enemies a few minutes before now laughed and hugged each other, wept openly on each others shoulders. Some prayed while others danced, their euphoria needing physical release as, at long last, they all came together on this night of *Rosh*

Chodesh Sivan. A single mind. A single heart. A single Israel.

He turned to Benyamin, that diehard cynic and sceptic, put his hand on his arm. 'So?' he asked. 'Are you coming with us?'

Tears were streaming freely down the big man's face. 'Yes,' he said. 'I'm coming with you.'

THIRTY-SEVEN

I

The wave of religious enthusiasm died quickly, leaving Croke feeling almost sheepish. He got back to his feet, brushed his knees, assumed his most purposeful expression, the one that said there was serious work to do. He checked his buttonhole camera then turned to Morgenstern, who was still murmuring a commentary to accompany his cameraman's footage.

This was no time for asking permission. He placed himself squarely in front of the lens, unplugged the microphone jack. 'Congratulations, Madam Vice President,' he said. 'The Reverend told me you were the new Esther. It seems he was right.'

A moment of silence; he began to fear he'd misjudged

this. But finally she spoke. 'Our task isn't complete yet, Mr Croke,' she said, in that distinctive voice.

'No, Madam Vice President.'

'You're delivering it yourself, I understand.'

Croke nodded. 'We'll take it to the airport now. We need to get it there by dawn.'

'I'll be watching. The whole world will be watching. Praying for your success.'

'Thank you.' He hesitated just a moment, then said: 'Madam Vice President, there's something I have to ask.'

'What?' she asked, her tone suddenly wary.

He dropped his eyes and nodded to himself, wanting to convey that he knew how far over the mark he was stepping. 'Madam Vice President, I've no illusions about the risks ahead. That's fine. This mission is worth it. But there's something I can't reconcile myself to, however hard I try.' He looked up again into the camera. 'My father has served our nation all his life. It would kill him to think I'd betrayed it in any way.'

'You know I can't publicly acknowledge our involvement.'

'No, Madam Vice President. Of course not. But he *trusts* you. He *admires* you. So if I don't make it back, I beg you please to find some private way of letting him know that I gave my life for a mission that had your knowledge and blessing. Just a word in his ear from someone he can trust, so that he can hold his head up high when the media goes to work on him.'

Her voice relaxed. Promises were cheap. 'Of course. I'll gladly let your father know.'

'Thank you, Madam Vice President.'

And he meant it. Her voice was far too well-known to be denied, and his buttonhole footage of Morgenstern and his NCT comrades was all the corroboration he'd need. When they tried to make him the fall guy now, as they surely would, they'd find themselves in for a nasty shock.

II

Jay wasn't among those who'd fallen to their knees. He'd known what they'd find, after all. And he knew the truth of it, too.

After he'd discovered the faint traces of a schematic hidden beneath one of Newton's religious texts in Jerusalem's Yahuda archive, he'd come to believe that the great man had somehow discovered the true Ark, had analysed its workings and then restored it. And his uncle Avram had joyfully agreed, for it had long been an article of his faith that the Ark would be found and returned to Jerusalem before the Third Temple could be built. This discovery, therefore, had seemed more than happy providence. It had seemed like the hand of God at work.

Luke's find yesterday, however, had made him question this assumption. For in his cryptic note, Newton had acknowledged receipt of 12 plain panels and blocks of SW. SW, in such a context, could surely only stand for shittim wood, the material from which the Ark had been fashioned. If this had been the original Ark, the panels would therefore already have been worked, not plain or still in blocks. And so Jay had been forced to a different conclusion: that Ashmole had bequeathed Newton not the true Ark itself, but merely the materials and concept necessary for building a perfect replica.

Jay hadn't shared this revised theory with anyone. He owed it to his uncle to tell him first, and he hadn't yet had the chance. And, to be honest, he wasn't sure he'd tell him anyway. It would only dismay and dispirit him, and what difference did it truly make? To Jay, an Ark by Newton was as wondrous and ordained as one by Moses. Besides, this was what destiny had written, and who were they to argue?

The schematic strongly implied there should be other materials here. Jay couldn't see them inside the Holy of Holies, so he went around back and there they were: three oak chests, a large one with two shrunken versions of itself in front, like a mother posing with twin daughters.

'What are they?' asked Luke, at his shoulder.

'Let's find out,' Jay said.

The boxes' sides and lids were elaborately fashioned with scenes from Genesis, Exodus and Kings. He opened one of the smaller ones first. It was tightly packed with vestments. The topmost robe was so heavy that it was an effort to hold it up. It was fashioned from purple, violet, white and scarlet cloth embroidered with gold thread and decorated with thin golden plates and bells. But what really caught Jay's eye were the four rows of precious and semi-precious stones sewn into its bodice. He turned with delight to Luke and Rachel. 'The ephod,' he said. 'The robe of the Kohen, High Priest of the Ark of the Covenant.' He held it against his chest to show them the stones. 'Sardius, topaz and carbuncle.' He moved his finger down a row. 'Emerald, sapphire and diamond.' His finger moved to the third row. 'Ligure, agate and amethyst.' And finally the fourth. 'Beryl, onyx and jasper.'

'The initials from the Newton papers,' said Rachel.

'The initials from the Newton papers,' nodded Jay. 'The twelve stones that Ashmole left Newton so that he could make himself an ephod. It proved this was for real, not some intellectual exercise. Why else would he have needed them otherwise?' He shook his head in awe. 'But he wasn't a Kohen, Luke. That was the fact of it. He needed a Kohen like me.'

'Jay Cowan,' murmured Luke. 'Jakob Kohen.'

'It was my great-grandfather,' said Jay. 'He thought

that Cowan would be a more prudent name for travelling here from across Europe. But we're Kohens all the same.'

'So that robe is yours, is it?'

'Made for me by Newton himself,' said Jay. 'Think about that. All my life, people have told me that I was a freak. Yet now it turns out I was made this way for a reason. Now it turns out that I have a destiny. That's quite something, don't you think? To have a destiny?' He folded the robe back in its chest, turned his attention to its twin. Its interior was divided into two; on the left were sheets of some dull metal; on the right were glass flasks with encrusted stoppers three-quarters full of some clouded liquid. He closed it, turned to their mother. Its lid, however, wouldn't lift. He frowned and walked around it, looking for a way in. It had sturdy brass handles set into its sides, but they didn't give when he pulled. And the oak panels fitted so perfectly together that they gave no hint of how they might open. Out of frustration as much as anything, he pushed each of the sides in turn, and finally one of the end panels sank in a little way. He pushed harder and a slot opened in the lid, allowing him to slide the panel up and out. There was a second panel immediately behind it, covered in rich blue cloth and fitted with a pair of leather handles. He pulled them and an interior compartment slid sweetly towards him, like a drawer on oiled castors. He pulled it all the way out, turned it around. It was perhaps two and a half feet long, half the length of the chest. Its sides were covered in the same blue cloth, but its interior was finished with brown and white fur, and it was as obviously shaped to accommodate the Ark as a glove is to fit a hand.

He knelt to look inside the hollowed chest. A mirror twin of brown and white fur was fitted to the far end, so that the two halves together would form a perfect womb for its precious cargo. He reached inside to see if the far end pulled out too, but it appeared to be fixed in place. He looked up at Luke. 'You can't carry the Ark openly,' Jay told him. 'It's against Jewish law. If you need to move it, you first have to wrap in *tachash* and blue cloth.'

'*Tachash*?' asked Luke.

'It's a kind of fur,' said Jay. 'Though no one's quite sure from which animal.' He stroked it against its nap to raise it. 'But Newton followed the King James Version of the Bible, and the King James translates it as badger.'

'So they built this to bring it here?' asked Rachel.

Jay didn't answer, his attention seized instead by a large oval cut in the bottom of the chest, the exact same shape and size as the base of the Ark itself. He smiled when he saw how it worked. He found and released a pair of latches holding the front half of the floor panel in place, then slid it out and set it aside. Now the chest could be carried over to the Ark and fitted snugly around it. The floor panel would then slot back in and lock around the base of the Ark like the collar of a guillotine around the neck of its next victim. Slide the velvet mould back in and fix it in place with the front panel and the Ark would be ready for moving without anyone having touched it at all.

The thought reminded him that he was here for a reason. He went around to the front and found the *goyim* with their hands all over the Ark. 'Stop that!' he commanded, his voice sounding imperious even to himself. 'Put that lid back on.'

Croke gave him a sour look. 'You're here to observe,' he said.

'Don't you realize what this is?' asked Jay. 'We take our time with it. We handle it with respect. And no one touches it. No one but me.'

'But—'

'Only a Kohen may touch the Ark, on pain of death. *On pain of death.* I am a Kohen. Are there any other Kohens here?' And he looked so belligerently around the chamber that no one said a word.

THIRTY-EIGHT

I

Luke and Rachel watched anxiously as the Ark was packed into the large oak chest and was then hoisted by crane up to the crypt. Whatever fate Croke had planned for them, they were surely about to discover it. So it came as an intense relief to learn they'd be going with it. Walters covered Luke with his taser while Kieran cut a fat strip from a roll of surgical tape and made to gag him. 'There's no need for that,' Luke assured him. 'I gave you my word.'

'Sure,' snorted Walters. 'And if you think we trust you . . .'

Kieran stuck the tape across his mouth, then did the same to Rachel. He and Walters then manhandled them up the ladder, handcuffed them when they got to the top, then took them out of the cathedral. A vast white canopy had been rigged up over the front plaza, large enough for two heavy vehicles to be parked inside it: a lorry hauling a container emblazoned with nuclear hazard warnings and a windowless white security truck, to which they were now taken. The three oak chests were already loaded along its spine, constricting the legroom of the bench seats that ran down either side. Walters herded them all the way in, made them sit side by side facing the largest chest. He briefly undid one of Luke's cuffs to loop the chain through a brass handle, thus securing him to it. He did the same with Rachel, then checked to make sure his team were all inside. Satisfied, he closed and bolted the rear doors then gave the side of the truck a loud double thump.

It was time to roll.

II

Croke put on a yellow police bib before climbing into the front of the security truck. 'Another quiet night in, eh, boss?' said Manfredo, already at the wheel.

'Another quiet night in.'

Morgenstern was on the cathedral steps. He'd be staying behind to supervise the re-plugging of the crypt floor before taking a chopper to USAF Lakenheath to meet the convoy. Croke waved to let him know they were ready, and to thank him for his help. Morgenstern relayed the signal to the driver of the nuclear container. Its lights came on. Its engine started to rumble. It began slowly to move, nudging its nose like a curious dog against the parting curtains of the canvas canopy then slipping out between them.

The security truck followed immediately behind. The sun had set, and they were greeted by a dazzling wildfire of camera flashes that made Croke blink despite their tinted windscreen. The first eruption died away; it grew diffuse. The spotlights of TV helicopters tracked them as a police escort formed around them. Blue lights flashed in synchrony as they forced a path through the crowds to Ludgate Hill, and sirens suddenly began to blare in a hideous concerted screech of noise. They picked up speed, though not too much. They were, after all, supposed to be carrying a dirty bomb.

All the feeder roads had been closed off by the police, so that there was no traffic to negotiate, no need to wait for lights. They reached the Limehouse Link and plunged down into its mouth. The white-tiled walls and compressed space reflected their sirens and lights, like some devilish nightclub. The tunnel was a mile long, with lay-bys for breakdowns every hundred yards or so. Two nondescript vans were waiting in the first. Manfredo braked sharply to drop off the back of the convoy and pull in beside them. A second security truck, indistinguishable from their own, was parked in the next lay-by along. It began to pull out the moment the last police outrider had passed, then accelerated to catch up with the convoy before it left the tunnel. In the nocturnal gloom, surrounded by this riot of noise and light, it would take a freakishly smart-eyed observer to notice the switch.

Croke opened the passenger door, jumped down, went around back. Working together, they all heaved the two smaller chests into the first van; the larger, along with Luke and Rachel, into the second. They locked up the security truck, covered it with a blue tarpaulin, then they divided into the two vans, Manfredo and Kieran taking the respective wheels. They drove on a short distance and pulled into another lay-by halfway along the tunnel. Then they waited.

It was another five minutes before the police opened their roadblocks and the first few headlights appeared in their rear-views. Manfredo and Kieran now pulled out well ahead of them, emerging unheralded and unobserved from the eastern mouth of the tunnel a minute later, before proceeding in a far more discreet convoy to City Airport.

THIRTY-NINE

I

There were no benches in the back of the new van, so Luke and Rachel had to kneel on the bare metal floor as though in supplication to the Ark. It was gloomier here than in the truck too, with only a single, low-powered roof light. Luke raised an eyebrow at Rachel, about the only communication available with his mouth still taped. She raised both hers in response. The way the skin crinkled around her eyes made it look almost as though she were smiling. Her courage was astonishing to him, and gave him heart. He leaned forwards, looked around the van. Walters and Kieran were here, of course. And Jay, too, his eyes fixed on the chest. He noticed Luke looking his way and coloured a little, then he rose to his feet and crouched his way towards them.

'Where the fuck are you going?' growled Walters.

'I want to speak to my friends,' said Jay.

Walters laughed. 'In your dreams, mate.'

'I can still put a stop this mission,' Jay told him. 'Would your boss thank you if I did?'

To Luke's surprise, Walters shrugged and let him by. He knelt beside Luke, picked at the tape over his mouth until he'd got enough up to strip it off. It was a day and a half since Luke had shaved, so that it felt like flame on his skin, but the pleasure of being able to breathe and talk made it more than worthwhile.

'Do Rachel's,' he said.

Jay complied. The skin around her mouth was as red as smeared lipstick. 'Thank you,' she said.

'You mustn't be afraid,' said Jay. 'You're both still under my protection.'

'And what happens when that runs out?'

'It won't,' said Jay. 'Not before Israel. They can't move the Ark without a Kohen, you see.'

Luke shook his head in disbelief. 'You can't honestly believe these people care about that.'

'Maybe not. But my uncle does. How many times do I have to tell you? Tonight won't happen without him. It *can't* happen without him. Besides, I'm not just here to *escort* the Ark. I have a far more important job. Something no one else can do, not these people here, not even my uncle. Something that requires a true adept.'

'And what's that?' asked Luke.

Jay dropped his voice. 'I know how it works,' he murmured.

'How what works?' frowned Rachel.

'The Ark, of course.'

She shook her head. 'What are you talking about?'

Despite the gloom, Jay's skin seemed to flush. 'Do you honestly think this is just some ancient chest of wood and gold we've found? Why would Ashmole and the others have needed Newton for *that*? It's described in great detail in the Book of Exodus, after all. Any craftsman worth his salt could have knocked one up.'

'Then why did they need him?'

'Because the Ark is what the Bible says it is, Luke. It's a *weapon*. And not just *any* weapon. It's the original weapon of mass destruction.'

'For God's sake, Jay!'

'Do you know what they called it, Luke?' he asked. 'They called it the Ark of the Strength and Glory of the Lord. They carried it seven times around Jericho and it brought its walls tumbling down.'

'Jesus, Jay.'

'And it wasn't just cities it destroyed. It took out *armies*. The first Book of Samuel, chapter 6, verse 19. The Ark slew seventy nobles and fifty thousand commoners just for looking wrongly upon it. *Fifty thousand*. Or the second Book, where the Ark slipped and

Uzzah tried to stop it from hitting the ground, and was killed instantly. Or Leviticus 10.' Jay stood unsteadily, spread his feet and hands wide like a ham actor delivering his big speech. '"And Nadab and Abihu, the sons of Aaron, took either of them his censer, and put fire therein, and put incense thereon, and offered strange fire before the Lord, which he commanded them not. And there went out fire from the Lord, and devoured them, and they died before the Lord."' He knelt again, looked fiercely back and forth between Luke and Rachel. 'Strange fire before the Lord. *Strange fire*. Doesn't that remind you of anything?'

'What the hell—'

'Newton and the other alchemists were after *sacred* fire. Don't you think that it's at least *possible* that sacred fire and strange fire might be one and the same? That what they were really after was the secret of the Ark of the Covenant? A source of power that could bring down cities, that could destroy armies tens of thousands strong? A source of power that would change the world forever?' He leaned towards Luke again, lowered his voice. 'Do you know what alchemical tradition says about how Solomon built his temple? It says he cast spells that trapped djinns and other powerful spirits in magical amphorae, then forced them to do his bidding. Djinns trapped in jars. Strange fire in chests of wood and gold. A source of power to change the world.' His expression was by now both manic and exultant. 'Newton understood how it worked, Luke. And so do I. And tomorrow morning I'm going to prove it. Tomorrow morning I'm going to show the world the face of God Himself.'

'How?'

Jay opened his mouth to answer, but then he blinked and hesitated as he realized how close he'd come to letting on more than he should. He gave Luke a knowing smile, as though to congratulate him for almost tricking him. 'You'll find out soon enough,' he said.

'Tell me, Jay.'

But he only shook his head again, his fervour dissipating by the moment, shrinking him as it went, leaving him a smaller and a lesser man. 'Soon enough.'

II

Croke fell silent in the front of the van as they neared City Airport. He was all too aware how critical the next few minutes were. Without the direct protection of the NCT, their little convoy was now far more vulnerable to misadventure, even betrayal. But Morgenstern had done him proud. Two airport security officers were waiting in a marked car as promised. They led them down a supply road to a security fence topped by triple strands of barbed wire, where another guard opened the gate for them as they approached, then closed it again behind them.

They drove across tarmac to the private jet concourse. The security car flashed its lights at a partially open hangar door. Manfredo flashed acknowledgement and drove inside. Croke's jet was waiting there, his pilot Craig Bray by the open cargo bay, checking pallets of supplies. They pulled up beside him, jumped down. 'All good?' asked Croke.

'Better than good,' nodded Bray. 'They signed off our paperwork blind. And they've given us priority clearance. They must think you're God Himself.'

Croke laughed. 'Closer than you'd think.'

Bray kicked one of the pallets. 'We're to load these, yeah? They were sent for my attention by some guy called Jakob Kohen. Only there's enough acid in here to bathe all the brides you could ever ask for.'

'Give me a moment,' said Croke. He went around the back of the van, found Kohen chatting with Luke and Rachel. 'What the fuck?' he asked Walters.

'He threatened to scupper the mission.'

Croke scowled. The little prick was getting on his nerves. 'Okay,' he said. 'Put his friends on board. And stay with them. I don't want them trying anything.'

'You got it, boss.'

Croke beckoned to Kohen. 'Your supplies are here,'

he said. 'Do you want to double-check them or shall we just load?'

'I want to double-check them.'

'Fine,' said Croke. 'But first we need to talk to your uncle.'

FORTY

I

It was past midnight in Jerusalem when Avram finally received his nephew's call. 'It's real?' he asked.

'It's real, Uncle,' Jakob assured him, his excitement audible despite the distance. 'I saw it. I *touched* it.'

'You touched it?'

'Only to pack it. We're loading it on to the plane now. We'll be in the air soon.'

'Good. And well done.'

'Thank you, Uncle.'

'Is the man Croke with you? I need to speak with him.'

'He's here. I'll put him on now.'

'I trust you're satisfied,' said Croke when Jay handed him the phone.

'I'm satisfied,' said Avram.

'Then you're going in?'

'When people are asleep. But please remember that I'll wait until the Ark is here before I bring down the Dome.'

'I know the plan,' said Croke.

'I know you know the plan,' said Avram. 'I want to make sure you bear the plan in mind as you're flying across the Mediterranean with the Ark in your hold. I want you to remember that I'll be monitoring your course all they way on a flight-tracking website, and that I'll call my nephew should I see any deviation.'

'I said I know the plan, Avram. I'll see you in Jerusalem.'

'In Jerusalem,' agreed Avram.

II

Luke watched warily as Walters crouched his way inside the van. 'I'm not to hurt you,' he told him and Rachel, showing them the taser. 'Not unless you try something. So please try something. Pretty please.' He unlocked Rachel's right cuff, released her from the chest handle, cuffed her to Luke instead. Then he removed and pocketed Luke's cuffs. 'On your feet,' he said.

Getting down from the back was awkward, attached together as they were. They found themselves in an aircraft hangar so vast that it made the sleek white jet inside it look small. Walters herded them to and up the forward steps. They turned away from the cockpit, passed between toilets and some kind of hi-tech comms' suite into a passenger cabin opulently fitted in white leather and polished walnut. There were two banks of seats on either side. They currently all faced forwards but Walters swivelled the front left bank one hundred and eighty degrees, locked it in place. 'Sit,' he said. They sat. He took out the second pair of cuffs, closed one around the central seat-belt fitting, the other around the chain of the handcuffs shackling Luke to Rachel, thus securing them neatly to their seats. 'Comfy?' he asked.

'A glass of champagne wouldn't hurt,' said Luke.

Walters snorted. 'I'm going to enjoy how this flight ends,' he said.

'Why's that?' asked Luke, striving to sound casual, not quite succeeding.

Walters sat sideways on the facing bank, put his right foot up on the white leather to flaunt his freedom. 'All in good time.'

Luke nodded. 'I have to tell you something,' he said. 'I think your loyalty does you credit.'

'My loyalty?'

'Sure. Your boss is bound to need a scapegoat when all this is over. And it's got to be you, right? I mean you're already up to your neck in shit for murdering Rachel's aunt, so you're—'

'I didn't murder her.'

'. . . the obvious candidate and I—'

'I never even touched her.'

'. . . just think it's commendable that you'd sacrifice yourself so that he can—'

Walters leaned forwards, jabbed his taser into Luke's chest and gave him a vengeful two-second burst that made him arch and yell in pain. 'Do you honestly think you can drive a wedge between me and the boss?' Walters asked rhetorically, tucking the weapon back into his waistband. 'Think a-fucking-gain.' But there was a more reflective look in his eyes, for all the bravado of his words. Not much. But something, perhaps, for Luke and Rachel to work with.

III

There were advantages for Avram in leaving the assault until the last moment before the first call to prayer of the new day. People would be at their sleepiest. It would mean having to hold the Dome for a shorter time before dawn and Croke arrived. But there was one major disadvantage too. Jerusalem's Old City virtually closed down by night, so that the later they left it, the more conspicuous they'd be, the more likely to attract the attention of the IDF and the police.

'It's time,' he said.

They headed out in small clusters, leaving Benyamin behind with Shlomo and his men. Ana and Ruth were waiting by the truck. Danel told them what they'd seen in London, but the two women weren't overly impressed. They had their own motivations for being here. Avram drove the truck into a darkly shadowed area of the car park and opened up the rear. They shifted furniture and fridges, heaved the dust carts down onto the tarmac. They armed themselves and put on sanitation worker jackets and caps.

Nathaniel, Ruth and Ana were taking the truck on for their own part of the mission. They all now hugged farewell and wished each other luck. Avram led the way into the Old City. He passed safely through Zion then called Danel with the all clear. He kept the line open in case of mishap, but luck was with them. He reached the basement apartment without incident, nodded down to Shlomo. A deep breath, then a deeper. A last check of his watch. After all these years, it seemed extraordinary to Avram that the time of preparation should finally be over and that the time of truth had come.

But it had.

FORTY-ONE

I

The intercom came on and the pilot announced departure. Walters leaned forwards to pull down the window blind. 'Don't want us waving to the crowds, eh?' asked Luke.

'Something like that,' agreed Walters. He fastened his seat belt, ostentatiously nestling his taser in his lap. Lights dimmed. A lurch of movement, though their engines weren't yet on, then a soft bump of wheels as they were towed over the hangar's door-rails. They stopped again. Now their engines came on, whining like teenagers on a museum trip. They began to move under their own power and were soon taxiing briskly. They turned into the runway, paused. Their engines roared and they hurtled into take-off. Acceleration pushed Luke a little from his seat. His heart sank as hope faded of some last-moment miracle intervention. Rachel slipped her hand into his. He interlaced his fingers with hers, gave a gentle press of gratitude and reassurance. They lifted sharply. Walters pushed the blind back up. The scattered lights of East London shrank beneath them. They banked into a turn that stole the city from their view and gave them night sky instead. It was moonless but spilled with stars, and just for a blink Luke was back beneath the Ashmolean, staring up at the wondrous galaxies of its ceiling. Then the cabin lights came on, extinguishing the night and prompting Rachel to take her hand from his, as though suddenly feeling shy.

Walters stood and stretched. 'Champagne, wasn't it?' he mocked.

'And some dry-roasted peanuts, if you've got any.'

Walters laughed. 'Back before you know it.' He went to the bar to fix himself a drink, then settled down across the aisle with his mates and Jay. He didn't have their company long, however, for Jay said something to Kieran and the two of them stood and made their way to the rear of the cabin. There was a door there with an embedded handle that Kieran had to pull out and twist to unlock and open. It was thick and heavy and surrounded by rubber seals; and it swung out towards him when surely a sliding door would have made a better use of space.

Luke frowned. Air pressure at altitude was so much greater inside a modern passenger jet than outside that their external doors and hatches invariably opened inwards. That way, even if someone tried to open them during a flight, whether by mistake or in an act of sabotage, they simply wouldn't have the strength. So that door seemed designed to separate a pressurized from an unpressurized compartment. But if that were truly the case, then Kieran and Jay wouldn't have been able to get through to the cargo hold at all. He was still puzzling over this when Rachel touched his arm. 'It's back there, isn't it?' she asked. 'The Ark?'

'I think so.'

'What's going on? Are we off to Israel?'

'As far as I can tell.'

'But *why*? All this mayhem, all this secrecy . . .' She shook her head. 'It makes no sense.'

Luke grimaced. 'There's a Jewish tradition that the Third Temple won't be built until the Ark has been found and returned to Jerusalem. But the Ark isn't enough by itself. The ground has to be cleared first. There's a Dome on it, remember?'

'Oh, Christ,' muttered Rachel. 'You think that's what Jay's uncle is up to?'

'Can't you imagine it?' said Luke. 'The Ark arriving at the Temple Mount at the very moment Jay's uncle brings down the Dome? It will look as though it was the

Ark that did it, just like at Jericho. True believers everywhere will see it as the will of God.'

'Muslims won't,' muttered Rachel. 'There'll be war.'

'Armageddon, more like,' said Luke. 'If ever there's
been a self-fulfilling prophecy, that's the one.'

'They *can't* be that crazy, can they?' asked Rachel,
looking around. 'I mean Jay and his uncle, maybe. But
these other guys, they hardly seem like religious fanatics,
do they?'

'I guess they do whatever Croke tells them.'

'But he doesn't look that way either.'

'He must have his reasons.'

'Yes. But what?'

'I don't know.'

'Maybe we should ask him when we next see him,'
suggested Rachel wryly.

'Yes,' agreed Luke. 'Maybe we should.'

II

The al-Haddad Gate was in the Muslim quarter of the
Old City, making it more difficult for Avram and his
comrades to reach unnoticed. But it was worth the extra
trouble, for the approach had a kink in it, depriving the
Waqf nightwatchmen of line of sight on the Israeli police
guardpost at the other end.

Avram shuffled his way past the mouth of the alley, an old man of no conceivable threat making his way home after a late dinner. A short distance behind, Danel and his teams of street-cleaners rattled their dust carts across the old stones. Danel paused for a cigarette as he passed the guardpost, but his lighter only sprayed sparks. He glanced at the policemen, held up his cigarette, raised an eyebrow.

'You guys are working late,' grunted one of them, taking a matchbook from his pocket.

'This damned earthquake,' said Danel. 'No one knows what's going on any more.'

'Tell me about it.'

The clatter of carts drowned out the faint noise of Shlomo and his men approaching through the shadows. The guardpost was swarmed in an instant, hands over all the policemen's mouths.

'Don't be heroes,' warned Danel.

Tranquilliser guns spat into their necks. They held them till they slumped, laid them in the shadows. Up went the dust cart lids, out came the assault weapons and the packs. They peeled off and discarded their outer garb, put on body-armour and infrared bibs that looked dark to the naked eye but which glowed brightly through their night-vision goggles, cutting the risk of friendly fire. They shouldered their packs, tightened straps. The moment Danel gave Avram the thumbs-up, he sent his prepared text message winging through the night to the Mount of Olives, where Ana, Ruth and Nathaniel were waiting.

Just a few more seconds and the fireworks would begin for real.

FORTY-TWO

I

Walters tried to kill time with a movie, but nothing held his interest. Luke and Rachel were like food stuck between his teeth – impossible to get out of his mind until they'd been dealt with. They'd be landing in Israel soon, and the Israelis weren't exactly famous for letting aircraft in without knowing exactly who was on board. And how the hell were they going to make Luke and Rachel disappear after that?

He headed forwards, knocked on Croke's door, and went in. Croke looked up irritably from some paperwork. 'What?' he asked.

'Our guests,' said Walters.

'I told you I'd take care of them.'

'Yes, but if the Israelis find them on board, we—'

'They won't. They'll be gone before then.'

'How?'

Croke sighed. 'Haven't you noticed our cargo hold? We can depressurize at altitude, dump stuff out; stuff that's been wrapped well and weighted to sink and stay sunk. Then we can pressurize again before we land.'

'We're dumping them? Where?'

'Where do you think?' His TV was tuned to a 24-hour news channel, its volume down. Now he flipped to a flight map showing their position and course. A single glance was all it took to see that there was only one body of water up to the job: the Mediterranean. 'The Aegean's no good,' said Croke. 'Too many islands. Too many shallows. So we'll have to wait until we're somewhere south-west of Cyprus.'

'What about Kohen?' asked Walters. 'He'll squeal if his friends go missing.'

'Not if we dump him too.'

'What about his uncle?'

'He won't give a shit, trust me. He only cares about the Ark. Once he sees it on Jewish soil, he'll do his part.'

'You're sure?'

'I'm sure.'

Walters nodded. 'Until the Mediterranean, then.'

II

Nathaniel had jacked up the right back wheel of the truck in order to change the tyre and so give Ana and Ruth cover to unload the Predator missiles and carry them down into the Jewish cemetery. It was a delicate operation, for a contingent of Israeli Defense Force light infantry were stationed in the Valley of Jehoshaphat, close enough that Nathaniel and the women could hear snatches of their conversation and laughter, see the occasional orange firefly of a cigarette.

Nathaniel had set his cellphone to mute. Now it began to vibrate. His heart seemed almost to vibrate in sympathy with it. He checked the message to make sure. Yes. His hands were clammy as he made his way to join the women.

'Is it time?' asked Ruth.

'It's time,' said Nathaniel.

This latest generation of Predator missiles had GPS capability. All nine were already on, programmed and ready to fire. They shouldered one each. The night was sparkling clear, the golden bulb of the Dome brilliantly lit. It usually made Nathaniel feel sick to see it, to see Islam lording it over Judaism like that; but tonight it felt righteous.

Ana gave the countdown in a quiet, calm voice:

'Three.

'Two.

'One.

'Fire.'

The noise of the triple discharge was quite something. The cemetery lit up orange and the three fat missiles flew with surprising slowness across the valley. They didn't watch them, however, but threw away the empty Predator husks, shouldered and fired another missile each. Now they unleashed the third and final set. Remarkably, all nine were on their way before the first ones struck.

Electricity for the Temple Mount was routed through two generator buildings on the northern wall. Both buildings were destroyed in an instant by the first salvo. The whole Temple Mount lit up like a fiesta in silent eruptions. The spotlights on the Dome stuttered and went dark. Only now did the triple booms reach them across the valley. By coincidence, they synchronized almost perfectly with the impact of the second volley. The Temple Mount's Golden Gate had been walled up centuries before. As the second tranche of missiles slammed into it, the vast old stones staggered yet somehow stayed standing. Then the final volley struck and the ancient structure collapsed in an avalanche of rubble that cascaded down through the Arab cemetery onto the road below.

The last of the explosions died away. The noise of gunfire reached them. It sounded strangely trivial in comparison. At first it was erratic but they quickly got a fix on their position. They knelt and raised their hands high above their heads. 'Don't shoot!' they yelled. 'We surrender! We surrender!' Their voices were drowned out by the thunder of copter blades. Spotlights dazzled them in the darkness. They braced themselves for bullets; but the bullets never came. Soldiers swarmed up the hillside and slammed them face-first into the ground. They tied their wrists behind their backs with flexi-cuffs and marched them down the slope. But the three of them smiled in triumph as they went. Their job was done.

It had started.

FORTY-THREE

I

Croke flipped through channels for breaking news from Jerusalem, but there was still nothing. It should be any moment now, yet he felt too restless to stay watching. He went forward to the cockpit, where he found Manfredo chatting away with Craig Bray and Vig, who had a pilot's licence of his own and so sat co-pilot on these trips. 'You need me, boss?' he asked.

He shook his head. 'I need our pilot.'

'Everything's sweet,' said Bray, glancing around. 'We're even a few minutes ahead of schedule.'

'It's not that,' said Croke. 'It's the depressurisation job I mentioned earlier. We're going to need to do it.'

Bray grunted. He was under no illusions why he was paid so well. 'It's a bugger at thirty thousand,' he said.

'Puts too much stress on the fuselage. Best to drop to twenty.'

'Won't that get us noticed?'

'Not if we wait until we've started our descent.'

'I need it dark and over water.'

'It'll still be dark enough, trust me; and we'll be coming in from due west, so we'll be over the Med until the last couple of minutes.'

'Okay. Good.' He went back out. There was still nothing on the news. He went through to the cargo hold to check on Kohen, found him trimming a wooden panel with a plane. 'How's it coming along?' he asked.

Kohen didn't even bother to look up. 'It would be coming along better if I didn't keep having to answer silly questions.'

'Fine,' said Croke. Until that moment, despite what he'd said to Walters, he hadn't fully resolved to kill Kohen. But this show of disrespect made up his mind for him. He returned to the main cabin, fixed himself a drink, then checked the news on one of the screens there. Still nothing.

'Maybe they've been caught,' said Luke.

Croke squinted around at him. 'What are you talking about?' he asked.

'Jay's uncle and his Third Temple friends. Maybe they were caught on their way to the Dome.'

Croke glanced towards the hold. 'Your friend's been shooting his mouth off, has he?'

'He told us nothing,' said Luke. 'It's the only way this makes sense. Though there's one thing we can't work out.'

'What?'

'We get why *they're* doing it,' said Luke. 'They want a Third Temple. But what's in it for you?'

'You're the ones with the letters after your names,' said Croke. 'Surely you must have some ideas.'

It was the girl who answered. 'Money,' she said.

The contempt in her voice nettled Croke. And he was curious, too, about how much they'd deduced, how much others might deduce. 'Who'd pay me for such a thing?' he asked, sitting down opposite them.

'Whoever benefits from Armageddon, I'd guess,' said Luke. 'Arms manufacturers. Oil companies with reserves outside the Middle East.'

'Why pick on oil?' asked Croke. 'Nobody benefits from Middle Eastern wars like renewable energy. Being green isn't the same as being ethical. Then there are the logistics suppliers and communications companies and mercenary groups – or security subcontractors, as I believe they like to call themselves these days.'

'Well? Which?'

Croke shrugged. 'All of them. None of them. Does it matter?'

'And they hired you to recruit fanatics to bring down the Dome?'

'The fanatics were already there, believe me. They've been there forever. Trouble is, while they talked a good game, nothing ever happened. And it's not *will* they lack. It's resources. Skills. *Professionalism*, you might say. My clients found that . . . *intensely* frustrating.'

'So that's your job?' snorted Luke. 'Project manager?'

'If you like.'

'And how much does an apocalypse cost these days? Fifty million? A hundred? What does that work out as? A dollar a life?' He turned to Rachel. 'You want to know who to blame for your brother? You're looking at him.'

'I didn't make the world this way,' said Croke tightly. 'I just live in it.'

'Is that how you sleep at night? By telling yourself that?'

'You want me to be ashamed? Is that it? Well, I'm not. There are finite resources in the world. There's only so much land and gold and oil. Every time someone takes a larger share for themselves, someone else goes short. I'm okay with that. I'm okay with other people going short. But here's the thing: *so are you*. You're fine with other people going short, you're fine with starvation, mutilation and massacre, just so long as it happens off-screen, just so long as you don't have to watch.'

'That's some philosophy,' said Rachel.

'It's called realism.'

'It's called narcissism,' said Luke. 'Caring about nothing but yourself. Though I do admire you for one thing.'

'I'm flattered. What?'

'Your sort usually leave the dangerous work to the flunkies. Yet here you are.'

'I like to see a project through,' nodded Croke. 'Besides . . .'

'Besides what?'

Croke hesitated. The truth had been eating away at him for two days now. He hankered to tell someone, even if only these two. 'You think me a narcissist,' he said. 'But it's just possible that someone way more important than me wants me here. That they've been planning on my being here for a very long time.'

'Like who?' frowned Luke.

Croke smiled as he leaned back in his seat. 'Like God,' he said.

II

The moment Avram saw the Jerusalem sky turn orange, he gave the order to go. His own legs were too old to lead the assault itself, so he left that to Danel and Shlomo. They had charges ready to blow the al-Haddad Gate, but the *Waqf* guards fled through it at the first sight of them, leaving it open behind them. They poured on through as the second volley of Predators struck, making silhouettes and easy targets of the *Waqf* guards. No point making martyrs of them, so they aimed bursts at their legs until they tumbled prostrate before their precious Dome. They raced up the steps onto the plaza. The generator annexe and the Golden Gate were ablaze, and guards were running about like termites from a scattered mound, blinded and deafened by the explosions, crying out in pain, outrage and terror.

The third and final volley struck. The east lit up like sunrise, engulfing a man in its flames like some primeval sacrifice. The shockwave buffeted Avram and he stumbled and went down. Heat scorched his cheek, but with only rock to feast on, the flames died quickly. Danel set charges and blew open the Dome's northern door. They hurried inside. A few old men were cowering in the shadows, but it was the work of a moment to round them up and send them on their way.

Everyone knew their role. Shlomo and his men took the doors and windows, securing them and establishing lines of fire over the whole Mount. Danel and the others collected the packs and made a mound of them beneath the Dome. For his part, Avram took a bullhorn to the door. He was about to speak when a group of young Arab men armed with pickaxe handles and the like yelled out and charged. Avram watched in satisfaction as Shlomo and his comrades scythed them down. They writhed on the ground, weeping and wailing, before dragging themselves back into cover, their crippling agony certain to give other potential heroes pause for thought.

He turned the bullhorn to maximum, spoke in Arabic and English. The Dome, he vowed, would be surrendered intact once their demands were met in full. But it would be destroyed instantly at any attempts to retake it. He repeated the message until satisfied it had got through. He set a satellite modem on a ledge, acquired a signal, tuned three laptops to the news, and arranged them so that everyone could watch or at least listen. He photographed the explosives being strapped to the Dome's pillars, then copied the images onto his own laptop. He checked Croke's current location on a flight-tracker website. He wouldn't be landing for a while yet, so he opened the Word document he'd written earlier, the one with the demands for the prisoner releases and for the military escort for Croke and his cargo. He cut the second demand and pasted it into a new Word document for sending out later. He made a few final tweaks to the prisoner list, composed an email to all the recipients in his address book, then attached the photographs and the prisoner list and sent it on its way.

He allowed himself a private smile. That should keep them on their toes.

FORTY-FOUR

I

'So you're on a mission from God,' mocked Luke. 'What are you? A Blues Brother?'

Croke felt himself flushing. Perhaps foolishly, he'd expected his revelation to evoke awe rather than ridicule. 'Aren't you *curious*?' he asked. 'Aren't you even the slightest bit curious?'

'About what?'

'About *everything*. About us finding the Ark today, for example. Today of all days.'

Luke frowned. 'What's so special about today?'

Croke squinted at him. 'You don't know? I thought you were a Newton scholar.'

'What are you talking about?'

'I'm talking about his *Observations upon the Prophecies*

of Daniel and the Apocalypse of St John. Haven't you read it?'

'Not for a while. It's more Jay's area than mine.'

Croke nodded. 'We spent an afternoon together at the start of all this. I found his interpretation of the prophecies amusing at first. But the more he showed me, the less sceptical I became.'

'You should check out the moon landings,' said Luke. 'They never really happened, you know.'

Croke turned to Rachel. 'Were you aware that Newton predicted the date of Armageddon? That he predicted the time of the Second Coming and the end of the world as we know it? I wasn't. I never even knew he was interested in such things. But he was. And he was very specific about them too. He stated that all of this would come to pass once the Whore of Babylon had held earthly power for a specific number of years. The Whore of Babylon, to Newton, was the Catholic Church. The Church acquired earthly power when Pepin first gave them lands to administer. And how many years were to pass from that moment until the Second Coming? I'm glad you ask. The answer doesn't appear just once in the Books of Daniel and Revelation. It appears *five times*. Twelve hundred and sixty years. And when is 1260 years since the Second Donation of Pepin? What date does Newton predict for Armageddon and the end of everything we know? Yes, you've guessed it. *This* year.'

'Is that really the best you've got?' asked Rachel. 'A prophecy from the Book of Revelation?'

'Look around you,' said Croke. 'Earthquakes, wars, famines, pestilence, hurricanes, turmoil in the Catholic Church. All exactly as predicted for the Last Days. And then there's the big one. Another prophecy of Daniel as interpreted by Newton, but even more specific this time: Armageddon is to take place seven weeks after the return of the Jews. Seven weeks is forty-nine days. A day in prophecy equates to a year in the real world. And do you know what was happening in Israel forty-nine years ago today? Forty-nine years ago today was the *exact moment* the Jews regained control of Jerusalem for the first time in two thousand years. *Forty-nine years ago today*. And when do we find the Ark? Today, of all days. And you still think it's *coincidence*?'

'Yes,' said Luke.

Croke smiled and forced himself to relax. 'It's not just Judaism and Christianity that believe in the Messiah, Armageddon and the End of Days,' he said. 'They all appear in Islam too. Did you know that? All these great religions with a shared vision of a final battle between good and evil, the coming of a saviour. Do you know what the main difference is? The main difference is which faiths the various armies profess.'

'People are tribal. What's your point?'

'You wouldn't believe how many different scenarios

have been predicted. Hundreds of them, all based on slightly different readings of the Tanakh, the Bible and the Quran. But there's one tradition in particular that caught my fancy: that the Ark will be discovered and brought to Jerusalem by the Antichrist himself, enabling the Third Temple to be built. And then this Antichrist will be crowned king in the rebuilt Holy of Holies, and he'll rule the earth for seven years.' He leaned a little closer to them both. 'That would be quite something, don't you think? To be crowned king in the Holy of Holies? To rule the earth for seven years? Especially as one man's Antichrist is really only another man's Messiah, except with worse P.R. Though he does have the better titles, to be fair. The Man of Sin. The Son of Perdition. The Dragon. They have a certain ring to them, don't they? You know what my favourite is? My favourite is the Prince of Rome. That has some real swagger to it, wouldn't you agree? The Prince of Rome.'

'And you take this stuff seriously, do you?' asked Luke.

'Don't you ever get tired of your own scepticism?' sighed Croke. 'Doesn't there come a point when the signs so mount up that belief becomes the rational option? Don't you ever look up at the sky and get overwhelmed by the sheer scale of it all? I do. I'll be thinking about orbits or gravity or electromagnetism or one of the myriad other things that have to be *exactly* as they are for us even to exist, and I'll get dizzy.'

'You should take a pill.'

'So you're immune to it, are you?'

'People have been predicting Armageddon for two thousand years. Yet somehow we're still here.'

'You're a scientist,' suggested Croke.

'I'm a believer in the scientific method,' replied Luke.

'Me too,' said Croke. 'Me too. I was raised that way. My father really is a scientist, you see. Not some wannabe hanger-on like you. A physicist, to be precise. He taught at MIT for a while, which you don't get to do unless you're very, very good, as I'm sure you appreciate. But then the US Air Force came calling, and he was too much the patriot to say no. He's been with them ever since, developing surveillance, intelligence and weapons' systems, that kind of thing. That's how I got started in my line of work, if you're curious. All those men with wings and stars on their uniforms who came visiting while I was a kid. I couldn't have asked for a better contacts list.'

'Your father must be *very* proud of you,' Luke said.

Croke laughed. 'He is, as it happens. But that's not what's under discussion right now. I'm trying to explain why I don't share your certainty, though I largely share your outlook. And I'm also trying to answer your earlier question, about why I'm on this flight.'

'Go on, then.'

'There's a town called Rome in upstate New York. Maybe you've heard of it?'

'What if I have?'

'The USAF has an important research base there. That's where my father went when he left MIT fifty years ago. It's where he's spent his whole career. He's actually run the place for the past three decades. He's been running it so long, do you know what they call him?'

'What?'

'They call him the King,' said Croke. 'The King of Rome.' And he laughed at the shock on Luke and Rachel's faces, and he pushed himself to his feet and sauntered back to his office.

II

Benyamin had fallen behind the others on the race to the Dome. He was older than everyone but Avram, and far less fit. The intoxication of seeing the Ark had worn off too, leaving him wondering what the hell he'd let himself in for. He arrived inside as Danel pulled the fuses of two construction flares that he'd set up on the carpet beneath the cupola, banishing the great darkness with their fluttering orange light, lighting up the gigantic space above them. Benyamin had seen countless pictures over the years, of course. He'd seen videos. But it was an Arab achievement and so he'd always dismissed it as nothing, as swimming pool architecture. But standing here, staring upwards, it was impossible to dismiss. Impossible to feel anything other than awe. He'd had no idea at all it would look like this, that *anything* could look like this. He felt giddy. He remembered why he'd wanted to become an architect in the first place.

A pair of doves had found their way inside – always a hazard with such vast spaces. Startled from their roost by the sudden noise and light, they flapped around the cupola, seeking escape from this most gilded of cages. One of them shat in fear even as Benyamin watched, spattering the Foundation Stone itself. His heart went out to it, to them both; and just for a blink he saw his daughters in their last moments, trapped in the rear of that Haifa bus while his wife did her best to comfort them and shield them with her body, and the gunmen outside discharged their magazines, then coolly clipped new ones in.

The terror they must have felt.

'Snap out of it,' said Danel. 'I need you.'

Benyamin's legs weren't working properly. Too much lactic acid from all the running he'd done. He had to look down at his feet as he followed him to a pillar, half concealed by steel scaffolding pipes, on which explosive charges had already been placed. 'Well?' asked Danel. 'Will they bring it down?'

A single glance was all it took. The scaffolding was clearly there to facilitate repairs, not to buttress the Dome.

'They'll bring it down,' Benyamin said. And that was that, his entire purpose for being here.

He stood by a pillar, wanting to be inconspicuous, watching as they went to work on the Foundation Stone. First, they covered the exposed rock itself with a double layer of blue silk. Then they unrolled two neoprene air mattresses side by side, zipped them together into a single large mat. They carried this mat over to the Foundation Stone and set it carefully down on it, then tied it to the surrounding pillars with a series of ropes.

The neoprene mattress had numerous internal compartments, each with its own intake valve. Danel and his team now fetched canisters of industrial foam, fitted nozzles to these valves, and pumped the compartments full. The foam expanded inside the neoprene before setting into a hard honeycomb shell capable of absorbing the impact of falling rubble, thus protecting the Foundation Stone from the coming demolition. There was still a risk that something sharp might stab its way through, however, so they stripped off their bullet proof vests and fitted them together with Velcro straps to make a Kevlar blanket that they laid across the neoprene carapace.

The Foundation Stone was now as safe as they could feasibly make it. They were ready to bring down the Dome.

FORTY-FIVE

I

'Oh sweet Jesus,' said Rachel. 'He thinks he's the Prince of Rome. He thinks he's the fucking Antichrist.'

'He's crazy,' agreed Luke. 'He's completely crazy.'

Rachel pulled an anguished face. 'But what if there's something to it? I mean, he's got a point, hasn't he? The Ark, the Newton prophecies, all the wars and earthquakes, the disease and famine. How many coincidences can there be before they stop being coincidences?'

'There are always wars and earthquakes. Always disease and famine. And when are the Catholics not in turmoil? And forget Newton's prophecies. He wasn't a date-setter. He abhorred that kind of thing. He made his predictions to tamp down Second Coming fervour, not to exacerbate it. Anyway, he always said that the End

Times couldn't begin until certain things had come to pass – not that they would begin when they had.'

'What about the 1260 years? Is that true?'

Luke grimaced. 'Yes. But so what? Newton never linked it to the Second Donation of Pepin. He mentioned Pepin, yes, but only along with Phocas and Charlemagne and plenty of other possibilities. All Jay did was pick his preferred date, subtract 1260 from it, and see what fitted.'

'And how about us finding the Ark today of all days?'

'We found it today because these people went to extraordinary lengths to make sure we did. You think they'd have dug up St Paul's if they hadn't needed it till next year?'

'I suppose.'

'Listen to me,' said Luke. 'There's nothing ordained about all this. There's nothing destined. We can still stop it. We *have* to stop it. If we don't, it'll be a bloodbath. Millions of people will die.'

She rattled her handcuff. 'Fine. But how?'

'By keeping our nerve. By waiting for our moment. It'll come. And when it does, we have to seize it. No hesitation. No holding back. No regrets.'

Rachel gave a determined nod. 'No regrets,' she agreed.

II

The Prime Minister of Israel still had sleep in her eyes as she arrived in the cabinet room. The Interior Minister and the Ministers for Foreign Affairs, Finance and Intelligence were already there, while the Defence Ministry was represented by the Chief of the General Staff. And each of them were attended by flurries of frantic aides checking their devices and whispering breaking news into their bosses' ears.

'Are our captives from the Mount of Olives talking yet?' she asked.

'Not yet, Prime Minister,' said Interior.

'How are Gaza and the West Bank?'

He nodded briskly. 'We have multiple reports of disorder, including several settlers' homes on fire. At least a dozen rockets have been fired. No word on casualties yet.'

'We're taking fire in the north too,' said the Chief of the General Staff. 'Mortar shells mostly.'

'Hezbollah?'

'We imagine so.'

'Any casualties?'

He shrugged. 'If not yet, then soon.'

'This is going to turn hot?'

'It's already hot. How much hotter it gets depends on the Dome. If these people bring it down . . .' He shook his head. 'We have to mobilize,' he said.

'If we mobilize, all our neighbours will mobilize too. It'll only make things worse.'

'With respect, Prime Minister, things already are worse. The moment the Dome comes down, we'll be at war. We need to be ready.'

She looked around the table. Intelligence, Finance and Interior nodded, but Foreign Affairs was occupied with passing out copies of some new briefing paper. 'What's this?' she asked.

'Excuse me, Prime Minister,' he said. 'That list of prisoners they want released: these are their biographies.'

'Any pattern?'

'Not that we can tell.'

The Prime Minister studied her copy of the list. She recognized most of the names, and the ones she didn't recognize fell into similar categories: Israeli citizens held on various charges in Egypt, Lebanon, Syria and Jordan. A mix of soldiers, spies, criminals and ordinary citizens who'd become victims of the region's power games. 'What do you think?' she asked. 'Manageable?'

Foreign Affairs nodded. 'We're already in the middle of exchange talks for many of them. We should be able to expedite.'

'Prisoner exchange?' scowled Interior. 'It's *their* damned Dome.'

'We have to give up something,' said the Prime Minister, 'or they'll blame us for it.'

'They'll blame us anyway. They always do.'

Intelligence had just received a briefing paper of his own. 'Excuse me,' he said. 'But I think we may have found out who's behind this.'

'And?'

'His name's Avram Kohen. We've had our eye on him for some time.'

'You've had your eye on him?' said Finance. 'And yet he's taken the Dome?'

'With respect, if you didn't keep cutting our budget—'

'Enough!' said the Prime Minister. This was no time for turf wars. 'What makes you think it's this man Kohen?' she asked.

'We've put equipment in the homes and offices of various people we're watching. The moment this broke, we ran a roll-call. All were accounted for, except Kohen and some of his suspected associates. And we have an additional asset for Kohen: a live-in nephew. He assured us just a fortnight ago that nothing imminent was planned.'

'He was lying?'

'Maybe. Or maybe they rumbled him and were using him to feed us misinformation.' He looked up from his notes. 'He's supposed to check in every other day, if he can; but we didn't hear from him last night and he's not answering his cell or his home phone. And, like I said, several of Kohen's other suspected associates have also vanished.'

'It's them, then.'

'Yes, Prime Minister.' He grimaced to indicate worse to come. 'The thing is, Kohen isn't a settler or a nationalist, the kind who might credibly want Jewish prisoners released. He's an out-and-out Third Temple fanatic.'

She slapped her hand on the list. 'Then why these demands?'

'A smokescreen, Prime Minister,' said the Chief of the General Staff. 'He wants us negotiating rather than sending in Special Forces.'

'Yes. But if he wants the Dome down, why not just bring it down? We're assuming it's already rigged to blow, right? Why play for time?'

'Maybe they're waiting for the media to get there,' suggested Foreign Affairs. 'Prime time in America.'

'Or maybe they're hoping to spark some kind of popular uprising.'

Intelligence had just received another memo. He scanned it and looked up. 'Prime Minister,' he said. 'We've been running checks on all Kohen's known associates. He has links to a group of American evangelists. They want a Third Temple for their own reasons, as I'm sure you're aware.'

'Fucking rapture-heads,' muttered Interior.

'One of their go-betweens is an arms dealer called Vernon Croke. He has close ties to the CIA, so we can't *do* anything about him; but we keep an eye on him all the same. The thing is, he was seen with a senior American counterterrorism officer during yesterday's dirty bomb flap in London. And then he left City Airport on his private jet late last night. He's due to land at Ben Gurion around dawn.'

Silence fell around the room. No one here believed in coincidences, not on days like this. '*That's* what Kohen's waiting for,' murmured the Prime Minister. 'He's waiting for Croke.'

'Or for whatever he's bringing,' said the Foreign Secretary. 'But what?'

The Chief of the General Staff leaned forwards. 'When those three on the Mount of Olives took out the generator buildings, they also brought down the Golden Gate. According to our soldiers in the valley, they hit it at least six times. Predator missiles are GPS controlled; they're accurate to a metre. That is to say: they hit the Golden Gate because the Golden Gate was what they were aiming at.'

The Prime Minister shook her head. 'What's your point?' she asked.

'The Golden Gate is the one prophesied by Elijah,' said Interior. 'That's why the Arabs blocked it up five hundred years ago. That's why they built a cemetery in front of it, to render unclean anyone passing through.'

'Prophesied by Elijah?' She looked utterly perplexed.

Foreign Affairs coughed into his hand, a little

embarrassed by her ignorance. 'Prime Minister, Elijah prophesied that when *he* came, he'd enter Jerusalem by the Golden Gate.'

'When *he* came? When *who* came?'

'Prime Minister,' said the Chief of the General Staff. 'He was talking about the Messiah.'

III

At last the story broke. Red banners announcing an incident in Jerusalem's Old City appeared at the foot of Croke's TV screen. He turned up the volume. The first reports were ambiguous enough that he feared the assault had failed. Then a news camera arrived near the Temple Mount and it became obvious that it had succeeded to perfection.

He'd already drafted his message to Grant, prodding him for the next set of passwords for the Rutherford & Small's bank account. Now he sent it on its way.

The TV reporter handed back to her studio. A harried-looking anchor attempted to make sense of the information pouring in. The Dome had been seized by up to thirty armed men. The Golden Gate was a smouldering ruin. Two *Waqf* guards were confirmed dead, and many more were grievously injured. There were reports of arrests on the Mount of Olives.

Croke checked his inbox. Nothing. He wasn't anxious, though. Seventy million was a fleabite to Grant's friends, and they weren't stupid. They knew he had the Ark in his hold; and while it might not fetch his full fee on the black market, it would still do him nicely.

Live feed now appeared from East Jerusalem. Thousands of Muslims were marching on the Temple Mount. The reporter stopped several for their opinions. Most sounded angry beyond control, but others strove for calm, citing rumours of a threat to destroy the Dome at any attempt to storm it.

He checked his inbox again, sighed. Looked like he'd have to give Grant a nudge. Every plane was, by law, fitted with GPS. Plug an aircraft's registration number into a flight-tracking website, therefore, and you could follow its progress live. Grant would doubtless be following him right now, so a change of course was certain to get his attention. But even as he was about to give Craig Bray the order, the new passwords arrived. He typed them in, clenched a fist in quiet satisfaction when they worked, giving him irrevocable joint authority over the $70 million.

So close now. So very, very close.

FORTY-SIX

I

'So the Messiah is about to arrive on a plane from London,' said the Prime Minister. 'Is that what you're telling me?'

'I'm telling you that these people didn't take down the Golden Gate on a whim,' said the Chief of the General Staff. 'Predator missiles are costly and hard to get hold of. To use so many on a single target . . .'

'Let's send up fighters,' said Interior. 'Let's shoot them down before they land.'

'What if he really is the Messiah?' muttered Foreign Affairs.

The Prime Minister silenced the snickering with a glare. 'If Kohen and Croke are together on this, they're bound to be in contact. What if they take the Dome down in revenge?'

'And kill themselves in the process?'

'If they have to.' But the question made her think. 'Kohen and his friends inside the Dome, they'll want to get out alive, right?'

'So one would imagine.'

'Which means they'll have to leave the Dome before they blow it.' She slapped the table. 'That's what this list is for. We get the prisoners released; they say thank you and give themselves up. And then, while we're escorting them away . . .'

Silence greeted this analysis. It sounded too horribly plausible. 'What do we do?' asked Finance. But no one answered.

Intelligence had left his seat to take a call. Now he returned. 'Forgive me, Prime Minister,' he said, holding out the phone.

'What is it?'

'Maybe nothing. But we found a letter in Kohen's house. A hospital appointment. This is his doctor now. He won't tell me what the appointment was about. Patient confidentiality. But he says he'll tell you, if you assure him it's a matter of national security.'

She nodded and took the phone. 'This is the Prime Minister,' she said. 'This is a matter of extreme national security. Tell me about Kohen.' She felt the blood draining as he talked, but she thanked him when he'd finished, passed back the phone. 'Kohen's dying,' she announced flatly. 'Two days ago, he found out he was dying.'

'He's Samson,' murmured Foreign Affairs. 'He's bringing the temple down on himself.'

'What do we do?' asked Finance again.

The Prime Minister glanced sharply at him. For all his reputation as a hawk, this crisis had exposed him as bewildered and feeble. If they survived tonight, she was going to need someone tougher. She turned to Foreign Affairs. 'Misdirection works both ways,' she said. 'Have your people contact the foreign and interior ministries of everyone holding these prisoners. Plead with them. Haggle. Make offers. Brief reporters. Give interviews. We have to assume that Kohen will be monitoring your efforts, so do everything you can to convince him that we've fallen for his plan.'

'Yes, Prime Minister.'

'They're waiting for this man Croke,' she told Interior. 'We need to delay his arrival. Stack him. Make him circle. Just buy us time.'

He nodded and rose to his feet. 'I'll get on it now, Prime Minister.'

'Nothing obvious. We don't want them knowing we're on to him.'

'No, Prime Minister.'

She turned to her Chief of the General Staff. 'We can't risk waiting,' she said. 'You're going to have to storm the Dome.'

He gave a grimace. 'It won't be easy,' he warned. 'It's surrounded by wide-open spaces. They have line of sight from doors and windows. They appear to be well-armed, well-trained, and they're certain to be anticipating some kind of action.'

'What if we drop in from above?'

'That would mean helicopters. They'd be sure to hear them.'

'The TV stations have been clamouring for us to let them put their choppers up,' said Interior, pausing at the door. 'We've told them no so far. If we gave them permission, would their noise cover ours?'

'What if one of them broadcasts us doing the drop?' asked Finance.

'Then they'll lose all future use of their testicles,' said the Prime Minister curtly. She turned to General Staff. 'Well? Could you make it work?'

'This kind of operation,' he said unhappily, 'it takes precise intelligence. It takes planning. It takes training.'

'I know it does. But we don't have time. It'll start getting light soon. Your men need to be in place before then.'

'Yes, Prime Minister. I'll set it up now.'

'Thank you. And General . . .'

'Yes?'

'Your best people. Your *very* best. Let them know that these fanatics want to start a war that could mean the end of Israel. Our nation's survival depends upon them. So they have my authority to do whatever it takes. *Whatever it takes*. If they see even a glimmer of an opportunity, *any* glimmer, they're to take it.'

He nodded soberly. 'Yes, Prime Minister,' he said. 'I'll let them know.'

II

Walters found himself watching the flight-map obsessively. Finally they passed south of the Aegean and reached unbroken deep water. Croke nodded when he went to notify him. 'Craig says we shouldn't depressurize at thirty thousand,' he said. 'Too much stress. He says to wait until we're on our descent.'

'Won't we be too close to the coast by then?'

'Apparently not. We'll be coming in over water. And it will still be dark enough. Okay?'

'Okay,' said Walters. But he was fuming as he left, angry at himself more than anything. It was clear to him now that Croke had been stringing him along. He'd never intended to get rid of Luke and Rachel. Why should he care if Walters went down for murder, after all? It would just mean one less salary to pay.

Bollocks to that, thought Walters. Croke liked his *faits accomplis* – it was time to give him one.

He made his way back to the cargo hold, found Kohen kneeling before the Ark, cleaning it with swabs of cotton wool dabbed in solvent. 'Take a break,' he told Kieran, who was on watch.

'It's okay,' said Kieran. 'It's pretty interesting, actually.'

'I said take a break.'

Kieran hesitated, then nodded. 'Yes, boss.'

Walters walked him to the door and closed it behind him, leaving himself alone with Kohen. He hadn't come equipped for this, but there were abundant raw materials to hand. The shrink-wrap and other packaging materials from the pallets had been stuffed between the oak chests and the wall. He found a length of five feet or so of woven blue polythene strapping, tugged it to make sure it was fit for purpose. 'How's it coming along?' he asked Kohen.

'Nearly ready,' nodded Kohen. 'I've tested all the components. They each do precisely what they're supposed to do. And the design itself . . . it's *brilliant*. I honestly think it's going to work.'

'Is that right?' asked Walters.

'It's been three hundred years,' said Kohen. 'So there's no way to know for sure until we try it. But yes, I think so.'

Walters wound the polythene strapping twice around each hand to give himself a good grip, while leaving enough free in between to do the grim business. He crossed his arms as he walked up behind Kohen, making a loop of it. 'Why not try it now?' he asked.

'At thirty thousand feet?' scoffed Kohen. 'What if I've misread the plans? What if we hit turbulence? No, thanks. I vote we wait until we land. It won't take long, after all. Just pour in the acid and—'

Walters brought the loop of strapping down around Kohen's throat and pulled it tight before he could cry out. Kohen dropped his swab and tried to claw his fingernails beneath it, but the garrotte was a cruel weapon: it didn't allow for comebacks. And Kohen was far too late, too slow and too weak. Already he was struggling for air. His face turned hideous colours, he flapped his arms, he kicked. A wet patch appeared on the crotch of his trousers. His struggles weakened into spasms that became twitches and then even those stopped.

Walters laid Kohen on his back. He pulled the blue strapping as tight around his neck as he could, then tied a knot in it, like a macabre string tie. He flapped out a tarpaulin, dragged Jay onto it, then folded it back over him so that he couldn't be seen from the main cabin. Satisfied, he wiped his hands on his trousers then went to find a fresh length of strapping.

It was time for the girl.

FORTY-SEVEN

I

Galia Michaeli had dreamed all her young life of being at the heart of a breaking news story. Now, in just her second week of work experience at the Tel Aviv studios, she was at the heart of the breaking story of the decade. And her main task had been made very clear to her three times already. It was to make coffee on request, and otherwise stay out of the way.

The news channel had a generic email address, but no one ever used it. No one who mattered, at least. It was, however, one of Galia's jobs to check it every morning, just in case. She did so now. It included another copy of the already notorious email from the Dome assailants. They'd obviously sent it to everyone they could think of. She opened the various attachments out of curiosity. Most were photographs that had already been shown on the news. And there was also the list of prisoners to be released. Without any great expectation, she checked this Word document to see if it had its Track Changes feature on, and whether she'd therefore be able to see earlier drafts. She sat up a little when she noticed a few minor changes in formatting. And then, as if by magic, a whole extra paragraph suddenly appeared.

Our final demand: Aircraft registration number N12891F has now landed at Ben Gurion Airport. Its passengers and cargo are to be escorted by military convoy to the Golden Gate on the Temple Mount. Failure to comply will result in the immediate destruction of the Dome.

Her mouth was dry as she copied the aircraft registration number into a search engine. The second result was for a flight-tracking website. She clicked on the link. A map of the eastern Mediterranean appeared, then a dotted line heading straight for Israel. Contrary to what the paragraph claimed, the aircraft hadn't yet arrived at Ben Gurion.

In fact, it wasn't due to land for the best part of another hour.

II

Something was going on in the cargo hold. Rachel was sure of it. Something bad. The look on Walters' face as he'd gone in there; the look on Kieran's after he'd been turfed out; the way Kieran had gone to Pete, was now murmuring with him and casting worried looks at the door.

She glanced at Luke. He nodded to let her know he'd seen it too.

The door opened. Walters came out, trying to look casual, but failing. She took and squeezed Luke's hand. His answering squeeze made her feel incomparably better. 'No hesitation,' he murmured.

'No regrets,' she agreed.

Walters went to join Pete and Kieran. They held an intense conversation in low voices. Kieran shook his head angrily and walked off towards the cockpit, but Pete nodded. Walters passed him the taser and then they came over to Luke and Rachel.

'Your friend Jakob wants a word,' Walters told Rachel, nodding at the cargo bay.

'With me?' she asked.

'He has a question about the Ark, apparently.' He reached into his pocket for the handcuff keys. 'Didn't understand it myself, to be honest. But I'm sure he'll explain.'

'Maybe I should go,' said Luke. 'The Ark's more my field than Rachel's.'

'He asked for her,' said Walters. He inserted the key into the cuff, turned it and released her wrist. She threw a beseeching glance at Luke; this had to be their moment. It seemed he agreed. He lunged forwards and smashed his knee up into Pete's crotch. Pete yowled and tried to fry him with the taser, but Luke anticipated him and slapped it against Walters instead. Walters screamed and fell to the ground, convulsing and clutching his chest. Pete tried to turn the taser on Luke, but he managed to hold him off long enough for Rachel to retrieve the dropped handcuff keys and release him. He instantly propelled himself from his seat, crunched his head up into Pete's jaw, sent him sprawling. He wrested the taser from him as he went down, gave him a squirt. 'The hold,' he yelled at Rachel.

She nodded and leapt over the white leather seat onto the carpet behind, heaved the door open. Luke was close behind, but Kieran had obviously heard the commotion for now he charged into the cabin and rugby-tackled Luke, took him down onto the carpet. Luke tried to taser him but Walters was already up again. He kicked the taser from Luke's hand then laid into him with his boot, and Kieran and Pete quickly joined in.

There were plastic bottles of solvent and sulphuric acid on the floor by the Ark. Rachel picked up one full of acid, uncapped it and swung it in a backhand arc, spraying it over the three men's throats and faces as Luke rolled away from them. Walters turned his back in time but Pete and Kieran felt the sting of it at once, screaming in pain and rage as it scorched their skin. She grabbed Luke's hand and dragged him into the hold then tried to slam closed the door behind her. Walters stuck his foot in the gap, however, and hauled it open again, aiming the taser at her. She grabbed a bottle of solvent and squirted it over his chest and face as he fired. The jolt stunned her and flung her onto her back, but what shocked her more was the way the sparks ignited the solvent as it spurted over Walters, erupting into a violent blaze. He shrieked and dropped the taser, tried to slap out the flames on his throat and chin and clothes and hair, but too late, they were already in his mouth, each breath drawing them further down into his chest and lungs.

Luke shoulder-charged him and knocked him backwards out of the hold. He grabbed the door by its interior handle and slammed it shut. Rachel was still trembling from the jolt, but she struggled to her feet to help him hold it. There was no lock on this side, no way to block it, opening outwards into the main cabin as it did; but there was a length of blue strapping on the floor, and Luke used it to tether the door to the base of the Ark, pulling it as taut as it would go. He found two more lengths of tape among some discarded packaging and anchored the door even more firmly.

'Will that hold?' asked Rachel.

'It'll give us time to find something better.'

'Like what?'

He waved a hand to indicate the whole cargo bay: the Ark, the pallets of supplies, the overhead lockers and the oak chests. 'I'll take a look,' he said.

FORTY-EIGHT

I

Galia Michaeli printed off the flight map and the amended prisoner release document and hurried into the control room. Everyone was far too frantic to pay any attention to someone as lowly as her, however. They all waved her away. Her nerve failed her. These people were experienced journalists, after all. They knew what mattered and what didn't. She was probably overestimating the significance of her find, she told herself. She retreated and went back out.

The editor of the morning show was on his mobile in the corridor, bawling out their hapless Jerusalem reporter for letting himself be scooped by Channel 2. He was infamous for his temper, her editor, for firing staff on the spot for the most innocuous offences. For all she knew, he'd seen the extra paragraph when the email had first arrived, had discarded it as nothing. The temptation to pretend she hadn't found it at all, to keep her head down and not be noticed, almost overwhelmed her. But this was news, she realized; and news was her vocation.

She went to stand in front of him, nervously held out the two pages. He took them, scanned them, frowned. 'What the fuck are these?' he demanded.

She did her best to explain, though her tongue was a small mammal in her mouth. He glared at her as she spoke; he looked incandescent.

'You're trying to tell me this extra paragraph was in that fucking email?' he asked.

She nodded, aware her eyes were watering. 'They must have deleted it before they sent it out,' she managed. 'But not properly.'

He nodded. If possible, he looked even angrier. He marched straight into the control room, held the sheets up high. 'Why the fuck did none of you pricks spot this?' he yelled.

'Spot what?'

They checked their own copies of the document as he explained, verified her story for themselves. For the first time, they looked at Galia with something approaching respect. It made her feel ten feet tall.

'I want cameras in the air now,' the editor said. 'I want this fucking aircraft filmed all the way in.'

'At this time of morning?' asked Lev, his deputy, the only one who ever dared stand up to him. 'Forget anything fixed wing. We'd never get it prepped and up in time. But maybe we could use the traffic chopper.'

'What's its ceiling?'

'Three thousand metres, give or take. Enough to film their approach.'

'Put them up now,' he said. 'I want to skull-fuck those Channel 2 bastards. You understand? It's payback time.' He turned to Galia. 'You're our new work experience girl, right?'

'Yes, sir.'

'And all the shit we give you, it hasn't put you off?'

'I want to work here, sir. More than anything.'

'Then congratulations,' he told her. 'You're hired.'

II

Croke was checking the latest bulletins from Jerusalem when he heard the commotion outside. He ignored it at first, assuming it would sort itself out. But then came the shrieks. He opened his door to see Walters staggering backwards out of the cargo hold, his whole upper body ablaze. He fell onto his back and lay there screaming, his face charred and flames flickering from his mouth as if from some vanquished dragon as he died. Croke whirled on Pete and Kieran, washing their arms and faces in the galley sink. 'What the hell happened?' he demanded.

'Acid,' said Pete succinctly, turning to show Croke his blotched and blistered face, the frightening red of his corneas.

The sight shocked Croke into silence. But not for long. 'Get in there,' he said. 'Finish them.'

'You're kidding, right?' snarled Kieran. 'They've got acid, solvent and a taser.'

'We can cover up your exposed skin.'

'We can cover up *your* exposed skin.'

'That wasn't a request,' said Croke. 'That was an order.'

'Stuff it up your arse.'

'Jesus!' said Manfredo, arriving with Vig at that moment. 'What happened?

'They're in there,' said Croke, nodding at the door. 'Go get them.'

'No need,' said Vig. 'Easier just to lock them in, then depressurize. We'll starve them of air in no time.'

Croke frowned. 'We can do that from out here?'

Vig nodded. 'Sure. It's all controlled from the cockpit.'

'What about breathing masks? Won't they drop down?'

'We stripped them out last year,' said Vig. 'It was too much grief having them deploy every time we depressurized. Anyone who wants air back there has to take it in themselves.'

'And we have enough time before we land?'

Vig shrugged. 'You don't want to hurry something like this, not at thirty thousand. It risks all kinds of shit. But we can still make it nasty back there pretty damn quick. Ten minutes and they'll be struggling. Fifteen and they'll be unconscious. Twenty and they'll be dead. Then we close the vents, pump some air back in, open the door and dump them during our approach. ' He gave Walters a prod with his foot. 'But we'll need to start now.'

Croke nodded. 'Then get busy,' he said.

III

Compared to the main cabin, the cargo hold was all functionality. There were bench seats along either side, but they were folded up to make room for the Ark, the chests, assorted luggage and the pallets of supplies. Luke tried the chests first. The end panel of the largest had been removed, leaving its innards exposed; but there was nothing inside. He tried the two smaller ones next. The first contained vestments, including the robe Jay had held up earlier; the second contained some old bottles of liquid, some thin squares of wood and sheets of white linen along with dented and misshapen coils of some soft, grey metal, probably lead to judge from their weight.

A tarpaulin near the tail had been folded back over itself. The shape beneath was unmistakeable. Luke felt a mix of grief and anger as he pulled it back. He'd already braced himself to find Jay dead, but not for the blotching of his skin or the broken, torn fingernails, nor for the blue strapping around his throat. He couldn't leave him with that grotesque garrotte, so he found a box-cutter by the pallets and cut it away before folding Jay back beneath his shroud. Then he rummaged fruitlessly through the suitcases and the overhead lockers, finding nothing but blankets and life-jackets.

'Was that Jay?' asked Rachel, when he rejoined her.

'Yes.'

She touched his forearm. 'I'm so sorry,' she said.

Some kind of plan or chart was unrolled beside the Ark, its corners pinned down by bottles. Luke crouched to study it. It proved to be a schematic with a photograph of a Newton text clipped to a corner. Luke freed the photograph and took it to better light. There were ghostly lines beneath Newton's handwriting, very similar to those in the larger schematic. The implication was clear. The great man had drawn the schematic himself, then he'd erased it and reused the paper for a religious text. Jay must have spotted the faint traces in Jerusalem, enhanced them with modern photographic techniques, then recreated this larger, cleaner version. It showed the Ark from front and side and top, and not as a religious relic, but as some kind of machine. No wonder Jay and his uncle had got so excited. No wonder they'd resolved to double-check every known Newton paper, and find all the missing ones too. He looked at Rachel. 'Nikola Tesla,' he said.

She shook her head. 'What about him?'

'Jay had a picture of him on his wall. And I studied him as an undergraduate. Your archetypal crackpot inventor. Bankrupted himself trying to invent an electrical super-weapon. He claimed that it would make whole armies drop dead in their tracks.' He put his hand on the Ark. 'The thing is, it's possible he got the idea from this. There's this bizarre paper he wrote, claiming that the Ark wasn't a religious artefact at all, but rather an incredibly powerful capacitor.'

'A what?'

'A capacitor. It's a device that can hold a huge electrical charge. Like a battery, except designed to discharge in a single great jolt, like thunderclouds in a storm. That's what would have made it so lethal.'

'The ancients didn't have that kind of technology,' said Rachel. 'We'd have found evidence if they had.'

'What else are your Baghdad batteries?' asked Luke. 'It's the same basic principle, only taken up a few notches. Anyway, I'm not saying he was right. All I'm saying is that maybe Newton came to the same conclusion: that the Ark was some kind of super-weapon, just as the Bible describes. An *alchemical* super-weapon. Because gold wasn't merely a metal to people like Newton, remember.

It wasn't even *primarily* a metal. It was a *symbol*. It symbolized the sun. It symbolized light. It symbolized the sacred fire itself, which Newton believed was electricity. And what was alchemy, after all? At its simplest, what was its purpose?'

'I don't know.' Rachel shook her head. 'I guess to turn base metal into gold.'

'Not quite,' said Luke. 'It was to turn base metal into gold *by treating it with sulphuric acid*. And if gold was really *light*, if gold was really *electricity*, doesn't that pretty much describe a lead battery?'

FORTY-NINE

I

Rachel stared at Luke as if he was crazy. 'A lead battery? You're not serious?'

'Why not?' said Luke. 'Forget about what the Ark really was, or whether it even existed. That doesn't matter, not for this. All that matters is what Newton believed it to be. And Newton believed that Moses had been a great alchemist, one with access to all kinds of lost knowledge. So *of course* Moses would have known the secret of sacred fire; *of course* he'd have harnessed it in his Ark. And Newton saw himself as Moses' successor, so *of course* he'd have set himself to rediscover those secrets, *of course* he'd have wanted to create his own Ark. And then Ashmole and Wren showed him the panels of wood and the twelve stones for the high priest's robes and maybe some crude instructions for a Baghdad battery that Tradescant had picked up on his travels. It must have felt like destiny.'

'But electricity was a nineteenth century technology, wasn't it?' frowned Rachel. 'I know Newton experimented with it, but surely a device like this was way beyond even him.'

'Van Musschenbroek invented Leyden jars a couple of decades after Newton,' said Luke. 'He coated the inside and outside of a bottle with foil to create positive and negative plates, then he put a metal rod inside them and generated a charge by rubbing glass with silk. They could knock a man out cold. Benjamin Franklin recommended them for killing turkeys.'

'Killing turkeys isn't destroying armies.'

'Van Musschenbroek wasn't Newton.' It hadn't just been his intellectual prowess that had set Newton apart. He'd also been a fantastically talented craftsman. Sightseers had travelled miles to see his childhood contraptions; and it had been his reflecting telescope, rather than his theories, that had first won him election to the Royal Society. 'All that effort working out the length of the sacred cubit. Who cares if the Temple's out by a foot or two? But the Ark was measured in cubits too. Electrical equipment has to be perfect.' He gave a dry laugh. 'Think about it: the greatest mind in scientific history working flat out on a single problem for twenty years. Would you honestly bet against him having come up with something of enormous power and originality?'

'He'd have told someone,' she protested.

'No,' insisted Luke. 'He *hated* sharing his ideas. Every time he did, it inevitably kicked off some new controversy. With Hooke, with Flamsteed, with Leibniz. Besides, he was head of the Royal Mint, remember? And he believed he'd discovered the philosopher's stone. Imagine the panic there'd have been if word had got out that the man in *that* job had discovered how to turn base metals into gold. And when he was dying, he went through everything he'd ever written and made a great bonfire of all the papers he didn't want outliving him. No one knows what they were, but I'll bet they were about the Ark, about electricity. He'd have been terrified of people using them to trash his reputation and denounce him as a sorcerer and a heretic.'

'But he missed two sets of the papers,' murmured Rachel, finally coming around. 'And Jay found the first in Jerusalem.'

'And I found the second in your aunt's attic.' He checked the Ark. Its lid looked like solid gold, but it wasn't heavy enough for that, so it was presumably wood covered by gold leaf. Rachel helped him remove it and set it down on the floor. Then they both looked inside.

'What the hell?' muttered Rachel.

But Luke only nodded. It was much as the schematic

depicted: a honeycomb of cells separated by wooden panels and fibreglass mats. A lead coil stood on its side in each compartment. He picked one up. Not pure lead but an alloy formed into a thin grid then stuffed with metallic paste and covered with cloth before being rolled. He peered down into the vacant bay. A sheet of wood riven by filaments of gold lay a few inches down, hinting at a second and maybe even a third layer of cells beneath.

'How does it work?' asked Rachel.

Luke returned the coil to its berth. He put his finger and thumb on it and its neighbour. 'Each of these pairs form a single electric cell,' he said. 'Combine them with other cells and you have a battery.' It was actually how batteries had got their name, because they worked so much more effectively in parallel, like cannon. 'Twenty cells on top. At least twenty more beneath. That's forty minimum, maybe sixty.'

'Enough to kill a turkey?'

'God, yes. And see these mats? Fibreglass is porous enough to allow liquid to seep through.'

A wry smile. 'So Newton had fibreglass now?'

Luke nodded at the oak chests. 'There are lots of linen sheets in there. They'd have worked fine. But acid degrades linen pretty quickly, so Jay must have used Newton's specs to create modern versions of everything. New coils, new dividers, fresh chemicals. But the wiring is all Newton's.'

'Wiring?' frowned Rachel.

'Wood doesn't conduct electricity. Gold is about the best conductor there is. Put the two together and you've got wiring.' He patted the sides of the Ark. 'I'll bet there's more inside these walls.'

'What does it do?'

'I don't know. I'd have to strip it down.'

Rachel touched her forehead, as if she had a headache coming on. 'You must have some idea.'

'I know how to start it,' he said. 'Just pour in sulphuric acid and distilled water and then turn on this electric motor.' He kicked it with his foot.

'The Ark won't generate its own power?'

'Capacitors and batteries are typically storage devices, not generators. Newton would have used some kind of friction machine. He had this saying as an old man: if you want to keep your legs, you have to use your legs. So maybe he invented the treadmill or the exercise bike; I wouldn't have put it past him.' He frowned, developing a headache of his own now. And each breath was taking more effort. 'Oh, hell,' he said, when he realized the implication. 'They've turned off our air.'

'How do you mean?'

'They can depressurize back here. They must be doing it now.'

'No!' cried Rachel. 'What'll happen?'

'I don't know. Altitude sickness, I guess. Headaches. Nausea. Unconsciousness.'

She gave him a fierce look. 'Death?'

He felt wretched. He wanted to comfort her. But she deserved the truth. 'Eventually,' he said.

'We have to fight back,' she said grimly. 'How can we fight back, Luke?'

He placed his hand on the Ark. 'This is a weapon, isn't it?' he said. 'I think it's time we found out what it can do.'

II

Avram glanced down at the remote control trigger in his left hand. It gave him an intoxicating sense of power. All he needed to do was pop the safety catch and press the red trigger and the world would be transformed.

But not yet . . .

Another tour of the walls, exhorting Shlomo and Danel and their men to stay alert for movement outside, for possible counterattacks. Not that they needed telling. They were all pumped up by adrenalin and success. Only Benyamin was looking miserable. 'Aren't you glad you came?' Avram asked.

The big man just shrugged.

Avram returned to his laptop, checked for latest news. It amused him to hear the Minister for Foreign Affairs gabbling about the prisoners whose release he had already secured. And it thrilled him to see aerial footage of the Dome from the very same helicopters he could hear thundering above. He flipped through his rota of news shows, going so fast that he passed one channel before he realized something wasn't right. He went back. Yes. Until now, every one of them had been all Dome all the time. But this one had split its screen. One half showed the Dome; the other showed only empty sea and sky. But a red banner ran across its foot.

Dome conspiracy aircraft arriving Ben Gurion shortly

Avram's heart squeezed. *How the hell had they found out? Had someone talked?* But then the anchor explained about Track Changes in the prisoner-release demand. He felt furious with his own sloppiness, but he couldn't see how it changed anything. The Israelis had to realize that shooting the plane down would mean instant and catastrophic consequences. But he kept a wary eye on that screen from then on, all the same.

III

There was no time for finesse, for working out in which order to do things. Luke and Rachel tore open crates of bottled sulphuric acid and distilled water, uncapped them and poured them in roughly equal measures into the Ark's cells. The liquid vanished as fast as they glugged it in, seeping through into the cells beneath. The floor quickly became littered with empties, and still it wasn't full.

'What will it do to the plane?' asked Rachel. 'Aren't they built to withstand lightning strikes?'

'Only because their outer hulls are insulated from their inner hulls,' said Luke. 'So lightning can't get through. But that also means that an electrical surge inside can't escape so easily. Everything could get frazzled.'

'Including us?'

He grimaced. 'It's our only chance.' The air was thin and vaporous. Their movements grew increasingly clumsy from lack of oxygen, their eyes watering with migraines. But they kept disgorging bottles until finally the Ark was full. They heaved its lid back on, then Luke stooped by the electric motor. 'Ready?' he asked.

'Ready,' said Rachel.

He flipped the switch and took a step back, fearful of something extraordinary. But nothing happened. Rachel looked at him. 'It'll take time,' he said.

The Ark began to steam and smoke, filling the hold with noxious fumes. Then it seemed almost to crackle. The air, despite its thinness, became increasingly charged. Luke's skin began to tingle. The tingling turned to itching, his skin infested by swarms of invisible insects that now burrowed inside him, squeezing his organs, pumping his heart, making his blood fizz like some madcap experiment.

'What's it doing?' asked Rachel, rubbing her forearms.

He looked down at the floor where threads of cheap carpeting stood up like wires. They needed to get off it. They needed insulation. He was about to tell Rachel when the Ark unleashed a violent spark that jolted up his arm and into his chest like some angelic taser. He fell to the floor. Rachel tried to catch him but he took her down too. His limbs wouldn't work. He couldn't breathe. Something was lodged in his throat. He began to gag, fighting for breath. Rachel turned him onto his back and hooked a finger into his mouth, pulled his tongue free. He rolled onto his side. 'The pallets,' he gasped. 'Wood.'

She nodded and helped him onto their insulated sanctuary. They turned to look at the Ark, flaming and sparking wildly. An electrical arch sprang up between the twin golden cherubs kneeling on its lid, glowing and fizzing like the filament of some impossible bulb, so that they had to close their eyes and turn away. Then a brilliant single blaze of light burst forth, bright as the sun, so bright that Luke could see it even through his tightly clenched eyelids and the noise it made was like nothing he'd ever heard before, a crackling kind of boom that made the whole aircraft shudder.

Both engines instantly sputtered and then failed. The plane began to plunge. The humpback-bridge moment of weightlessness went on and on and on. Everyone shrieked, in the hold and in the main cabin, a feedback loop of terror at the certainty of imminent violent death. But the pilot was still fighting and he managed to wrest back some measure of control. An injured engine whined as it strained heroically against gravity and momentum. The wings and fuselage shuddered as they fought horrific loads. Lockers fell open, disgorging their contents. The oak chests rattled and empty bottles danced crazily. Then gravity returned with a vengeance, pressing Luke and Rachel down on the pallet. Their trajectory flattened and they pulled up level. They'd lost so much altitude that the air was thicker here and began to reverse its flow, making breathing easier, blunting the sharpest edges of their headaches.

It was Rachel who heard the noise. 'What's that?' she asked.

'What's what?'

'That whining,' she said. 'Can't you hear it?'

Luke looked at the electric motor. 'Oh, Christ,' he said, as the Ark began to glow once more. 'It's recharging.'

FIFTY

I

Avram watched in horror as the plane plunged towards the sea. It was too far away to identify, but what else could it be but Croke's jet? What else could it be but the Ark? He cried out in anguish and rage.

They'd shot them down. They must have known what the consequences would be but they'd shot them down anyway.

He looked at the trigger in his left hand. He steeled himself to release the safety and press it. But then, like a miracle, the plane began to pull out of its dive. It was at an angle to the camera so that he could watch it fighting gravity until finally it levelled off. He cried out again, but in exaltation this time. What more proof could anyone want that the Lord, praise His Name, was truly on their side? Tears prickled his eyes as—

The plane's rear windows began to glow, as though reflecting the dawn. But it couldn't be. The sun wasn't up yet. And anyway, the light seemed to be coming from inside the plane. The camera zoomed in closer. The light grew brighter and brighter and then the whole plane lit up like a star going supernova. The flare lasted barely a second before it died away, leaving the morning darker than before. Flame flickered from both the aircraft's engines and twin trails of thick black smoke scoured the grey sky. The plane began to lose altitude once more. It wasn't quite in free-fall, but with both engines on fire even Avram could see that there was only one possible outcome now: its crash into the sea and total obliteration. His heart seemed to break apart inside his chest. The Ark was lost. Without it, no Jewish uprising. Without it, no Third Temple. Without it, his Lord was nothing but a sham.

His wail echoed through the Dome. He glared down at the remote control. He released the safety then made to stab the trigger with his thumb.

II

Luke took Rachel in his arms as the Ark discharged a second time. He didn't need to look outside to know that the engines were gone, that the plane had received its death blow. He couldn't believe it was going to end like this. He couldn't accept that he was responsible for bringing this on Rachel. He looked around for some glimmer of hope, saw it in the large oak chest. He grabbed her hand and pulled her to it. 'Get in,' he said.

'It won't be strong enough.'

'Newton built it to protect the Ark,' he told her. 'It will be strong enough.'

She nodded and climbed inside, fitted her feet into the hollow at the far end. The plane was hurtling downwards, wreaking havoc on the hold. He picked up the mirror half of the Ark's protective moulding and made to enclose Rachel in its protective womb, but she fought him off. 'No! You have to get in too.'

'There isn't room. Not for both of us.'

'There is if we use life jackets.'

He felt a fierce surge of joy and pride and hope. The overhead lockers had all tumbled open and spilled their guts onto the floor. He grabbed life jackets from all around and tossed them into the chest. Through a window, the sea was rushing up fast. No more time. He grabbed the chest's end panel, fitted it into its grooves then climbed inside and let it drop down like a portcullis behind him, enclosing both him and Rachel in its protective walls. The chest was too short for him and he had to bend his knees, adopt the brace position. The life jackets were all around them. In the darkness they felt for and pulled toggles, inflating the jackets like balloons, creating a buffer between themselves and the chest walls, packing themselves tighter and tighter until they couldn't move, and his chest was pressed against hers, and his chin was on her shoulder. The screaming of their descent grew louder as it echoed off the water. Any second now. Any second. He wrapped his arms around Rachel and hugged her hard, felt her hugging him back with equal intensity, and if it had to end for them both, then best like this, best like this, best like—

A deafening crash. The fuselage jumped and shuddered. The oak chest was flung forwards, spinning and tumbling like a die cast by some outraged god. They crashed into and through the internal bulkhead, would surely have broken apart had the Ark not already smashed a path for them. The impact was still so violent that Luke banged his head hard even through the life jackets, leaving him dazed and only vaguely aware of hideous noises all around him, of shrieking metal and things breaking and popping and splintering. Their forward motion stopped abruptly. He felt utterly disoriented and for a moment wondered whether this was what death felt like. But then he realized he was merely upside down, that blood was rushing to his head and pain was reporting in from the various parts of his body, telling him that he was very much alive.

Rachel was still in his arms, still pressed against him

by the swell of life jackets. 'Are you okay?' he asked. His voice was slurred and disembodied, but the biggest surprise was hearing it at all.

Rachel didn't reply. His hand was pinned behind her back but some of the life jackets had punctured and were slowly deflating, allowing him to work it free. He touched her throat, felt nothing. His heart twisted. 'Rachel!' he cried.

He tried her wrist instead and this time felt something, not strong but steady. No time to celebrate, however. Metal groaned outside, stretched beyond its capacity. The chest lurched and tipped onto its side. He heard splashing. His right hip grew wet; then his thigh and calf. And he realized, belatedly, they were shipping water fast through the hole Newton had cut in the chest's floor in order to accommodate the base of the Ark.

III

Benyamin had vowed to attend every minute of the trial of the four young Palestinian men who'd murdered his wife, two daughters and seven others. But it had proved a farce. They hadn't even offered a defence. At least, their defence had been a simple political statement: they were soldiers fighting a war in which they themselves had lost parents, brothers, sisters, children and friends. And there'd been no trials for *those* killings. No justice for *their* bereavements.

To his surprise, Benyamin had found this line of defence deeply disturbing. It had troubled him enough that he'd skipped the foregone conclusion of the verdict and the sentencing. It was easier to hate people when you didn't know them; it was easier to believe that your lust for vengeance was somehow different, nobler. But it wasn't different. He saw that now. He saw it in the sheer ugliness of Avram's expression as he released the safety and made to press the trigger.

Benyamin didn't even think. He simply hurled himself at him and they tumbled together onto the Foundation Stone. The impact knocked the remote from Avram's hand and it skittered away across the Kevlar blanket. They both went after it, scrambling on their hands and knees, while everyone looked around to watch.

That was when it happened. All the windows burst open at once, raining glass on the floor. Stun grenades exploded in midair, a compressed storm of light and thunder. Figures swathed in black swarmed in through doors and windows, firing as they came, punishing each and every hint of resistance with instant death. The shock of it made Benyamin falter, allowing Avram to reach the remote first. He raised his hand and was bringing it down to slap the trigger when the fusillade of high velocity rounds shredded him and flung him onto his back, his eyes wide and staring upwards, so that the last thing he'd ever have seen was the Dome towering high above him, still standing.

IV

The seawater was already up to Luke's chest. He put his hands above his head and fumbled through the deflating life jackets for the sliding end panel. He'd been twisted around so much that he couldn't be sure which way was up, which way to push. Panic got to him; he kept trying different directions, hoping one might work. None did. Maybe the impact had jammed it. Maybe he was only making it worse. He forced himself to calm down, to think. He felt around and quickly found the hole in the chest's floor. Now at least he could orient himself with confidence. The end panel slid upwards. He pushed it hard. Nothing.

Water reached his throat. He had to lift up Rachel's face so she could breathe. He remembered Jay finding this chest earlier, how he'd struggled to open it until he'd tried pushing the panel inwards and *then* lifting it. There was nothing on the inside for Luke to pull towards him. He tried to grip its edges with his finger-nails, but it was useless. Water rose above his mouth.

The pressure was building on his sinuses too. As the chest had enough air in it to float, the implication had to be that they were still trapped inside the fuselage, and sinking with it.

He let go of Rachel. The only thing he could do for her was to get them both out. He took a deep breath from the small pocket of air, fitted his right foot through the hole in the floor, felt fuselage. He pushed the chest along until something outside stopped him. He took another breath then pushed as hard as he could, using whatever obstacle he'd encountered outside to depress the end panel. It yielded and slid upwards, but only a little way. And it let out the last of the air, so that the urge to breathe became almost irresistible. He pushed against the chest's wall until it tipped onto its side, allowing him finally to slide the panel free.

Luke hauled himself out, dragging Rachel with him. They were already deep enough underwater for it to be almost dark. His eyes were so blurry that he could only gain the vaguest impression of his surroundings. The tube of the passenger cabin, a carnage of dead bodies strapped into white leather seats in a doomed effort to survive the impact; but also a jagged-edged ring of lighter blue above him, where the jet had sheared in two, offering a glimpse of surface high above.

He kicked towards it, fighting the screaming of his

lungs, and finally he breached the surface and opened his mouth and gasped the air and kept on gasping until his need was sated. He turned belatedly to Rachel, lifted up her head. He'd never had CPR training, had only seen it in the movies, but he understood the principles: chest compressions and assisted breathing. He couldn't lay her down on her back to press on her chest, so he hugged her tight three times instead, pinched her nostrils, put his mouth to hers, breathed into her. He hugged her again. On the second hug her mouth opened and she coughed and choked and spluttered and then vomited out a small stream of discoloured seawater, and then she gasped and began breathing by herself, replenishing her oxygen-starved body.

Life jackets were bobbing all around them, rubber ducks in a giant bath. Luke grabbed the nearest. It was a struggle to fit it around Rachel's neck and clip in the straps. He cursed himself for all those safety demonstrations he'd ignored over the years. But finally she was in. He blew into the intake valves to inflate it as far as it would go then he found a life jacket for himself. His right arm was growing increasingly numb from some blow he couldn't even remember having taken. But finally he had it on. Blood was streaming from a cut in Rachel's scalp. He wiped it away just as she opened her eyes. She looked pale and groggy, but she raised an eyebrow even so, making it instantly clear that she recognized him, that she was going to be okay, and the relief was so intense that it wasn't just the sting of salt water that made his eyes tear up.

She tried to say something, but it was beyond her for the moment. He put a finger to her lips. A slick of oil was spreading on the sea, calming it like the proverb, creating an iridescent haze all around them. Its vapour was somehow reassuring, like hospital disinfectant. The sun was rising on the horizon, a new day dawning. And Luke was suddenly suffused by an extraordinary and unexpected gladness to realize that now it would merely be another in the usual sequence. Not the End of Days. Not Armageddon. Just Tuesday.

'Is it over?' murmured Rachel.

'It's over,' he said.

As if to underline his words, the noise of a boat's engine reached them at that moment, rising and fading with the swell. They had to be closer to the coast than he'd realized. Its white fibreglass bow slapped water as it slowed for the debris field. He called out and waved to it and it picked its way carefully through the flotsam, looking in vain for other survivors, then cut its engine and let momentum bring it alongside.

Friendly hands reached down to take hold of him and Rachel and haul them aboard. And then there was the sound of jubilant, relieved laughter; his, Rachel's or the crew of the boat, he simply couldn't tell.

EPILOGUE

Downing Street, three days later

Luke felt intense pride as he watched Rachel negotiate. Or maybe it was just happiness at seeing her again. They'd hardly spent ten minutes together since the crash. Her concussion and near drowning had been severe enough for her Israeli doctors to insist on keeping her in hospital and under observation for an extra couple of days, so by default he'd been the one speaking to the police, the intelligence services and the media, first in Israel, then back here in England.

The Prime Minister sighed as he flipped through the settlement agreement once more. 'These are difficult times,' he said. 'Everyone's having to make sacrifices.'

'Yes,' agreed Rachel. 'And this is yours.'

His cheeks pinked a little. He uncapped his pen, wrote his name with a flourish on each of the copies. 'There,' he said. 'Satisfied?'

'Thank you, Prime Minister.' She took three sets, passed two to her lawyer, then held a brief whispered conversation with him.

Luke looked around. The walls of the conference room were hung with portraits of great men in dark suits. He'd had his fill of self-important people recently. All the manoeuvring. All the excuses. All the blame shifting. He looked out through the facing windows instead; a sunlit garden with magnolias and cherry trees in magnificent blossom. And he had a sudden wild hankering to be out of here, just him and Rachel and the open road.

His new mobile buzzed in his pocket. He'd turned the ringer off for this meeting, but the police had insisted he keep it on at all times in case of urgent questions. He checked it; it could wait. But developments were breaking all the time. Just this morning an Israeli dive team had found the front half of Croke's jet on the sea floor, five bodies still trapped inside. But no sign yet of the Ark. Not that it mattered much any more. With the full story out, it had lost its power to do harm. It almost certainly wasn't the real thing, after all, but a scientific curiosity barely three hundred years old. Yet the leaders of Israel and her neighbours had still been sufficiently sobered by their closeness to catastrophe to adopt a new spirit of cooperation, even an eagerness to talk.

Other investigations were on-going in England. The vaults beneath St Paul's and the Museum of the History of Science were being thoroughly and carefully explored. And everyone wanted to know exactly how the National Counterterrorism Taskforce had been able to take over Crane Court and then tear up the cathedral floor with so little supervision. Questions had been raised in Parliament; an emergency session in the House of Commons had left the government in turmoil and the Prime Minister fighting for his political life. Hence his desperation for some of Luke and Rachel's new stardust. Hence today's announcement of substantial and immediate new funding for veterans' care and homes, and the photo-op that would accompany it.

It wasn't just in England that powerful people were fighting for their careers, even their lives. A Washington DC lobbyist had been arrested on suspicion of bankrolling Croke's operation. An evangelist with ties to the White House had hanged himself in his garage. And the President had declared himself fit ahead of schedule, and had ordered the Vice President to clear her desk.

The Prime Minister capped and put away his fountain pen, rose to his feet. He looked decidedly chipper now that the unpleasant business was done, bouncing up and down on his toes. 'Are they ready for us outside?' he asked.

An aide took half a pace forwards. 'Five minutes, Prime Minister.'

'As well to make them wait,' he confided to Rachel. 'It lets the excitement build.' He gave her an avuncular smile and added: 'And you'll probably want to let me field the questions. These media packs can be quite intimidating, if you're not used to them.'

'Yes,' said Rachel. 'Because Luke and I clearly scare easily.'

His lips went tight. He raised an eyebrow at an aide.

Luke went to join her. 'So what are your plans?' he asked. 'After this press nonsense, I mean?'

She held up her copy of the agreement. 'I promised Bren we'd go celebrate,' she said. 'You want to join us?'

'I'd love to,' he said. 'But I can't. Not this afternoon. I've another meeting with the police and then I've got a month's worth of phone calls to return.' The whole affair had rehabilitated him. His old university had offered him his job back, and he'd been invited to multiple interviews elsewhere. He needed to take advantage before his popularity faded. 'But I'll be heading down your way tomorrow. I promised Pelham I'd drop by.'

'Ah, yes,' she said. 'I've had about thirty messages to call him. He insists I go out with him. Says it's the least I owe him after the way he sacrificed himself for us and had to endure being driven around Birmingham for a day.'

Luke's mouth felt unaccountably dry. 'And? What are you going to tell him?'

She shook her head emphatically. 'I think I made it pretty clear where I stand on going out with anyone called Pelham, don't you?'

'Damned right,' he grinned. Without really thinking, he touched her hand, felt a delicious tingle at the contact. These past few days, he could scarcely touch anything without a spark of static, as though the Ark had charged him to overflowing, and he was still shedding. 'Speaking of which,' he said.

'Yes?'

'The name Luke,' he said. 'You never said where you stood on going out with someone called Luke.'

'No,' she agreed. 'I didn't.'

'Well?' he asked, his heart in his mouth. 'Would you?'

And there it was at last, that smile from the photograph. 'Yes,' she said. 'I rather think I would.'

AUTHOR'S NOTE

Newton's Fire is, of course, a work of fiction. That said, I've tried to stay as true to the historical background as a story of this nature allows. Sir Isaac Newton did indeed make predictions about the date of the Second Coming. He was fascinated by Solomon's Temple and he worked for many years at the Royal Mint. He drove himself into a breakdown in 1693, in part due to his alchemical experiments, and he claimed in *Praxis* to have achieved multiplication. He was also very good friends with Christopher Wren, who in turn was close to both Elias Ashmole and John Evelyn. And Conrad Josten really did discover an anomaly beneath the basement of the old Ashmolean with a metal detector, yet he lacked the funds and opportunity to explore further.

I have deliberately avoided saying in which year the action takes place, in the hope that readers will find it more immediate that way. That said, the story is anchored to certain historical events (the climax takes place exactly forty-nine years after the Six Day War of 1967, for example), so it's not very hard to work out for those readers who so wish. Incidentally, the day in question genuinely does enjoy a rare conjunction with *Rosh Chodesh Sivan*.

As ever, I'd like to thank my agent Luigi Bonomi for his invaluable advice and encouragement during the writing of this book. I'm extremely grateful to Thomas Stofer for his insightful feedback on the first draft, and to Kati Nicholl for her excellent fact-checking and copy-editing. I'd also like to thank the whole team at HarperCollins for helping to make this book look so good and read so well; and most especially I'd like to thank my editor Jamie Cowen for his encouragement, hard work and willingness to fight for changes that I wasn't certain about at the time, but which in retrospect were right.

I had surprisingly good fun researching this book, not least because of the many kind and knowledgeable people I met along the way. I'd like to thank all those at the Museum of the History of Science, the National Library of Israel, St Paul's Cathedral, the Monument and else-where for giving me so much of their time and expertise.

But I'd particularly like to thank Stephen Snobelen of the History of Science and Technology Programme at the University of King's College in Halifax, Nova Scotia, who not only advised me during the writing of this book, but was also kind enough to read an early draft of the manuscript to let me know where I'd gone too far off my Newtonian rails. I've followed his guidance in most, but not all, cases, so any mistakes that remain are most definitely mine and mine alone.